THE PRETENDER

A
Mifflin
County
Mystery
Book 3

The Pretender

Wanda E. Brunstetter

Barbour Publishing

© 2025 by Wanda E. Brunstetter

ISBN 979-8-89151-034-0
Adobe Digital Edition (.epub) 979-8-89151-035-7

All rights reserved. No part of this publication may be reproduced or transmitted for commercial purposes, except for brief quotations in printed reviews, without written permission of the publisher. Reproduced text may not be used on the World Wide Web. No Barbour Publishing content may be used as artificial intelligence training data for machine learning, or in any similar software development.

Scripture taken from the New King James Version®. Copyright © 1982 by Thomas Nelson. Used by permission. All rights reserved.

All German-Dutch words are taken from the *Revised Pennsylvania German Dictionary* found in Lancaster County, Pennsylvania.

This book is a work of fiction. Names, characters, places, and incidents are either products of the author's imagination or used fictitiously. Any similarity to actual people, organizations, and/or events is purely coincidental.

No medical advice in this work of fiction is intended as a substitute for the medical advice of physicians. Readers should consult a physician in matters relating to their health, particularly with respect to any symptoms that may require diagnosis or medical attention.

For more information about Wanda E. Brunstetter, please access the author's website at the following internet address: www.wandabrunstetter.com

Cover model image: Richard Brunstetter III

Cover Design: Kirk DouPonce, DogEared Design

Published by Barbour Publishing, Inc., 1810 Barbour Drive, Uhrichsville, Ohio 44683, www.barbourbooks.com

Our mission is to inspire the world with the life-changing message of the Bible.

Printed in the United States of America.

DEDICATION

In loving memory of Thiel Kauffman.
His love for Jesus spilled out on so many people
in and around Mifflin County, Pennsylvania.

*"And you shall know the truth,
and the truth shall make you free."*
JOHN 8:32

CHAPTER 1

New York City

*D*ING*! D*ING*! D*ING*!* "O*RDER UP*!"
Despite the tantalizing aroma of zesty lasagna waiting to be served, Anthony Reeves cringed, and his teeth clicked as he clamped his mouth shut. He hated the sound of that irritating bell whenever he was on this side of the kitchen and it wasn't him ringing the bell. Anthony had been hired here to cook, not wait on tables while filling in for a tardy waitress. Where was Eileen Peterson this afternoon, and what excuse did she have for yet again being late? This was getting old, and Anthony was fed up.

I should say something to Eileen about her tardiness, Anthony told himself. *But I don't like to be mean, and she may have a legitimate excuse. Besides, this is not my restaurant, so it's up to my dad to keep things running smoothly and make sure the help is here on time. I'm really surprised Pop hasn't fired Eileen by now. Maybe he's softhearted toward her because she does a good job when she's here waitressing.* Anthony frowned. *Of course I do a good job when I'm cooking in the kitchen, and what thanks do I get? Guess maybe my dad thinks my paycheck every week is all the appreciation I need.*

Anthony glanced at the clock, and he focused on the problem of Eileen again. She was an attractive young woman with russet, shoulder-length hair and expressive brown eyes. But it wasn't the young woman's lovely features that made her a customer favorite here in his parents' Italian restaurant. Anthony figured it was a combination of things—Eileen's attentiveness to their patrons' needs, the pleasant smile on her face as she conversed with them, a good memory when it came to keeping track of the names of frequent customers, and the fact that she checked in regularly with those at her tables to see if they were satisfied with their meals. Eileen had also been good about asking if the people she served needed a beverage refill. There was no doubt about it: She was one of the best waitresses Anthony's parents had ever hired to work here, and because of that, Eileen received better tips than anyone else on staff. The young woman's only downfall was being late more often than she should, which meant someone had to fill in for her. So today, in addition to waiting on customers due to Eileen's absence, Anthony was also stuck with clearing off tables, because the busboy who normally worked this shift had called in sick.

Ding! Ding! Ding! Ding! Anthony's father rang the bell with more gusto this time.

Like a dutiful son, Anthony turned his head toward the kitchen and hollered, "I'm coming, Pop! I just need to clear off one more table!"

Anthony saw his petite, dark-haired mother step out from behind the serving area. "Don't worry about it, Son. I'll see that the couple sitting at the booth near the front window gets their lasagna right now."

He nodded and winked. "Thanks, Mom." If there was one parent Anthony could count on to look after him, it was his mother. Whenever Pop became cranky or expected too much from Anthony, Mom was there to smooth the waters and fill in as needed. She had always been a good mother, and Anthony felt grateful. Some people weren't so lucky. Pop wasn't a bad parent, and he'd always worked plenty hard to provide for his family. But he wasn't a nurturing kind of man, and often expected more from his children than those who weren't related to him.

While his mother took care of the customers awaiting their order, Anthony scooped up the dishes and silverware from another table and wiped the tabletop and benches clean. He hauled everything to the kitchen sink so that Sam, the dishwasher, could take care of the job he'd been hired to do.

Anthony had just stepped back into the dining room when their tardy waitress entered the restaurant with slow footsteps and drooping shoulders. "Where have you been?" he asked, approaching her. It was then he noticed Eileen's disheveled appearance and tearstained cheeks.

Eileen sniffed, and as she dropped her gaze to the floor, her thick lashes swept across the lower rims of her eyes. "S–sorry I'm late. I had a rough m–morning." Eileen's chin trembled, and her voice cracked. "My life is over, Anthony. I'm toast."

Feeling the need to offer the poor girl a bit of support, he gave her shoulder a few gentle taps. "Come on now. It can't be all that bad."

She looked up at him, and a couple of tears rolled down her cheeks. "A lot you know."

"You're right, I don't know. So let's go in the break room, and you can tell me all about it."

She glanced around the room with a panicked expression, and then her gaze went to the clock on the far wall. "I. . .I can't. I'm already late for my shift, so—"

Anthony clasped her arm. "It's all right. My mom will cover for you—and me as well. Mom's good about that kind of thing, you know." He peered in his mother's direction and was pleased when she nodded. He was glad someone had a little compassion here. Pop was certainly short on patience. Meanwhile, things in the kitchen were heating up, and Pop was still dinging that infernal bell.

Quickly, Anthony led Eileen to the other room, before his father could say anything inappropriate to either of them. Of course, Anthony figured if Pop were to sound off, it most likely would have been directed at him.

<hr />

When Eileen took a seat at the small table where employees often sat to eat their meals during breaks, Anthony pulled up a chair beside her. "Now, what happened this morning that brought you to work late and in tears?"

She reached into her denim jacket pocket for a tissue, dabbed the tears beneath her eyes, and blew her nose. "I...I'm pregnant, and when I told Jeff that he's the father of my unborn child, he called me a liar and fired me on the spot."

Anthony blinked in succession. "The guy whose kids you've been taking care of in the evenings while their mother is pulling night duty at some nursing home?"

"Yeah, but it's not a nursing home. Jeff's wife, Penny, is a certified nurse, and she works the night shift at one of the hospitals in the area." Eileen paused a minute, drew in a quick breath, and blew it out with a *whoosh*. "I used to just stay until Ronnie and Andrea were tucked into bed, but for the last couple of months I've been staying longer."

"As in overnight—till their mother came home?"

"Uh-huh. There was an attraction between me and Jeff, and even though I fought it, we drew closer. When he declared his love for me, one thing led to another and then. . ." Eileen's voice trailed off. She couldn't help noticing the defined muscles in Anthony's cheekbones tighten as his blue eyes flashed with what she assumed was anger.

"Didn't you have the good sense to realize that the jerk was just playing the 'I love you' card in order to get what he wanted?" Anthony waved one hand about, as if to emphasize what he'd said. "Oh, and I'm guessing the guy probably promised that he would leave his wife and marry you."

She moved her head slowly up and down. "He did—until I told him I was pregnant, at which point he denied we'd ever had an affair."

"You could get a paternity test to prove that he's the baby's father."

This time she shook her head. "He ordered me out of his house and said if I ever came back or tried to prove that he'd fathered my child, he would call the police."

"And you believed him?"

"Yes, I was scared. And the truth is, I didn't want to hurt Jeff's wife with a scandal." Eileen drew her fingers into the palms of her hands until the nails dug into her skin. "I can't make it on just what I earn here at the restaurant. If I even still have a job, that is. I wouldn't be surprised if your dad fired me for being late again." Her last word ended on a sob, and she had to catch her breath before going on. "As much as I dread the thought of it, there's only one thing left for me to do."

"What's that?"

"I have to go back to my hometown and plead with my parents to take me in." Every muscle in Eileen's slender body quivered. "The only thing is, once they find out that I'm pregnant but not married, they—at least my father—will throw me out."

Anthony's long fingers slid though his thick crop of dark, curly hair as he stared at Eileen with an intense gaze. "But if you had a husband, they'd be okay with that, right?"

"Well, most likely, but—"

He smacked his hands together, causing Eileen to nearly jump out of her chair. "So there's your answer."

She jerked her head back. "What answer?"

"You need a husband."

"Yeah, right! Should I take out an ad in the newspaper, asking someone to volunteer to marry me?" She pursed her lips. "That's a brilliant idea, Anthony. Yeah, a really great one, all right."

He leaned closer to her and said firmly, "Hear me out on this suggestion before you say anything negative, okay?"

"Go right ahead."

"I have a two-week vacation coming up, beginning next week, and I can use those days to help you."

Her auburn brows lifted slightly. "How will that help me?"

"I will pretend to be your husband, and at the end of two weeks, we'll have a big fight, at which time I shall announce that I made a mistake marrying you, am moving back to the city, and will be getting a divorce." Anthony patted her shoulder, as if for emphasis. Or was it in sympathy of her plight? "Your folks will think I'm a horrible person, of course, but their sympathies will be toward you and the unborn baby." He snapped his fingers. "So there you go, Eileen Peterson—end of problem."

She drummed her knuckles along the tabletop, mulling over Anthony's very generous but preposterous offer. She couldn't believe that a man she'd only known a few months would even make such a crazy suggestion.

What should I do? Eileen asked herself. *Should I take Anthony up on his unexpected offer or try to find some other solution to my problem?*

CHAPTER 2

Belleville, Pennsylvania

It was time to start supper, but Elsie Petersheim wasn't in the mood to cook anything. A first glance at the calendar this morning had reminded Elsie that today was Rosa's birthday. It had been a little over two years since her and Mahlon's eldest daughter had disappeared, and Elsie's heart still ached. Not knowing whether Rosa was alive or dead had plagued Elsie every single day since she'd first realized her daughter had gone missing after attending a young people's gathering with her boyfriend, Ephraim Peight. So much had happened since then, including the fact that in a week and a half, Ephraim would marry Rosa's best friend, Ada Detweiler.

If Rosa knew about the wedding, I wonder what she would think, Elsie pondered as she stared out the kitchen window at a female cardinal eating from the new feeder her daughter Tena had recently hung on a shepherd's hook. *Would Rosa be happy for the betrothed couple, or would she be upset, believing Ada had stolen her boyfriend?*

Elsie sucked in her bottom lip as she rubbed her chin. *Guess it really doesn't matter now, does it? Rosa is obviously not coming home, or she would have been here by now.* She looked away from the window and sighed. *Or at the very least, we would have heard something from her.*

Elsie had known for some time before her daughter's disappearance that she was unsettled and did not wish to join their Amish church, of which Mahlon was the bishop. Whether it was due to Rosa's wild streak or her desire to go against her father's wishes, Elsie could never be sure. She just knew that Rosa had a mind of her own and had been more headstrong and defiant than their other four children. The oldest, Norman, was now happily married to Salina, and had been living in her parents' home temporarily. The only ones left at this house were Susan, Tena, and Alvin. Although neither Susan nor Tena had boyfriends right now, Elsie figured it was just a matter of time before the girls would be married and making homes of their own. Alvin, the youngest, was still in school, so at least he wouldn't be moving out anytime soon, and for that, Elsie was thankful. She was in no hurry to be an empty nester, and if Elsie had her way, she would keep all her children and future grandchildren living close by so she could see them as often as possible.

"What are you doing, Mom?" Susan asked when she and Tena entered the kitchen.

"Not much," Elsie replied. "I came here to start supper, but now I can't figure out what to fix, and it doesn't help that I'm not in the mood to cook."

"You look *mied*, so why don't you go relax in the living room and let us do all the cooking?" Tena suggested.

"You're right," Elsie agreed. "I am tired, so I will take you up on that offer." Forcing a smile she didn't really feel, Elsie ambled into the living room and sank to the couch. At least here she could close her eyes for a bit and enjoy the warmth of the fireplace. Soon Alvin and Mahlon would be in from doing their chores, and they would all gather at the table for supper.

~

"Wow, Eileen! I've never been to this part of Pennsylvania before." Anthony looked over at her as she sat straight as a board in the passenger seat of his sporty sedan. "The countryside is so beautiful. I can't believe you would leave all of this to move to a big, noisy city like New York."

"I needed a change."

He gave a nod. "Yeah, who doesn't?"

"You seem to be pretty satisfied cooking at your parents' restaurant." She was glad for the topic change. It helped take her mind off a more pressing matter.

"I do enjoy wearing my chef's apron whenever Pop lets me do the job I was hired there for."

The bitterness in Anthony's tone was obvious, and Eileen could relate to the way he felt. To her way of thinking, working for one's parent was not ideal, even in the best of circumstances. That's how it had once been for her, at least.

Eileen bit down on her lower lip until she tasted a hint of blood. *When we get to my folks' house and I introduce Anthony as my husband, I wonder if we'll be welcomed, or will the door be slammed shut in our faces?*

She licked the moisture off her lips and swallowed hard. "Before we arrive at my parents' home, I need to tell you a few things."

He bumped shoulders with her. "I figured you'd get around to that."

"You did?"

"Yeah. Thought you'd want to fill me in a bit about your family so it would appear as if I know you real well and you'd previously told me about your relationship with them." He thumped the steering wheel with one hand while keeping his other hand firmly in place. "Let's start with this—do you have any siblings?"

"Um. . .yes. . .two brothers and. . ."

"Oh, hey! Would you look at that gorgeous sunset?" Anthony pointed to the west. "Looks like it could've come straight out of a magazine cover."

"Yeah, we get some nice ones here in the Big Valley. Sunrises from the east too."

"Big Valley?" He glanced at her and tipped his head to one side.

"I'll explain it another time. Right now, I really do need to fill you in on a few important details concerning me and my family."

They passed a horse pulling a carriage with blinking lights on the back, and Anthony let out a whistle. "Was that a horse and buggy? Are we in Lancaster County where all the Amish people live?"

"No, this is Mifflin County, and Amish people, as well as other Plain groups, live here."

"Interesting."

"Yes, and as a matter of fact—"

The car swerved suddenly and Anthony hollered, "Oh, wow, that was close! I almost hit a dog!"

She looked out the front window and squinted. "That looks like my little brother's mutt, and that driveway up ahead leads to my parents' place."

Anthony made a sharp right and drove up the wide gravel path, stopping in front of a rustic-looking two-story white house. "I don't see any cars or a garage either," he commented. "Maybe no one's at home."

Eileen was on the verge of commenting when the dog Anthony had almost hit dashed into the yard, barking frantically. *Oh great, now he's gonna alert the whole house.*

Before she could say anything to Anthony, he jumped out of the car and came around to open the door for her. She was barely on her feet when he stepped onto the front porch and knocked on the door. On trembling legs, she joined him there, leaving no more time to explain anything about the family who lived here.

A few awkward moments passed, and then the door swung open. A slender middle-aged woman with strands of graying hair peeking out from under the sides of her white, heart-shaped head covering stood looking at them with wide eyes and quivering lips. "Rosa? Is. . . is it really you?"

CHAPTER 3

Anthony's muscles tensed as his thoughts tangled into knots. He'd seen pictures of Amish women before and had even seen a group of Plain people when he'd visited Niagara Falls a few years ago, and the lady who'd answered the door was definitely Amish or at least belonged to one of the Plain groups. What really puzzled him, though, was why she'd called Eileen "Rosa," while looking at her with an incredulous stare. Could Eileen resemble someone the woman knew? Or perhaps the woman dressed in Plain clothes might be here visiting Eileen's parents and had Eileen mixed up with one of her siblings who may have looked similar to her.

The answer to his questions came as quickly as they had appeared. The Amish woman pulled Eileen into her arms, and the two began to sob.

"Oh, Rosa, my dear daughter." She held both hands against her chest. "My mother's heart just knew you couldn't be dead." The older woman reached out and touched Eileen's shoulder-length tresses. "You've cut your hair, and you're wearing English clothes, but I would know my daughter anywhere." Tears coursed down the woman's cheeks. "I've missed you so much. Where have you been all this time?"

Daughter? Anthony blinked and turned to face Eileen as she pulled slowly away from the older woman. He wanted to ask her right then and there if she'd lied to him about her name or the woman who'd called her Rosa. Something was definitely wrong, and he needed some answers quickly before he continued the charade of posing as her husband. But how could he get her alone to ask the necessary questions?

He was surprised when Eileen, Rosa, or whoever she was looked at her mother and said, "Can we talk about this later? Anthony and I drove a long ways to get here, and we're really tired." She finally gestured to him and said, "Mom, this is my husband, Anthony Reeves."

Her mother's mouth opened wide. "Seriously? You're married?"

Anthony stepped forward and shook the woman's hand. "That's right, and we're expecting our first child." *Might as well get straight to the point,* he decided. *I'm here as a pretender, but Miss Rosa obviously lied to me about her real name as well as her family heritage. I wonder, who's really the one pretending?*

"You're going to have a baby?" A wide smile swept across the mother's face when the daughter responded with a nod. "Oh, that's *wunderbaar!*"

Although not familiar with the Pennsylvania Dutch language, Anthony figured the word must mean "wonderful," but he would ask Rosa about that later.

~

Rosa was glad that Anthony seemed to have composed himself and was going along with the story they had concocted. At least that much was out in the open now. She was about to ask if she and Anthony could go upstairs and freshen up when her two sisters stepped into the hall. They looked at Rosa as if they were seeing a ghost. Tena was the first to speak.

"Oh my—what a surprise! You look so different in jeans and a sweatshirt, Sister, but I'm so glad you're alive." She gave Rosa such a big welcoming hug that it brought tears to her eyes. "And it's even more special that you came home on your birthday."

Mom nodded vigorously. "Happy birthday, my dear Rosa. What a gift you have given me, even though it is I who should be showering you with gifts on this most special day."

"It's your birthday?" Anthony questioned in a hushed tone. "How come you never said anything to me about it?"

She shrugged and whispered, "It's not important."

Rosa glanced at Susan, who stood nearby with her mouth still agape.

Rosa stepped forward to embrace her sister, but Susan remained firmly in place, with her back straight as a rod. *She's obviously mad at me for leaving, or maybe Susan would have preferred that I had stayed gone.*

"Let's all go into the living room so we can talk," Mom suggested. "Your *daed* is in the barn doing chores, and Alvin went with him, but they should be in soon."

Rosa glanced at Anthony, and when he gave a brief shrug, she looked at her mother and said, "I think my husband and I would like to freshen up first. Is that all right with you?"

"Of course." Mom pulled Rosa in for another hug. "I am so thankful to God that you are home, safe and sound. I still can hardly believe that you're actually standing here with us right now." She shook Anthony's hand for a second time. "Thank you for bringing your wife here to see us."

Anthony gave a nod. "She wanted me to meet her family."

Mom smiled and blotted the tears from her face. "You two go on upstairs now and make yourselves comfortable in Rosa's old room. We'll make sure the sheets are changed before bedtime, but you can rest for a while on top of the bed if you like, and the upstairs bathroom is free for your use as well."

Rosa couldn't miss the way her sister's features had tightened. *Has Susan taken over what used to be my room? Would Mom have allowed her to do that?*

Rosa gave Anthony's arm a tug. "Come on, Husband—follow me to my room upstairs."

At the top of the stairs, he turned to her and, with his nostrils flaring, said, "You've got a lot of explaining to do, Eileen—Rosa—or whatever your real name is."

She put one finger to her lips. "*Shh...* Let's talk about this in my room, where we can't be heard."

Rosa opened her bedroom door and stepped inside. When Anthony followed, she asked him to take a seat on the end of her bed, and after a quick glance around the room, she sat down beside him. "I'm sure you have lots of questions."

"You've got that right." His chin jutted forward. "Let's start with what your real name is."

She clasped both hands in her lap and swallowed hard. "My name is Rosa Petersheim, and I'm sure you must now have come to the conclusion that my family is Amish."

"Yeah, the Plain dresses and head coverings your mother and sisters wore were kind of a red flag." Anthony reached up and rubbed the back of his muscular neck. "So did you change your name legally to Eileen Peterson?"

She shook her head. "Eileen is my middle name, and I chose *Peterson* because it's similar to my last name, Petersheim."

"So you used a fake ID to get the job working for my folks?"

"Yeah, I met someone soon after I ran away from home a little over two years ago, and they helped me get what I needed."

He scratched behind his right ear and frowned. "What exactly were you running from?"

As Rosa squirmed atop the quilt on her bed, her heartbeat picked up speed. "Everything—my overbearing father, who is the bishop of our Amish community. My pushy boyfriend, who wanted me to join the Amish church so we could be married. And all the expectations placed on me by each of the church rules."

"Did your family know why you left home?"

"Of course. Before heading to a young people's gathering with Ephraim, I left a note in my room, letting them know that I would most likely not be coming back and explaining my reasons for taking off."

"Ephraim. Was he your boyfriend?"

She bobbed her head.

"Did he know you were planning to leave home?"

"No, but I was going to tell him and see if I could talk him into leaving with me for a new beginning." She paused for a breath. "Then before I could tell him my plan, we had a big fight as the gathering was winding down, and I took off on foot and never looked back."

Anthony gave a strong shake of his head. "You're kidding."

"It's true. I had my purse with me, so I wasn't without money, and I caught a ride with someone who was heading up to State College. From there, I got on a Trailways bus and went to a small town not far from New York City. I found my first job there, and then moved from job to job until I ended up getting hired at your father's restaurant."

Anthony sat in silence several minutes before posing another question. "How long ago did this take place?"

"A little over two years ago. Didn't you hear what was said before?" She gave a dry laugh. "Time spins by quickly when you're havin' fun."

"Did you connect with anyone in your family—let them know where you were living and that you were okay?"

"I tried to call a couple of times but never connected with anyone. Finally gave up and decided to move on with my life, since I had no plans of joining the Amish church." Rosa swallowed hard. "And I sure wasn't about to become a member so I could marry some guy who kept begging me to do so."

"Did you love him?"

She gave a noncommittal shrug. "Guess it all depends on your definition of love."

"What's yours?"

"I'm not sure. I suppose genuine love would mean a commitment to someone that was so deep you'd be willing to do anything—go anywhere—to make them happy."

"And you didn't love Ephraim enough to do that?"

"No, and he didn't love me enough to leave our Amish heritage and explore the English world." Rosa got off the bed and wandered over to the window to look out at the darkening sky. "I probably never would have come back if I hadn't gotten pregnant and needed my family's support." Unbidden tears welled in her eyes. "I foolishly thought the jerk I gave myself to really loved me and would accept responsibility for the baby he'd fathered." Rosa whirled around to face Anthony. "But I guess no man can be trusted, and now that you know the truth about me, you'll probably head straight back to New York and forget about the promise you made to pretend we are married."

"I'll keep up with the ploy like we planned," he said. "And I won't leave till I'm sure your folks are committed to taking care of you and the baby." He took hold of her hand but then quickly pulled it away.

"What are we going to do about our sleeping arrangements if they ask us to stay here at the house?" she questioned. "Since they believe we are married, we can hardly put in a request for separate rooms."

"We can share the same room, but I'll sleep on the floor." His answer was given quickly.

She tipped her head and looked directly at him. "You would really do that for me?"

He thumped his chest. "I'm not the kind of guy who fails to keep his promises."

"Thank you. I appreciate that." Rosa heaved a sigh of relief. Now all she needed to do was secure her father's blessing. If she couldn't do that, she'd be out on the street, trying to figure out some other way to support herself and the baby growing inside her.

⸺

"Whose vehicle is that parked in front of our house?" Mahlon asked upon entering the living room where Elsie sat with Susan and Tena. She still felt a bit dazed from seeing Rosa and coming to grips with the reality that her eldest daughter was still alive and had returned home as a married woman with a child on the way.

A sense of joy and relief spread through Elsie, such as she had not known in a good many years—not since her and Mahlon's youngest child was born. *And to think, we will become grandparents for the first time.* She couldn't contain the deep sigh welling in her chest. *Oh, what a blessing that will be.*

Mahlon moved closer to Elsie's chair. "Did you hear my question about the car parked in our front yard? I don't recognize it as belonging to any of our drivers—or English neighbors, for that matter."

She shook her head. "No, it's not either of those." Elsie rose from her seat and lifted both hands to her husband's broad shoulders. "Oh, Mahlon, we've experienced a miracle in this family today. Our missing *dochder* has come home."

Mahlon's arms hung loosely at his sides as he stared at her, blinking slowly as if in disbelief. "Rosa is here? Is that what you're saying?"

Tena leaped to her feet and dashed across the room. "That's right, Dad! Isn't it exciting?"

His head swiveled from right to left. "Where is she?"

Susan, who remained on the couch with a stoic expression, pointed to the ceiling. "She and her good-looking English husband are upstairs."

Mahlon's posture stiffened. "Husband?"

"*Jah*, and they are expecting a baby. And just think, Husband, we are going to be grandparents for the first time." Elsie clutched his arm. "Isn't that exciting?"

"What's exciting?" Alvin asked when he entered the room, holding a pure white kitten in his hands.

"Our missing sister came home," Tena said.

His eyes widened. "Rosa?"

"That's right, Son." Elsie smiled. "Isn't that the best news ever?"

Alvin bobbed his head and glanced around the room. "Where's she at now?"

Susan pursed her lips and pointed up again.

Just then, Rosa made an appearance with Anthony at her side. She gave Alvin a hug then moved toward her father. "Dad, I'd like you to meet my husband, Anthony Reeves."

Holding her breath, Elsie waited for Mahlon's response. Surely he would be happy to see their daughter and meet the man she had chosen to marry.

Anthony stepped forward and extended his hand. "It's nice to meet you, Mr. Petersheim."

Mahlon's eyes narrowed as he tapped his right foot, refusing to shake the young man's hand. His piercing gaze turned to Rosa. "Where have you been? Do you have any idea what you've put this family through?"

She lowered her head, as though hurt by his harsh tone. "I'm sorry, Dad. Let's all take a seat, and I'll explain things to you."

He glared at her like an angry bull about to charge. "You'd better have a mighty good excuse for your absence or you'll be heading right out the front door with no chance of ever coming back!"

Elsie swallowed around the constriction that had formed quickly at the back of her throat. Losing Rosa once had torn her heart asunder. She couldn't imagine losing her dear daughter a second time, not to mention never getting to know Anthony or hold Rosa's baby.

CHAPTER 4

Dad lowered himself into an overstuffed chair and folded his arms. Meanwhile Mom, with her mouth quivering slightly, took a seat in her rocker, while Alvin stood close by. Susan and Tena filled up the space on one end of the couch, and Rosa and Anthony sat together on the opposite end.

"Well, let's have it," Dad said, looking at Rosa with his nose scrunched up. "Where have you been all this time, and why haven't you contacted any of us until now?"

Rosa cleared her throat and glanced around the room at each of the solemn faces looking at her. "Where's Norman?" she questioned. "I would like for him to hear this too."

"Your *bruder* and Salina's wedding took place a few weeks ago, and they are currently living at her parents' place until the home they have rented is ready for them to move into," Mom was quick to say.

"Oh, I see. Well, I always figured they'd end up getting married." Rosa glanced at Anthony as he removed his leather jacket and laid it across his knees. She wondered if he felt as uncomfortable as she did right now. It would not be easy for her to divulge all the information her folks sought, but she had to begin somewhere, so she plunged ahead. "As I'm sure you must know, I left a note in my room explaining why I had decided to leave home."

Dad shook his head vigorously, and Mom emitted a strangled-sounding squeak.

"You did find the note, didn't you? I put it on my nightstand so it wouldn't be missed."

Mom looked at Rosa's sisters. "Did either of you girls find a note in Rosa's room?"

With solemn expressions, they both shook their heads.

Dad pointed to Alvin. "What about you, Son?"

"No, Dad." Alvin lifted his chin. "I'd never go into Rosa's room without her permission, and I don't go in now that it's Susan's room either."

So Susan did take over my room after I took off. Rosa's fingers clenched, and she winced when her nails bit into the flesh. *I wonder if she found the note and won't own up to it. If so, would Susan do such a thing?* Rosa decided that the first time she had a chance to speak with Susan alone, she would get to the bottom of this. In the meantime, she had some explaining of her own to do.

"So if there really was a note, what did it say?" Dad asked, pulling Rosa's thoughts back to their discussion.

"It said that I couldn't live here anymore because of all the pressure being placed upon me to join the church. I also stated that I wanted to explore some things in the English world and would let you know when I got settled somewhere."

Dad's face reddened, and he pointed a shaky finger at her. "Which you did not! In all the time you've been gone, we haven't heard one single word from you!"

"I did call a couple of times and left messages, plus I sent a few postcards and letters, but no one ever responded. So I figured you did not want to hear anything from me." Rosa's voice quivered, and she felt a sense of comfort when Anthony took her hand and gave it a gentle squeeze. It seemed as though someone in this room was on her side. Or at least she hoped he was. After Anthony's reaction when she'd come clean with him about her true identity, Rosa couldn't be sure of anything right now.

"As far as I know, there were no messages from you, Rosa." Mom looked at the girls once more, with her head tilted slightly. "Did either of you discover any messages from your sister on our answering machine or in the mailbox?"

They both shook their heads again.

"Well, there you have it!" Dad shouted. "You're lying, just like you have done often in the past."

Rosa's internal temperature rose. "No, Dad, I am telling you the truth. I really did leave a note, and I made those calls." *I can't believe they never received my phone messages.* She glanced at Susan, who now sat with her head down. *Could Susan have heard those few messages I left on our folks' answering machine to let them know I was okay, but then not told them about the calls? If so, I would like to know why. I'll add that to the list of questions to ask her.*

Dad's eyes seemed to bulge as he glared at Rosa. "Do you have any idea how your disappearance has affected this family? We didn't know if you were alive or dead, and at the risk of his relationship with Salina, Norman spent many hours trying to find you." His voice rose even higher. "And your poor *mamm* was so distraught and filled with grief that she became physically ill."

Rosa blinked back the tears burning her eyes. "I'm so sorry, Mom. I had no idea you never received any of my messages or that you had taken ill. If there was some way I could make it up to you, I surely would."

"It's too late for that now," Dad said without giving Mom a chance to respond. "What's done is done, and there's no going back."

"I realize that, but—"

"There are no buts about it," Dad cut Rosa off. "You messed up our lives and now you come waltzing back in here like nothing ever happened at all."

"That's not true, Mr. Petersheim," Anthony spoke up. "Eileen—I mean, Rosa—wanted to see her family."

Once more, Rosa appreciated her friend Anthony's support.

Dad grunted like a grizzly bear as he folded his arms. "Well, she's seen us now so she can move on with whatever life she has created without us."

Mom practically jumped out of her chair and hurried over to Dad. "No, Mahlon. Rosa and her husband are welcome to stay here for as long as they want. There's plenty of room for them in Rosa's old room, and Susan can move across the hall with Tena again."

"But Mom, that's not fair," Susan argued. "After Rosa disappeared, you said I could have her room."

"I also stated that if Rosa came back, that room would be hers again, so please go upstairs and change the sheets on the bed and remove your clothes and personal items. Then after we've all had supper, Rosa and Anthony can bring their things inside and get settled in."

Susan's lips curled as she plucked at her apron band, but she gave no argument and ended up stomping out of the room like a sullen child.

Rosa also stood and said to her mother, "I'd be happy to help you get supper going."

"Susan and I have the meal in the oven," Tena said, "but you can help Alvin by setting the table."

"Sure, no problem." Rosa followed her mother, sister, and young brother out of the room. She hoped Anthony would be okay staying alone with her father.

~

The icy stare he'd received from Rosa's father since she, along with her mother and younger sister and brother, had left the room was enough to freeze a tray of water in less than a minute.

"What do you do for a living, Mr. Petersheim?" Anthony asked, hoping to break the ice and get a nice conversation going.

Mahlon sat several seconds before opening his mouth to speak. "I own the Meat and Cheese Store here in Belleville. My son Norman and daughter Susan work there with me." He reached around and rubbed the back of his neck. "Rosa used to be an employee before she went missing."

Anthony's lips compressed. *Hmm...one more thing Miss Rosa never told me about. I wonder how much more there is that I don't know concerning her past. Maybe it doesn't matter. Once my two weeks' vacation is over, and Rosa and I have had our separation blowup, I'll be heading back to Mom and Pop's restaurant in New York. Then I can put all thoughts of Rosa Petersheim to rest and move on with my life.*

"So what kind of work do you do?"

Mahlon's question pushed Anthony's contemplations to the back of his mind.

"I'm a chef at my parents' Italian restaurant in New York City." *At least I cook until Pop decides I need to do something else.* Anthony saw no reason to voice his most recent thoughts.

"So your parents are Italian?"

"Only Mom. My dad has a British heritage, but he likes Italian food real well, and my mother's a great cook, which might be why he married her." Anthony chuckled, hoping to bring some lightheartedness into the room. It didn't work. Rosa's father sat slouched in his chair with his eyelids half closed. Surely there had to be some topic they could find to talk easily about.

Anthony perused the sparsely decorated room. With the exception of the couch, chairs, two small end tables, fireplace, and gas lamps overhead, there wasn't much to look at. The wooden floors were bare, without even any throw rugs covering them, and there wasn't a single picture on the wall. Anthony didn't know much about Amish rules, other than what he'd heard on a few reality shows that he figured were probably not all that accurate. He was full of questions and wanted to ask about several things, but he didn't want his curiosity to be seen as prying into someone's life that was none of his business. Even so, he needed to find something to talk about until they were called to the supper table.

If Anthony had been a praying man, he would have sought guidance. Instead, he threaded his fingers through the front of his thick, curly hair and blurted, "How many horses do you have?"

Mahlon's eyes opened fully, and he muttered, "With the exception of Alvin, everyone in this family has their own horse."

"Did Rosa have one when she lived here?"

"Of course, and her mare is still with us." He looked toward the ceiling with a shake of his head. "My wife, Elsie, insisted that we keep the horse in case Rosa ever returned. Rosa's sisters took turns using the mare, but it's doubtful that Rosa will ever really take possession of the horse again." He flapped a hand. "I mean, she'd look pretty silly drivin' a horse and buggy wearing jeans and a sweatshirt. Besides, you have a car, so what use would Rosa have for our slow mode of transportation?"

Anthony wondered what Rosa's dad would have to say if he knew about their plan to split up in a couple of weeks. Would it give Mahlon some hope that his wayward daughter might return to the Amish way of life and join the church? If Rosa was planning to stay with her parents and expected them to help her raise the baby, wouldn't it make sense that she would become a church member and dress in Amish clothes, accordingly?

Anthony felt relief when Rosa's mother came into the living room and announced that supper was on the table. She also stated that Susan had come downstairs and Rosa's room was now ready for Anthony and Rosa to occupy the space.

Anthony said, "Thank you," got up, and followed Rosa's father out of the room. He could hardly wait to see how the conversation around the table would go as he shared a meal with this Amish family.

Susan took her seat at the table next to Tena and closed her eyes for silent prayer. She had quit praying after her boyfriend, Ben Ebersol, went to prison for setting fire to several barns in the area. Susan had known Ben was on the wild side, and she'd been attracted to his good looks and carefree personality. If she had known from the beginning of their relationship that he would be capable of destroying someone's property and animals and nearly causing Ephraim Peight to perish in a fire, Susan would have broken things off with Ben and never allowed herself to fall in love with him.

And now, she just went through the motions of praying to keep up appearances where her dad was concerned. *Nothing ever works out well for me,* Susan thought bitterly as she waited for Dad to signal, by the rustle of silverware, that his prayer was over. *Rosa has always been Mom's favorite daughter, and now she's back with a good-looking husband and a baby on the way, and I have nothing, not even her old room anymore. It's not fair that I'm stuck sharing a bedroom with Tena again. I wish Rosa had never come back so Mom would still depend on me.*

Susan's eyes snapped open when she heard Dad clear his throat. If he'd rustled his silverware, she must not have heard the familiar sound. Now she had to force herself to eat the meat loaf she and Tena had prepared, as if nothing was wrong and her appetite was hearty, which was anything but the truth.

From his place at the head of the table, Dad began dishing up from the platter and bowls closest to him and passing them along to Mom, who sat to his left.

"Everything sure smells and looks delicious," Anthony commented when the meat loaf had been handed to him.

"My husband is a chef," Rosa said, "so he appreciates good food."

The sappy look on her sister's face was enough to make Susan's stomach churn. *Is she really as happy as she looks, or is Rosa merely putting on an act for Mom and Dad's sake? Maybe she and Anthony have no place else to go, and she wants to make a good impression so Dad won't kick them out of our house.* Susan dished up a few peas and rolled them around on her plate. One small slice of meat loaf and a blob of potatoes filled out what Susan thought was all she could manage to get down. She hoped that no one would notice or comment about it. Everyone except for Dad seemed to enjoy asking Anthony about his job as a cook and questioning him, as well as Rosa, concerning what it was like to live in New York.

Susan wished she could take off for someplace like that, or even the big city of Philadelphia—anywhere but here. *Maybe someday, when I have enough money saved up, I'll leave Mifflin County and start a new life somewhere else, like Rosa did. Only, I would not look back once, and I sure wouldn't return home and expect my Amish family, who don't care about me anyway, to take me in.*

CHAPTER 5

New York City

"Would you please hand me the saltshaker? You didn't add enough to the green beans."

Lavera looked across the table at her husband, Herb, and calmly said, "I didn't add any salt while steaming the veggies, because as you may recall, due to your high blood pressure, the doctor wants you to limit salt intake." She pushed a bottle of garlic powder in his direction. "Why don't you sprinkle some of this on for added flavor?"

"I like garlic well enough, although it's not the same as salt. But I guess it's better than nothing at all." Herb picked up the bottle, opened the lid, and gave it a shake. "I suppose the next thing I know, the doctor will want me to give up eating pasta, red meat, and my favorite desserts." He groaned. "Talk about a boring diet."

"Try not to be so negative. When your health is at stake, you should be willing to make any helpful changes if needed."

"Yeah, well, I don't need some guy with a stethoscope and a tongue depressor telling me what I should or shouldn't eat." Herb cut into his steak, cooked medium rare, just the way he liked it, and smacked his lips. "Perfecto."

Lavera shrugged in response. Any further comments on her part would probably fall on deaf ears. She loved this man she'd been married to for nearly twenty-six years, but he could sure be stubborn and had always made it clear that he didn't want anyone telling him what to do.

Of course, Lavera could be the same way when it came to certain things.

"I wonder how things are going with Anthony right now. He said he would call when he and Eileen arrived at their destination," Lavera said after putting a dollop of sour cream on her baked potato.

Herb glanced up from his plate and frowned. "And where would that be? Did he ever say exactly where they were going in such a hurry and why he had to take his full two weeks' vacation on such short notice?"

Lavera shook her head. "He only said that Eileen wanted to go home to see her folks, and he'd agreed to drive her there."

"Well, unless they live on the other side of the country, it shouldn't take him two weeks to get there and back to New York."

"Maybe they've already arrived at their destination, and she invited him to stay awhile."

Herb grabbed a paper napkin from the wicker basket in the center of the table and wiped his mouth. "What for? Those two barely know each other. It's not like the two of them are dating or anything."

"True, but she has been working at our restaurant for nearly six months, and you know our son—he's the friendly type, who has always seemed to care about people he knows who are hurting."

"Yeah, alley cats included." Herb cut another piece of steak. "I can't tell you how often I've caught him feeding stray cats that hang out near the back door of our restaurant."

"You can't compare a nice young woman like Eileen to a hungry cat."

"Can if I want to. I've never cared much for Miss Peterson and her sultry-looking eyes. Don't think I haven't seen the way she flirts with the male customers."

"It hasn't affected our business, has it?"

"Guess not, but it could have if Eileen had continued to show up late, like she did the week before she and our Anthony took off for parts unknown with little or no explanation." Herb pounded the table with his fist, jostling the silverware. "I came real close to firing them both on the spot."

"You couldn't very well fire her after she'd already told us she was quitting." Lavera rested both elbows on the table and leaned closer to her husband. "And since Anthony is our only son—who's a very fine cook, I might add—firing him would not have been a smart decision. Especially since he'd said that he would be coming back when his vacation ended."

"Yeah, well. . .that remains to be seen. I wouldn't be surprised if that young woman ends up convincing him to stay with her, and then he'll never come back to New York." Herb pursed his lips. "Then I'll never be able to retire and give him the business we've worked so hard to build."

Lavera squinted her eyes as she pointed at Herb. "You're kidding, right?"

"Why would I kid about something like that? Haven't we talked about taking an extended trip to Italy so you could see all the places where you grew up and, at the same, visit some of your cousins?"

"Well, yes, but that was supposed to be a vacation, not a permanent move. Besides, no way could we take off and leave Anthony here to run the place by himself."

Herb grunted. "If Connie had shown some interest in learning the restaurant business, instead of running off and marrying the first guy who came along, and Eva wasn't in college, we'd have more family to count on."

Lavera rolled her eyes at him. "When are you going to let that go, Herb? Shouldn't our grown children have the right to choose their own path in life, like you and I did?"

He shrugged his shoulders. "I guess so. Sure don't have to like it, though."

She hid a smile behind her open hand. Whatever choices their grown children made, like it or not, Herb would have to learn to accept it, because it was all a part of life.

Belleville

After supper that evening, Rosa's mother brought out two pies she'd made earlier in the day and placed them on the dining room table. One was chocolate, and the other was banana cream, which she placed in front of Rosa. "It's not a birthday cake, but I'm happy to be able to serve you a special dessert in celebration of your birthday today, in addition to your miracle homecoming this evening." Her smile stretched wide. "Those are certainly good reasons to celebrate, jah?"

"Thank you, Mom. The pies look delicious, and I can't wait to try a piece of the banana cream." Rosa looked at Anthony. "How about you? Which flavor might be your favorite?"

Susan sat on the other side of the table with her arms folded. *They're a married couple, for goodness' sake. Why wouldn't my sister know what kind of pie her husband likes? That seems kind of odd to me.* She shifted on her unyielding wooden chair. *I wonder how long these two have known each other. I don't recall either of them saying anything about when they started going out or even mentioning what day they'd gotten married.*

It aggravated Susan that Rosa and her good-looking husband had shown up here unannounced—and on Rosa's birthday, no less. And what really irritated Susan was that Mom had welcomed them both with open arms. *And not nearly enough questions.* Susan figured if it had been her who'd been missing all that time and she'd returned unexpectedly, her welcome would have been meager at best. Rosa needed to pay for the way she'd upset the whole family by running off. So rather than eating a piece of pie, Susan sat quietly, thinking things through.

I know something that might get a rise out of my sister. Jah, think I'll see if a little unexpected news will rain on her parade.

"Guess who's getting married soon?" Susan directed her question to Rosa.

"I have no idea," her sister responded after taking a bite of banana cream pie.

"Your best friend, Ada, and her groom-to-be is none other than your ex-boyfriend, Ephraim. Now, isn't that a big surprise?"

⸺⸺

Rosa gave a sharp intake of breath. "Are you sure about that?" It didn't seem possible that while she'd been gone, Ada and Ephraim could have developed a serious relationship that led to their marriage. She remembered how Ephraim used to insist that he would never love anyone but her. Did he still feel any love for her? Had he picked Ada as a second choice? Would he feel differently if he knew that Rosa was back home now?

With her enthusiasm over the pie all but gone, Rosa toyed with the napkin by her plate. *Even if Ephraim did still have feelings for me, or I for him, it's too late for us now. I'm here with a pretend husband and Ephraim's on the brink of marrying my best friend.*

During the years she and Ephraim had gone out, Rosa had never suspected that Ada might have become interested in him, although Rosa did recall several occasions when her friend had commented that Rosa was lucky to have a boyfriend who loved her so much. Rosa hadn't thought much about it at the time, but now she found herself wondering if Ada might have been envious because she wished Ephraim had chosen to court her instead of Rosa.

Well, it doesn't matter now, she told herself. *If I had wanted to marry Ephraim, I shouldn't have run off. I should have stayed here, joined the church, and married him.*

"So do you think you'll go to the wedding?"

Susan's unexpected question drove Rosa's thoughts aside, and she pressed her spine firmly against the back of her chair. "Of course not. I wasn't invited."

"I'm sure you would have been if you hadn't run off, and I'm almost certain that if Ada and Ephraim knew you were here, they would want you to be present at their wedding." With her shoulders pushed back, Susan looked directly at Rosa.

Rosa shook her head. "It would be rude to show up unexpectedly, without an invitation, and I'm sure the bride and groom would not like it."

"Well, don't you think you should at least tell them you're here? Maybe even give them the opportunity to let you know about their upcoming wedding?"

"Susan, please stop pressuring your sister with questions and allow her to make her own decisions."

Rosa was glad when their mother spoke up. She was stressed out enough and didn't need Susan giving her the third degree about this—or anything else, for that matter.

"Your mamm's right," Dad put in, much to Rosa's surprise. "It's her choice whether she wants to attend the wedding, and you need to mind your own business."

"Fine, then!" Susan pushed her chair aside and stormed out of the room.

Anthony leaned close to Rosa and said quietly, "Maybe we should go find us a hotel for the night."

"Absolutely not!" Apparently Mom had heard what he'd said, because she gave a vigorous shake of her head. "I want you both to stay right here and make yourselves comfortable in Rosa's old room, like I said earlier. And you're welcome to stay just as long as you like. Is that understood?"

Anthony looked at Rosa, and when she nodded, he said, "Okay then, I'll get our luggage from my car and bring it inside."

After he went out the front door, Rosa stood and picked up her plate with the unfinished slice of pie, as well as the one Anthony had yet to finish. "I'll take these out to the kitchen."

"Don't take my plate," Alvin quickly announced, "'cause I ain't done."

"You are not done," Tena corrected.

He bobbed his head. "Jah, that's what I said."

"And I'm not finished either." Dad grabbed the trim stainless steel spatula and dished himself another piece of chocolate pie.

"What about you, Daughter?" Mom questioned, looking at Tena, who seemed to be staring at her now-empty plate.

"One piece was enough for me. I'll help you and Rosa in the kitchen, and then I'm going up to bed. Although I'm not lookin' forward to sharing a room with Susan tonight," she muttered.

Rosa bit the inside of her cheek as she fled to the kitchen. *Maybe I made a mistake coming back here to seek the help and support I want from my folks. I'm wondering if they weren't better off without me.*

"Where are you going?" Anthony asked after Rosa hung her clothes in the closet and moved toward the bedroom door with a canvas bag in one hand.

"To the bathroom to brush my teeth and get ready for bed. Then I'm going downstairs for a glass of water. Would you like one too?"

"No thanks. I'll be okay."

Rosa gestured to the thin piece of foam she'd taken from the attic when no one was looking, along with two blankets and a pillow she had placed on the floor for him to sleep on. "Are you sure you're gonna be comfortable there?"

"Probably not, but I'll make do. It'll only be for a couple of weeks, after all."

"Yeah, that's true." She grabbed a flashlight, put her hand on the doorknob, and paused. What a mess she'd gotten herself into—first by running away from home, then getting involved with a married man, and now dragging Anthony into her web of deceit. He was a decent guy and deserved better, and yet here he was, about to make his bed on the floor for the night, in order to keep up appearances with Rosa's family and protect her honor. Tomorrow morning, they would need to hide the evidence of his makeshift bed underneath her bed frame.

Rosa glanced briefly over her shoulder, then went out the door.

When Rosa approached the upstairs bathroom and found the door closed, she descended the stairs, in the hope that the downstairs bathroom was not occupied. As she moved slowly down the hall, guided by her flashlight, and approached her parents' bedroom, Rosa heard voices. She paused and listened.

"What do you mean I haven't been cordial enough to Rosa and her curly-haired English husband?" Dad's booming voice rang out. "Do I need to remind you, Elsie, that I had previously stated when our wayward daughter went missing that unless she came home with a good excuse, Rosa would not be welcomed?"

"I know what you said, Mahlon, but her main reason for leaving was because you pressed her too hard to join the church," Mom responded.

"That's not true. I only tried to make her see the folly of her ways, and—"

"Our daughter is home now, with a husband and baby on the way, and I will not allow you to chase her off again!"

As she stood listening to her parents discussing this, as though they were playing on opposite teams in a game of competitive volleyball, Rosa's guilt increased. *What can I do to make things better?* she asked herself while moving up the hall to continue her trek to the bathroom. *If I leave home again, it will break my mother's heart. If I stay, Dad may never welcome me into the family, and I'm sure that Susan won't either.*

⁓⁓

Anthony reclined on the floor in Rosa's bedroom, trying to find a comfortable position and wondering if he'd made the wrong decision regarding her. *If I had known what I was getting myself into, would I have thought it through a bit more before I suggested that I play the role of her husband?*

He lifted his head from the pillow and reached around in an attempt to fluff it up a bit, thereby giving himself more support. Rosa had been gone awhile, and he wondered if she'd gotten lost in this big drafty house with no electricity. How was he supposed to charge his cell phone or plug in his electric shaver? *Guess I'll just have to take it out to the car when necessary and use my power cord for charging as needed.* Anthony could not understand why the Amish would intentionally choose to live this way, with all the conveniences of the modern world available to them. Was it their need to hold on to old-world traditions, or did the meaning of their lifestyle go deeper than that?

The house seemed deathly quiet, and the only source of light in the room was a glimmer of the moon shining through a small tear in one corner of the window shade.

The bedroom door squeaked open, and Anthony turned his head in the direction of the sound. Then he heard footsteps padding across the bare floor.

"Rosa, is that you?"

"Of course it's me. Who else would it be?"

When she leaned close to Anthony and spoke, he felt her breath blow against his face, leaving him feeling a bit rattled. "Oh, umm...I thought it might be your sister—the one who used to occupy this room."

"Yeah, well, it was my room way before it was Susan's, and she is clearly having trouble accepting the fact that I have returned home."

Anthony heard the bed creak and figured Rosa had reclined on the mattress. "You're probably right," he agreed. "But hopefully it won't take her long to move past those feelings."

"I wish that were true, but you don't know my sister. She's always been jealous of me."

"You shouldn't give up hope, at least not yet. Maybe things will change in your favor."

"Yeah right. Now that is wishful thinking."

CHAPTER 6

THE FOLLOWING MORNING, ANTHONY awoke to the sound of a blaring rooster's crow and a sore, stiff back. Every muscle in his body ached from having slept on the floor. The thin foam beneath his body had done little to offer comfort and give him a good night's sleep.

He groaned, sat up, and glanced at the bed. It was empty and appeared to have been neatly made, with the top end of the colorful quilt pulled perfectly over the pillow. There was no sign of Rosa, and he figured she must either be in the bathroom or have gone downstairs. Despite the uncomfortable makeshift bed he'd slept upon, Anthony assumed that he must have been so tired he'd slept through whatever noise Rosa had made when she'd gotten up, made the bed, and left the room.

He stood and stepped into his jeans. After opening the door, Anthony was greeted with the familiar aroma of coffee brewing. *Ahh* . . .at least something in this house seemed familiar to him. During his childhood years, Anthony recalled that the first thing his mother had done every morning was to get a pot of coffee going. Pop always said that he couldn't start his day without a kick start of caffeine. Mom liked coffee too, but she never drank more than one cup each morning. Anthony and his sisters had begun drinking coffee when they were teenagers, so Mom had increased the size of her coffeepot to accommodate the family.

Anthony pushed his thoughts aside and padded down the hall in his bare feet to the bathroom. At least this old-fashioned home had running water with indoor plumbing. He'd half expected he'd have to carry water in from outside and heat it on the stove to wash up, or worse, take a bath in some galvanized tub, like the ones he had seen in some of the old western films.

As Anthony stood at the bathroom sink washing his face, he thought about his motorcycle, sitting in the parking garage of the building where his one-bedroom apartment was located. He had rented the place after moving out of his parents' house a few years ago and paid a steep price for the two parking spaces he needed to accommodate both of his vehicles. Without that, he would have stayed put at Mom and Pop's place, where they could scrutinize everything he said or did.

Anthony pulled a comb through the thick curly hair that fell across his forehead. He'd definitely been blessed with his mother's full head of dark hair. Pop, on the other hand, was nearly bald. He claimed it was heredity, from his grandfather, but Anthony figured his father's loss of hair might have more to do with the stress he put himself under, always shouting orders and worrying about who was doing what in the kitchen and dining room of the restaurant. Sometimes the place felt like a three-ring circus. For that reason alone, it was nice to be away for a couple of weeks. Maybe by the time Anthony returned, Pop would be more appreciative and stop asking Anthony to wait on tables or fill in for the busboy.

Sure wish I had a restaurant of my own, Anthony mused. *I could be the head cook, serve whatever I wanted, and make all the decisions about hiring, firing, and decorating the place.*

He set his comb down on the counter and frowned at his reflection in the small mirror above the sink. *Guess that's not likely to happen, though. It's probably nothing but a pipe dream, or as Mom would call it, "wishful thinking."*

⁓⁓

"This ham is real tasty," Anthony commented as he forked another succulent bite into his mouth. "Do you raise the hogs here on your property?" He directed his question to Rosa's father, who sat at the end of the kitchen table.

"No, I don't," Mahlon said after he'd eaten the remainder of his scrambled eggs. "We get our pork from a local Amish farmer and sell it in my Meat and Cheese Store."

"Oh, I see." Anthony was pleased with the man's response, because it was the first full sentence he'd uttered since the Petersheim family had sat down to eat breakfast. Anthony figured either Rosa's dad was a man of few words or he clearly didn't care much for him, because he rarely looked Anthony in the eye.

"Where's your store located?" Anthony questioned, hoping to continue the conversation. "Do you sell from a building here on your property or do you have a store someplace else?"

"Nope, it's not here." Mahlon gave a quick shake of his head. "My place of business is in town, where it's visible and more people come through on a daily basis. Our property here is too far from town, and in my opinion, it's too out of the way for a business to flourish. Plus, if I'd chosen to locate it here, I would have needed to build a separate building on a section of land that's closer to the road so people driving by could see it."

"I see. I'll have to stop by there sometime and check it out." Anthony was pleased that Mahlon had not only answered his question but also given some details. It was a start, at least. Anthony hoped that from this point on, Rosa's dad might be a little more cordial toward him.

"We can go there today," Rosa spoke up. "I would like to show you a few other things in our area, and a stop at my dad's store will give me a chance to see my brother Norman and introduce him to you." She smiled at Anthony and then looked at her dad. "I know you're closed every other Saturday, but will the store be open today?"

"Jah," Mahlon responded. "Norman and Susan will be working there, as usual, but I'll be staying home today to study for Sunday's sermon if I'm the one chosen to preach."

"Lucky me." Susan looked at Rosa with a slight scowl. "You want your old job back? If so, I'd be happy to step aside and look for something that suits me better."

Rosa opened her mouth like she was about to offer a response, but her mother spoke first.

"Your sister's in a family way, Susan. If she continues to suffer with nausea, like she did earlier this morning, there's no way she'll want to work outside the home, much less at the Meat and Cheese Store with all the pungent cheese and meat odors that might make her feel even worse."

Susan gestured to Rosa with her index finger. "Well, if you're feeling so *grank*, maybe you oughta spend the day in bed instead of showing your husband around town."

Anthony couldn't miss the sneer on Susan's face. She obviously had a grudge against her older sister. *Not like my two sisters, who have always gotten along so well with each other—and with me as well. I wonder what Susan has against Rosa.*

༺ ༻

"So what do you think of our little town of Belleville?" Rosa asked as Anthony pulled his car out of the parking lot at the grocery store, where they'd picked up a few nonperishable items for her mother.

"It's small," he responded, "but there seems to be enough places of business here for a person to survive."

"Yeah, but we lack exciting entertainment, and there aren't a whole lot of restaurants to choose from."

"No Italian cuisine I'll bet."

"Just a pizza place. They also sell sandwiches as well as a few other items on their menu. It's nothing like your mom and dad's place in New York, though."

"I suppose not." Anthony tapped the steering wheel with the knuckles on his left hand. "What else is there to see of interest in this town?"

Rosa was tempted to direct him to the greenhouse so she could see if Ada still worked there, but she wasn't ready to see her friend yet, so she changed her mind. On the other hand, Rosa realized that after her fake breakup with Anthony took place in a couple of weeks and he left town, if she chose to remain in her parents' home, then she would be forced to see others in their community and provide an explanation as to where she'd been all this time. Simply put, there was no way she could remain in Belleville and hide out indefinitely. Even so, today she was not up to facing Ada and hearing about her upcoming wedding to Ephraim. Rosa did want to go see Norman, however, so she gave Anthony directions to the Meat and Cheese Store.

"I thought you weren't coming to work today, Dad," Norman commented when his father entered the store with Susan.

"I won't be here long," Dad responded. "Just came to do a little paperwork and give you some surprising news."

"Oh? What news is that?"

"The prodigal daughter came home," Susan blurted before their father could respond.

Norman's brows lifted high on his forehead. "Huh?"

Susan leaned against the front of the checkout counter with her arms folded. "Rosa showed up last evening with some leather-jacket-wearing English fellow she said was her husband."

Norman blinked in succession as he stared at his sister in disbelief. "Is this some kind of a joke?"

Susan shook her head, and then Dad stepped forward and put his hand on Norman's shoulder. "It's true, Son. Your wayward sister, who you spent so long trying to locate, showed up right out of the blue."

"Wh–where's Rosa been all this time, and why hasn't she ever contacted any of us to let us know she was okay?"

"I don't know all the places she's been since she ran off that night over two years ago, but she did say she had left a note for us before she left for the young people's gathering," Dad responded. "She also said she left messages on our phone's answering machine so we would know she was okay." He paused and gave his full beard a good tug. "I don't believe her, of course, because if there had been any kind of note, someone would surely have found it. And if Rosa had left messages, one of us would have heard them and shared the news with the rest of the family."

Norman's stomach tightened. He was stunned by this news but also relieved. After all these months of hearing nothing from his sister, he'd finally accepted the fact that she must be dead and they would never see her again.

"I'm eager to see Rosa and meet her husband."

"Figured you would be, and I guess your mamm thought so too. She asked me to invite you and Salina to join us for supper this evening. Will you be free to come, or have you made other plans?"

Norman shook his head. "No plans that I know of. I'll call Salina and let her know right away. What time should we be there, Dad?"

"We'll probably eat by six thirty, but feel free to come earlier if you like."

"Okay."

"I need to get my paperwork done and head back home to study for tomorrow. My driver will be back to pick me up soon." Dad headed for the back of the store and disappeared into his office.

Susan nudged Norman's arm. "You'd better be prepared for when you see Rosa tonight."

"Prepared for what?"

"Rosa doesn't look like she used to."

"In what way?"

"She wears English clothes now, and her hair is much shorter." Susan held her hand against her shoulder. "On top of that, there's something about the guy Rosa married that Dad doesn't like."

"Such as?"

"For one thing, he wears a dark leather jacket and looks like he belongs on the back of a motorcycle, not on the brink of becoming a father."

Norman's mouth dropped open. "Rosa's expecting a baby?"

"That's right." Susan's lips curled. "I think the only reason they showed up at our place is because her husband's out of a job and they don't have anywhere else to go."

"Did they say that?"

"Well, no, but—"

The bell above the door jingled and a young English couple entered the store. Norman had to do a double take when the young couple moved toward him, and the woman held her arms outstretched.

"Rosa?"

"Yes, it's me, in the flesh."

"Dad told me you had come back, but I could hardly believe it." Norman gave his sister a hug, and then he stepped back to study her hair and clothing. "Wow, you've really changed, Rosa. You definitely don't look Amish anymore." Before she could respond, he turned to the young man who stood near Rosa and extended his hand. "I'm Rosa's brother Norman. And I'm guessing you must be my sister's husband."

"Uh, yeah. My name is Anthony Reeves." He gave Norman's hand a hearty shake. "Nice to meet you."

"Same here."

Rosa swiped at the moisture on her cheeks. "I'm really sorry for everything I put our family through during my absence."

"Yeah, some of us thought you were dead, and our poor mom was really a wreck. You shouldn't have put her through that, Rosa." Susan got right in their sister's face, causing Rosa to take a step back.

"I told you all last night that I'd left a note and also some messages on the recorder in our folks' phone shed."

Susan gave a huff. "Yeah, so you said."

"What I said was true. When no one responded to my messages, I finally gave up, thinking I had been disowned for good."

A mixture of thoughts swirled through Norman's head. During Rosa's absence, he remembered that he'd seen Susan in the phone shed several times and she'd acted strangely when he'd questioned her about it. He really wanted to discuss this with Susan right now, but he figured it would be best to wait until they were alone to quiz her on this topic.

That evening when Norman and Salina came for supper, the joy Elsie had felt since Rosa returned to them increased. How wonderful it was to have their whole family together around the dining room table. And the addition of Rosa's husband made it even more complete. Despite what Mahlon thought, Anthony seemed like a nice man. The only flies in the ointment were that he wasn't Amish and apparently Rosa still had no desire to join their church. If she did, wouldn't she be wearing one of the Amish dresses in her bedroom closest instead of a pair of jeans and a T-shirt? Did she enjoy dressing in what Elsie considered to be men's apparel?

I hope Rosa and Anthony remain here in Belleville and don't move back to New York, Elsie thought. *It would be so hard to see them go, and once their baby comes, we would rarely see the child unless they came back here for a visit. I can't imagine that Mahlon would ever hire a driver to take us to the big city to see our daughter whom he has still not truly accepted.*

Elsie looked at Norman and Salina, sitting on the other side of the table with smiles on their faces as they conversed with Rosa and her husband. After all the time Norman had spent fruitlessly searching for his sister, he could have been bitter about not hearing anything from her during the time she'd been gone. If he was upset with Rosa, he certainly hadn't let on. Alvin and Tena had seemed happy to have Rosa back too, but not so with Susan, which saddened Elsie.

She glanced to her right, where Susan sat with slumped shoulders and not a hint of a smile on her face. What a shame her daughter didn't seem the least bit happy to have her sister back. Elsie wondered if it might have something to do with Susan having to give up the room she'd been occupying in Rosa's absence. Elsie remembered well how Susan had asked numerous times if she could move her things into Rosa's old room. At first, the answer had been no, but Elsie had finally given in and allowed Susan to do as she wished, but with the understanding that if Rosa ever came back, the room would be hers again.

Susan will just have to get used to it and stop being resentful, Elsie told herself. *Life is too short to hold grudges.*

CHAPTER 7

THE FOLLOWING MORNING, BEFORE ROSA and Anthony headed downstairs for breakfast, she informed him that they would be expected to attend church with her family today.

Anthony's dark eyebrows shot up. "Say what?"

"My folks expect the whole family to go, and since they believe we are married..."

He rolled his eyes. "Do you know how long it's been since I've entered a church building?"

"Well, no, but..."

"I was around eight when my grandma dressed me up one Sunday while I was staying with her. Then she took me to church, and I hated it, so she never got me to go there with her again. Furthermore, I don't have a suit or tie to wear, and I don't think I'd be able to sit for a whole hour and listen to some dry preacher go on and on about things I couldn't care less about."

Rosa wondered if she should prepare Anthony by telling him that their worship services were often held in a barn or someone's shop, and it would be for three hours, not one, but she decided against saying anything for now. She also didn't mention the seating arrangement or the type of benches they would sit upon. If her pretend husband knew those things, Rosa was sure he would refuse to go, so it was best to wait until they arrived and let him find out all the details for himself. Their lengthy songs found in the *Ausbund* hymnal would most likely be another thing Anthony wouldn't care for, in addition to listening to the sermons preached in German.

Rosa moved across the room, opened her closet door, and took out one of her Plain Amish dresses—a black dress, with no frills whatsoever, not even any buttons or snaps. The bodice was held together by enough straight pins to keep it modestly closed.

Anthony's eyes widened. "What are you gonna do with that?"

"I'm going to wear it, along with a white cape, apron, and head covering. Oh, and I'll also be wearing black shoes and stockings."

"To church?"

"Yes. My folks—especially my dad, will expect me to be dressed in the appropriate attire."

He looked down at the pair of jeans he'd put on soon after getting up this morning. "What about me? Do I have to borrow some of your father's clothes, which I'm sure would be too big for me, in order to attend church with you?"

She shook her head. "Of course not. You're English and will be seen as a visitor, so you can just wear a pair of dressy slacks and a nice button-down shirt."

"What about my leather jacket? Can I wear that too?"

"Umm. . .sure, I guess so. It's a chilly fall day, so you'll probably need it—at least while you're outside."

"What will you wear to keep warm?" he questioned.

Rosa reached into the closet again and pulled out a black woolen shawl, which she wrapped around her shoulders. "Lovely, isn't it?"

Anthony gave her a crooked grin. "Yeah, straight from Paris."

"Absolutely!" Rosa twirled like a dancer she'd seen on the TV at the home where her baby had been conceived. A sudden pang of nausea swirled through her belly, and she took a few deep breaths, hoping she wouldn't throw up.

Anthony stepped forward and clasped her arms. "Are you okay? Your face looks kind of pale all of a sudden."

"I–I'll be fine. Just feeling a little nausea right now."

"Can you take something for it?"

Rosa heard the concern in his voice, and she appreciated it. No doubt he would make some woman a good husband someday. He'd never really said, but maybe Anthony had a serious girlfriend waiting in New York for him, and for all Rosa knew, they might even be engaged. "If the sick feeling doesn't go away soon, I'll drink a cup of mint tea or nibble on a few saltine crackers," she responded. "In fact, I'll take some to church and keep them in my purse, just in case."

"If you're not feeling well, maybe you should stay home today," Anthony suggested. "I'm sure your parents would understand. And I'll remain here with you," he quickly added.

Rosa shook her head. "Not my father. A family member would have to be really sick before he would look favorably at them missing church." She placed one hand against her stomach. "Besides, if I'm going to have the privilege of remaining here with my family and expecting them to help me raise this baby, then I need to gain my father's approval."

"Guess that makes sense, but shouldn't it be more about your welfare and that of the unborn child than trying to please your dad?"

"Of course I am concerned for my baby, which is why I must keep the peace around here. If you were actually a part of my family, you'd understand." Rosa pointed to the closet. "Now please choose some clothes to wear and go change in the bathroom while I put on my Amish clothes and try to put my hair in a bun so I can slip my head covering on. We'll be leaving for church soon, and I don't want to be late."

"Okay, whatever you say," Anthony called over his shoulder as he pulled out some clothes before going out the door.

"This day can't be over soon enough," Rosa muttered as she sank onto the end of her bed. Although her nausea had subsided a bit, which should have lessened her nerves, Rosa feared that after attending their church service this morning, Anthony might hop in his car and head straight back to New York.

Anthony's back muscles tightened as he struggled to find a comfortable position on the backless wooden bench he'd been directed to sit on over an hour ago inside this quaint-looking barn where the odor of straw and horseflesh permeated the air. Was this really the biggest or best building the group of Amish people could find to hold their service today? And for goodness' sake, why did the men sit on the opposite side of the room from the women? Apparently they believed in segregating the congregation, but with the women sitting directly across from the men, Anthony could see Rosa sitting between her two sisters. Her blank expression and continued yawning indicated that she was either tired or bored. He figured it was probably the latter, since that was certainly the case for him.

On top of that, Anthony felt like a sore thumb, sitting here among these strangers, all dressed pretty much alike. He figured every eye must be on him, since his appearance didn't fit in with the rest of them here. Coming into the building, he'd noticed lots of folks staring at him. No doubt they all wondered about the stranger who had invaded their space. Perhaps some in the congregation had already heard that Rosa Petersheim had returned home—and with a husband who wasn't one of them.

He glanced at his watch, which also set him apart, since none of the Amish people he'd seen wore any kind of jewelry. The songs the people had been singing during this hour were slow and drawn out. There was, however, a distinct blending of voices in rich tones that he found to be quite interesting. Anthony wished he could understand the words. One thing he did understand, however, was that he could never be Amish. Besides the language barrier, horse-and-buggy transportation, and Plain clothing worn by both the men and women, it would be hard to give up the use of electricity along with the modern conveniences such as television, air-conditioning, and computer games—although Anthony rarely watched TV or played games. His world involved trying out new recipes to offer the customers who ate at his parents' restaurant and riding his motorcycle on days when he wasn't working.

A sense of relief flooded Anthony when the singing finally ended, but the building had become too warm from all the body heat, and he felt a need to take off his jacket. The problem was, in order to do so, he would need to stand up, because two young Amish men were sitting so close to Anthony that their shoulders pressed against his.

I can't stand up, he told himself. *Everyone would be watching me, and I'd feel like a bug under a microscope. Guess I'll just have to sweat it out till this church service is finally over and I can go outside.*

When everyone stood for the reading of scripture, Rosa chanced a peek at Anthony. She felt sorry for him as he rubbed his hands down the sides of his trousers while turning his head from side to side. The poor guy was probably bored and stiff from sitting for over an hour on the unyielding bench. She certainly couldn't blame him for that. In the two years Rosa had been gone, she'd nearly forgotten how tired she used to get during the three-hour services that took place every other Sunday in a different church member's home or outbuilding. She had always looked forward to the noon meal afterward, though, when she could sit with and visit other girls her age.

Rosa thought about her friend Ada and wondered if she might be here today. Perhaps Ada could be sitting a row or two behind her, or maybe she was visiting Ephraim's church. Rosa was tempted to turn around, but she squelched the desire and kept her focus straight ahead. There was no point in drawing attention to herself. A good many people had already looked at her strangely when she'd walked toward the barn with Anthony beside her. Although no one had said anything to her, there'd been lots of quizzical stares, and a few folks had made eye contact and then quickly looked away.

What does it matter what they think of me anyway? Rosa placed both hands against her still-flat belly and swallowed down the bile rising in her throat. *Wait till they find out I'm pregnant and my pretend husband walks out on me and ends our fake marriage.* Rosa knew that even if she never joined the Amish church, at least she and her baby would have the support of her family. *Maybe not Dad's, though,* Rosa thought bitterly. *He may always be disappointed in me.*

⁓⁓

Susan was about to head for her parents' buggy when a firm hand took ahold of her shoulder. Startled, she whirled around. "Norman! You scared me."

"Sorry, didn't mean to. I just wanted to talk to you before our folks head home." His forehead wrinkled.

"You look so serious. What's up?"

"It's about that note Rosa said she left in her room before heading out to the young people's gathering with Ephraim the night of her disappearance."

"That was over two years ago, and there's no telling what happened to the note—if she left one at all."

"I'm well aware of how long it's been."

"Then why are you bringing it up now?"

"Because you're the one who took over Rosa's room, and if anyone had the opportunity to discover her note, it would have most likely been you."

Susan's fingers curled into her palms. "I didn't, though."

"What about the messages Rosa said she'd left on our recorder so we would know where she was?"

"She could be lying about that too."

"What reason would she have to lie?"

Susan shrugged. "Who knows? Maybe she made the whole thing up to get back in Mom and Dad's good graces. I'm sure she doesn't want them to think she left home and deliberately didn't try to contact them."

Norman looked like he was about to say something more, but she cut him off.

"Listen, I've gotta go. Dad went to get his horse, and Mom, Tena, and Alvin are probably waiting for me in the buggy by now. Enjoy the rest of your day, and tell Salina I said hello." Susan hurried off at a fast pace.

Norman's questions had irritated Susan. It felt like he'd been accusing her of something, but without coming right out and saying it.

She lifted the hem of her dress a bit and ran for the carriage. *Well, Norman is not my keeper, and I don't have to answer any more of his questions.*

⁓

Anthony opened his car door and collapsed onto the front seat, then leaned forward, grasping the steering wheel with both hands. He didn't know how he'd made it through the three-hour service or the noon meal that had followed. Strange Amish men looked at him with obvious curiosity, and a few of the younger ones had actually introduced themselves and made some small talk. One guy, who'd introduced himself as Noah Esh, had asked where Anthony was from and what had brought him to their Amish church service. Noah had seemed surprised when Anthony mentioned that he was here with the Petersheims and that he was married to Mahlon and Elsie's daughter Rosa. The young man's mouth had dropped open, and then he'd said, "I—I didn't know Rosa had returned to Belleville. She's been gone a long time, and I thought she must be dead."

Anthony had given the man a brief update and quickly excused himself to go find his "wife." He didn't know how much data Rosa wanted him to share about where she'd been all this time and did not wish to be accused of spreading information about anything regarding her personal life. So after thinking it through a few seconds, he'd played it safe.

Anthony sat up straight and looked back over his shoulder to see if there was any sign of his pretend wife. The last time he and Rosa had conversed, she'd said there were a few people she wanted to speak with and suggested that Anthony wait for her in the car. Eager to get away from the people still lingering about in the yard, he'd happily agreed.

I'll be glad when all of this is over and I can head back to New York. Although, I will miss the quiet, peaceful life here in the Big Valley, where I'm sure there's a lot less crime than we have in the big city. Anthony rubbed his forehead with circular motions. *And truthfully, I might even miss Rosa when I'm gone.* One thing was for sure: He figured most of the regular customers at his folks' restaurant probably missed her already, since the young woman they all knew as "Eileen" was a favorite waitress for many.

Anthony watched as Mahlon drove his horse and buggy out of the yard and onto the road. Although a bit curious about what it would be like to ride inside the man's black-top carriage, he was glad there hadn't been room for him and Rosa to accompany her family in the buggy. Anthony had much preferred to drive them to the church service via the comfort of his own car.

During the noon meal, Rosa had spoken to several women. Each of them had been kind and said they were glad she was back, safe and sound. It made it easier that no one had said anything negative to her, and she was glad she hadn't been asked to provide too much information about her whereabouts over the past few years. She was not about to give a full account to people outside the family regarding everything that had occurred while she'd been on her own. Besides, even Rosa's parents didn't know every detail about where all she'd been or what she had done since running away from home. And she certainly didn't want anyone to know that she and Anthony were merely pretending to be married. It would be bad enough when he abandoned her and the gossip began to circulate throughout their community. She could almost hear the talk now. *"Can you believe that our bishop's daughter ran away, married an English man, and is now caught up in a nasty divorce?"* Oh yes, there would be plenty of talk all right, but Rosa would bear up under it. She had to, for her baby's sake.

Rosa left the circle of women she'd been talking to and was about to head for Anthony's car when she came face-to-face with Ada Detweiler's mother, Alice.

"I spoke to your mamm earlier," the middle-aged woman said. "And I am sure you can imagine what a shock it was to learn that you had returned home after such a long absence and without a single word to your family, letting them know that you were alive and well."

Rosa wanted to defend herself, but she chose to hold her tongue, figuring Alice probably wouldn't believe her anyhow. Instead, she forced a smile and said, "I thought Ada might be here today, but I haven't seen any sign of her."

Alice shook her head. "My daughter attended services with Ephraim Peight this morning, in his church district." The woman folded her arms and stared directly into Rosa's eyes. "They're to be married the week after Thanksgiving."

Rosa gave a quick nod. "So I heard." Then, after a glance in the direction of where Anthony waited in the car, she said, "It was nice seeing you again, Alice. Please tell Ada that I said hello."

"Don't you think maybe you should tell her yourself? After being gone all this time, without bothering to contact your best friend, the very least you can do is stop by the greenhouse and let her know you are home."

"Is she still working there?"

Alice bobbed her head.

"Won't you be telling her that you saw me today?"

"I could, but it's not really my place to do so. I think it would be best if she heard it from you. Don't you agree, Rosa?"

"Yes, I suppose." Rosa's stomach roiled, and she feared she might lose what little bit of lunch she'd eaten. So without even managing a goodbye, she turned and ran for Anthony's car as fast as her wobbly legs would allow her to go. She didn't know which was worse—the nausea she felt, knowing she had to face Ada soon, or listening to what she felt sure that Anthony would have to say about the church service he'd been forced to attend.

CHAPTER 8

Rosa looked over at Anthony as they headed toward the greenhouse in his vehicle the following morning. She should have apologized sooner, but after they'd arrived home from church yesterday afternoon, he'd gone straight to her room and taken a nap, while Rosa sat in the living room visiting with her mother and Tena. Susan had been invited to join them but declined the offer, saying she was going to take a walk. Meanwhile, Dad snoozed in his recliner, and Alvin went out back to play fetch with his dog. By suppertime, when the whole family gathered in the kitchen for a light meal, Rosa wasn't about to bring up the topic of Anthony's experience at church. If she had asked how he felt about the service, it would have probably embarrassed him, because she felt sure that he hadn't enjoyed one moment of the three-hour service, or the simple fellowship meal that had followed. Rosa couldn't blame him. It had to have come as quite a shock for him to have witnessed the way the Amish people worshipped compared to most Protestant churches. Rosa would have discussed it with him on the drive home from church, but he'd said he had a headache and didn't feel like conversing. Now was the time, though, so Rosa plunged ahead.

"I'm really sorry about yesterday; I should have given you some advance warning about what to expect during our church service and the simple meal that was served afterward."

"Yeah. Why didn't you prepare me for all of that?" Anthony's sharp tone and deep frown let Rosa know he was none too happy about what had occurred.

"I was afraid if you knew how long you'd be expected to sit on a hard bench with no back for three hours, you'd either refuse to go with me or head straight back to New York and call our whole charade off."

He nodded. "I might have done either, but it wasn't just the length of time I had to spend on that unyielding bench that bothered me so much. It was the strange-sounding singing that I couldn't understand, along with two messages that were spoken in a foreign language, and on top of that—the curious stares sent in my direction throughout the day."

"I received plenty of stares too," she acknowledged. "But at least I could understand the German words being said during the service. I'm sure as an outsider, it must have all seemed pretty strange to you."

"You got that right."

Anthony remained quiet for several minutes, and then he spoke again. "There were a lot of things I didn't understand about the service, but one thing in particular puzzled me the most."

"What was it?"

"How come the men and women sit on different sides of the building?"

"It's my understanding that separating men and women helps to ensure that everyone's attention remains on the service and to avoid distractions."

Anthony gave a shake of his head. "I wouldn't be too sure about that. From where I was sitting, I could see the women's section perfectly, and I'm sure that all the other men could too."

Rosa rolled her tongue around in her mouth before responding. "You do have a good point. Even so, that's just the way it is, and as far as I know, it's always been so. I seriously doubt that things will ever change in that regard," she added.

"I see." He glanced at her quickly then back at the road. "Remind me—why are we on our way to a greenhouse? Are you planning to buy some flowers or plants for a family member or someone you know?"

"Nope. I just need to go see one of my friends. In fact, she was my best friend until I left home and ventured out on my own."

"Did you keep in touch with her while you were gone?"

"No, and I owe her an apology for that. Hopefully, she will accept it when I tell her my reasons."

When Rosa entered the greenhouse, she spotted Ada, bent over a golden-yellow mum. Rosa swallowed hard as she watched her friend pick up the pot. She missed their carefree days, when the biggest problem they'd faced was deciding whose team they should be on when playing volleyball or baseball.

Rosa glanced over her shoulder and saw Anthony watching her from where he stood several feet behind. She figured he probably wondered why she was just standing there, unmoving.

Gathering her courage, Rosa stepped up to Ada and gently tapped her shoulder.

Ada set the pot down and whirled around as though she'd been stung by a bee. Her mouth opened slightly, and she stared at Rosa with eyes wide. "Rosa?"

"Yes, it's me—although I do look a bit different than the last time you saw me." Rosa gestured to her dark-colored jeans and olive-green sweatshirt. "Did your mother tell you that I spoke to her after church yesterday?"

"No, for whatever reason, she did not say a word about it." Ada breathed in and out as though struggling to find her breath. "Where have you been all this time, Rosa? When no one heard from you, we all thought you might be..."

"Dead?"

"Jah." Tears sprang to Ada's eyes and quickly rolled down her cheeks; then she grabbed Rosa and hugged her tightly.

Rosa sniffed deeply, and tears followed. "I'm so sorry, Ada. I should have contacted you."

"Why didn't you? Surely you must have realized I'd be worried sick about you. Ephraim was too, and he kept asking if I'd heard anything from you." Ada blinked rapidly. "Speaking of Ephraim, there's something you need to know. The two of us—"

"Yes, I heard. You're planning to marry him next week."

Ada moved her head slowly up and down. "I'd like to explain how this all came about."

"You're not obligated to give me the details. When I took off, I gave up my relationship with Ephraim." Rosa shrugged. "Besides, the night of the young people's gathering, we had a big argument, and we ended things."

"So you don't still have feelings for him?"

"No, not at all. Besides, I'm a married woman now." Rosa motioned for Anthony to join them, and when he did, she introduced him to Ada.

Anthony shook Ada's hand and said it was nice to meet her, and she reciprocated, adding, "Congratulations. How long have you two been married?"

Rosa looked at Anthony, hoping he would respond, but he just stood there with his hands in his jacket pockets. She figured she'd better come up with an answer quickly, so Ada didn't catch on to the fact that this was only a pretend marriage.

"We've been married almost a year, and we're expecting our first child." Rosa glanced at Anthony again. "Isn't that right, honey?"

She felt relief when he gave a nod.

"A baby on the way? Oh, how wonderful!" Ada beamed. "You two must be so happy."

"Couldn't be more joyous." Anthony's tone was subdued, and Rosa hoped Ada didn't catch on to the fact that he was faking it.

Rosa hated bold-faced lying to her friend, but this was the lie she'd told her parents, so she had to tell Ada the same story.

"Are you in Belleville just to visit your folks, or do you plan to stay here permanently?"

Her friend's question caused Rosa to pause and think of the best way to answer. Even though she did plan to stay and raise her baby, in a couple of weeks, Anthony would be returning to his home and job in New York. She didn't dare reveal that part, however.

"I think we're planning to stay here in Mifflin County." Rosa slipped her hand in the crook of her pretend husband's arm.

Ada gave Rosa another welcoming hug. "That's wonderful. It will give us plenty of time to catch up with each other. I'm eager to hear how the two of you met and learn where you have been all this time." She looked in the direction of the checkout counter. "Right now, though, I need to get back to work."

"Oh, of course. We can talk more some other time." Rosa was about to walk away when Ada spoke again.

"Ephraim's and my wedding is next Tuesday. I would be pleased if you and your husband could be there, Rosa."

The invitation took Rosa by surprise, but after Anthony gave a nod, she offered Ada a smile and said, "We'd be honored to attend your wedding."

"Great! The service begins at 9:00 a.m., and it will be held in the shop at my parents' house. You're invited to the meal afterward too," Ada quickly added.

"All right. We'll see you then. Oh, and if I don't see you before, I hope you have a nice Thanksgiving."

"You as well."

When Rosa and Anthony left the greenhouse and approached his vehicle, she looked up at him and said, "I was surprised you agreed to attend my friend's wedding, since you don't even know Ada or her future husband."

He shrugged his broad shoulders. "I figured it would help us keep up the appearance of being a happily married couple. And since weddings are usually quite festive, it will no doubt be kind of fun."

Rosa grimaced. "Umm...there are a few things I think you should know about Amish weddings."

Anthony tipped his head. "Such as?"

"I'll tell you all about it on our drive back to my folks' house."

⁓

Ada stood watching as Rosa and her husband left the building. Seeing her friend show up out of the blue had raised strong emotions. *If Rosa left home of her own accord, then why hadn't she made any contact with me?* Ada pondered this question a few minutes. *Maybe we weren't as close as I thought. Sure wish I'd been free to talk with her longer so I could ask a few more questions. I'd like to know where she's been all this time and how she met Anthony.* A lump formed in Ada's throat. *Wouldn't Rosa have wanted me to be at her wedding?*

It had also been a shock for Ada to see her friend dressed in English clothes and wearing her hair shorter than it had ever been before. If she hadn't recognized Rosa's pretty face, she wouldn't have known who she was.

Another thought popped into Ada's head. *It's a shame that Ephraim wasted so many months pining for Rosa and hoping for her return. If he'd known that she was alive and had married a good-looking English fellow, I bet he would have set his feelings for Rosa aside much sooner and maybe seen me in a different light right away. Well, better late than never,* Ada told herself. *At least he will soon be my husband, not hers.*

Ada carried the pot of mums over to another area where more fall flowers had been displayed and set it down. *I wonder if Ephraim knows Rosa is back in town, and if so, what was his reaction? I think I'll go over to the harness shop to see him when I get off work this afternoon. If he hasn't heard about his ex-girlfriend's unexpected return, he will need to be told. It would be a shock if Ephraim didn't find out until the day of our wedding. I can't imagine what he would think when he looked out at the group of people there and saw Rosa sitting in the area reserved for English guests, with a handsome, curly-haired man sitting beside her.*

⁓

As soon as they got into his car, Anthony looked over at Rosa and said, "I'm hungry. Where's a good place we can go to get some lunch?"

"There's the Taste of the Valley, which my mother mentioned had recently been renamed the Pinewood Café. They serve soups, salads, and sandwiches. Or at least they did when I lived here."

"Any place else you would recommend?"

"There's also Richie's. It's a family restaurant and pizzeria."

"Let's try there. It's always good to check out the competition."

Rosa rolled her eyes. "Your folks' restaurant is in New York, silly. So Richie's hardly qualifies as competition."

He gave her a thumbs-up. "Point well taken. Even so, I'd like to check the place out and see how good the food is there."

"Okay, that's fine with me. Just head back the way we came, and we'll see it on Main Street. While we're eating, I'll fill you in on what to expect from an Amish wedding."

⁓⁓

As they sat at a table inside Richie's, waiting for their Sicilian deep-dish pizza, Rosa decided this was a good time to bring up Ada and Ephraim's wedding, because it was only fair that Anthony should know what to expect during the service.

She took a drink of water and cleared her throat. "About the wedding service we've been invited to attend...it's nothing like a traditional English wedding."

"I figured it would be different, but I'm not sure how," he responded.

"For one thing, the bride does not wear a fancy white wedding dress. She'll be dressed in her modest Amish clothes, much like she would wear to church. The groom will wear similar attire to what he'd wear in a church service too."

"Where will the wedding be held?" Anthony questioned.

"Ada said it would be at her parents', which means it will most likely take place in her father's shop, or perhaps the basement of their home, which is quite large."

He leaned forward with both elbows on the table. "I see."

Rosa paused to take another drink. "There's no music or fancy decorations, and the bride does not walk down the aisle. The couple will walk in together, along with their witnesses—they will each have two—and then they all will be seated near the center of the room, with the bride and her witnesses facing the groom and the men he's chosen."

"Interesting."

"Also, the three-hour service is similar to one of our regular church services, with singing, scriptures, and sermons preached. The emphasis of those messages will be on the topic of marriage, and the bishop, who in this case will be my father, delivers the final sermon before the bride and groom stand before him to acknowledge their vows."

"After that he probably pronounces them man and wife, and the groom kisses the bride. Right?"

Rosa shook her head. "There are no kisses, or even a hug. Once the bishop gives his pronouncement, the bride and groom return to their seats for the remainder of the service."

Anthony tapped his knuckles against the tabletop. "Hmm. . .that all seems pretty strange to me."

"I figured it would, because you didn't grow up in an Amish home."

"Yeah, thank goodness. Don't think I'd do well with all those strange customs, and if I were getting married, I'd want music and would definitely want to kiss my bride." Anthony wiggled his dark brows, causing Rosa to feel the heat of a blush.

"I'm sure you'll enjoy the lavish meal served after the wedding, though. There's no way anyone in attendance could leave there hungry."

His thumped his belly. "Speaking of which. . .where's our pizza? I'm starved."

"I think it's ready right now." Rosa gestured to the pizza being carried out to their table. After describing a traditional Amish wedding to Anthony, she was glad he hadn't protested and said he wouldn't go. Her biggest concern now was how it would feel to watch her best friend marry the man who had once proposed marriage to her.

Allensville, Pennsylvania

From the back room of the harness shop, where Ephraim was working with his father's other employee, Noah, Ephraim heard the bell above the front door ring, indicating that a customer had come in.

"Want me to get that?" Noah asked.

"No, that's okay." Ephraim gestured to the leather harness Noah had been working on. "You can finish up with that, and I'll go see who came in."

When Ephraim entered the front part of the building, he was surprised to see Ada waiting by the counter. The sunlight streaming in through the nearby window made her light brown hair appear almost golden, and his breath caught in his throat. No matter how many times he saw his bride-to-be, Ephraim never tired of looking at her pretty face. But it wasn't just Ada's beauty that had captured him. It was her sweet demeanor, her sensitivity, and the way she cared about others.

"Well, this is a surprise," he said, eagerly stepping up to her. "What brings my soon-to-be bride here this afternoon?"

She looked up at him and smiled, although it didn't quite reach her eyes. "I came to see my soon-to-be groom. There's something important I need to talk to you about."

He stroked her cheek with his thumb. "Is anything wrong?"

"Not wrong, exactly—just unexpected, and a bit disconcerting."

His brows furrowed. "What's up?"

"Rosa's back. She came to the greenhouse earlier today to see me."

Ephraim blinked several times as a chill ran up his back. "Seriously?"

"Jah. All this time she's been gone, she was perfectly fine, and yet no one heard a word from her."

He drew in a deep breath and let it out in a rush. "What was her excuse for running off and not telling anyone where she was?"

"She didn't really offer an excuse, but she did apologize."

"We all thought something bad may have happened to her, and that she might even be dead." Ephraim's muscles quivered as he held his palms tightly against his thighs.

"There's more," Ada said.

He tilted his head in her direction. "Oh?"

"Rosa is married to an English fellow, and he wears a black leather jacket and has a head full of dark, curly hair."

"Did she tell you that?"

"She told me she was married, and she didn't need to describe her husband because he was with her." Ada reached over and clasped Ephraim's hand. "I told her about us, and I hope you don't mind, but I invited them to our wedding."

Ephraim's face heated until it felt as warm as if it had been a hot summer day. "What? Why would you do that, Ada?"

"Well, because I felt an obligation, since she and I were good friends for so many years, and you—"

"Yeah, yeah, I know. I was her boyfriend who she didn't want to be with, and then when she disappeared, many people, especially her brother Norman, blamed me for her disappearance." Ephraim's eyes narrowed into tiny slits. "If you had consulted with me first, before extending an invitation to Rosa to attend our wedding, I would have said no."

Tears formed in Ada's eyes, and she sniffed. "I...I'm sorry, Ephraim. I was caught off guard and blurted it out before taking the time to think it through. If you prefer, I'll get ahold of Rosa and tell her that it would be best if she and her husband didn't come to the wedding."

Feeling overcome with sympathy for this special woman whom he loved so much, Ephraim pulled Ada into his arms and gently patted her back. "No, don't do that. It would be rude, and Rosa might start a round of gossip about us."

"I don't think she would do that."

"She ran off without telling anyone where she was going, didn't she? I wouldn't put anything past Rosa Petersheim—or whatever her last name is now."

"It's Reeves, and her husband's first name is Anthony." Ada paused. "Oh, and there's one more thing."

"What would that be?"

"Rosa and Anthony are expecting their first baby."

Ephraim's muscles tensed. He needed to calm down but couldn't seem to help himself. "Well, good for them. I hope they'll be as happy as you and I will be when we start our family."

CHAPTER 9

Wearing a pair of sweatpants and a T-shirt, Anthony bounded into the kitchen, his mouth watering, while he sniffed the air. "Oh boy, something sure smells good in here! Can I help you with anything, Elsie?"

"Well, it's too soon to set the table," she replied.

"No, I was actually referring to helping with the meal."

Rosa's mother turned from her place at the counter, where she appeared to be mixing some savory-smelling stuffing, which Anthony assumed would go inside the turkey once it had cooled adequately. It wasn't safe to stuff a cold bird with hot stuffing. It could cause food poisoning.

"I appreciate the offer," Elsie said, "but I'm sure you could find something more enjoyable to do than hang out in this overly warm kitchen with me and my daughters." She gestured to Rosa, Susan, and Tena, all busy with various jobs for their afternoon Thanksgiving meal preparation.

"Hey, I can't think of anything I'd rather do than be right here where the action is. I'm a chef, after all, so I know my way around the kitchen quite well." He looked over at Rosa and winked. "Isn't that right, honeybunch?"

Tena giggled, Susan rolled her eyes, and Rosa nodded. "Absolutely, dear husband. You're the best." She set her fruit-cutting job aside and moved over to stand beside her mother. "You should take Anthony up on his offer, Mom. I promise you won't be disappointed."

"All right then, Anthony," Elsie said with a pleasant smile. "Why don't you come take a look at the list I have for the items we plan to serve for dinner today?" She gestured to the piece of paper on the table. "And then you can choose whatever you'd like to make."

Anthony didn't have to be asked twice. He stepped right up to the table and grabbed the list. "You know what?" he said after studying the piece of paper. "Think I'll make a dessert when there's a break in the dinner preparations, if that's okay with you, Elsie."

She nodded. "Feel free to make whatever you want, and Rosa can help you find everything you'll need. She's a pretty good cook too, and has enjoyed creating new dishes in my kitchen since she was a young girl."

He eyed Rosa curiously. In the time he'd known her, she'd never let on that she had a flair for cooking. As far as he knew, she'd only been good at waitressing. Anthony looked forward to seeing what his pretend wife ended up making to serve at their Thanksgiving meal.

New York City

Leaning both elbows on the table, Lavera looked over at her husband and commented, "Without Anthony here, it doesn't feel like Thanksgiving."

Herb grunted. "Well, if he hadn't run off to who knows where with that flighty waitress, he'd be sitting here right now, enjoying our hearty meal."

"I feel bad that our daughters aren't here with us today either." She sighed. "Since they both had other plans for today, whether we like it or not, it's just the two of us at our Thanksgiving table this afternoon."

Herb nodded and forked a hunk of turkey into his mouth.

Lavera picked up her glass and took a drink of water. "You might think I'm paranoid, but I have this horrible feeling that our son might never come home."

Herb's brows squeezed together. "What would give you that crazy idea?"

"Well, for starters, he's only called us once since he and Eileen hit the road. I can't help but be worried about him."

He shrugged his shoulders. "No news is good news, right?"

"Maybe. It could also mean that Anthony's having a good time and isn't thinking about us at all."

"He'd better not forget that he has a job here. That son of ours knows we're counting on him to get back to work as soon as his two-week vacation ends." He reached for the bowl of mashed potatoes and piled two hefty spoonfuls onto his plate, then poured plenty of thickened turkey gravy over the top.

"But what if he doesn't return after two weeks?"

"Then we'll have twice as much work to do at the restaurant, and like it or not, I might have to find a cook to replace Anthony."

Lavera leaned closer to Herb and touched his arm. "Surely you wouldn't do that to our son."

"I would if I needed to. Business is business, you know, Lavera. That restaurant is our livelihood, and we wouldn't function well if we became shorthanded in the kitchen." He dropped a few peas onto his plate and mixed them in with the potatoes and gravy. "I'll do what I have to if it becomes necessary." Herb gestured to Lavera's plate. "You need to eat the dinner you took the time to cook and stop worrying so much. Our son's not stupid—I'm sure he'll be back here on time."

Lavera hoped her husband was right, but she couldn't let go of the nagging feeling that clung to her thoughts and seeped all the way into her soul.

Belleville

Susan watched with envy as Rosa and Anthony chatted with Norman and Salina. Both couples were married, and one of them was expecting a baby, but Susan had no one. When Ben had been convicted of arson and sent to prison, all hopes of getting married and raising a family with him had been washed down the drain like dirty soap water. It wasn't fair that she had no boyfriend or promise of marriage. It didn't seem right that her runaway sister had been welcomed back into the family with open arms. *Why does Rosa get away with everything, and I'm always in trouble—especially with Dad?*

Susan scrunched up the napkin in her lap between her fingers. *I bet if I'd done something like that, I'd be getting the cold shoulder from both of our parents and maybe all my siblings too.*

It was difficult for Susan to sit here and eat when her appetite had been squelched with all the jealous thoughts circling around in her brain. *No one even seems to care about me, nor do they ask any questions about my life.* She stabbed at the piece of dark turkey meat on her plate and rolled it around in the gravy she had previously poured over her potatoes. *Of course, even if someone were to ask about me, there's not much I'd have to say that would be worth sharing. My life consists of working at a job I don't like, doing mundane chores around here, attending church regularly, and going to an occasional young people's gathering when Dad pressures me to go.* Susan pursed her lips. *Big deal! I lead the most boring life of anyone I know. At least when Ben and I were together, we had the pleasure of doing some exciting things.*

Susan nearly bounced out of her chair when Tena bumped her arm and said, "Would you please pass the tray of cut-up veggies?"

"Yeah, okay—sure." Susan handed the tray to her sister and forced herself to eat the piece of turkey still on her plate. *I wish Rosa had never come home. At least then I'd still have her bedroom, as well as a whole lot more of Mom's attention.*

꩜

Between the conversation with his new brother-in-law and an occasional glance in Susan's direction, it didn't take Norman long to figure out that she was in a bad mood. Was it the fact that Rosa was back at home and Mom seemed so happy about it, or did his younger sister have something else on her mind? Susan had always been the moody type, so with her, it was hard to tell what the problem was. One thing was for sure: She hadn't been the same since Ben was sent to prison. After Rosa showed up, Susan became even more sullen. Well, she needed to put it all behind her and move on with her life. Norman figured that maybe what his sister needed was a new boyfriend. Surely that would help to put her in a better mood.

When Anthony asked him a question, Norman's attention was diverted to him once again. "Sorry. What was that?" he asked.

"I was just wondering what there is to do for fun around here."

"For one thing, most of the young people, and even some of the older folks, enjoy playing baseball and volleyball," Norman responded.

Anthony leaned closer. "Baseball sounds like fun. I'm not sure about volleyball, though, since it's a sport I've never played."

"I'm sure Rosa could teach you," Tena volunteered. "She's always been good at that game."

"In Rosa's condition, I don't think she ought to be playing any contact sport," Norman's mother spoke up.

"You're right about that," Anthony agreed. He patted Rosa's shoulder. "There's no point in taking any unnecessary chances."

Rosa smiled but made no comment. She seemed preoccupied with eating the food still left on her plate. Or maybe she was thinking about the enjoyable times she had spent in the past, playing volleyball and, more often than not, helping her team win the game.

○‿○

Hearing the topic of volleyball and remembering how much she had loved playing the game put an ache in Rosa's heart. Her mother was right—she shouldn't be playing the game during her pregnancy, and maybe not for several months after the baby was born. It would be difficult to abstain from it, though, since Rosa loved playing so much.

Rosa let go of her fork and placed both hands against her stomach. *I wish I'd never gotten pregnant. I shouldn't have allowed myself to get involved with Jeff. I believed that he loved me and planned to divorce his wife so we could be married, but I was a fool. He only used me, and then as soon as he found out I was carrying his child, he threw me aside like yesterday's garbage.* Rosa looked away from her plate and massaged her belly. *Even so, this child is a part of me, and I am obligated to raise it, no matter what. Therefore, I shall love and nurture my baby and make sure that all his or her needs are met, because that's what good parents do.*

Rosa picked up her fork again and stabbed a hunk of steamed broccoli. *I will eat well and take care of myself so I can make sure that both me and my baby get all the nourishment we need.*

When Susan brought up the topic of Ada and Ephraim's upcoming wedding, Rosa stiffened. She hadn't told anyone in the family that she and Anthony had received an invitation to the event, and she had no idea if any of them had either. Since Ada's parents were in the same church district as Rosa's family and Rosa's father, as the bishop, would no doubt have a part in the wedding ceremony, she figured they would have been invited to the wedding. If so, it seemed strange that nobody in the family had mentioned it to her. She was tempted to ask, but with everyone enjoying the meal and talking nonstop about other things, this didn't feel like the right time to bring up the subject of Ephraim and Ada's wedding. She would wait for a better time, when she and her mother were alone. Her father would know, of course, but he still hadn't warmed up to either Rosa or Anthony.

And maybe he never will, she thought with regret. *Although he might allow me and the baby to live here in his house, my father might always remain distant toward me. I wonder what it would take to bridge the gap between us and make Dad love me again.*

When dinner was over and the dishes had been washed, dried, and put away with Tena and Susan's help, Elsie brought out three kinds of pie. When they were placed on the dining room table, Alvin scrunched up his nose. "Aw, Mom, do we hafta have that horrible-tasting mincemeat pie again? It makes me feel sick to my stomach just looking at it."

"Hush now," his mother said. "You know mincemeat is one of your *daed's* favorite kinds of pies." She gestured to the other two pies on the table. "Besides, your sisters and I also made two apple pies. You like those, don't you, Alvin?"

"Jah, but not near as much as pumpkin."

Elsie shrugged. "Well, it's all we have, so you'll have to be satisfied."

"Put some whipped cream on a piece of apple pie, and it'll taste delicious," Norman's wife, Salina, suggested.

Alvin folded his arms and dropped his gaze to the floor. "Still wouldn't be as good as pumpkin."

"Do you like any kind of pumpkin dessert, or just pie?" Anthony questioned.

"Mostly pie, but I also like pumpkin cookies and pumpkin bread with chocolate chips baked in."

"You have good taste, Alvin." Anthony leaned close to Rosa and whispered, "Shall we get the special dessert we made while the turkey was baking earlier and no one but the two of us was in the kitchen?"

She smiled and nodded. "Sure. I'd say that now's as good a time as any. We can put it on the table along with the pies Mom and my sisters made yesterday."

Anthony grabbed Rosa's hand and hurried off to the kitchen where they'd hid their dessert toward the back of the pantry.

When they returned to the dining room a short time later and placed their creation on the table, Elsie broke down in tears as soon as she laid eyes on it.

"Oh, you made Rosa's pumpkin rolls! What a nice surprise, and for sure it's the best dessert of all!"

Anthony looked at Rosa and noticed that there were tears in her eyes as well. She had told him earlier that before she'd left home, pumpkin rolls had been one of her special desserts to make. It had been fun to help her in the kitchen this morning with the recipe, but Anthony had never expected the pumpkin rolls would cause her mother to break down in tears. He couldn't help feeling a bit envious over the love he felt here with this Amish family—except for Mahlon, who hadn't talked much with anyone but his son Norman and occasionally with Alvin, who'd continually interrupted Mahlon and Norman's conversation. It wasn't that Anthony's own parents did not love him. They just didn't always show it—especially his dad. Anthony figured there wasn't anything he could do about it either.

Even though today had been most enjoyable and relaxing, he didn't dare get used to it, because in less than two weeks, after his planned breakup with Rosa, Anthony would be on his way home and his life would return to what his dad considered normal.

CHAPTER 10

ANTHONY COULDN'T BELIEVE HE WAS sitting on another uncomfortable wooden bench at an Amish service—this one for the wedding of a couple he didn't even know. He'd asked himself several times over the last week why he had been putting himself through all of this for a young woman he'd only known a short time.

I either have a tender heart, like Mom has often said, or I'm just a sucker when I see a woman in tears and in need of someone's help. Anthony shifted on the bench, hoping to find a more comfortable position. It was hopeless. Between the several hundred bodies producing heat inside this building and the discomfort of having no back on the bench, there was no way Anthony would ever find comfort. What he needed was to be outside in the fresh autumn air.

Maybe when these people decide to get on their knees and pray, I can sneak out of the building for a short while. Anthony scratched the side of his head where an irritating itch had plagued him for the last several minutes. Struggling to keep from scratching at it, he'd lost the battle and didn't care if anyone might be watching him.

Once he had the itch under control, Anthony's thoughts took over again. *But if I get up and go outside, I most likely will be noticed. Guess it probably wouldn't look good for Bishop Petersheim's phony son-in-law to make a quick escape in the middle of this solemn and very unusual service.* At least to Anthony, everything that had happened since he'd entered the building seemed strange. Why would the bride and groom sit in chairs opposite each other, rather than standing side by side, like the couples Anthony had seen at other weddings he'd attended? And no kiss exchanged between the bride and groom? That didn't seem right to him. Anthony figured there wouldn't be any clapping or cheering at the end of the service when the wedding couple exited the building either. To him, that didn't seem like much of a celebration. But then, he figured every church or religion had its own customs, and what seemed right for some might seem odd for others, like him. Anthony also assumed that if a person had grown up in an Amish home, none of the customs or rituals would seem strange.

Anthony wedged his index finger beneath his shirt collar and sucked in some stale air. *I wonder if after our made-up divorce, and a little time passes, Rosa will find a nice Amish man and become a church member.* His fingers traveled to the back of his neck, and he began to massage the kinks that had formed over the past two hours. Was it possible that the Amish church would not allow a divorced man or woman to become a member or get married in their church because of some religious teaching or certain rules? If so, by pretending to be Rosa's husband and then making it seem as though they'd be getting a divorce, Anthony might be putting Rosa in a terrible position. One that he'd never considered or talked with her about. He would need to do that before they proceeded with their plans to fake a breakup that would send him home to New York and back to the life he knew.

Rosa watched tearfully as Ada and Ephraim stood before her father to commit their marriage vows to one another. *If I hadn't run off to seek a new life of my own in the English world, it could me standing beside Ephraim right now. We would be on the verge of making a commitment to each other for the rest of our lives. For that matter, if we had gotten married when he wanted to, we could very well have a child by now, and I wouldn't be in the fix I'm in right now.*

Rosa swallowed past the lump that had formed in her throat. *Instead, I'm going to have a baby who will never have a father to love him or her.*

What chance do I have now of ever finding a husband who'd be willing to take on another man's illegitimate child?

She thought more about the relationship she'd once had with Ephraim, and how he'd proclaimed his love for her many times, even pleading with Rosa to join the Amish church with him so they could get married. Basically, their relationship had been one-sided, because Rosa had never loved Ephraim enough to set her worldly desires aside in order to do what he wanted. The bottom line was they'd wanted different things, and Ephraim was better off choosing Ada for his lifelong marriage partner than he ever would have been with Rosa. Despite the envy she felt at their happiness, Rosa was pleased for the two people who had been her friends since childhood. Now she had to figure out what to do with the rest of her life. Part of her felt it would be best to join the Amish church, but in order to do that she would need to confess that she and Anthony were never married, because as a divorced woman, she would not be allowed to become a church member.

Rosa looked down at the skirt of her dark green Amish dress. *What a predicament I have put myself in, and all because of my stupid, selfish desires. Oh, how I wish I could go back in time and start over. If it were possible, I would definitely do things differently. Even if I had chosen not to marry Ephraim, I should never have run away from my home and family.*

⁓℮⁓

Ada's heart swelled as she stood beside her groom in front of the bishop, prepared to answer his questions. In all the years she'd cared deeply for Ephraim, Ada had never expected that he would propose marriage and they'd be standing here today, on the brink of becoming husband and wife. Since Ephraim and Rosa had been a couple for a few years before her disappearance, Ada had never expected that she would be here in the place of her best friend. She still couldn't believe Rosa had refused to join the Amish church and marry Ephraim, but the truth was, her friend's loss had been Ada's gain.

Ada knew Rosa and her English husband were here today, because as she, Ephraim, and their witnesses came into the building at the appointed time, she'd seen the couple seated in the area set aside for visitors outside of the Amish faith. It was strange to see Rosa dressed in Amish clothes, while Anthony wore dress slacks, a pale green shirt, and a jacket that had obviously been purchased in a non-Amish clothing store. Did Rosa choose to wear Plain clothes to fit in here today, or was she considering the idea of joining the Amish church? If so, what about Rosa's husband? Would he be willing to join as well? It seemed doubtful; although a few people had made the change from English to Amish, it was not the norm.

Ada's attention was drawn back to Bishop Petersheim's words. "Can you both confess and believe that God has ordained marriage to be a union between one man and one wife, and do you also have the confidence that you are approaching marriage in accordance with the way you have been taught?"

Together, she and Ephraim said, "Yes."

The bishop looked at Ephraim and asked, "Do you also have confidence, brother, that the Lord has provided this, our sister, as a marriage partner for you?"

Ada held her breath. Ephraim didn't hesitate to say yes.

Next Ada was asked, "Do you have confidence, sister, that the Lord has provided this, our brother, as a marriage partner for you?"

Ada also was quick to say yes.

Once more, the bishop asked Ephraim a question. "Do you also promise your wife that if she should in bodily weakness, sickness, or any similar circumstances need your help, that you will care for her as is fitting for a Christian husband?"

Ephraim nodded, saying yes.

The bishop turned to Ada again. "Do you promise your husband the same thing, that if he should in bodily weakness, sickness, or any similar circumstances need your help, that you will care for him as is fitting for a Christian wife?"

She said yes.

"Do you both promise together that you will, with love, forbearance, and patience, live with each other and not part from each other until God will separate you from death?"

They replied, "Yes."

The bishop prayed, and following the prayer, he took the bride's hand and placed it in the groom's hand. As he did so, and while still clasping both of their hands, he said, "The God of Abraham, and the God of Isaac, and the God of Jacob be with you and help you together and give His blessings richly unto you, and this through Jesus Christ, amen."

As Ada and Ephraim returned to their seats, officially husband and wife, she said a silent prayer, thanking the Lord for her groom, and asking Him to shower them with His blessings.

⁓⁓

As Ephraim sat next to Ada at their corner table, or *Eck*, he looked out at the throng of people who had attended their wedding. Family and friends were enjoying the bountiful meal that followed the service. In addition to the bride's and groom's witnesses, Ephraim's family members, as well as Ada's, had all been seated at the tables closest to the Eck.

Across the room, Ephraim caught a glimpse of Rosa, dressed in Amish clothes. Seated beside her was a dark-haired English man who he figured must be Rosa's husband. Given Rosa's disinterest in joining the Amish church during the time that she and Ephraim had been going out, it didn't really surprise him that she'd chosen to marry an Englisher. What seemed odd, however, was the fact that she wore an Amish dress today. It would have seemed more fitting if Rosa had also been wearing modern clothes, like her husband.

I still can't believe Rosa ran off like she did and never made contact with anyone, Ephraim thought. *I was worried sick about her, and I know Ada was too. I'm sure Rosa's disappearance had an even bigger impact on her family than it did me. Not only was she inconsiderate of their feelings, but also, in my opinion, she showed a lack of maturity.*

While Ephraim hadn't been able to understand it then, he knew now, and without a doubt, that he was better off without someone like

Rosa in his life. Ada had been the best choice for him, and he would thank God for her every day of his life.

Reaching over to clasp his bride's soft hand, Ephraim leaned closer and whispered, "I love you more than words can say, and I look forward to every year we will have as husband and wife."

"*Danki*, Husband," she murmured. "I feel the same way."

Anthony helped himself to enough mashed potatoes to cover most of his plate and covered them with the thick gravy that followed, as more food was sent along the extended table where he and Rosa sat with several other non-Amish people he had not met. He figured they must be acquainted with Ada or Ephraim, perhaps through their workplaces. Or this group of people could include English drivers, or maybe just good neighbors.

Anthony noticed that Rosa's parents, as well as her siblings and Norman's wife, had been seated at another table, a little closer to where the newly married couple sat. He figured that since he wasn't Amish, and Rosa had never joined her family's church, they had been relegated to sit with the people at this table who, with the exception of Rosa, were all dressed in modern-looking English clothes.

"What do you think of all this food?"

Rosa's question drove Anthony's contemplations aside, and he pointed to a second piece of succulent chicken he'd taken and smacked his lips. "I think it's pretty tasty, and I'm enjoying every bite."

"When you eat everything on your plate, you can have more, because when the serving bowls are empty, the table waiters will pass out more for every table." Rosa grinned at him. "But don't stuff yourself too full, because there's still dessert to come."

Anthony groaned and held his stomach. "Oh boy! Sure hope I'll have room enough for that in my belly."

"And it won't be just one dessert, either," she said, bumping his arm with her elbow. "There will be a couple of different pies and sometimes a fruit or gelatin salad."

"I'm open to try any of those—especially the pies." Anthony chuckled.

"I figured you would be, since food is kind of your thing."

"No kind of about it. Before I became a chef, I had actually considered becoming a food critic."

She pursed her lips. "What would that involve?"

"Well, a food critic, who some also call 'a food reviewer,' is a professional who travels around to different restaurants and food establishments to evaluate the quality, taste, presentation, and portion sizes of food and drinks," Anthony explained. "Some critics might also specialize in certain cuisines or types of restaurants."

"That's interesting. Do the owners of the restaurants know the reviewer is there to analyze their food?"

"Not usually. Typically, food critics try to be anonymous so they don't receive any kind of special treatment that might bias their reviews."

"Guess that makes sense." Rosa picked up the napkin next to her plate and blotted her lips. "Does a food critic get paid by someone who sends them to the different restaurants?"

"Yes, they do. Food critics often work for newspapers or magazines, or they might have a TV show or publish a book."

"So what made you decide to become a chef instead of food reviewer?"

"For one thing, I enjoy cooking, and it's fun to try new recipes. I also like to eat whatever I make." Anthony thumped his belly and winked.

"Since you love to cook, maybe you should offer to make supper at our house one evening. I'm sure my mother would be more than willing to take a night off from kitchen duty. My sisters would probably like that too."

Anthony nodded. "You know, that's not a bad idea. Think I might bring the topic up to your mother when we get back to your home following this supergood wedding meal."

CHAPTER 11

"M OM AND I ARE GOING into town today to pick up a few things, and we're taking her horse and buggy," Rosa told Anthony shortly after breakfast the following morning. "Would you like to come along?"

"No way! If I was going anywhere, it would be in my car, which, in my opinion, is safer and much more reliable," he replied. "Besides, I need to stay here and make plans for what I'm going to serve you and your family for supper tonight."

"You really don't have to cook us a meal, Anthony," Elsie called from the other side of the kitchen. "You're our guest, after all."

"I'm well aware, but I'm also a chef who loves to cook, so the least I can do is fix a meal or two while Rosa and I are staying here."

Elsie smiled. "And you are more than welcome to stay with us for as long you like. In fact, we hope you'll find a job and settle here in the Big Valley so we can see you, Rosa, and the baby on a regular basis."

Anthony looked at Rosa, and when all he got from her was a brief shrug, he said, "That's a nice thought, but we'll have to wait and see how it goes."

"How what goes?" Tena questioned upon entering the kitchen.

"Oh, I was just saying how nice it would be if Anthony and Rosa decided to settle here in our community permanently," her mother responded.

Tena gave a vigorous nod. "Jah, I would like that very much. Besides being able to spend more time with my sister and brother-in-law, I can't wait to become an auntie and do some babysitting for my little niece or nephew." She stood beside Rosa. "Are you hoping for a boy or a girl?"

Rosa shrugged. "It really doesn't matter to me, as long as the baby is healthy."

"What about you, Anthony?" Tena asked. "Would you like a son or daughter?"

Anthony cringed inwardly, but he couldn't allow his feelings to show or say anything that might reveal the truth about the fact that the child Rosa carried inside her womb was not even his. He put on what he hoped was a pleasant smile and said, "Rosa is right. The only thing that matters is for her to give birth to a healthy child."

Seemingly satisfied with their answers, Tena told her mother that she would take care of doing the laundry while she and Rosa were out shopping.

"Danki," Elsie replied. "If there's something you would like for me to pick up in town, let me know before Rosa and I head out."

"I will, Mom." Tena gave her mother a hug and hurried out of the room.

"Well, Daughter," Elsie said, tapping Rosa's arm. "Should we put on our warm wraps and see about getting my horse hooked up to the buggy?"

"Sure, and maybe if I work with her awhile, one of these days we can drive my horse Daisy to town. It might take her a while to get used to me again, but I'm sure glad Dad kept her while I was gone."

"Actually, it was my idea to keep Daisy." Elsie brought one hand up to her chest. "In my heart, I kept holding on to the hope that you would return to us someday, and I begged your daed not to sell the horse."

Anthony noticed moisture in his pretend wife's eyes when she murmured, "I appreciate that, Mom, and as I've said before, I am sorry for all the stress and fear that I put you through while I was gone."

Using one corner of her apron, Elsie wiped her daughter's tears away. "All's forgiven now, so let's not dwell on that anymore, okay?"

Rosa nodded before turning to face Anthony. "Is there anything you would like us to pick up at the grocery store for whatever you're planning to make for supper?"

Anthony scratched behind his right ear as he contemplated. "I'm still not sure what I'm going to make, but once I figure it out, if I can't find the ingredients here in your mother's kitchen, I'll hop in my car and head to the store myself."

"Okay." Rosa moved toward him, like she might say something else, but then she gave a quick wave and followed her mother out of the room.

When the women were out of sight, Anthony leaned back against the counter and released a puff of air. He hated lying to Rosa's family. But he'd made a promise to Rosa and needed to see it through until it was time for him to go home.

※

"It feels strange to be driving a horse and buggy again." Rosa looked over at her mother, sitting in the passenger seat. "I was surprised when you suggested that I be the driver this morning."

"I thought you might like to get the feel of it again," Mom responded. "Especially if you're wanting to work with Daisy."

"You're right," Rosa agreed. "I'm definitely out of practice, and starting with your gentle mare was a good idea."

Her mother smiled and reached over to give Rosa's arm a gentle pat. "Words can't express the joy I feel having you home again."

"I'm glad to be back too, but to be honest, in some ways the time I spent away from here was good for me."

Mom tipped her head slightly. "In what way?"

"I got to experience some things in the English world, and in the process it made me appreciate my family and all the things I had grown up with living here in Mifflin County."

"Does that mean you and Anthony plan to stay?" Her mother's tone was hopeful, and Rosa chose her next words carefully.

"I—I hope so, but there are still a few issues that will need to be worked out."

"Such as?"

"I'm not sure life here in Amish country is what Anthony needs."

"He seems content, and even the fact that he wants to cook supper for us tonight is an indication to me that your husband enjoys spending time with our family."

"I suppose he does, but Anthony is used to a different kind of life in New York, and he enjoys his job there as a chef."

"What about you, Daughter? Do you miss the things you had in the big city?"

"No, not really." *At least that's an honest statement,* Rosa told herself. *I had a big awakening, when the father of my child made it clear that he wanted nothing more to do with me.*

Rosa wondered how her mother would respond if she knew the whole truth. *I'm sure Dad would disown me if he knew about my relationship with Jeff. Would Mom be so disappointed that she'd also disown me?*

As they approached town, the horse whinnied and picked up a bit of speed, bringing Rosa's thoughts to a halt. She took full control of the reins and guided the mare into the grocery store's parking lot and up to the hitching rail. *Good, we're here, and the trip didn't go too bad. Guess I haven't lost my touch when it comes to making a horse obey my signals and commands.*

"When we finish our shopping here," Rosa's mother said, "I'd like to stop by the Meat and Cheese Store before going home. Would you be okay with that?"

"Of course, Mom. We can go wherever you like."

"Before we get out of the buggy, I'd like to ask you one more question."

Rosa turned to face her mother. "What would you like to know?"

"I've noticed that you wore your Amish attire to church and to your friend's wedding. Did you do that so you would fit in, or do you have any plans of joining the Amish church?"

"I–I'm not sure yet, Mom. There are several things to consider."

"You mean because your husband isn't Amish, and would probably not be comfortable converting to our Plain way of life?"

Rosa held the reins firmly to keep the horse steady and prevent the animal from trying to back up. She wished this particular topic had not been brought up. Since she and Anthony weren't even married and he'd be leaving soon, the notion of him joining the Amish church was not a possibility. Besides, if they were actually a married couple, Anthony was used to modern ways, and it would be a huge challenge for him to adapt to the Amish lifestyle, even if he so desired.

"I've never discussed with Anthony the possibility of becoming Amish, but I'm almost 100 percent certain that he would not be willing," Rosa replied to her mother's question. *At least that statement wasn't a lie.*

Before Mom could offer a response, Rosa handed the reins to her and got out to secure the horse. Rosa wished she could reveal the truth about her and Anthony's situation, but if Dad knew the lie they'd told, he would be furious and might very well kick her out. No, it was best to keep playing along and follow through with the plans she and Anthony had made that would soon lead to their breakup and the end of their pretend marriage.

Susan had just begun cleaning the front windows at the Meat and Cheese Store when the door opened and Noah Esh entered the building. Although he and his family lived in Belleville, he worked at the harness shop in Allensville, so she rarely saw him except at the biweekly church services.

"My brother's near the back of the store, so if you need anything you can't find, I'm sure he can help you with it," Susan said, barely looking Noah's way.

"That's okay," he responded. "Just stopped by on my way home from work to get some cheese for my mamm."

She glanced at the battery-operated clock on the far wall, noting that it was half past noon. "Did you get off work early today?"

"Jah, I did. Ephraim, his parents, and Ada went with his grandma to Bird-in-Hand to attend a funeral for one of the grandmother's friends. So rather than close the harness shop for the entire day, I was asked to be there for the morning hours only." Noah removed his straw hat and fanned his face with the brim, which seemed strange to Susan since it was a chilly fall day. "I didn't do any actual work this morning, though. Just waited on folks who came by to either pick something up that they'd had repaired or to drop off an item."

Susan resisted the urge to tell Noah that she didn't care about that, but if Dad or Norman ever heard her talk to a customer in such a way, she might get fired, or at the very least, lose some of her weekly paycheck. Instead of commenting on what Noah had said, Susan sprayed the first window with the bottle of cleaner she held and began wiping it clean with a paper towel. She was relieved when he headed for the other end of the store. The last thing she wanted to do was make idle talk with him or anyone else right now.

Susan had finished the first window and was halfway through the second one when Noah returned and plunked several packages of cheese and meat on the counter.

She glanced over her shoulder, hoping either Norman or Dad would come up front to wait on Noah, but there was no sign of either of them, so apparently they were both still busy doing something they felt was more important than waiting on Noah—if they even knew he had come into the store. Since Susan was up front, it was probably assumed that she would wait on any customers who might come in.

Susan set her cleaning supplies aside and stepped behind the counter to ring up Noah's purchases. She hoped he would remain quiet this time, but no such luck.

"I haven't seen you at any of the young people's gatherings for some time. In fact, the last one I saw you at, Ben Ebersol was with you. Have you heard anything from him since he went to prison—a letter or phone call, maybe?"

Susan's back stiffened. The last person she wanted to talk about was Ben, and she told Noah so too.

"Oh, sorry. Sure didn't mean to make you *umgerennt*."

"I'm not upset. I just don't want to talk about Ben." She gave Noah the change he had coming from the money he'd given her. Then Susan bagged up his purchases and handed him the paper sack. "Have a nice day."

"You too, Susan." Noah was almost to the door but turned back around. "This Sunday evening there's supposed to be another singing. Think you might go?"

She gave a vigorous shake of her head.

"That's too bad. You'll be missed."

Susan held both hands tightly at her sides. *I bet no one will even notice I'm not there.*

~~~

When Elsie and Rosa got out of their carriage, she spotted Noah Esh getting into his buggy. He waved, and she followed suit. Noah was such a nice-looking man and always so polite. From what she had heard, he was also a trustworthy hard worker at the harness shop in Allensville. It was a wonder he didn't have a steady girlfriend. At least as far as Elsie knew, he didn't. But maybe he was seeing someone and she hadn't observed them together anywhere.

When Elsie and Rosa entered the Meat and Cheese Store, she saw Susan behind the counter wearing a frown that had created wrinkles in her forehead.

"Is something wrong, Daughter?" Elsie questioned.

"It's nothing worth mentioning," Susan replied.

"Your frown says otherwise. Have you had a stressful morning?"

"It was fine until Noah showed up and started asking me questions I didn't want to answer."

"What kind of questions?" Rosa asked.

Susan glared at her sister. "Why's that important to you?"

Elsie stepped forward and shook her finger. "That is no way to speak to your sister. Now please apologize."

Susan turned her head and looked toward the front window.

"It's okay, Mom. Don't worry about it." Rosa took off toward the back of the store.

Elsie stepped in front of Susan. "I think you need an attitude adjustment."

Susan plopped one hand against her hip. "And I think some people need to mind their own business."

"Are you referring to Rosa or me?"

"I meant Rosa and Noah Esh too. He was pressuring me to go to this Sunday night's singing."

"That's not a bad thing, Susan. You haven't been to one in a long time, and—"

"No! I'm not going, and that's final!"

Elsie's heart clenched. It saddened her to hear the sharp tone of her daughter's voice and to see Susan's pained expression. All she could do at this point was pray for Susan and hope that she would change her attitude and do what was right.

CHAPTER 12

Anthony couldn't control the urge to whistle a jovial tune as he moved about Elsie's large, well-stocked kitchen, making supper preparations for this evening. The main dish, which consisted of ground beef, onion, green pepper, salt, black pepper, butter, shredded raw potatoes, eggs, milk, and shredded cheddar cheese, was already in a pan on the stove, keeping warm. A tossed green salad with plenty of lettuce, tomatoes, carrots, cucumbers, and black olives that he'd put together a short time ago sat on one end of the counter, ready to serve. Anthony had also made his special recipe for cheesy breadsticks, which were in the oven turning nice and brown. While Rosa and her mother were in town shopping, Anthony had created a scrumptious-looking carrot cake with cream cheese frosting for dessert. It rested beside the salad bowl on a glass plate he'd found in one of the cupboards.

Sure hope everything I made today will be enjoyed by everyone in Rosa's family, he thought. For Rosa's sake, Anthony wanted to make a good impression on her relatives, not only with his cooking, but by the way he treated her family members. Anthony couldn't help feeling sorry for his make-believe wife and the situation she currently found herself in. It was bad enough that Rosa was pregnant and dealing with morning sickness and that her father had been so distant toward her since their arrival at his home. Rosa's sister Susan seemed almost hostile whenever she spoke to Rosa, or she looked at her with angry scowls. It made no sense. Anthony wondered what had happened between the two of them in the past to cause the animosity. Or maybe Susan's negative attitude was due to something that had occurred during Rosa's absence and she was using her older sister as a scapegoat for her own unhappiness.

And Rosa's father? Why wouldn't he have welcomed his daughter home with love and gratitude, knowing she was safe and had returned of her own free will? It seemed to Anthony that Mahlon, a preacher no less, would have been thrilled to have his eldest daughter back in his home.

Some people do strange things when they are miserable. Anthony continued with his contemplations. *I've often wondered if my dad's grouchiness has more to do with something that happened in his past than it does with his frustration toward me. Or maybe it's the business of running the restaurant that keeps him on edge. Too bad he won't take some much-needed time off once in a while. I'm sure my mom would enjoy taking a vacation.*

The portable windup timer positioned at the back of the stove went off, and Anthony let his thoughts dissipate in order to open the oven door and check on the breadsticks. Sure enough, they were nicely done. He grabbed a pot holder, pulled them out, and placed the tray on a cooling rack. Rosa had told him twenty minutes ago that she and Tena were going to set the dining room table, and Anthony figured that had probably been done by now. It was time to let the family know that supper was ready to be served.

꩜

"This meal is really delicious, and the fact that you made something similar to a pizza in a pan is most unusual," Elsie commented after taking a second helping of what Anthony had named German pizza.

"I'm glad you like it." Pleased with her comment, he offered Elsie a wide grin. "And since all the ingredients are cooked in one pan, it's quite easy to make. Also, without a crust made with high-carb flour like traditional pizzas, it's a healthy dish for those who are diabetic or simply watching their weight."

"Nobody at this table has diabetes, and none of us is overweight."

With puckered lips, Mahlon made a grunting sound. "And since we're eating it with a fork and not our hands, it doesn't seem much like a pizza to me."

"Maybe not the kind most folks are used to eating," Rosa interjected, "but it's certainly quite tasty. I also like the fact that the shredded potatoes make the texture seem almost like there is a crust."

"I like the German pizza dish," Tena chimed in, looking at Anthony. "It has lots of flavor, and so does the salad you made."

"Thank you." He handed the basket of breadsticks to Rosa's father. "Would you like one of these?"

Mahlon shrugged. "Guess it wouldn't hurt." He took two and passed the basket to Alvin. "How about you, Son?"

"Okay." The boy took a plump-looking cheesy breadstick, covered it with plenty of butter, and took a bite. "Yum! You're sure a good cook, Anthony. You oughta fix supper for us more often."

"Glad you like it." Anthony glanced over at Susan, who sat across the table, to gauge her reaction to the meal. But she said nothing and didn't even make eye contact with him. Instead, she reached for the ranch dressing he'd made using buttermilk and poured some on her salad.

Anthony appreciated the positive comments he'd received from Elsie, Rosa, Tena, and even Alvin. He wished he could say the same for Susan and Mahlon, but he would take whatever he could get. Maybe when he brought out the carrot cake for dessert, it would meet with everyone's approval. He'd certainly put his best efforts into making it and looked forward to eating a decent-sized piece of the cake himself.

⁓ↄ

"That meal I cooked for tonight's supper sure didn't go over the way I had hoped." Anthony sank to the foot of Rosa's bed and groaned. "I doubt that anything I could say or do would merit your dad's favor." He stretched his arms over his head and yawned. "I'm exhausted from trying to make conversation with him. He doesn't seem to care for me at all."

"Don't take it personally, Anthony. My father can be quite difficult at times, but I believe that somewhere deep inside, his heart is soft as a marshmallow."

"Really? Well, you could have fooled me. He seems kinda like my dad—they are both hard nuts to crack."

Rosa couldn't help but smile as she took a seat beside him. "I've never heard it put quite that way, but I guess you're right about that."

"I wonder how your folks will take it when we stage our breakup and I head back to New York to get the fake divorce."

She released a heavy sigh. "Maybe we should come clean and tell them the truth, that we're not really married, and you only came here as a favor to me."

Anthony gave a quick shake of his head. "No way! I promised to accompany you and pretend to be your husband so you didn't have to suffer the embarrassment of telling them the truth of how you got pregnant. If we stick with our original plans, your folks will be none the wiser. I have less than a week before my vacation is over, so we need to see this through until the day of our planned breakup. After that, I'm sure you'll have your parents' sympathy and full support, which is exactly what you want, right?"

"Yes, of course, but—" Rosa stopped talking when she heard footsteps in the upstairs hallway. "Oh boy, I hope nobody heard us speaking about this," she whispered.

Anthony flapped a hand. "Naw, I doubt it. We weren't talking that loud, so I wouldn't be concerned."

"I hope you're right." Rosa continued to keep her voice low. "The last thing I need is for the truth to come out—especially from someone other than me."

He leaned close to her ear—so near that she felt his breath blowing gently on her neck, which caused goose bumps to erupt on the upper half of her body. "Try not to worry, Rosa," he said. "It'll be fine."

Rosa hoped he was right, because she desperately wanted things to work out for both her and the baby, who would be born in about six months.

THE PRETENDER

A few minutes before, after hearing voices she recognized coming through the closed door of Rosa's bedroom, Susan had halted her footsteps to listen to what was being said. What she had heard Anthony and her sister saying was a shock, and she covered her mouth to keep from gasping out loud.

So Rosa and Anthony are not even married, yet they're pretending to be so she can worm her way back into this family. Learning that her runaway sister had been bold-faced lying to their parents since her return caused Susan's pulse to quicken. If Rosa was truly pregnant and Anthony was the father of her unborn child, why hadn't he done the right thing and married her? Why the big act, and why were they planning a fake breakup? It made no sense at all.

Susan leaned closer and put her ear right up to the door, hoping to hear more of their conversation. However, Anthony and Rosa had lowered their voices, and all she could make out now was some murmuring, but nothing clear enough to know exactly what else had been said. She stood there several more minutes, hoping their voices might get louder again, but all was quiet.

Figuring they had probably quit talking and had gone to bed, Susan turned sharply and entered the room across the hall that she had been forced to share with Tena. She felt relief to discover that her sister was already in bed and appeared to be sleeping. Susan was in no mood to engage in small talk with Tena, who could be a chatterbox at times. Besides, the teenage girl usually wanted to talk about things Susan had no interest in, like the so-called cute little squirrels she'd seen trying to get into one of Mom's bird feeders. Another topic Tena often mentioned was her hope of getting another bunny someday that she could keep as a pet.

How ridiculous! Susan thought about the last rabbit her sister had found and kept in a cage for a while, and how their little brother had set the rabbit free. At first, Tena had been quite upset when she'd discovered it was gone, but she had finally agreed that the critter was better off being outside where it could roam around, rather than living in captivity.

Susan removed her shoes, took off her dress, and slipped into a clean nightgown. After letting her hair down and brushing it for a good long while, she pulled back the covers on her own bed and slipped between the sheets. As her head reclined on the soft pillow and she closed her eyes, her thoughts returned to the conversation she'd heard across the hall.

Hmm. . .I wonder what I should do with the unexpected information I learned. Should I confront Rosa about it? Tell Mom and Dad what I know? Or would it be better if I keep quiet for now and wait to see how it all plays out when Anthony and Rosa have their so-called breakup?

Susan had several choices she could make, but for now, she would set her contemplations aside and try to get a good night's sleep. Tomorrow was another day, and after her body and brain had a chance to rest, she would hopefully be thinking more clearly and could make a proper decision.

She lay there several minutes and, when close to dozing off, gave a satisfied sigh. For the first time in a good long while, she was one up on Rosa. Susan felt sure that once the truth was revealed, her older sister would no longer be their mother's favorite daughter. Their father would probably kick both Rosa and Anthony out of the house. *After that happens, I will take my rightful place in the position of favored daughter,* she mused. *And then I shall be happy and satisfied at last.*

CHAPTER 13

During breakfast Sunday morning, Rosa noticed Susan staring at her intently, with her head tilted to one side and her eyebrows raised high. Was her sister on the verge of asking a question or just looking at Rosa with disdain? Rosa was preparing to pose that question when Susan quickly turned to face Anthony.

"So Anthony, are you excited about the prospect of becoming a father, and are you hoping for a son or a daughter?"

He looked up from his bowl of cereal and jerked his head. "Huh?"

Susan repeated her question.

Anthony glanced over at Rosa, as though hoping she might speak on his behalf, but she said nothing and hoped he would answer the question in a manner so that no one at the Sunday morning breakfast table would become suspicious.

Anthony reached for his cup of coffee, took a drink, and set it back on the table. Then he smiled at Susan and said, "When a new baby enters the world, it's always exciting, and it doesn't matter whether it's a girl or a boy."

Rosa felt her tensed shoulders relax. *Nice job, Anthony. I couldn't have said it better myself. After that answer, I don't think anyone could suspect that Anthony is not my baby's father or have any suspicion that we're not married.*

"Well," Rosa's father said, pushing away from the table, "we'd all best get ready to head for church services now."

Anthony's eyes widened and his Adam's apple became more prominent. Sunday from attending your church."

Rosa couldn't miss the pained expression on Anthony's face or his obvious gulp. The poor guy had already been forced to attend church twice with her family, and then there was Ada and Ephraim's wedding. Anthony had made it clear to Rosa that he was not a regular churchgoer, so sitting on a hard bench with no back for three hours among people he didn't know and listening to a language he didn't understand had to be difficult for him.

Feeling the need to come to Anthony's rescue, Rosa looked at her father and said, "Dad, I'm not feeling so well this morning, and I think it would be best if I stay home from church to rest." She gestured to Anthony. "I'd feel a lot better if my husband stayed right here with me."

Susan cleared her throat real loud and looked over at Rosa. "Maybe you ought to drink some of that peppermint tea Mom likes so well. I'm sure after drinking a few cups, you'll likely feel better."

"Mint tea doesn't do much for me," Rosa was quick to say.

Mom, who sat on the right side of Rosa, reached over and gave her hand a few gentle pats. "You do look kind of pasty white. I think you and Anthony should remain here today, so you can rest and try to get your stomach settled."

Rosa was relieved when Dad shrugged his shoulders and mumbled, "Okay, whatever. But the rest of us will be going to church, so let's get a move on."

Tena, Alvin, and even Susan jumped up and quickly cleared their dishes. Mom did the same. When she began running water into the sink, Anthony called, "Don't worry about the dishes, Elsie. I'll take care of them while Rosa rests on the living room sofa."

Mom turned and looked at him with the brightest smile. "Why thank you, Anthony. What a thoughtful son-in-law we've been blessed with."

He merely responded by mumbling, "Just trying to help out."

THE PRETENDER

As Susan sat stiffly on the back seat of her father's buggy, stuck between Alvin and Tena, she paid little heed to Mom and Dad's conversation up front and hardly noticed how bare the trees along this stretch of road appeared now that so many had lost their leaves. All she could think about was the conversation she'd heard behind Rosa's closed door last night. Susan had hoped that asking Anthony about becoming a father might cause him to trip up and reveal that he wasn't the baby's biological father, if that was even the case. The whole thing about Rosa and Anthony not being married didn't add up, and the fact that they'd been lying to Mom and Dad stunk worse than a dead fish unattended. Susan felt a desperate need to know the full story about why the tall, good-looking stranger had shown up with her sister a little over two weeks ago, pretending to be Rosa's husband. That fact Susan was sure of, but whether Anthony was the father of Rosa's baby was yet to be determined.

Susan's fingers clenched, causing her nails to dig into her flesh. *I need to get to the bottom of this once and for all, but I'd like a little more information before I reveal the truth to Mom and Dad.*

As Dad guided the horse and buggy up the driveway of the home where church would be held, another thought popped into Susan's head. *I will listen in on Rosa and Anthony's conversations every chance I get and try to ask more pertinent questions that might trip them up. Sooner or later, I'll have all the information I seek, and then we'll see how things play out for my sister Rosa.*

Rosa sat beside Anthony on the couch, drinking a cup of peppermint tea. Although she hadn't felt any nausea earlier, after the family left for church, she'd had a bout of morning sickness, no doubt brought on from the odor of coffee brewing in the kitchen. Anthony had poured himself a cup of the strong-smelling brew and brought it to the living room, along with tea for Rosa. Her stomach settled quickly, and the smell coming from his cup didn't bother her so much anymore.

"I wanted to thank you for getting me out of going to church today," Anthony said, moving a bit closer to her. "I really didn't feel up to sitting through another long, boring service."

"You might not think it was so bad if you understood what was being said."

He shook his head. "Even if I did know the German language, I doubt I'd get much out of the preaching."

"What makes you think so?" she questioned after setting her cup down on the low wooden table in front of them.

"Because I'm not interested in some minister's opinion of what's right or wrong. That's what they preach about—correct? All the dos, don'ts, and strict rules that people should adhere to. Am I right, Rosa?"

"Our preachers do often talk about what is right and what's wrong, but their messages come from passages of scriptures found in the Bible."

Anthony drummed the fingers on his left hand along the corresponding knee of his jeans, about the same time as the grandfather clock on the far wall struck ten. He set his cup down beside Rosa's, stood, and held out his hand toward her. "I've got an idea."

"Oh? What is it?"

"Why don't we get out of here for a while and take a Sunday drive somewhere in Mifflin County that I haven't seen before?"

"That's a good idea," she responded, clasping his hand and rising to her feet. "And I know just the place I'd like to show you."

"Turn left here and follow the signs to Reedsville," Rosa said as Anthony headed in the direction of the shops in downtown Belleville.

"What's in Reedsville?" he asked.

"You'll see when we get there."

As they rode along, Anthony listened with interest as Rosa told him how the Amish came to live in Mifflin County.

"In 1791 some Amish families from Lancaster County decided to leave that area and buy some land in what people often call the Big

Valley," she explained. "The Amish population grew via immigration from the southeastern part of Pennsylvania, and by the 1840s the congregation of people became so big that it was finally divided into three specific groups. I'm sure I mentioned that each of these groups drive different-colored buggies."

"Yes, you did," he agreed. "And the group your family belongs to drive only black-top buggies."

"Right. Then there's the yellow-toppers, which you've probably seen a lot of driving their horse and buggies in Belleville."

"Yep."

"So today, I'm going to show you where most of the white-top buggy-driving Amish live."

"And that would be in Reedsville?"

"Correct. The Amish who drive those carriages are called the Nebraska Amish."

"How come?"

"Because a big portion of their very conservative Amish group originally came from Nebraska."

"Guess that makes sense."

"The Nebraska Amish dress the most conservatively. The men wear plain white shirts, brown denim trousers, and no suspenders."

"Seriously? Not even one, like your dad and the other men from your community wear?"

"Nope. It's my understanding that their trousers are laced up somehow in the back."

"That seems really odd to me." Anthony glanced over at Rosa then back at the road. "What else can you tell me about the Nebraska Amish?"

"Let's see now... They don't have indoor plumbing, do not place screens on their doors or windows, and the windows have no curtains."

"Wow! I'm sure glad your folks allow indoor plumbing. I can't imagine going without a warm shower."

"Me neither."

"Any other interesting facts about the white-toppers?"

"Well, for the longest while, most of them only used kerosene lanterns on their buggies, as well as inside their homes. Recently, though, several minor changes have taken place within the Kish Valley Front Mountain Nebraska Amish."

"Such as?" Anthony found all this information Rosa was feeding him to be quite interesting. If he were writing a book, he'd probably include a chapter about this unusual group.

"Many white-topped Amish are now replacing their kerosene lanterns with LED lights. Also, the power tool batteries are charged using small solar panels."

"What's the reason for the change? Do you know?"

"I think one of the main reasons is because the cost of kerosene in the valley has increased a lot."

"Makes sense to me. The price of gasoline for motorized vehicles has gone way up from what it used to be as well."

"You're right, and the cost of living has gone up everywhere it seems."

As they approached the outskirts of Reedsville, Anthony caught sight of an unpainted barn near a plain white house with a blue door. Outside, in a field, not far from the barn, numerous buggies with white tops had been parked.

"Looks like something's going on at this place," Anthony commented.

"They're having church—most likely inside the barn."

He let go of the steering wheel with one hand and slapped his forehead. "Oh yeah! I should've realized that, since today is Sunday."

She chuckled. "Well, you can't be expected to remember everything."

Anthony elbowed her arm. "Very funny."

She continued to laugh. "Just admit it, Anthony. It's a little funny."

"Okay, whatever you say, smarty. You can make fun of me all you want. I'll get you back sometime, just wait and see."

Rosa leaned back in her seat and relaxed. It was nice to be out with Anthony today, while having the chance to show him around the area and offer some information about the Nebraska Amish and their ultraconservative ways. She was glad he had suggested they go for a ride. It almost felt like they were on a date.

Better not go there, she told herself, after they headed in the opposite direction from which they'd come. They were about halfway home, and Rosa wished the drive could last a bit longer.

Anthony is not my boyfriend, much less my husband, and this is definitely not a date, she reminded herself. *He'll be returning to New York soon, and I need to keep things in perspective. Even if I did have romantic feelings for Anthony, and him for me, it would never work out between us.* Rosa counted on her fingers while closing her eyes. *First of all, he has an apartment, plus a good job waiting for him in the big city. Second, I'm expecting a baby that is not his. Third, I am planning to stay here in Amish country, whether I join the church or not. And fourth, Anthony only sees me as a friend with a need to fool her parents so she can hopefully be accepted by them.*

Rosa's thoughts came to a halt and her eyes snapped open when the car gave a lurch and came to a complete stop.

"Wh–what happened?" she sputtered. "How come you stopped the car?"

"I didn't." His lips flattened as he tried starting the engine and nothing happened. "Well, that's just great." He gestured to the fuel gauge. "The tank's half full of gas, so that's not the problem."

"What do you think is wrong?"

"I have no idea, and I'm not a mechanic, so this could be bad."

Rosa bit down on her bottom lip. "Oh, I hope not. We need to be home before my family gets back from church. Otherwise, if they see that we're gone, they won't like it—especially my dad."

"Why would they care if we were not there?" Rosa heard the irritation in Anthony's tone.

"As you may recall," she reminded him, "I did fake feeling ill this morning so we didn't have to go to church with them. And if they—mostly Dad—believes we were out gallivanting around the valley, he might become suspicious and think we had deliberately skipped church."

Anthony looked at Rosa with a scrunched-up face and spoke with tension in his voice. "I don't really care what they would think, Rosa. I just want to get this car started so we can be on our way again." He tried the ignition one more time, but the engine did not turn over.

Anthony reached into his jacket pocket and groaned. "Now that's just great."

"What?"

"My cell phone's not in my pocket, so I can't even call AAA for assistance."

"Where's your phone?" she asked, dreading the answer.

"I laid it on the counter in your mother's kitchen while I did the dishes, and I must have left it there. Otherwise I would have it here with me right now."

She heaved a sigh. "Now what?"

"We walk—unless you have a better idea."

Rosa shook her head. "Perhaps we can catch a ride with someone passing by. Other than that, I have no ideas at all."

"Catch a ride in someone's Amish buggy?"

"Well, no. . .I mean, maybe. Actually, I was thinking another car might come this way. But if it was a buggy and they had room for us, then I guess we could—"

Anthony gave a shake of his head. "Uh, no. I'd rather walk than ride in a horse-drawn carriage." He opened the car door. "So come on, Rosa, let's get out and start walking."

CHAPTER 14

By the time Rosa and Anthony made it back to her parents' yard, she was tired and in dire need of something cold to drink. She wished that either she or Anthony had thought to bring a few bottles of water with them when they'd left for their Sunday drive.

"I'm going in the house to get a cold drink while you make your phone call. Would you like me to bring a glass of water out to the phone shed for you?" Rosa asked.

Anthony touched the base of his neck and blinked rapidly. "Why would I use the phone shed when my cell phone's right there in the kitchen?"

Rosa smacked her forehead with the palm of her hand. "Oh yeah—that's right. Don't know what I was thinking."

"My bet is that you were thinking like an Amish woman. It's in your blood, Rosa, whether you want to admit it or not."

She bristled. "I was raised by Amish parents, but I never joined the church, so I'm not officially Amish."

"That may be true, but you speak the Pennsylvania Dutch language, wear Amish clothes when you go to a church function, and I'm sure there are many other things about the Plain way of living that have been ingrained in you."

Rosa couldn't argue with that. There were lots of things about being Amish that she couldn't shake free from her life. The sense of stability and family roots went deep. During the two-plus years she'd been away from home, Rosa had experienced the modern English world and found something lacking. It wasn't that everything about that way of life was bad, for there were certainly some good things. But she'd never felt complete. It was as though an important part of her had been missing, which was partly what had finally brought her home.

Anthony followed Rosa into the house, and they went straight to the kitchen. Anthony suggested that she take a seat at the table while he filled two glasses with water, one of which he handed to Rosa. "Here you go. I'll take mine to the living room, along with my phone to search for the nearest towing company, and then I'll make the call."

"Okay. While you're doing that, I'm going upstairs to lie down for a while." She swiped a hand across her sweaty forehead. "The walk back just about did me in, and I'm exhausted."

Anthony took a step toward Rosa and touched her flaming cheek with his thumb. "You do look flushed. Guess I should have left you in the car and hiked back here on my own, but then I would have been worried about you sitting there all alone. I hope the long walk wasn't too much for you, Rosa."

She shook her head, feeling a sense of regret when he removed his thumb. "I'm okay. With a little rest, I am bound to feel better." Still holding on to the glass of water and with her heart pounding in her chest, Rosa hurried from the room and headed for the stairs. The look of concern she'd seen on Anthony's face, along with his gentle touch, had almost been her undoing. The last thing she needed was to fall for a guy who would be leaving in a few days. Rosa's emotions had been up and down like a yo-yo lately, which she figured had something to do with the hormonal changes that went with being pregnant.

I really don't wish that Anthony and I were a couple, Rosa told herself as she ascended the steps toward her room. *Even if by chance he did have feelings for me, it would never work out.*

༺ ༻

Anthony flopped onto the couch and picked up his phone. After searching for a towing service, he discovered one in the area and was about to give them a call when the phone's battery died.

"That's just great. Now I'll have to run out to the phone shed and charge it so I can make the call." He took a small tablet and a pen from his jacket pocket and scribbled down the number of the towing company.

Anthony drank the rest of his water, got up, and headed out the front door. He hoped it wouldn't take long to charge his cell phone because he didn't want to leave his car sitting along the side of the road much longer. No telling who might come along and fool with it. At least since it wouldn't start, he didn't have to worry about it being driven away. Some kids out for a good time could do other damage, though.

When Anthony approached the phone shack, he was greeted by a friendly black-and-white cat that had decided Anthony's pants would make a good scratching post. "Get lost," he mumbled, shooing the feline away. "You're nothing but an irritating nuisance."

The cat scampered away, and Anthony quickly entered the cramped building. After locating the power source and plugging in his phone cord, he seated himself on the folding chair in front of the small bench that held the family's phone and answering machine. "Duh!" He slapped his forehead with the palm of his hand. "Why wait for my cell phone to charge when I have access to the Petersheims' telephone?"

He picked up the receiver and dialed the number for the towing service. It rang several times before someone answered. When Anthony explained the situation, including the color and make of his vehicle along with where his stalled car had been left, the guy asked Anthony where he wanted the vehicle to be towed.

Anthony frowned. Since he wasn't familiar with all the businesses in town, he had no idea which mechanic to take the car to—if there even was anyone who repaired cars in this remote area. He was about to say so when the fellow on the other end suggested a place on Main Street in Belleville, where they sold tires and did vehicle repairs.

"Guess that'll work," Anthony responded. "I'd like to meet you where I left the car, but I'd have to walk back, and it'll take me a while to get there."

"That's okay. I have another stop to make, so it will probably be an hour or so till I can get there."

"Okay. I'll see you there in an hour then." Anthony hung up the phone and sighed. He'd hoped the guy would take pity on him and offer to pick him up.

Guess I oughta be thankful the guy will be meeting me there. He could have said he wasn't working today since it's a Sunday, or not answered his phone at all.

Anthony stepped out of the phone shed in time to see and hear a horse and buggy approach the driveway. When it turned in, he knew right away that it was the Petersheim family returning home from church. As much as he would have preferred not to ride in Mahlon's buggy—or any buggy for that matter—Anthony decided he would put his dislike of the idea aside and ask Rosa's father if he would give him a ride to his car to wait for the tow truck.

Mahlon stopped the buggy and hollered out the driver's side, "What were you doing in the phone shed?"

Anthony explained what had happened with his car and how his cell phone needed charging, so he'd used the phone in the shed to call a tow truck to pick up his vehicle. He also stated that Rosa was tired from the walk back and had gone up to her room to rest.

Mahlon's features tightened as he gave his beard a hefty tug. "See what can happen when you rely on a motorized vehicle, not to mention going sightseeing on a Sunday instead of attending church?"

As much as he didn't want to, Anthony ignored the man's comment and asked Rosa's father if he would mind giving him a ride back to his car to wait for the tow truck.

Mahlon scratched behind his left ear and said, "I'm tired, and I'd planned to take a nap this afternoon."

"Okay then. Guess I'll just have to walk back."

"I'll take him," Susan was quick to say. "Is it all right if I use your horse and carriage, Dad?"

Mahlon hesitated, but after Elsie leaned close to him and said something, he looked at Anthony and said, "All right then. My daughter will take you to your car."

"I wanna go too," Alvin piped up from the back of the buggy.

Mahlon shrugged. "That's fine with me, boy. I'll get a better nap if the house is quiet."

Susan got out and took her father's place, and Elsie and Mahlon headed for the house, while Alvin remained in the back seat. Anthony climbed in on the passenger side up front. They were about to head out when he remembered that he had left his cell phone in the shed. Even though it wouldn't be fully charged, he told Susan that he needed to get his phone, hoping it would have enough battery so that he could make a call if necessary.

"No problem," Susan said. "I'll just hold the horse steady until you get your phone and are back in the buggy."

⁂

A knock on the door roused Rosa from her sleep. She figured it might be Anthony coming to let her know if he'd been able to reach a tow company.

"Come in," she called as she pulled herself to a sitting position and leaned back with her spine pushing against the pillow.

A few seconds later, the door opened and her mother entered the room. "I hope I didn't wake you."

"I did doze off for a bit," Rosa admitted, "but it's okay. I'm awake now. How long have you and the rest of the family been home?"

"Not long. Maybe fifteen minutes or so." Mom sat on the edge of bed next to Rosa and reached out to hold her hand. "Are you feeling all right? Anthony said you had come here to rest, and from the look on your face, you appear to be a little peaked."

"I'm okay—just tired from walking home after Anthony's car broke down. Did he tell you about that?"

"Jah. He said he'd made a phone call from the shed and that a tow truck was going to pick up the car. He also mentioned that he wanted to be there to talk to the driver, so Susan volunteered to take him in your daed's rig to wherever the car had been left sitting."

"Oh, I see. I'm surprised Dad didn't take Anthony there."

A pink flush appeared on Mom's face and neck. "Well. . ."

"Don't tell me. I bet Anthony did ask Dad, and he declined."

Mom nodded. "He said it was because he was tired."

"Maybe, but I bet the real reason was because Dad doesn't care much for Anthony. On top of that, he was probably irked because the two of us didn't go to church and went for a Sunday drive instead." Rosa couldn't keep the irritation she felt out of her tone. If her father didn't like something or someone, he wasn't very good about hiding it.

"I'm glad you found a nice husband," Mom said, quickly changing the topic.

Rosa nodded and managed to put a smile on her face, knowing if she hadn't, her mother might have thought there was something not right between Rosa and Anthony. They had to keep up appearances until it was time for the breakup. After he left, no one, including Mom, would have a good opinion of him. Rosa felt bad about that, but they had to stick to their original plans. It was either that, or admit the truth and deal with the consequence of Dad's anger and Mom's disappointment.

⁂

Susan was thankful for this opportunity to speak with Anthony without Rosa being present. She hoped as they headed in the direction of Anthony's car that he would divulge some information about his relationship with her sister that would be helpful for her to put every piece of this mystery puzzle together once and for all. One thing was for sure: Susan knew the couple were not married. She'd heard them say so with her own two ears.

Susan glanced over at Anthony sitting straight and tall on the seat beside her. "So I've been wondering—"

"Hey, look over there!" Alvin hollered from the back seat of the buggy. See that *hund* sittin' by the side of the road? Sure hope he don't spook Dad's *gaul*."

"The horse won't be bothered, even if the dog barks," Susan said. "He's been trained not to, so just sit back and relax."

"I'm guessing *hund* means 'dog' and *gaul* means 'horse,'" Anthony commented.

"Right on both counts." Susan snapped the reins and the horse picked up speed, without shying or spooking at all.

She glanced at Anthony again. "So back to what I was saying before my little brother interrupted us—"

"I ain't little!" Alvin tapped Susan's shoulder. "And you ain't my mamm."

"Stop saying *ain't*," Susan scolded. "It's not proper English. You should have said, 'I am not little.'"

Susan was relieved when Alvin didn't respond. She wished one of their parents had told him that he couldn't come along. If Alvin kept talking, she'd never get any of the questions she wanted to ask Anthony answered.

She waited a few more minutes, then tried again. "I've been wondering, did you and Rosa have a big wedding?"

Anthony cleared his throat a couple of times before responding. "Uh...no. It was a small one, with just a few people."

"I guess Rosa didn't think any of her family should be invited." Susan gripped the reins a little tighter as anger set in. "Yet the two of you showed up here, right out of the blue, expecting everyone to welcome you both with open arms."

"Rosa hoped you all would."

"Yeah, I just bet she did. But how about you, Anthony? What did you expect when you got to our home?"

"Well, I'm not really sure. I hoped that—" Anthony stopped talking mid-sentence and pointed up ahead. "There's my car, and I'm glad to see the tow truck pulling up ahead of it. If you'll stop the buggy so I can get out, I'm going to talk to the driver and see where he plans to take my vehicle for repairs. I might just ride with him there and then see if he will drop me off at your folks' place after that. Thanks for the ride, Susan. I really appreciate it." Anthony hopped out of the buggy before she could respond.

Susan's shoulders slumped as she sighed. *That sure didn't go the way I'd hoped it would. And who knows when I'll get another chance to speak to Anthony without Rosa around?*

CHAPTER 15

Monday morning, Anthony received a call from the repair shop where his car had been taken, with the unsettling news that the fuel pump was shot and it could take a week or so for them to get the part needed.

He pounded his right fist in his left palm. "That's just super! This news is not what I need today."

"What's wrong?" Rosa asked, taking a seat beside him on the sofa.

Anthony flicked a lock of hair off his forehead and grimaced. "The guy at the repair place informed me that my fuel pump is shot and it could be a week or more before they get in a new one." He sagged against the back of the couch. "You know what that means?"

"That you're stuck here for another week?"

"Yeah, and boy is my dad gonna be mad when he finds out."

Rosa glanced toward the hallway outside the living room. "We need to keep our voices down," she whispered. "My mom's in the basement, but she could come up at any minute and hear what we're saying."

"Yeah, you're right, so let's go up to your room and we can talk more about this."

Anthony rose to his feet and extended his hand to help Rosa get up. They made a hasty exit and headed up the stairs. In Rosa's room, they both took a seat on her bed. Without thinking, Anthony flopped down and rested his head on her pillow. "Wow, this is a comfortable mattress. You must sleep pretty good in this bed."

115

"I'm sorry, Anthony. I can only imagine how uncomfortable it must be for you to sleep on the floor every night." Rosa swiveled around to look at him, and he saw a look of pity on her face. "And I'm sorry about your car. I should never have gotten you into this mess in the first place."

He sat up and put his hand on her trembling shoulder. "I volunteered to come here with you and pose as your husband, so you're not at fault. And don't worry about me sleeping on the floor. I'm almost getting used to that flimsy piece of foam," he added with a forced grin.

"Yeah, right." Her lips compressed. "So now what? Are you going to call your father and give him the news that you won't be back at work when you had originally planned?"

"Yep, and I'm gonna do that right now." He flapped his hand toward the door. "So you might want to leave the room, because I'm sure if you're anywhere near my phone, you'll hear Pop's loud response."

Rosa shook her head. "No, that's okay. I'll stay, because you might need some support."

He clasped her hand, enjoying the warmth of it and appreciating her willingness to sit here with him while he made the call.

New York City

The phone rang and Lavera picked it up. "Reeves Italian Diner. How may I help you?"

"Hi, Mom. It's good to hear your voice."

"Oh, Anthony, I'm so glad it's you. We haven't talked since you called on Thanksgiving."

"I know, Mom. Sorry about that. The days have gone by quickly, and now I need to talk to Pop."

"He's in the kitchen, cooking as usual. May I take a message?"

"No, it's important, and I need to speak to him myself."

"Okay." Lavera set the receiver on the counter and went to the kitchen. She found Herb dishing up a plate of spaghetti and meatballs. "You're wanted on the phone, dear."

"I'm busy. Take a message."

"It's our son. Anthony said he needs to talk to you."

"About what?"

Lavera shrugged. "He didn't say. Just said it was important."

Herb lifted his gaze toward the ceiling. "It better be him calling to let me know that he's gonna be here on the day he said, because I'm getting sick of holding down the fort." He handed the plate of spaghetti to Lavera. "You can take this out to table number five while I see what Anthony wants."

Belleville

Rosa sat close to Anthony, hoping her presence offered him the support he apparently needed as he held the cell phone close to his ear and rubbed his forehead. She figured that was probably better than putting it on speaker mode, just in case her mother decided to come upstairs for anything.

Even though the cell phone was not on speaker, Rosa heard the anger in the voice of Anthony's father after Anthony explained about his car troubles and said he wouldn't be back to New York for another week or so. She also saw Anthony's stiff posture and the tightened muscles in his arms as he held the phone. No doubt he was angry and even embarrassed that she sat here listening to him receive a tongue-lashing from his father for no good reason. After all, it wasn't like Anthony had planned for his car to die or chose for the new fuel pump to take a week or more to get here. Rosa thought Anthony's dad ought to be more understanding, especially in a situation like this.

Of course, she reminded herself, *my daed's never been understanding when I've done something he doesn't approve of. If he was honest with me, Dad would probably admit that he wishes I'd never come home. Most likely he prefers Susan's help at the Meat and Cheese Store than he ever did mine when I worked there.*

When Anthony finally clicked off his phone and dropped it on the bed beside him, he turned to face Rosa and said, "That went exactly like I figured it would. My dad is hopping mad, and he threatened to fire me and hire some other cook to take my place." He paused long enough to take a few deep breaths before continuing with his tirade. "I'm sure after I said I'd get there as soon as possible and hung up, Mom probably went to bat for me and tried to calm Pop down."

"I can't tell you how many times my mother has run interference between me and my father over the years." Rosa gestured to Anthony's phone. "Would it help if I called and talked to your father?"

Anthony gave a firm shake of his head. "That would undoubtedly make things worse. Remember, Pop wasn't too happy when you quit your job to make the trip here, leaving him short a waitress."

"True. I'm sure he won't fire you, though. That was probably just an idle threat."

Anthony's forehead wrinkled. "I wouldn't be too sure. But you know what, Rosa? I can't worry about that right now." He planted his feet on the floor and stood. "It's kinda stuffy in this room. Think I'll go outside for a breath of fresh air. You want to join me?"

"Not really. I'm too tired to do much of anything right now. Think I'll stay here and rest for a while." Rosa reclined on the bed.

He looked down at her with his thick brows drawn together. "You okay?"

"I'm fine—just tired."

Anthony leaned over and gave Rosa a peck on her forehead. "All right then, I'll see you later, Wife."

"Stop it! That's nothing to joke about."

When Anthony left the room, shutting the door behind him, Rosa closed her eyes and tried to relax. She wished there was something she could do to make things up to Anthony for the sacrifice he'd made in bringing her home. Once again, Rosa wished she had never agreed to let Anthony pretend to be her husband. Now they would have to keep up their charade until his car had been fixed and he could be on his way back to New York.

THE PRETENDER

Anthony put on his jacket and went out the back door. When he stepped into the yard, he realized that with Mahlon and Susan working at the store today, Elsie in the basement, Alvin at school, and Rosa in her room, he pretty much had the whole place to himself. It felt kind of good, and he wandered around the area, breathing in the cool, fresh air.

Elsie's garden, which he guessed must have been vibrant and full of fresh produce, was bare, except for the tops of carrots and other root vegetables. A few colorful mums still bloomed in the flower beds near the house, but those would be gone once winter brought snow and freezing weather.

Anthony stopped walking and flexed his fingers repeatedly. *Oh boy! Sure hope I'm not stuck here till the snow flies. I need to get back to New York before Pop carries through with his threat and I end up losing my job.*

Caw! Caw! Caw! A noisy crow flew overhead, scattering Anthony's thoughts and doing away with the peaceful moment he'd experienced when first stepping into the yard. There was no point worrying about his job right now, when there was nothing he could do about it. If Pop did end up firing him, he'd look for another position at some other restaurant. With the amount of eateries in New York, plus the experience Anthony had as a chef, he felt sure that someone would hire him. In the meantime, he might as well make the best of his situation here.

Anthony turned and allowed his footsteps to take him to Mahlon's rustic-looking barn. After stepping inside, Anthony paused to allow his eyes to adjust to the shadows in the main part of the building, devoid of light except for what little crept in from outside through the bare windows. He paused and lifted his head to inhale the aroma of the sweet-smelling hay that had been stacked neatly along one wall.

Anthony smiled when he heard some soft meows, along with the rustle of straw that had been spread on the floor in a spot where a mama cat lay with a batch of kittens. He remained in place several minutes, watching the little critters and wondering what it would have been like to grow up on the farm, with the option to play in the barn. Anthony assumed there would be lots of places in this building for a child to hide or play games. Of course, for someone like Rosa's brother Alvin, coming here wouldn't be all fun and games. He'd heard the boy's father remind him several times that there were chores waiting for him to do in the barn.

Anthony heard the soft nicker of a horse, and he followed the sound down a shadowy corridor where there were no windows at all. Before coming to the barn, he had seen a couple of horses grazing in the pasture and figured they were all out there, but apparently he'd been wrong.

As he approached the second stall, Anthony heard the stomping of hooves, followed by a series of snorts. No doubt the horse was keenly aware of his presence.

When Anthony drew closer, the chestnut horse stuck its head over the top of the gate. Surprised, Anthony jumped back. "Whoa now! Don't you go gettin' any ideas." In the dim light, Anthony wasn't sure whose horse this was, but he was glad it seemed to be gentle.

The horse nickered and shook its head, as though it understood what Anthony had said. He relaxed a bit and even chuckled. Anthony was glad no one had witnessed the alarm he'd felt when the animal had first made its appearance. Cautiously, Anthony reached his hand out and stroked the horse's nose.

"Too bad I don't have an apple or some other treat to give you," Anthony said as he continued to pet the horse. "If I'd have known I would end up in here, I'd have brought you an apple."

Anthony remained a while longer, stroking the horse and enjoying the moment before deciding it was time to head back outside.

Once he was in the cooler air again, Anthony strolled past the chicken run and watched as a couple of cackling hens took a dirt bath, while several others scratched for bugs. *Thanks to these plump chickens, we had fresh eggs for breakfast this morning,* Anthony mused as he moved on. *Guess that's one more positive thing about living the country life.*

Anthony shoved his hands into his pockets and moved toward the back of the Petersheims' property. He heard the high-pitched *maa-maa* bleat of several goats inside an enclosed area and went over to take a closer look. Goats were not something one would normally see running around New York City, and Anthony watched with interest as they pranced and frolicked around, some standing on their hind legs to reach and eat the leaves from the lower branches of the tree nearby.

Anthony noticed that one of the male goats was busy rubbing against the fence post, while another one nibbled on the wood. "Strange. Very strange critters," he mumbled with his arms folded.

Shaking his head, Anthony was about to walk away and return to the house when he caught sight of yet another male goat—this one with a white beard mixed with gray. The animal was foraging in the grass on the opposite side of the fence. Anthony's side, to be exact. *I wonder how that critter got out.*

Unexpectedly, and with its head down, the goat, coming at a good clip, headed right for Anthony. "Go back where you came from! You obviously jumped the fence once, you can do it again," Anthony hollered, waving his arms. Big mistake! The crazy animal gave a low guttural sound and charged.

Anthony did the first thing he could think of. He bent down, picked up some small stones, and pitched them at the goat. His aim was bad, and the rocks missed, but the action did not deter the goat. It made him more aggressive.

Anthony's adrenaline took over, and knowing he needed to take refuge, he ran for all he was worth toward the woodshed. Seeing a pile of logs on one side of the small building, he scrambled to the top and shouted for help. Meanwhile, the goat, with head down and making a threatening kind of grunting sound, came closer and closer. If someone didn't hear Anthony's screams soon and come to rescue him, he figured he might have to fight off the goat with his bare hands. "If I had a stick in my hand," he muttered, "I would definitely use it right now."

CHAPTER 16

As the aggressive goat came closer to the woodpile where Anthony stood, he didn't know which emotion he felt the strongest—anger or fear. Regardless of how he felt, he had to figure out a way to get out of this fix.

Anthony moved to the right, nearly losing his balance, and hollered at the goat. "Go away! Get lost! Go back to where you belong!"

"Hey, Anthony, what's goin' on? How come you're standing on the logs and hollering at Buster?"

Anthony's eyes widened as he caught sight of Alvin coming up behind the goat. "You'd better watch out, kid," he shouted. "That critter's a mean one."

"He could be, I suppose, but not usually. Even so, all goats are good jumpers, so you bein' on those logs is no protection. Any minute, he could leap right on up there and join you." Alvin set his lunch box on the ground and marched up to the goat. "He's got ya buffaloed 'cause he knows you're scared."

"You got that right." Anthony shifted his stance a bit, keeping both eyes on the bleating goat.

Alvin reached down and opened his lunch box. He grabbed an apple and approached the animal slowly. "You want this treat, Buster?" He held the apple close to the goat's mouth.

Anthony resisted the temptation to hold his breath as he waited to see what the goat would do. He hoped the critter wouldn't charge or butt the boy. It could spell disaster. To Anthony's surprise, however, that ornery animal took one bite of the apple and followed Alvin across the yard and all the way to the pen. When Alvin opened the gate and let the goat in, Anthony climbed down from his log perch.

"That was impressive," Anthony said when Alvin returned. "How'd you know the goat wouldn't headbutt you?"

The boy puffed out his chest a bit as his lips curved into a smile. "Buster's one of my favorite goats, and after school most days, I've been workin' with him and some of the other goats my dad bought a while back."

"You're sure a smart fellow, Alvin. I'm impressed."

The boy kicked at a couple of small stones beneath his feet. "Aw, it ain't no big deal. I like most animals, and I really enjoy workin' with 'em."

Anthony began walking with Alvin toward the house. "What else do you know about goats?"

"Well," Alvin said, "I'm sure they're not all as easy to work with as Buster. I am no goat expert, but I've heard that some of them can be real mean. But they also like to play, and in the process, they sometimes end up gettin' carried away."

"How'd you learn so much about goats?" Anthony asked.

"Mostly from workin' with the critters, but I've also read a book on raising goats that I checked out at the library in town."

"Sounds like you know what you're doing, then."

Alvin shrugged. "Don't know about that, but as I said before, I do like workin' with animals."

"Maybe you'll end up being a veterinarian someday," Anthony suggested.

The boy stopped walking and turned to look up at Anthony, who'd also halted his footsteps. "I can't be a vet if I'm gonna join the Amish church when I'm a bit older."

"Are you set on joining?" Anthony queried.

"I guess." Alvin shrugged. "If I don't join, my dad will be really disappointed. It's bad enough that Rosa ran off and never joined the church, and I'm pretty sure my sister Susan doesn't wanna become a church member either."

Anthony tilted his head toward the boy. "What makes you think so?"

"Because Susan hasn't taken any classes to prepare for it, and she does a lot of sneaky things that our folks don't approve of."

Anthony was tempted to ask for specifics, but he decided it was none of his business. If he truly was Rosa's lawful husband, it would mean he was actually Susan's brother-in-law. Only then would he take an active interest in her actions. Anthony figured he might even intervene if he knew she was doing something wrong. Under the circumstances, however, it was best that he keep any questions or opinions about Susan to himself.

"So tell me a little more about the goats you help to care for," Anthony said. "Are they dairy goats or being raised for the meat?"

Alvin gave a vigorous shake of his head. "Oh, no—we don't kill any of our goats for meat on the table. Mom likes to have them for milk and cheese."

"To sell at your dad's Meat and Cheese Store?"

"No, just for us. Dad gets his goat milk products for the store from an Amish man over in Allensville who has a big herd of goats. We don't have enough goats to provide what we need for the store."

"I see."

Walking slowly as they moved on, Anthony asked Alvin to share a little more information about the goats his family owned.

"Well, let's see. . .guess I could tell you how a sick goat will stand hunched, with its head lowered, but it may fake fitness if somethin' or someone surprises or comes after it."

Tilting his head, Anthony pointed at the boy. "Did you make that up, Alvin?"

"No way. It's the truth." Alvin snapped his fingers. "Oh, here's somethin' else that's kinda interesting. When a goat's hungry or wants a treat, it may root near the place where its food is usually dished out."

"So that's their way of letting you know that they want to eat?"

"Yep." Alvin's dimples deepened as he grinned widely. "Is that enough goat information for now?"

Anthony chuckled and tousled the boy's hair. "I think that'll do, but if I have any other questions, I'll know who to ask."

As they approached the house, Anthony looked up and noticed Rosa standing at her bedroom window. He wondered if she'd heard him hollering for help when the goat chased him onto the logs. But if she had, surely she would have come outside to see if she could help somehow.

Anthony waved and then smiled when Rosa returned the gesture. *She really is a beautiful woman. If Rosa decides to join the Amish church, I hope someday she will find a nice Amish man who'll gladly marry her and be a good father to the child she's carrying.*

༄

"We've had a busy day here, jah?" Norman's father asked as they prepared to close the Meat and Cheese Store for the day.

Norman nodded. "Seems like everyone who came in wanted the same thing, because we're running low on cheese sticks and pork links."

"I'm guessing the cheese sticks are for children's lunches, and a lot of our female customers are planning to cook pork links for supper tonight, or maybe for tomorrow's breakfast."

"You could be right, Dad." Norman glanced over at Susan, who stood quietly near the front door. No doubt she was eager to see the CLOSED sign hung in the window so the three of them could head for their homes. Susan had been in a sullen mood all day, which had been obvious by her lack of conversation with the customers she'd waited on. Norman suspected his sister's bad mood had something to do with the fact that Rosa was at home with their mother, while Susan was stuck here dealing with Dad's many requests and expectations.

If my sister dislikes working here so much, I wonder why she doesn't look for some other job, Norman pondered. *There are plenty of other things she could do, but then that would leave us shorthanded here at the store, at least till our daed found a replacement for her.*

Dad moved closer to Norman and elbowed his arm. "Did you hear what I said, Son?"

"Jah, you said something about it being busy here today."

"No, not that. I had moved on to another topic."

Norman blinked in succession. "Oh, sorry. Guess my mind was somewhere else. What was it you said to me?"

"I was telling you that I think that husband of Rosa's is freeloading on us. If he's gonna remain at our house, then he oughta get out there and find a job." Dad grunted. "I don't appreciate being taken advantage of, and I have to wonder what Rosa ever saw in the lazy fellow."

Norman wasn't sure how to respond to his father's tirade. If he took Anthony's side and suggested that the reason he hadn't looked for a job was because he and Rosa weren't sure if they'd be staying in the area permanently, Dad might go off on that too. He'd probably say something like, "Well, if they aren't sure, then they shouldn't have come here at all."

As Norman stood mulling things over and trying to decide how best to comment, Susan joined the conversation. "I totally agree with you, Dad. Anthony should be out looking for a job, and he and Rosa ought to find a place of their own." Her eyes flashed angrily. "It's not fair that we all have to work for a living while he lazes around at the house all day."

Norman wasn't sure why, because he didn't know Anthony very well, but he felt it necessary to come to his brother-in-law's defense. "I don't think it's a good idea to be judging Anthony, especially when he's not here to defend himself. Maybe it's going to take a little time for him and Rosa to decide where they want to settle down and raise their family." Norman looked first at his father and then Susan. "And maybe Rosa's husband isn't lazing around all day like you think. He might be doing all kinds of chores to help out at the house while we're here at the store. If you're so worried about it, you might want to check with Mom and ask what occupies Anthony's time during the daylight hours."

THE PRETENDER

Dad's brows furrowed, and Susan's mouth opened slightly, like she might say something, but neither of them commented. Norman was glad this discussion had ended. All he wanted to do was go home to his sweet wife and spend a pleasant evening with her. He was ever so glad that he was married and out on his own, because he could only imagine how much tension there must be in his parents' house these days.

※

During supper that evening, Alvin picked at his food as he slumped in his chair beside Anthony.

"What's wrong, Son?" Elsie questioned from across the table. "Did you snack too much after school and ruin your appetite?"

Alvin shook his head. "I only ate one cookie when I came inside with Anthony."

"So how come you haven't eaten much supper?" the boy's father questioned.

Alvin shrugged.

"This isn't like you at all," Elsie said. "Are you feeling grank?"

"I don't think I'm sick, Mom." Alvin reached for his glass of water and took a drink. When he set it back on the table, he grimaced. "My throat kinda hurts, though, and my belly aches too."

"How long have you felt like this?" his mother asked.

"My throat felt scratchy while I was at school today, but the bellyache didn't start till I sat down to eat supper."

"You might be coming down with something," Rosa interjected. "Has anyone in your classroom been sick?"

"A couple of kids were missing today." Alvin pulled a hand across his forehead. "Boy, it sure is hot in here. Can someone please open a window?"

"It's not hot in this room, Alvin." Susan glared at her brother. "You're just trying to get out of eating scalloped potatoes because it's not your favorite dish."

"I ain't either," he countered.

"*Ain't* is not good English, you know." Susan popped a black olive into her mouth. "What's that new teacher you have this year teaching you, anyway?"

"I don't like Mary Sue as well as Salina, but she's a good teacher."

"Not if she's allowing you to say words like *ain't*."

Mahlon held up his hand. "All right, Susan, that's enough! Finish eating your supper and stop nitpicking your bruder."

Anthony waited to see how Susan would respond, and he was surprised when she dashed out of the room like a child who hadn't gotten her way. Since that first day he and Rosa had arrived at the Petersheim home, he'd noticed that Susan seemed to have a chip on her shoulder. He wondered what the problem was and if Rosa might know. *Maybe I'll ask her when I get the chance—see if she can shed some light on her sister's actions.*

A few seconds passed, and when Alvin continued to sit there without eating, Elsie got up and came around to stand behind the boy. Reaching over the chair where he sat and placing her hands on Alvin's forehead, her brows drew inward as she declared, "You're burning up, Son. You need to leave the table and go straight to bed. I'll be up soon with something to hopefully bring the fever down and help your stomach stop hurting."

Alvin didn't have to be asked twice. He pushed his chair back and quickly fled the room. Elsie went to one of the kitchen cupboards, took out a few items, and asked Tena and Rosa to see about clearing the table when everyone finished eating. Then she too scurried out of the room.

"I bet I know what's wrong with Alvin," Tena said, looking at no one in particular.

"What would that be?" Rosa asked.

"When I was in town earlier today, I heard someone say that the *wasserpareble* is going around Mifflin County. The first symptoms for that are sore throat, fever, and sometimes a stomachache."

"Oh boy, I hope that's not the case," Rosa said.

Anthony leaned closer to her. "What's wasserpareble?"

"The chicken pox," Mahlon responded.

Anthony stiffened. He hoped that wasn't the case for Alvin, because if it was, that meant he'd also been exposed. As far as Anthony knew, and according to his mother, he'd never had the chicken pox.

CHAPTER 17

TWO DAYS LATER, ROSA INVITED Anthony to go for a ride with her by horse and buggy. He said he wasn't excited about it, but when she stated that she wanted to pay a call on her friend Ada, whom she hadn't talked to since the day of her wedding, Anthony said he'd put up with the smell of horseflesh and go with her.

Some friend I am, Rosa thought as she directed her horse toward the greenhouse where Ada worked. *I've been too wrapped up in my own problems to take time out to see how things are going for Ada. Of course,* she reminded herself, *I wasn't a good friend during the two years I was gone when I didn't contact my best friend. I'm surprised Ada's even speaking to me now. Ephraim either, for that matter. They both should be angry at me for not telling them where I was going or keeping in touch.* Rosa had consoled herself with the fact that she'd written a note before taking off, as well as calling home to leave a few messages during the time she'd been gone—although no one in the family seemed to know about the note, nor the phone calls that should have been on their recorder. Unless, of course, someone had erased them, which could have been done accidentally or on purpose.

"Hey, there's the greenhouse. If you don't turn in now, you'll miss the parking lot."

Anthony's statement caused Rosa to jerk her head and also the horse's reins. "Thanks for the heads-up. My mind was elsewhere, and I wasn't paying attention to how close we were to the greenhouse."

THE PRETENDER

Rosa guided the horse up to the hitching rail, and Anthony stepped down from the buggy to secure the animal. Once that was taken care of, she got out as well. Just then, a gust of wind came up, blowing leaves around like monarch butterflies swirling in a summer breeze.

Walking together toward the greenhouse, Rosa enjoyed the warmth generating from Anthony's skin as he clasped her hand. She figured the gesture was probably for show, in case someone Rosa knew saw them out together. If they'd been dressed in Amish attire and holding hands, anyone who was Amish might have been taken aback by their physical contact. But it was common to see English couples holding hands or with their arms around each other.

As they entered the building, Rosa spotted several pots of red poinsettias near the checkout counter. The lovely plants reminded her that Christmas was just a few weeks away. By then, Anthony would no doubt have his car fixed and be back in New York to celebrate the holiday with his parents and sisters.

Rosa thought about the Christmases she'd spent away from her own family and how lonely she'd felt without them. Drifting from town to town and working at various positions had not filled her with the joy she'd hoped for when she'd first left home to explore the modern English world. At times Rosa had wanted to leave it all behind and return home. But her pride got in the way, and she would move on to a new town instead, with the last one being New York City.

"I don't see your friend anywhere," Anthony commented, breaking into Rosa's thoughts.

She looked out at the expansive greenhouse, her gaze flitting from aisle to aisle. "I'll ask the woman at the checkout counter where Ada is working right now," she responded.

"Yeah, that's probably a good idea," he agreed.

Rosa approached the counter and waited until the Amish woman ahead of her had paid for her items. "Could you please tell me where I might find Ada Detweiler—I mean, Peight?" she asked the woman who stood near the cash register.

"Ada's not working today or tomorrow. She asked for a couple days off to help her mother-in-law do some cleaning."

"Do you mean at Dorothy Peight's house?"

"Yes, that's right. Ada said her in-laws will be hosting church at their place this Sunday, and since many hands make light work, I'm sure there will be plenty of others helping there today as well."

"Thanks." Rosa turned to face Anthony. "Since we don't really have any other plans for the day, would you mind if we stop by the Peights'? I'm sure Ada will be busy cleaning and such, but it would be nice to at least say hello and let her know that I've been thinking about her."

Anthony shrugged his shoulders. "Sure, whatever you like. You're the driver, after all."

Rosa smiled. She was glad he had no objection to stopping by a place where he didn't know the people. It was just one more thing that reflected Anthony's easygoing ways.

Allensville

Coming up the driveway leading to the home of Ephraim's parents, Rosa was surprised to see an elderly Amish woman jumping on a trampoline that had been set up in the side yard. Three young Amish children were leaping up and down with her.

Anthony looked over at Rosa with raised eyebrows and pointed. "I can't believe my eyes. Sure never expected to see anyone that old on a trampoline, let alone an Amish woman."

Rosa clicked her tongue against the roof of her mouth. "Me neither."

"Do you know who she is?"

"No, but I'm guessing it might be Ephraim's grandmother," Rosa replied. "During the time Ephraim and I were going out, he often mentioned his grandma who lived in Lancaster County. From some of the things he shared about her, I was led to believe that she is quite the character, with lots of determination, and he had said that she's a bit feisty too."

Anthony chuckled. "Guess there's nothing wrong with that."

"Agreed." Rosa guided the horse to the rail and held firmly to the reins while Anthony got out and secured the mare.

"I'm going up to the house to see if Ada's here," Rosa said after joining him near the horse. "Are you coming with me?"

He shook his head. "Think I'll stay out here and go watch that Amish woman playing leapfrog on the trampoline for a while. In fact, I might even join her and the kids."

Rosa tipped her head as she placed both hands against her hips. "You're kidding, right?"

"Nope, I'm totally serious. Growing up, I had a friend whose parents bought him a trampoline for his birthday one year. I went over to his house as often as I could, and both of us got pretty good at doing flips and some other tricks."

She rolled her eyes. "Well don't do anything foolish. It's bad enough that my little brother is down with the chicken pox. Sure don't need you getting injured and ending up in the hospital."

Anthony lifted Rosa's chin with his thumb and looked directly into her eyes. "It's nice to know you're worried about me, but I'm a big boy, and if I decide to have a little fun on the tramp, I'll be fine."

"All right, whatever you say. Just be careful, okay?"

He gave her a thumbs-up. "Sure, whatever *you* say."

Rosa stood watching as Anthony's long legs took him swiftly across the grass. Before he reached the trampoline, she turned and headed for the house. She had no plans to remain here and watch him relive his childhood. Besides, if he was going to do something stupid, she didn't want to be a witness to it.

When Rosa knocked on the door, she was greeted by Ephraim's mother, Dorothy. "Oh, I'm surprised to see you here." The woman spoke in a cool tone, and her eyes held no sparkle.

Rosa swallowed hard. *Dorothy doesn't want me here. She's probably peeved because I broke up with her son, ran off for two years, and never contacted Ephraim. Well, guess I can't blame her for that.* Rosa shifted uneasily, wondering if she should turn around and head back to her horse and buggy. But she'd made the trip to see Ada and didn't want to leave without at least saying hello.

"I'm sorry to bother you," Rosa said. "But when I stopped by the greenhouse a while ago, I was told that Ada might be here."

"Jah, she is. We're having church at our place this Sunday, and my thoughtful daughter-in-law came to help me clean and get everything ready."

Rosa crossed her arms over her stomach as she struggled with a feeling of agitation. *Is Ephraim's mother trying to rub it in my face that her son married someone better than me? Dorothy probably thinks I'm far from being thoughtful.*

There had been a time when Rosa thought Dorothy cared for her. Of course, that was when she and Ephraim were going steady and seemed to be heading down a path that could have led to marriage. *I messed that up when I ran away and left Ephraim and my family behind*, Rosa admitted to herself.

"Would you please let Ada know that I'm here and would like to speak with her?" Rosa forced herself to offer Dorothy a pleasant smile, hoping it might soften things between them a bit.

No such luck. Looking directly at Rosa, the woman tapped her foot and said, "Why did you come back here to the Big Valley, Rosa? I hope it wasn't to cause any problems between my son and his wife. They are very happy together, and—"

Rosa held up one hand. "I have no intention of causing Ada or Ephraim any problems. I am sure they must have told you that I am married now, and my husband and I are currently staying at my parents' house."

"For how long?" Dorothy's eyes narrowed. "Do you plan to stay in the area for good or run off again when things don't go your way or you become dissatisfied with the Plain way of living?" She gestured to Rosa's jeans and sweatshirt. "It's clear that you're not Amish anymore and don't wish to be."

At this point, Rosa was tempted to turn right around and tell Anthony that she was ready to go home. But no. She came here for a reason, and she was not going to leave until she'd seen Ada. Instead of responding to Dorothy's question or commenting on the woman's assumption that she was no longer Amish, Rosa asked the question again. "Would you please let Ada know that I'm here?"

"As you wish." Dorothy whirled around and headed down the hallway behind her with the hemline of the dark green dress she wore swishing.

Rosa poked her tongue against the inside of her cheek and inhaled a long breath. In the past, Ephraim's mother had never been rude to her. *But maybe I deserve it*, she told herself. *I did disappoint her son by refusing to join the church and marry him, and I'm sure he had plenty to say about it to his parents when I ran away.*

Several minutes passed, and Ada stepped out onto the porch with outstretched arms. "Oh, it's so good to see you, dear friend." She gave Rosa a welcoming hug.

"It's good to see you too. I went by the greenhouse to say hello and see how you've been doing and learned that you were here, helping out."

Ada nodded. "Jah, there are several other women here today as well, including Ephraim's grandmother." She grinned and gestured to the trampoline. "Of course, right now she's taking a little jumping break, and it looks like your husband has joined the fun."

"Yes, I noticed the older woman on the trampoline. It was a surprise to see her out there," Rosa commented.

"Sarah is quite the character," Ada said. "She's in her late seventies but still quite active and ready to try almost anything."

"I hope when I'm her age, I'll be courageous enough to do a few daring things. . .although it might not include jumping on a trampoline."

"I'm with you on that." Ada grasped the handle on the front door. "Should we go inside where it's a little warmer to visit?"

"No, that's okay," Rosa was quick to say. "I think it might be better if we do our talking out here."

"Are you sure?"

"Definitely. Your mother-in-law wasn't too friendly when she answered the door and saw me, so I think it's better if I don't go in."

Ada clasped Rosa's arm. "I'm sorry if Dorothy made you feel uncomfortable. She's been working hard to get things ready for Sunday, and I'm sure she must be exhausted."

Rosa was on the verge of telling Ada that she was sure there was more to it than that when a ruckus erupted out in the yard. Turning around, she was surprised to see Anthony in the middle of the trampoline, with the children and Ephraim's grandmother gathered around him as he leaped like a frog high into the air above the trampoline.

Anthony couldn't remember the last time he'd had so much fun. It had been a good many years since he'd jumped on his childhood friend's trampoline, but apparently he hadn't lost his touch, because he still remembered one of the best ways to make himself jump higher. What made it even better today was that he had a captive audience who stood on the edges of the trampoline, clapping and cheering him on as he lifted his hands high over his head and pushed off the trampoline with his feet.

"Now it's your turn to try it," Anthony shouted to the eager-looking children, as well as the Amish lady, whose name he had learned was Sarah.

He stopped jumping and stood off to one side as each of them took a turn. There was plenty of laughter and squealing, but no one could even come close to the height that he'd been able to jump.

I wonder if I can still do a flip in the air and land on both feet. Anthony braced himself and gulped in some air as he first did a back drop. *So far so good.* Next, he moved to an over-the-shoulder handspring, a back handspring, and finally, a backflip. As he landed, one leg angled to the left, and he wobbled. The next thing Anthony knew, he was off the tramp and lying on the ground on his back with spots before his eyes. A searing pain shot through his left ankle, and it was all Anthony could do not to scream. Groaning, he rolled to one side and tried to sit up, but the pain was too intense. Anthony knew he'd either broken his ankle or sprained it badly. He certainly wasn't about to try standing on his own, and much as he hated to admit it, he needed some help.

CHAPTER 18

With her heart pounding so hard she thought it might explode, Rosa hurried down the porch steps and ran to the place where Anthony lay. Ada was at her side, and they dropped to the ground at the same time.

"Are you hurt, Anthony? Did you break anything?" Rosa's mind skipped ahead to all the possibilities.

"Mostly my pride for showing off." He touched his ankle and winced. "Got the wind knocked out of me, and I think I may have sprained or even broken my ankle."

"Oh my!" Ada put one hand against her mouth. "Should I go to the phone shed and call for emergency help?"

Anthony gave a vigorous shake of his head. "The last thing I need is a trip to the hospital in an ambulance. I can only imagine how much that would cost." He moved his foot slightly and winced.

"You should definitely have it looked at," Rosa said. "If it is broken, you'll need to have it tended to, and without an X-ray we won't know for sure how serious the injury is."

By now, Ephraim's grandma and the children who had been on the trampoline with Anthony were off and standing around him with wide eyes and mouths open, like a bunch of baby birds waiting to be fed.

"Young man, you need to be seen by a doctor right away. That's all there is to it!" Sarah shook her finger at Anthony. "That trick you tried to do on the trampoline was reckless, but if you don't get your ankle looked at right away, it will be just plain foolishness."

"Why don't I call one of my drivers to come and take you to one of the area clinics so you can be seen today?" Ada was quick to say. "I will be happy to pay the driver."

Rosa shook her head. "That's okay, Ada. I have enough money to pay the driver, but I would appreciate it if you made the call for us."

"Sure, no problem." Ada hurried off in the direction of the phone shed near the front of the Peights' property.

Rosa hoped it wouldn't be long before a driver pulled in, because the grimace on Anthony's face made it clear that he was in a lot of pain. She hoped the injury wasn't serious. Anthony had done a lot for Rosa by coming to Mifflin County and pretending to be her husband. So she would do whatever she could to see that he got the proper care he needed. It was the least she could do to make up for the sacrifice he'd made.

Belleville

Susan stood with her arms folded and her back firmly against the inside area of the checkout counter, staring at the clock in front of her. They had seen fewer customers than normal this morning, and she wished she could go home. Boredom had quickly set in with no one to wait on and no questions to answer. Susan's father had let her brother go at noon, since things were slow and Norman had mentioned that Salina had an appointment and he wished to go with her.

I wonder what kind of appointment she'd have that would require Norman to be with her? Susan blew out a puff of air. *Sure wish I had some excuse to leave the store early. I bet Dad could handle things here by himself for the rest of the day. But I guess there's no point in asking, because he would most likely say no, like he usually does whenever I want something.*

"What are you doing standing there with your back to the counter?" Dad's booming voice pushed Susan's thoughts aside, and she whirled around to face him.

"I was just looking at the clock and thinking what a slow morning we've had."

"Jah, that's true, but this afternoon, business could pick up." He moved toward the front window to look out and made his way back to where she stood. "You need to find something to keep yourself busy for the rest of the day. No more standing around with a mopey look on your face."

"I can't help the way my face looks." Susan lifted her hands and touched both cheeks. "I'm bored and wishing I was anywhere but here."

"Is that so?" His nostrils flared as he planted his legs in a wide stance. "Seems to me that you're an ungrateful daughter who doesn't appreciate the job that's been provided for her."

Susan jerked her head sharply as a flush of heat converged on her face. "That's not true, Dad. I do appreciate the chance to earn money. I just don't enjoy the work I'm expected to do here in the Meat and Cheese Store."

He eyed her intently. "I think your biggest problem is you don't socialize enough with other young people your age. It's been a long time since you went to any of the young people's gatherings. While others are out having fun, all you do is sit around home with a sour expression and complain."

Susan was about to respond, but he spoke before she could get one word out.

"So hear me well, Daughter. The next time there is a young people's singing, you will be attending the gathering. Is that understood?"

The warmth Susan felt on her face increased. "That's not fair, Dad. I'm not a child anymore, and I shouldn't have to go to any of the social gatherings if I don't want to."

Dad stepped forward and jabbed a finger close to her nose. "Listen here, young lady. As long as you are living under my roof, you will do as I say. End of story."

Elsie made her way up the stairs to check on Alvin. For the last two days she'd kept him home from school, and she would continue to do so until he was well enough to return. Her dear, sweet boy had definitely come down with chicken pox, and he had the irritating, itchy eruptions on his body to prove it.

Elsie entered her son's room and found him lying on the bed with his eyes closed. Believing he must be sleeping, she decided it would be best for her to go back downstairs rather than wake him. Rest was good for the boy, and when Alvin slept he didn't scratch. Elsie had warned him about the dangers of scratching, stating that the pox could get infected.

The red skin rash had shown up last night on his stomach, and by this morning they had spread to Alvin's back and face. It looked like pimples or insect bites. Elsie knew they would appear in waves over two to four days, after which they'd develop into thin-walled blisters filled with fluid. The blister walls would break later, leaving open sores, which ended up crusting over to become dry, brown scabs. Chicken pox was contagious, so Alvin should stay home from school until the rash was gone and all the blisters had dried, which usually took about a week.

She remembered how miserable she had felt when she'd come down with the chicken pox at the age of seven. She hadn't heeded her mother's advice about not scratching and had a few scars to prove it. Thankfully, they weren't in obvious places, so at least she didn't have to offer explanations to anyone who might see them and ask what had happened.

Elsie set the glass of water she'd brought for her son on the small table beside his bed and quietly left the room. She would check on Alvin again in an hour or so, unless she heard him hollering for her sooner.

Back downstairs, Elsie went to the kitchen to fix herself a glass of apple cider. She had just taken a seat at the table when she heard the front door open and close. A strange rhythmic tapping accompanied by a slight scuffing sound traveled into the kitchen. Curious, Elsie rose from her chair and left the room to see who had come in and what the odd noise was all about. Upon entering the front hallway, she was surprised to see Anthony hobbling on a pair of crutches while Rosa walked beside him.

Elsie's eyes widened as she stared at him in disbelief. "Forevermore, what happened to you?"

⁓⁓

Anthony grimaced. "I sprained my ankle pretty good."

"Pretty good? Don't you mean, pretty bad? At least that's what the doctor said, Anthony." Rosa led the way to the living room and gestured to her father's recliner. "Better sit down and put up your feet like the doctor said you should."

Anthony hobbled over, and with a groan, he lowered himself into the chair and then leaned the crutches against it.

Rosa stood on one side of him, and her mother on the other, both wearing anxious expressions.

"How did it happen?" Elsie questioned.

Anthony explained how he'd been jumping on the trampoline in the Peights' yard and bounced a little too exuberantly while trying to show Ephraim's grandmother and a few children how to do a backflip.

Elsie's eyes opened wide again. "Sarah was on the trampoline?"

"That's right, Mom," Rosa said before Anthony could respond. "She wasn't just *on* the tramp either. That brave woman was actually jumping when we pulled into the yard."

Elsie gasped and put a hand to her mouth. "Oh my! Sarah's lucky she didn't fall and break a bone or suffer a bad sprain too."

"Tell me about it," Anthony said as he raised the foot end of the recliner. "That woman is quite a character. I don't know her personally, but she seems to have twice the energy of someone half her age."

Elsie nodded. "That's for sure. I hope when I'm as old as Sarah, I'll have even half the get-up-and-go she has." She motioned to Anthony's swollen ankle. "Would you like me to get an ice pack for you?"

"That would be much appreciated. I also have some pain meds I need to take, but it's supposed to be with food."

"No problem, Anthony. I'll get the medication from my purse and then go to the kitchen to get you a glass of water," Rosa said. "And then I'll make you a sandwich. Would you like bologna and cheese or tuna fish?"

"My first choice would be bologna and cheese." He wrinkled his nose. "Never did care much for smelly tuna fish."

"I'll take care of it right away." Rosa hurried from the room.

Elsie looked at Anthony and smiled. "I've never seen my daughter so eager to please. She obviously loves you very much, and I'm so glad that the two of you found each other. Some people are just meant to be together, and I believe you and Rosa are one of those fortunate married couples." Elsie pulled a throw pillow off the couch and placed it gently under Anthony's swollen ankle. "It pleases me to see how happy you've made my eldest daughter."

Anthony lowered his gaze, unable to look at Elsie's tender expression. He felt like a heel leading her and the rest of Rosa's family on and making them believe that he and Rosa were married. It had also surprised him when Elsie said that she'd never seen Rosa so eager to please and that he and Rosa were meant to be together.

Guess we're both good actors, Anthony thought. *I'm quite sure that Rosa doesn't have deep feelings for me. She's only putting on an act for the sake of fooling her family into believing that she and I are happily married.* Then another thought popped into Anthony's head. *What if Rosa does have strong feelings for me?* He squeezed his eyes shut, hoping to remove the crazy notion. *No, that's not possible. If Rosa ever loved anyone, it may have been the man who fathered her child. But when the idiot broke things off with her and made it clear that he wanted Rosa out of his life, refusing to acknowledge the baby, any feelings she had for him should have died.*

Anthony clenched his hands together until his nails dug into the flesh. *Selfish so-and-so, who not only cheated on his wife but led Rosa on until he got what he wanted and then dumped her flat when he found out she was carrying his child. A guy like him deserves a good punch in the nose. Maybe it would knock some sense into his thick head. If I knew where he lived, I might knock his block off or at the very least let the guy know exactly what I think of him.*

"I suspect that you're trying to sleep," Elsie said after Anthony opened his eyes. "I'll let you rest while I go upstairs to check on Alvin. He's definitely got the chicken pox and has many skin eruptions to prove it." She shook her head slowly. "Poor boy is absolutely miserable."

"Sorry to hear that. I hope he feels better soon." Anthony cringed inwardly. It was bad enough that his ankle was throbbing like crazy and his vehicle still wasn't drivable. The last thing he needed was to come down with the chicken pox, which would keep him here in the Big Valley that much longer. Anthony hoped his mother was wrong and that he'd already had the pox when he was a young child. But if that were so, then why didn't he or Mom have any memory of it? If Anthony hadn't come down with the pox before, then he'd gone all these years without contracting the disease, which he supposed could mean that his body was immune to the illness. He hoped it was the case and that he wouldn't get sick, but right now he had other things to be concerned about. More than anything, Anthony wanted his ankle to heal and his car part to come in, so he could get back on the road and return to New York, which would make his parents happy. Above all else, Anthony needed to get as far from Rosa Petersheim as he could, before he ended up getting sucked into the vortex of a permanent relationship with someone he couldn't see himself spending the rest of his life with. He also realized he was beginning to care about some of Rosa's family members, like Elsie and Alvin.

No, I can't stay here, Anthony told himself. *The best thing for me and Rosa, as well as her family, is for me to take myself out of the picture and move on with my life without any emotional attachments or complications.*

CHAPTER 19

It had been two and a half weeks since the part for Anthony's car had been ordered, and it still had not come in. Although his ankle was somewhat better, he'd awakened during the night with a fever and sore throat. Rosa had kindly given up her bed and slept on the thin piece of foam she'd placed on the floor next to the bed. Anthony had argued with her when she'd first insisted on him taking the bed, but feeling so weak and miserable, he'd finally given in to Rosa's request. As he sucked on a piece of ice to help soothe his throat, he was thankful for the comfort of the soft mattress beneath his aching body, nearly drenched in sweat.

Anthony had never been a sickly person, and he hated lying around and doing nothing but sleeping or staring at the ceiling. But at this moment, if he'd been a praying man, he would have asked God for a miracle healing so he could carry through with his plans to have a falling-out with Rosa and be on his way back to New York. Anthony had come to the conclusion that he needed to accept the fact that he was stuck in Mifflin County, whether he liked it or not. Trouble was, he actually liked a few things about being here with Rosa and her family. Maybe more than a few things, but he'd never admit that to himself or Rosa. Anthony didn't want her to think he might be willing to marry her and settle down here. Giving up his hopes and dreams of opening his own restaurant in New York would be ridiculous. Mingling with the Plain people or even becoming one of them was even more absurd. Anthony wasn't cut out for the simple life in such a rural part of Pennsylvania. Becoming a father to a child who wasn't his or marrying a woman he didn't feel committed to would make no sense at all.

Anthony closed his eyes and tried to block out the vision of Rosa that seemed to be stuck in his head. What was it about the young woman that made him feel like a better person when he was with her? Why did the touch of her hand on his hot forehead feel so good? And how come the conversations they'd shared since coming here made Anthony feel like Rosa was his best friend? He wondered but hadn't asked if she felt it too.

Anthony rolled over onto his side, trying to find a more comfortable position. *I wonder if my fever is making me delirious and unable to think clearly. Yep, that's probably all it is.*

Although Rosa hadn't said anything, she was fairly certain Anthony's symptoms were an indication that he'd come down with a case of the chicken pox. The poor guy was miserable, and Rosa was glad she'd convinced him to take the bed where he could rest a lot better than if he'd been sleeping on the floor.

She turned on the warm water to fill the plastic tub in the kitchen sink, added liquid detergent, and then swirled it around the dirty breakfast dishes she had volunteered to do while Mom went to the shoe store with Tena. Although Alvin was doing better, he still had some skin eruptions that hadn't crusted yet, so he, along with Anthony, had been served his breakfast in bed again this morning.

Rosa was glad she'd had the chicken pox when she was a young girl. It wouldn't be good to come down with them while she was pregnant.

She paused from her work and glanced down at her stomach. She felt love for the unborn baby, even though he or she had been conceived in the wrong way and with the wrong man.

How could I have been so foolish? she asked herself for the umpteenth time. *I've made so many stupid decisions, even before I left my family and ran away from home. Sure wish I could go back and do things over, making wiser decisions instead of trying to prove something to myself and everyone else.*

Rosa knew that all the guilt and sorrow she felt for her mistakes could not undo the past, and she needed to look toward the future rather than looking back and blaming herself for everything. The biggest issue, however, was she wasn't sure what the future would bring, or what direction to take, especially concerning the situation she'd created by allowing Anthony to pose as her husband. When he returned to New York, Rosa would have two choices. She could either continue with the lie, and allow her family to believe that she and Anthony had gotten a divorce, or come clean and admit that they'd never gotten married at all. That would also mean admitting that Anthony was not the baby's biological father and telling her folks that she'd had an affair with a married man who was not going to leave his wife in order to marry Rosa.

It's a catch-22, she reminded herself. *I will lose either way in my father's eyes, and maybe in Mom's too. They'll be disappointed in me and think I'm a sinful person, and it's true. They could very well kick me out of their house, and then when the baby comes, I'll have no other place to go. I can't return to New York when Anthony leaves. Even if I could get my job back at the restaurant, I wouldn't make enough money to support myself and the baby, let alone pay someone to watch the child while I'm at work.*

Rosa swallowed against the pressure building up in her throat as she pulled the wet, soapy sponge across one of the soiled dishes. *If I stick with the story that Anthony and I are married but have decided to get a divorce, I will not be allowed to join the Amish church. If I admit that we never got married and have been pretending, that won't go over well either. Dad has made it clear many times over the years that lying is a sin and he will not let any of his children get away with telling untruths.*

Rosa grabbed one of the glasses and scrubbed the inside with the sponge. *On second thought, maybe when Anthony gets his car back and is feeling better, I could ask him to take me with him when he returns to New York and see if I can get my job back at his father's restaurant. I could at least try to find a cheap place to rent and make do until the baby comes. After that, I don't know what I would do, other than pray for a miracle.*

Tears slipped from Rosa's eyes and dribbled down her cheeks. She needed to remain here where she had the help and support of her family, but in order to do that, she would have to own up to the truth and beg their forgiveness. She needed to decide at what point she should confess and hope that it didn't backfire on her. Would it be better to wait until Anthony headed back to New York or make the confession soon, while he was still here and could help her explain why they had lied to her parents? Up and down, back and forth, Rosa couldn't seem to make up her mind about anything at all.

Even if I decided to go that route, Rosa thought, *with Christmas just a few days away, I should probably wait until the holiday is over, because there's no point in ruining everyone's special day.*

CHAPTER 20

Anthony groaned, sat up in bed, and rubbed his eyes against the invading light coming into the room, where the shade had been partially opened. It was hard to believe this was Christmas Day, and here he was still sick as a dog with itchy blisters covering many parts of his body.

I should never have come here, he thought. *If I'd stayed in New York instead of taking pity on Rosa and bringing her here, I wouldn't have been exposed to her little brother and ended up with a nasty case of chicken pox—or wasserpareble or whatever the Amish call it.*

Anthony reached for his glass of water and took a drink. *Who am I kidding? I could have been exposed to the pox or any other disease while living and working in New York City. Besides, staying here with the Petersheim family hasn't been all bad. Rosa and I have done a few enjoyable things together, and I've been given the opportunity to use my culinary skills for her family, which has been nice.*

Anthony placed the empty glass back on the nightstand beside his bed and grimaced. He wanted a refill but didn't have the energy to go downstairs or make his way to the bathroom sink. Anthony couldn't remember the last time he'd felt so zapped of energy. No doubt Rosa and her family members were gathered around the table about now, enjoying their Christmas feast. A meal Anthony wished he could have fixed for them and been able to partake of himself.

He figured Rosa might bring him up a plate of food sometime

today, but the truth was, he didn't have much of an appetite. The only thing Anthony really wanted at the moment was for the terrible itching to stop so he wouldn't be tempted to scratch. "I'll probably end up with all kinds of scars from my scratching," he muttered. Sometimes Anthony would wake up from a deep sleep, scratching at places that itched so bad he couldn't help himself.

Anthony's cell phone vibrated on the table beside his bed. He'd turned the ringer off so he wouldn't be disturbed while trying to sleep and hadn't taken the phone off vibrate mode yet. He reached for the device and clicked it on. "Hello," he rasped.

"Merry Christmas, Son. How are you doing?" Mom spoke a little louder than usual, and Anthony figured she was making an effort to sound upbeat—maybe hoping to cheer him up—since he'd told her during their last conversation that he was down with the chicken pox and felt miserable.

"Hey, Mom, I hope you and Pop are with my sisters today and having a special Christmas."

"We all gathered at our place for part of the day, but your sisters had both made some other plans too, so they left a while ago." There was a pause. "You were missed."

"Thanks. I miss not being with all of you too."

"Now, back to my question that you've yet to answer. How are you doing? Are you feeling any better since the last time we talked?"

"Not really. I'm still spending most of my time in bed, and those pesky pox marks have continued to itch like crazy. Sure wish I'd had the chicken pox when I was a kid. Probably could have dealt better with it back then."

"No doubt it would have been better, but life doesn't always give us what we want or think we need. I guess the good days help to prepare us for the not-so-good times and teach us to appreciate those times when things are going well for us."

"Yeah, right." Feeling an itch coming on behind his right ear, Anthony switched the phone to his left ear, hoping the change might make the agonizing itch stop or at least help him to focus on something else.

"Were you able to eat a nice Christmas dinner with your friend's family today?" Mom asked.

"No, I've spent the day in bed." Anthony released a noisy yawn. "There's not much for me to do but sleep and try not to scratch."

"Rest is good," she said. "And you definitely shouldn't scratch the blisters. You could end up with an infection, which would leave a nasty scar."

"I know, Mom, and I'm doing my best not to let that happen." Another yawn came, and he tried to suppress it by covering his mouth.

"You sound tired, Anthony. I should let you go so you can sleep if you wish."

"Yeah, okay. Tell Pop I said hello, and my sisters too, next time you see them. I'll talk to you again when I'm feeling better. Bye, Mom." Anthony clicked off the phone, and he'd just placed it back on the end table when a knock sounded on the bedroom door. He hoped whoever it was didn't want to talk, because he was not in the mood for conversing with anyone. Just the few short minutes with his mother had about done Anthony in.

He hitched a breath and called, "Come in."

༺༻

"I'm glad to see that you're awake," Rosa stated upon entering the room with a tray, which she placed across his lap. "Since you didn't feel up to coming down to eat with the family, I brought you a little of everything that was on the table for our Christmas meal, including a slice of pumpkin pie."

He offered her what appeared to be a forced smile. "I appreciate the gesture, but I'm really not *hungerich*."

Rosa blinked a couple of times and tilted her head. "Oh, so now you're talking the Dutch, is that how it is?"

"I've just picked up a few words here and there, like the one for *hungry*, but I definitely can't speak full sentences or understand most of what I hear you or your family saying to each other."

"I'll give you credit for trying." Rosa gestured to the food on his tray. "Now, how about eating a little bit, even if you aren't hungry? If you don't eat, you'll never regain your strength."

"Okay, I'll try." Anthony picked up the fork and stabbed a small piece of turkey. He put it in his mouth, chewed, and then swallowed. "Not bad. Who did the cooking today?"

"Mom baked the turkey. Tena and I each made a few pies, and the three of us worked together on the rest of the meal."

"What about your sister Susan? Didn't she help with any part of the meal?"

"Not with the cooking, but she did set the dining room table and help us serve the meal." Rosa heaved a heavy sigh. "In case you haven't picked up on it, I am not one of Susan's favorite people."

Anthony ate some of the mashed potatoes before responding. "Yeah, I've gotten that impression, based on some of the comments she's made, not to mention the way she often glares at you. What's up with that, anyway? Isn't she glad that you're home safe and sound?"

Rosa walked over to the window and lifted the shade the rest of the way, bringing more light into the room. When she moved back to stand by the bed, she was frowning. "Susan and I have never gotten along very well. Even when we were children she seemed to be jealous of me and often accused our mother of caring more for me than she did her."

"Do you think that was true?"

Rosa shook her head. "I doubt it. Mom's always been pretty fair with the way she's treated all of us. But I suppose there were times when she spent more time with me—especially in the kitchen, since we both like to cook. Even so, that didn't justify Susan believing I was the favored one. She had the same opportunity to spend time in the kitchen with our mother if she'd chosen to."

Anthony grunted. "Sibling rivalry—it's not a good thing."

Rosa folded her arms and moved closer to the bed. "It sounds like you may have had a little experience with that."

"Yeah, what kid hasn't? I thought my two sisters were Pop's favorites, and they believed that Mom cared more about me." His thick brows rose. "Go figure."

"Would you like me to stay while you finish your meal?" Rosa asked, switching to another topic. "If you'd rather eat in peace and not have to engage in conversation, I can go back downstairs and help with the dishes."

Anthony rolled his eyes. "I'm sure you're real excited about doing that chore."

"Not really," she admitted. "But I don't want to make a pest of myself hanging out here if you'd rather be alone."

He shook his head. "No, please stay and keep me company. It gets pretty boring lying in this bed most of the day with nothing to do but think about my predicament and try not to scratch."

"I hear what you're saying. When I had chicken pox during my childhood, I scratched even when my mother warned me not to."

"And now she's warning me." Anthony ate a few peas and then set his fork down. "When I spoke to my mother on the phone before you came in, she also cautioned me about not scratching the blisters. I'm sure she's worried about me and wishes I could have been there with the rest of the family to celebrate Christmas."

Rosa took a seat on the end of the bed, being careful not to jostle the tray. "You should feel better in another week or so, and then as soon as you get your car back and running in good shape, you'll be on your way home."

"Yeah, I guess. Sure never expected that I'd be here this long."

Rosa bit the inside of her cheek and swallowed hard. "I'm sorry, Anthony. You're probably wishing that you'd never agreed to come here with me and pretend that we are married."

"It was my idea, you know."

"I realize that, but it doesn't make me feel any less guilty for keeping you here so long."

"You're not to blame, Rosa. It's just some unfortunate circumstances that have messed up our plans."

"Speaking of which…" Rosa paused, searching for the right words. "Once you're over the chicken pox and your car's been fixed, we're gonna have to come up with the best way to tell my folks that we're splitting up and you're leaving me to get a divorce."

Anthony sat quietly for several seconds before he spoke again. "No matter how we make it happen, it won't be easy. I'm sure your parents, and maybe your siblings, will be quite upset."

Rosa nodded. "But they'd be even more upset if they knew that we aren't even married and devised this plan so that I could come back here and have a place to live and raise my baby."

He grimaced. "Either way, it's a no-win situation, but we'll get through it when the time is right."

Susan headed down the hall to use the bathroom, but hearing voices from Rosa's room, she paused outside the bedroom door and listened intently to Rosa and Anthony's conversation. Upon hearing everything they'd said, her upper arm muscles twitched and her lips pinched tightly shut. Susan felt more certain than ever that what she'd heard before was true. Anthony and Rosa really weren't married, and their relationship was nothing but a scam.

Planting her feet in a wide stance, Susan leaned in closer to the door. *Now all I need to do is figure out the best way to share this news with Mom and Dad. I'm sure they'll ask Rosa to leave once they find out the truth. Then I'll be the favored daughter, and everything will finally be as it should.*

New York City

"Who were you talking to on the phone?" Herb asked when Lavera left the kitchen and joined her husband in the living room.

"It was Anthony. I called to wish him a Merry Christmas and see how he's feeling."

"Well, he's certainly not feeling homesick, or he'd be here with us right now," Herb muttered.

Lavera frowned. "He has chicken pox, Herb. I told you that when I spoke with our son the last time. Do you not remember?"

"Yeah, yeah. Guess I do, but I wouldn't be surprised if he's just using it as an excuse not to come home and face the fact that he's been replaced at the restaurant."

Lavera moved closer and placed her hand on Herb's shoulder. "He doesn't know you hired another cook. I didn't have the heart to tell him." She shrugged. "Besides, I figured you'd probably reinstate Anthony as the head cook when he comes back, and let Billy be his assistant, the way he's doing for you now."

Herb folded his arms and huffed. "And where would that leave me if I let Anthony take the lead cook position? What do you want me to do, Lavera—retire and stay home all day with nothing to do?"

"No, of course not," she was quick to respond. "I just thought maybe—"

"I told that son of ours that if he didn't return home by the date he said he'd be back, his job would be gone, so he has no one to blame but himself."

"But Herb, it's not like Anthony planned to have car troubles, or sprain his ankle and then end up getting chicken pox. Those are extenuating circumstances, and you should be more understanding." Lavera struggled to keep her voice down and prevent the tears filling her eyes from spilling over. Herb was being unreasonable, and he needed to realize that and have some understanding for their son's position right now. *Surely once Anthony returns home, my husband will give him his old job back at the restaurant.* She swallowed against the pressure in her throat. *If he doesn't, we might lose Anthony altogether, and he could end up moving from New York City permanently.*

༄

Belleville

Elsie was about to clear away what was left of the desserts from the dining room table when she heard footsteps coming down the stairs.

Assuming it must be Rosa returning after taking food up to Anthony, she placed the apple pie she'd picked up back on the table. Rosa had only cut herself a small piece of that pie before announcing that she was going to take a tray up to Anthony. So Elsie figured when her daughter came back, she'd want to try some more of the delicious dessert.

Elsie waited near Rosa's chair but was surprised when Susan entered the room, wearing a solemn expression.

"What's wrong with you, Daughter?" Mahlon asked before Elsie could voice the question.

"Yeah," Alvin put in. "You look like you've been suckin' on a piece of lemon."

Tena snickered, but Susan held her stoic expression. Apparently she didn't think her younger brother's comment was funny.

Susan moved close to the table, where Mahlon, Tena, and Alvin sat, playing one of their card games. "Umm. . .I have something very important to say, and I think you're gonna be quite surprised by this news."

Elsie tipped her head. "Can it wait until after these three finish their game?" She gestured to the card table. "Your daed's getting ready to make his next move."

"That's right," he said, staring at the cards he held. "And I believe I'm on the verge of winning, so whatever you have to say can wait."

Susan gave her head a vigorous shake. "No, it can't, Dad. It's about Rosa, and I know once you find out the truth, you'll be very upset."

Elsie gestured to Tena and then Alvin. "Why don't you two put on your jackets and go out to the barn to make sure the *katze* have all been fed? When you come back inside you can have another piece of pie and finish your game."

"Okay!" Alvin jumped up right away and raced to the door, but Tena remained in her chair.

Before her daughter could say anything, Elsie looked at her and said, "You too, Tena. Alvin might need your help, and I don't think it's a good idea for him to go outside in the dark alone."

Mahlon laid his cards down with a huff. "Do as your mamm said, Tena."

Without a word, she got up and left the room.

Elsie waited until she heard the front door open and close before she turned to face Susan. "Now, what's so important that you had to interrupt their game?"

CHAPTER 21

Susan pulled out the chair where Tena had been sitting and sat down.

"Well, what is it you need to say to us?" her father asked.

Susan saw by the narrowing of his eyes that he was annoyed with her for interrupting the game he'd been playing with Tena and Alvin. So she decided it would be best to say what was on her mind quickly before he lost his temper—or she lost her nerve. Susan also knew that she had better speak before Rosa came back downstairs.

She moistened her lips with the tip of her tongue and plunged ahead. Looking first at her mother and then her father, Susan announced: "Rosa and Anthony have been lying to you."

"About what?" Mom questioned with furrowed brows.

"They're not married—they are just pretending to be husband and wife. And I'm not even sure if Rosa is actually pregnant. If she is, I doubt that the baby is Anthony's." Susan paused to inhale a quick breath before continuing. "And to top it off, those two liars are planning to stage a fake breakup so it will look like Anthony is going to return to New York to get a divorce."

There, it was out, and Susan felt pretty good about it. Now Mom wouldn't think Rosa was so wonderful anymore, and Dad was bound to kick the pretenders out of his house.

Susan waited wordlessly for their response, but when neither of them said anything, she spoke again. "So what are you gonna do about it? Don't you think you oughta confront Rosa and her so-called husband regarding the trick they've been playing on all of us?" Susan's voice rose higher with each word she said.

Mom opened her mouth as if to say something, but Dad spoke first. "I don't believe you, Susan. I think you made this ridiculous story up."

Susan's defenses rose as her voice rose higher, and she blew out a noisy breath. "Wh–why would I do that? With my own two ears, I heard them talking about it. So why don't you believe me?"

Dad leaned forward and placed both elbows on the table as he stared hard at Susan. "Because you have developed a habit of lying to us."

Mom bobbed her head, as if in agreement with what Dad had said.

"No, Dad, I'm not lying. I am telling the truth." Susan knew she needed to stand up for herself and try to convince her parents that she hadn't been lying about this.

"Your daed is right," Mom spoke up. "When you were going out with Ben Ebersol, you lied to us on more than one occasion." She paused a few seconds and rubbed an area on her forehead where her fine wrinkles had deepened. "How can you expect your daed and me to trust your word when you deceived us concerning your relationship with Ben? Besides," she quickly added, "you have been snappish with Rosa ever since she returned home, which leads me to believe that you are not happy to have your sister back, safe and sound."

Susan couldn't deny her mother's last statement. The truth was, she was anything but happy to have Rosa living in this house again. It angered her to think that it was Rosa who was lying to their parents now, and she was getting away with it. Susan held her hands stiffly at her sides while clenching her jaw. *I need to try again—say something to make them believe I'm telling the truth about Rosa and Anthony. But they think I'm a liar, so what can I say to make them believe me?*

⁂

Elsie's pulse raced, and she felt palpitations within her chest. It saddened her to think that Susan would make up such a ridiculous story about her own flesh-and-blood sister who had been missing for over two years. *Susan should be as happy as we are that Rosa came home and is happily married with a child on the way. What's come over my daughter to make up such a story and expect us to believe it? If what she said about Rosa and Anthony not being married is actually true, it would make no sense whatsoever. I can't think of any reason why they would tell us they were husband and wife if they weren't.*

"Susan, your mother and I do not wish to hear any more of your tall tale. Is that clear?" Mahlon spoke with obvious conviction as he pounded his fist on the tabletop.

"But Dad—"

He gave a firm shake of his head. "We've heard enough. Now please go to your room and don't speak of this again. Is that clear?"

"So you're not even going to ask Rosa if what I said is true?"

"No, we are not. I'm not particularly fond of the man your sister chose to marry, but if you had any sense at all, you would see from the way Anthony and Rosa act toward each other that they are in love." He touched his nose with one finger. "In fact, it's plain as the *naas* on your face."

"Is that really what you see?"

"Jah, Susan, it's quite obvious to me that they are a happily married couple." Mahlon pulled his fingers down the side of his face and into his full beard. "End of discussion. Now get on up to your room!"

Susan gave a huff, turned on her heels, and tromped out of the room and straight up the stairs. Elsie cringed when she heard Susan's bedroom door slam shut with such force that it could have woken anyone in the house who was sleeping.

I hope Anthony isn't trying to sleep right now, she thought with regret. *I wish Susan would have held her temper and accepted what we said without noisily stomping up the stairs. I wonder sometimes if that girl will ever grow up.*

⁓⁓

After Susan reached the top of the stairs and entered her room, slamming the door, she remembered that when she'd first come upstairs, before hearing Rosa and Anthony's discussion, she'd been on her way to use the bathroom.

Guess I'd better head in there now, she told herself. *Then I'm going to get ready for bed, because I am not about to go back downstairs and face Mom and Dad's accusations again.* Susan hurried her footsteps as she headed in the direction of the bathroom. *I don't understand why they didn't believe what I said about Rosa and Anthony's deceit. All they had to do was confront Rosa, and I bet she would have crumbled and admitted the truth.*

Tears welled in Susan's eyes as she opened the bathroom door and stepped inside. *I wish Dad hadn't mentioned anything about all the lies I'd told them when Ben and I were going out. Now they don't trust anything I say.*

As much as Susan hated to admit it, lying had become part of her life from the day Rosa went missing. She had lied about other things that she wasn't ready to admit, and they had nothing to do with her relationship with Ben. Even so, what Susan heard Rosa and Anthony talking about was not something she had made up. She didn't know how she could make her parents believe her, but she wasn't about to give up.

Susan squinted at her reflection in the bathroom mirror. Sooner or later, the story Rosa and Anthony had made up was bound to be found out as a lie.

―――

Rosa sat with Anthony until he finished his food. When he said he was done, she noticed his eyelids flutter. "You look tired," she said. "I should go now and let you get some more sleep."

Anthony yawned. "You're right, I am exhausted. The meal was good, but now I feel like I could use a nap."

Rosa lifted the tray from his lap. "I'll take this back down to the kitchen, but I'll return to check on you in an hour or so."

He offered her a feeble smile. "Okay, thanks. You're an angel."

She shook her head. "Far from it, but I appreciate the kind words." Rosa felt the temptation to kiss Anthony's forehead where no chicken pox had formed, but she held herself in check. If she did something that bold, he might take it the wrong way and think she had feelings for him that went beyond friendship.

"Sleep well," Rosa said before opening the door. She stepped out into the hallway, nearly colliding with Susan.

"Watch where you're going," her sister snapped. "You could've smacked into me and dumped everything on that tray all over the floor."

"Sorry, I didn't know you were standing there."

Susan's lips curled. "I wasn't standing. And for your information, I was on the way to my room to get ready for bed."

"It's kind of early to call it a night, don't you think? Are you feeling all right?"

"I'm fine, physically. Just tired and want to be alone to do some thinking." Susan gestured to Rosa's bedroom door, then looked back at Rosa with arms crossed and brows wrinkled. "How's your *husband*? Did you take him some food?"

With the emphasis Susan had put on the word *husband*, Rosa wondered if her sister might suspect something—like the fact that she and Anthony weren't actually married.

But if Susan believes that, then I'm sure she's only guessing. A ripple of apprehension ran up Rosa's spine. *What if Susan was out in the hall the whole time I was in my room with Anthony? What if she heard our conversation concerning the fabricated story we've been telling?*

Rosa's tongue rolled around in her mouth as she reflected on that thought. *If Susan did hear what Anthony and I said, then why doesn't she come right out and say so? I'm sure she would like nothing better than to bring Mom and Dad in on our little secret, but I'm sure if she knew, she'd say something to me first.*

"You haven't answered me, Sister. How's your husband?"

Susan's question pushed Rosa's contemplations aside. "Oh, umm . . .Anthony is still pretty miserable, but at least he was willing to eat something, and now he's resting peacefully."

"Yeah, I'll bet."

Rosa held tightly to the tray. "What's that supposed to mean?"

"I'll let you figure it out." Susan turned sharply, opened her bedroom door, and stepped inside, closing it with a bang.

Rosa flinched. *I wonder what her problem is. Hopefully it doesn't involve me and Anthony. I especially don't want her knowing that we only have a pretend marriage. If she knew, she'd be the first person to run and tell our folks.*

～～

Rosa entered the dining room, and when she observed her parents sitting at the table with tension-filled expressions, she felt concern. The muscles in her arms tightened as she gripped the tray she'd brought down from her room. *Could they know something? If Susan heard Anthony and me talking and she knows we aren't married, did she tell Mom and Dad?*

"How is Anthony doing?" Mom asked. Before Rosa had a chance to respond, her mother pointed to the empty plates on the tray. "I assume he must be feeling a little better since it looks like he ate all the food you took up to him."

"At my prompting, he did eat, but Anthony is still quite miserable." Rosa placed the tray on one end of the table where there were no cards or board games.

"I know you're concerned about your husband," Mom said, rising from her chair and placing both hands on Rosa's shoulders.

"Yes, I am," Rosa admitted as her mother began to massage some of the tension Rosa felt in her tight muscles. "Anthony wishes he could have joined the family to celebrate Christmas today, but unfortunately, he didn't feel up to it."

"Can't blame him for that," Dad said. "A case of the wasserpareble can be mighty unpleasant even for a child, not to mention a full-grown adult."

"Tena and Alvin are still out in the barn," Mom stated, "but when they come back in, we'll probably continue playing games. Would you like to fix yourself a cup of tea or some eggnog and join us, Rosa?"

"What about Susan?" Rosa asked. "I would think she might want to take part in the games."

Mom gave a quick shake of her head. "Your sister has a bee under her bonnet right now, so she's upstairs in her room, probably pouting because she didn't get her way."

"Yes, I nearly ran into her in the hall after I left my room with the tray, and it seemed like she was not in the best of moods."

"You got that right," Dad interjected with a swift wave of his hand. "Susan got mad at us for not believing some unbelievable story she'd made up, and when we reminded her that she's told us too many lies on several occasions, that ended the conversation." He looked pointedly at Rosa. "After all, why would we want to believe anything your sister says now?"

"That's right," Mom agreed. "Susan needs to grow up and prove to us that she can be trusted."

Rosa cringed inwardly. *If Mom and Dad only knew the web of lies Anthony and I have been weaving, they would probably throw us both out on our ears.* She glanced toward the front door when Alvin and Tena entered the house. *They'll all have to know eventually—just not today. There's no point in ruining my parents' Christmas, because it sounds like Susan already has.*

As Rosa headed to the kitchen with the tray, she wondered yet again if Susan knew the truth. If so, perhaps she'd been trying to tell their parents about it, but they hadn't believed her. One thing was certain: Whatever Susan had said to their parents, they didn't believe her, so at least for now, Rosa had nothing to worry about. The bottom line, however, was that as soon as Anthony felt better and his transportation was no longer an issue, the two of them needed to initiate their breakup, which would send him on his way. Once that was done, Anthony would no longer be a part of the lie they'd conjured up. After that, all Rosa needed to do was stay in her parents' good graces so she could keep staying with them and receive their support when the baby came.

Rosa set the tray on the counter near the sink and placed Anthony's dishes in a tub of soapy water to soak awhile. Then she rinsed her hands and dried them on a clean kitchen towel before turning on a gas burner on the stove. While the water in the teakettle heated, Rosa stood in front of the window, looking out at the star-studded night sky. A little flutter in her belly caused her to tremble, and she placed both hands against her abdomen. "I would do anything for you, my precious little one," she murmured. *Even tell the biggest lie so you could live here safely with your grandparents, who I am sure will love and care for you as much as I do already.*

Tears welled in Rosa's eyes, and she soon felt moisture on her cheeks. Gently rubbing her belly, Rosa lowered her gaze. *I wish you could grow up with a loving father. Maybe someday I'll find a caring man who'll be willing to raise another man's child.*

CHAPTER 22

By the end of January, winter had definitely settled within the hills and valley of Mifflin County. Heavy snow had fallen last week and continued with each passing day. Anthony was glad to be over the chicken pox, but unfortunately, his car was still in the shop, awaiting that part the mechanic kept saying he hadn't been able to get. Anthony was beginning to wonder if the guy had even tried to secure the part. Surely it couldn't have taken this long to get his car up and running again.

"Even if I did have my car back," Anthony muttered as he tromped through the snow on his way out to the barn, "it would be hard to get home in this nasty weather—especially without snow tires, which I will probably need to buy once the car is finally repaired." Anthony figured he could probably catch a bus home or even hire a driver, the way the Amish did when traveling any distance where they couldn't take their horse and buggies. But if he did that, once his car was ready, he'd have to find someone to give him a ride back to pick it up. On top of that, it would involve seeing Rosa and her family again, which could lead to a discussion he didn't want to have about the divorce Rosa's parents would have been led to believe must have occurred.

"Everything's such a big mess!" Anthony kicked a clump of snow off his waterproof boot that he'd gone to the Amish shoe shop to purchase when the weather had turned bad. *I have to wonder if I'm destined to remain here for the rest of my life. Sure seems funny that I haven't been able to carry through with the plans Rosa and I made before coming here. If I were a betting man, I'd probably believe that the deck has been stacked against me.*

When Anthony approached the woodshed near the barn, he was stunned to see that the entire roof of the small wooden building had caved in. *No doubt from the heavy snow that has fallen,* he concluded. *I wonder if Rosa's dad knows about this. If so, I'm surprised he didn't mention it before leaving for work this morning. I'm sure he will want the roof replaced as soon as possible. Otherwise, all the nice firewood that's been stacked inside the building will get wet and laden down with snow.* He heaved a sigh and kicked at a chunk of ice this time. *Guess I'd better start working on this project as soon as I get the chores done in the barn that I promised Mahlon I would do this morning.*

Anthony looked up at the cloudy sky, which he hoped wouldn't bring more snow today. With any luck, and a break in the weather, he might have the roof repaired by the end of the day. Of course, he'd have to find the right roofing materials and tools for the project first. And that could take some doing.

Being careful of his footing lest he fall, Anthony made his way to the barn, shivering with each step he took. *I'm not cut out for this kind of life. I'm a cook, not a carpenter, and I wish I was inside right now, whipping up something good to eat instead of out here in the cold with chattering teeth and frozen fingers and toes.*

"Are you feeling all right, dear one?" Elsie asked when she entered the living room and found Rosa lying on the couch with her head propped on a pillow.

"I'm okay, Mom. Just dealing with some nausea again and feeling a bit stressed out."

"Because of the stomach upset?"

"Partially, but a lot of other things are bothering me too."

Elsie took a seat on the opposite end of the couch and began rubbing Rosa's bare feet. "Care to talk about it?"

"There really isn't much to say, Mom." Rosa put her hand to her mouth and yawned.

"Something must be upsetting you or you wouldn't be stressed."

"Yeah, that's true."

Elsie didn't want to push too hard, but she felt the need to encourage Rosa to talk about whatever was on her mind. She knew from experience that it always felt better to discuss one's feelings or share a problem with someone else.

Elsie sat quietly for a few minutes, wondering if Rosa might say more and hoping she would. It wasn't good to keep things bottled up inside. But at the same time, she didn't want to pry. To her surprise, Rosa finally sat up and spoke again.

"Anthony and I are dealing with some issues, Mom."

"Like what?"

"For one thing, he's not happy living here."

"I'm sorry to hear that. Has anyone in the family said or done something to offend Anthony or hurt his feelings?"

"No, it's nothing like that."

"Maybe it's because he doesn't have a job," Elsie suggested.

Rosa shook her head. "No, that's not it either."

"What is the problem, then, Rosa?"

"It's kind of hard to explain."

"Is he not happy about the baby? Does Anthony think he won't be able to support you and the child?" Elsie moved closer to her daughter and lifted Rosa's legs so that her feet were in Elsie's lap. "If that is the problem, then maybe your daed can find something for Anthony to do at the Meat and Cheese Store."

"I can't imagine what there would be for Anthony to do at Dad's place of business," Rosa said. "Anthony's a cook, not a salesperson or a bookkeeper. Besides, Norman and Susan are already working at the store with Dad, and I doubt that he'd need another employee for any position."

Elsie bobbed her head. "Guess you're right. Well, maybe one of the restaurants in Belleville or one of the surrounding towns might be in need of a cook. It would be worth Anthony checking into, don't you think?"

"I don't know—maybe." Rosa rolled her neck from side to side, and then she pulled herself up and rose from the couch. "I'm really not up to this discussion right now, Mom. Think I'll go upstairs to my room and lie down for a while. Give me a holler when you're ready to start lunch, and I'll come down to help you fix the meal."

"Okay." Elsie watched as Rosa ambled out of the room. The poor thing looked beyond tired, and if she and Anthony were having marital problems, that was no doubt taking its toll on her too. Perhaps what the couple needed was some marriage counseling—if not from Mahlon, then maybe one of the other ministers in their church district. Mahlon had make it clear that he didn't care much for Anthony, and his relationship with Rosa wasn't as good as it should be either. So it might not be in the couple's best interest if he was the one to counsel them. For now, though, Elsie determined that she would speak to Anthony when he came inside and see if she could find out what the problem was between him and Rosa. If it was a simple matter, Elsie thought she might be able to help them work through it. Otherwise, she would see about talking with one of the ministers on behalf of her daughter and son-in-law. It was the least a concerned mother-in-law could do.

⁓⁓

Rosa lay on her back, pressed against her mattress, while staring at the ceiling overhead. She couldn't believe all the questions her mother had asked, and worse yet, she'd almost blurted out the fact that she and Anthony were not married. Truth be told, if Rosa hadn't left the room when she had, she might have done just that. This secret was getting harder and harder to keep. And to compound the problem, the longer Anthony stayed, the more Rosa wanted him to remain here.

She rolled onto her side, facing the window, and blinked against invading tears blurring her vision. *I should never have involved him in my problems. It would have been better for both of us if I hadn't told Anthony I was pregnant and fearful of going home to tell my parents that I was an unwed mother. Anthony is too nice a guy to just shrug his shoulders and walk away. He's the kind of person who would never have said the situation I had found myself in was my problem, not his.*

Rosa swallowed the bile rising in her throat and sat up quickly, hoping she wouldn't throw up. *I've made such a mess out of my life, and there's no way to go back in time and fix any of it. Instead of being fearful of my parents' rejection, I should have returned to the Big Valley alone and begged for their forgiveness for running away. Then I should have told Mom and Dad the truth about the baby and pleaded with them to take me in.*

Rosa rose from the bed and moved over to the window to look out at the wintry scene in the yard below. She spotted Anthony standing near the barn with both hands on his hips. *He's such a great guy,* she thought ruefully. *Some woman will be lucky when he falls in love with her and proposes marriage.*

Frustrated and cold, Anthony entered the kitchen, hoping to fix himself something warm to drink to take off the chill and give him a much-needed break. He found Elsie there and promptly told her about the collapsed roof on the woodshed.

"I'd planned to at least get started tearing off what's left of the roof," he said, "but I couldn't find any tools to do the job, and since I have no transportation, I can't go to town for the things I would need to do the job."

"I could call one of our drivers to take you there. Several of them have vans, and one fellow we know has a pickup truck, so that would be a good option, since he'd have plenty of room to haul whatever you need."

Anthony pulled his fingers down the side of his bristly face, which he hadn't taken the time to shave that morning. "Guess that might be a good idea. Right now, though, I want something warm to drink. It's freezing out there this morning."

"Well, of course." Elsie scooted over to the stove and turned on one of the gas burners. "Would you like me to fix you a cup of tea or maybe some hot chocolate?"

Anthony licked his chapped lips. "Hot chocolate sounds great. Would you have any marshmallows to put on top?"

She grinned at him. "Alvin loves marshmallows in his hot chocolate. He also likes to eat them straight out of the bag," she added with a chuckle. "Of course, I have to stop him before he ends up on a sugar high."

"Makes sense. Most kids like to indulge in anything that's sweet." Anthony pulled out a chair and took a seat at the table. It sure felt good to be in out of the cold for a while. He figured the warmth here in Elsie's kitchen would have him thawed out in no time.

"You don't have to fix the shed roof by yourself," Elsie said after she'd poured milk in a kettle and started heating it on the stove. "I'm sure Norman would be willing to help, and Mahlon too."

"Actually, after looking things over, I came to the conclusion that it needs a whole new roof," Anthony stated. "And I figured if I could at least get started on that today, it would be one less thing for your husband to worry about."

"That's very kind of you. I'll go out to the phone shed and see if I can find a driver who's free to take you into town today."

Anthony shook his head. "Just give me his number and I'll make the call on my cell phone. There's no point in you going out there in the cold."

"I don't mind. Besides, I have a few other calls I need to make, so as soon as your hot chocolate is made, I'll head out there while you warm up with your drink."

Anthony could see by the determined set of the woman's jaw that she was going out to the phone shed regardless of what he'd said. So he gave an agreeable nod and waited patiently for the milk in the pan to heat. He did, however, think it was a shame that this family didn't have a phone inside their house and had to brave the elements to make phone calls or listen to any messages that may have come in.

Just one more thing about the Plain life that I don't understand, Anthony thought, diverting his gaze from the stove to Rosa, who had just entered the room. Her face looked kind of pale, and her shoulders were slumped like a cake that had fallen. Anthony figured she probably wasn't feeling well.

"I'm making hot chocolate for Anthony," Elsie said, turning from the stove to face her daughter. "Would you like some too?"

"Jah, Mom. That sounds good to me." Rosa took a seat at the table beside Anthony.

A few minutes later, Elsie handed them both large mugs full of creamy, fragrant hot chocolate. She also placed a bag of marshmallows between them and grinned.

"Thank you," they said in unison.

"So now I'll be off to the phone shed." Elsie moved across the room, where several outer garments had been hung on wall pegs. She removed one of the jackets and slipped it on, along with a pair of gloves she pulled from the jacket pocket. "I'll just put my boots on in the utility room and be on my way. While I'm gone, I hope you two will enjoy your beverages, as well as your cherished time together." She gave a small wave, turned, and hurried out of the kitchen.

Rosa leaned closer to Anthony and whispered, "While my mom is at the phone shed, I want to talk to you about something important."

The way Rosa clasped her hands together while biting on her lower lip let Anthony know that she must be worried about whatever she wanted to tell him. "Is there a problem?" he asked.

―⁂―

"Yes, there's definitely a problem." Rosa heaved a sigh. "While you were outside and I was resting on the couch, my mother came in and brought up a topic I did not want to talk about."

Anthony took a sip of his drink, set the mug down, and tipped his head in Rosa's direction. "What'd she say?"

Rosa repeated the conversation she'd had with her mother and frowned. "I was hoping to prepare her for the day when we would announce that our marriage is over and that you planned to leave here to get a divorce. But I guess that wasn't such a good idea." Rosa picked up her spoon and stirred the marshmallow around in her beverage. "I never got any of that said, because I didn't know what to say when Mom started making suggestions about our marriage."

"What kind of suggestions?"

"She thinks you might not be happy here because you don't have a job, and she went so far as to suggest that you help out at my dad's store."

Anthony's dark brows lifted higher than usual. "Seriously?"

"Yeah, and when I said that I doubted Dad would have enough work for you to do there, then Mom mentioned you trying to get a cooking position at one of the restaurants in our area."

"What'd you tell her?"

"I said I wasn't up to talking about it right then and went upstairs to rest in my room." Rosa clutched Anthony's arm. "I never meant for my mother to try and fix our problems. I just wanted to give her a heads-up that things aren't going well between us so that when we do make the official announcement before you take off, she wouldn't be completely surprised."

"I see your point, and it was a good idea, but—"

"Sorry. I should have talked to you about it before I said anything to Mom. Maybe you would have had an idea as to what my response should have been when she started making suggestions."

He shook his head. "How could I have known what you should say when I had no idea you were going to talk to your mother about us?"

Rosa thumped the side of her head. "You're right. Don't know what I was thinking." She wasn't sure from Anthony's placid expression whether he was irritated with her or not. The only thing she knew for sure was that they needed to have their pretend breakup, and soon.

CHAPTER 23

When Elsie woke up the following day, a decision had been made. She would go see Melvin Peachey, who was married to her good friend Doris and was one of the older ministers in their church district. He and his wife owned an herbal and supplement store, and she hoped they wouldn't have too many customers today and Melvin would be free to talk with her for a few minutes.

There was very little wind, and the temperature had risen to thirty-eight degrees, so Elsie felt confident enough to make the trip by herself. Rosa had stated during breakfast this morning that she was planning to go someplace today as well, but not until this afternoon.

It shouldn't take me long to tell Melvin what's on my mind and ask if he is willing to speak to Anthony and Rosa, Elsie told herself as she guided her horse down the road toward the Peacheys' store. Melvin and Doris had been happily married for a good many years, so Elsie felt confident that he would offer them good counsel.

There were two things Elsie was concerned about, however: One, Anthony and Rosa might not appreciate the minister's counsel and could be too embarrassed to share their problems with a stranger. And two, if Mahlon found out she'd asked Melvin to speak with the couple instead of him, he'd probably be quite upset, since he was Rosa's father, not to mention the head minister in their church district.

"Well, all I can do is ask Melvin not to mention our conversation to my husband and hope that he doesn't find out," Elsie spoke aloud as the horse and buggy neared the herbal store. A few minutes later, she pulled into the parking lot, climbed out of the buggy, and secured her horse to the hitching rail.

When Elsie entered the store a few minutes later, her senses became filled with a combination of interesting odors. She recognized right away the familiar sweet-smelling scent of basil, which she had planted in her garden last spring. With any luck, it would come back this spring and provide her with all that she needed.

Moving toward the checkout counter, where her friend Doris stood, Elsie smiled as the citrusy scent of lemon balm overwhelmed her senses.

"What a pleasure it must be for you and Melvin to work in this store," Elsie commented as she approached Doris and gave her a hug.

Doris' twin dimples deepened as she nodded. "The only problem is that some of the odors, like basil and oregano, cause me to feel like I should be at home cooking." She gave a small laugh, and Elsie joined in.

"What brings you into our store on such a cold winter day?" Doris asked with a slight tilt of her head. "Are you in dire need of some herbs for cooking?"

"It's not as cold as yesterday, so I figured I could venture out without freezing to death." Elsie removed her dark outer bonnet and placed it on the counter. "Actually, I came here to speak with your husband. Is he in the store today?"

"Jah. Melvin's in the back room, looking for something I misplaced. I can go get him, or if you prefer, you can wander back there to talk to him."

Since Elsie wanted to speak to the minister in private, she figured that might be the best option. "If a customer comes in you'll be needed, so I'll just go on back there and seek Melvin out."

"Okay. When you're through conversing, stop back here and I'll give you a start from the pot of peppermint that is growing freely."

"That would be lovely." Elsie smiled and headed for the rear of the store. She found Melvin exiting the storage room and asked if she could speak with him for a few minutes.

"Jah, of course," he responded. "Are you in need of some herb that you couldn't find up front?"

Elsie shook her head. "We have a family matter that I would like to talk with you about."

"Oh, I see." He opened the door to the room he'd come out of and gestured at the folding chairs located near an old-looking relic of a desk. "Please, take a seat."

Elsie did as he suggested, and after Melvin seated himself in another chair, she cleared her throat and got right to the point. "My daughter, Rosa, and her husband, Anthony, are having marital problems and could use some counsel."

He gave his thick gray beard a quick tug. "Shouldn't your husband be the one to do that? As the bishop, he's our head leader, and I would think—"

She lifted a hand. "No, I believe he would be too close to the situation to be neutral." Elsie leaned slightly forward. "Besides, Mahlon hasn't fully accepted Anthony yet, so anything he might say to the young man could cause more dissension between the two of them, and maybe even between Anthony and Rosa."

"I see."

"So if you are willing to talk with my daughter and son-in-law, I think it would be best if you didn't mention it to Mahlon."

The chair Melvin had chosen to sit in had rollers, and he began moving it back and forth with the weight of his feet. Elsie figured the man was mulling things over and perhaps wondering how it might affect his relationship with their leader if he went behind his back and counseled Rosa and Anthony.

After several minutes, Melvin stopped rolling his chair and looked directly at Elsie. "If I agree to do this, when would be the best time for me to speak to the young couple? Would you send them here, or would it be better if I went to your home during a time when Mahlon is working at his store?"

"I was thinking you could come to our house, and since Mahlon won't be home until late this afternoon, now might be a good time, if you're not too busy here and can get away for an hour or so." Elsie figured in this case, the sooner the better.

Melvin tipped his head from side to side, as though contemplating things more. After a few more minutes passed, he finally gave a nod and stood. "All right then, Elsie. I'll head over there right now."

She offered the minister an appreciative smile. "Danki." Elsie rose from her chair. "I'll stay here and visit with Doris, because I don't think it would be good if I was there when you spoke to them, and I definitely don't want Anthony or Rosa to know that I asked you to counsel them."

⁂

Rosa held the reins tight as she headed for the greenhouse, which was about three miles from her folks' house. Since she was finished running her errands and Anthony was working on the shed roof, Rosa had decided to pay a call on Ada. Although the greenhouse was open fewer hours during the winter months and had fewer employees during the offseason, Rosa hoped her friend would be there today. If not, she would seek Ada out at the home she and Ephraim had recently rented in Allensville, not far from the harness shop. Hopefully, Ephraim would be at the harness shop today, because if Rosa did end up going to their house, she didn't want him to hear what she planned to say to Ada. Rosa was a ball of nerves, but she felt a strong need to confide in her friend. There were so many things she needed to get off her chest by speaking to a person with an unbiased opinion on what she should do. Ada had always been a levelheaded person, and she had a talent for listening and offering good advice.

Maybe she'll have some helpful ideas for me, Rosa thought as she guided her horse and buggy into the greenhouse parking lot and up to the hitching rail.

When she entered the building, Rosa was pleased to see the owner and his wife up front by the checkout counter, but after glancing around, she saw no sign of Ada.

"Excuse me," Rosa said, stepping up to the counter. "Is Ada Detweiler—I mean Peight—working here today?"

The man's wife gave a nod. "She stepped into the restroom a few minutes ago, but she should be out soon and will be working over there for a while." She pointed to a row of several pots filled with all types of indoor plants in various sizes.

Despite her nervousness, Rosa managed to offer the woman a smile. "Okay, thanks." She turned and headed down the aisle to wait for her friend.

A few minutes passed, and then Ada showed up, wearing a grin that stretched wide. "It's so good to see you, Rosa. I was just thinking about you the other day and wondered how you were doing." She gave Rosa a hug.

"I'm okay. Still having some morning sickness, but it comes and goes." Rosa stepped back a little and repositioned her purse strap that had slipped halfway down her arm. "We haven't talked in a while, and I was hoping you'd be working here today." She glanced toward the front of the building. "I don't want to get you in trouble with your boss for visiting a friend when you should be working, though. So if this is a bad time. . ."

"It's all right. We're not that busy today, and I can work on rearranging these plants while we talk."

"Okay, good." Rosa was on the verge of telling her friend the reason for her visit, but Ada spoke first.

"I have some good news to share with you."

"Oh?"

Ada placed one hand against her flat stomach. "Ephraim and I are expecting our first child, and we are so excited." She clasped Rosa's hand. "Just think, our little ones won't be too many months apart. I'm hoping they will grow up to be good friends."

"Congratulations, Ada. I'm happy for you." Rosa pushed aside the reason she'd come here today. No way would she burst Ada's happiness bubble by blurting out the truth about her and Anthony's pretend marriage. At a time like this, the last thing Rosa wanted to do was burden Ada with a problem that was not her own and that she could do nothing about.

Rosa's thoughts turned inward. Even though she was happy for her friend, she couldn't help feeling a bit envious. Ada was married to a man she loved and was now looking forward to the arrival of their firstborn child.

A lump formed in Rosa's throat. *If Ada knew the truth about me and Anthony, she'd probably be too ashamed to even call me her friend.*

―――

Anthony was about to pick up his hammer to continue working on the shed roof when his thoughts overtook him, so he paused and stood up straight. He reflected on the conversation he'd had with Rosa yesterday and wondered if there was any way they could make Rosa's mother believe that things were okay between them.

Or maybe it would be better to start quarreling in front of Rosa's family now, so that they won't be shocked once we finally announce that we're splitting up.

Anthony's thoughts came to a halt when his cell phone rang. He pulled it out of his pocket but wasn't able to answer before it went to voicemail. Anthony punched the button, and after listening to the message, he felt a huge sense of relief. The mechanic he'd left his vehicle with said that the part for Anthony's car had finally come in and he now had the vehicle running and ready to be picked up.

Anthony's excitement over hearing this news pushed him to work even harder on the roof, which meant that he would probably have it done in plenty of time before he took his leave.

―――

Anthony had been working about two hours, trying to put the finishing touches on the shed roof, when a horse and buggy pulled into the yard. Glancing up, he expected to see Elsie or Rosa returning home, but it was an older Amish man who guided his horse to the hitching rail and then climbed down from his carriage.

A few minutes later, Anthony was taken by surprise when the man introduced himself as Melvin Peachey and explained that he was one of the ministers in the Petersheims' church district.

Anthony set his tools aside and shook the man's hand. "Nice to meet you. I'm Anthony Reeves."

Melvin nodded. "Yes, you're Rosa's husband, right?"

"Yes, that's correct." What else could he have said? Anthony sure couldn't blurt out to the minister that he'd only been pretending to be married to Rosa.

"How are things going between you and your wife?" Melvin questioned.

"Umm. . .okay, I guess."

Melvin reached into his jacket pocket and pulled out a hankie. After blowing his nose on it, he stuffed it back. "I'll get straight to the point, Anthony. The reason I came here today is because someone mentioned that you and Rosa might be having some marital discord." He took a step closer to Anthony. . .so close that Anthony could detect the odor of peppermint on the man's breath.

"Someone?" Anthony repeated. "And who might that be?"

The minister shuffled his feet a few times, looked down at the ground, and then looked back at Anthony. "Well, it was your mother-in-law."

Anthony's arm muscles tensed. "She did, huh?"

"Yes, she's concerned. So I came here with the hope that I could talk to both you and Rosa, and maybe be of some help concerning your situation."

"Actually, Rosa isn't here right now," Anthony stated. "And the truth is, we don't need any outside counseling, because Rosa and I are working things out between us."

"Oh, I see. Well, that's a good thing." The minister clasped Anthony's shoulder. "Please remember, though, that I'm available to talk anytime if you should ever need me."

"I'll keep that in mind. Thanks for coming by, Minister Peachey."

"Melvin. Just Melvin," the man said before he turned and headed back to his horse and buggy.

Anthony watched Melvin free his horse, get into his buggy, and back away from the hitching rail. *Wow! I can't believe Elsie would go to the minister behind our backs and tell him that Rosa and I need to be counseled. I hope he doesn't speak to anyone else about this, because it seems that things are getting messier all the time.*

When Rosa got home, she saw Melvin Peachey's horse and buggy pulling out of the yard and wondered why he had come here. It wasn't likely that he'd wanted to speak to her father, because everyone in the valley knew that at this time of day, Dad would be at the Meat and Cheese Store.

She spotted Anthony working on the shed roof, and when he saw her, he waved and came right over to the hitching rail where Rosa had directed her horse. Anthony secured the animal and then hopped into the buggy to sit beside Rosa. "We've got problems," he said.

"What's wrong?"

Rosa listened with interest as Anthony told her what the minister had said to him. "I couldn't believe it when the man said that your mother asked him to come by here and counsel the two of us because we were having marital problems."

The muscles on both sides of Rosa's back tightened. "I can't believe she would do such a thing."

"Well, she did, and if that man tells anyone else what she said to him, soon your whole church district will know about it." Anthony rubbed his forehead where there was a sheen of sweat. "Pretty soon, we'll have more visitors trying to solve our marriage problems for us."

Rosa drew in a quick breath and released it slowly in an effort to relax. "We can't go on like this any longer, Anthony. We either have to tell my parents the truth now or stage our fake breakup. Then you will have no other choice but to go home, even if you have to find some other way to get there."

"I already have the means to travel home, Rosa," Anthony stated. "I got a call from the mechanic this morning, stating that my car is ready. I just have to figure out some way to pick it up."

"Oh, that's good news. I can take you there by horse and buggy."

"Thanks, Rosa." Anthony touched her arm gently. "Say, an idea just came to me."

"What's that?" she asked.

"I'll write a note for your parents, grab up my clothes and personal items, and stuff them in my duffel bag. Then I will leave the note on the kitchen table, or just give it to you, saying that things aren't working out between us and I'm going back to New York to see a lawyer so I can file for divorce. I'll even say that you're better off without me. You can share the note with your parents this evening."

Rosa's eyes widened. "You're going to just take off like that and leave me here to face my parents and deal with all their questions alone? I thought we were going to do this together."

"I figured it would be better this way. Less chance of a big scene, don't you know?"

"So you think there won't be a scene if you're not here when they read the note, huh?" Rosa's face felt like it was on fire, despite the cold air that had begun blowing since her arrival. She placed both hands on her hips and glared at Anthony. "For your information, Mr. Reeves, my mother's going to be very upset, and Dad will most likely be furious."

"Yeah, I know." Anthony pointed at Rosa. "But he'll be angry at me, not you. You'll have their pity, and I'm sure they would never toss their pregnant daughter out of the house. They'll be loving and encouraging, and you can join the Amish church and be part of their happy family. That is what they've always wanted for you, right, Rosa?"

"Well, yes, but there's one big issue you're not aware of, Anthony."

"Oh yeah? What's that?"

"If they continue to believe I am a married woman, and your letter says you'll be getting a divorce, I will not be allowed to join the Amish church." She smacked her forehead with the palm of her hand. "We didn't think this one through very well."

"How come you wouldn't be allowed to join the church?"

"It's one of our church rules, because the Amish don't allow divorced church members."

"Another man-made rule of the church, huh?"

She shook her head vigorously. "It's God's rule, by which all Amish church rules have been established."

Anthony reached under his stocking cap and scratched his head. "So if we go with our original plan, and if they believe I'm leaving you to get a divorce, then what?"

"I just told you—I won't be able to join the church."

"Would they allow you to continue living with them?"

"I–I'm not sure. Maybe—at least till the baby is born and I can find a job to support myself and the child. Then I might have to move out."

"Would you stay here in Mifflin County?"

"I–I don't know. I want to, but—"

Anthony clasped Rosa's arm and pulled her close to his side. "And we thought we had this plotted out so well. You know what? We've put ourselves right in a box with no way out."

She gave a quick shake of her head. "No, Anthony. I'm the one in the box. As soon as you pick up your car, you're free to go back to your job and family in New York. Then I won't be your problem anymore. You can be well rid of me and this mess I created by leaving home in the first place."

Anthony's long lashes blinked rhythmically as he stared at her. "Then there's only one thing we can do, Rosa, because I cannot leave you in the position where you won't be able to join the church." He leaned closer and stroked her face gently with his thumb. "We'll tell your folks the absolute truth, and we'll do it tonight, right after supper."

CHAPTER 24

ANTHONY DROVE SLOWLY BEHIND Rosa's horse and buggy. It felt good to have his car back, and it meant that he could finally go home.

He rapped the steering wheel with the knuckles on his left hand. *Then why am I not filled with excitement?* he asked himself. *I'll tell you why*, his inner voice said. *You dread telling Rosa's parents the truth, and you know when you leave you'll miss Rosa.*

Anthony had not fully admitted it to himself until now, but he'd come to care deeply for Rosa. "I might even be in love with her," he murmured. Anthony wasn't sure how she felt about him, but even if Rosa returned his feelings, they could never be together. Her family was Amish, and she planned to join their church. Anthony couldn't imagine setting his English ways aside and becoming Plain. It would be too drastic a change, and he enjoyed many things about the modern way of life that he wouldn't want to give up.

Rosa will be better off without me in her life anyway, he thought. *The fact is, we were never meant to be together. After I'm out of the picture, some nice Amish guy will no doubt come along and steal her heart. She'll forget she ever met me. Maybe it'll happen sooner than she expects.*

For most of the drive back to the Petersheims' house, Anthony managed to get himself pretty worked up, but by the time he pulled into the driveway behind Rosa's horse and buggy, he'd calmed down and accepted the way things were. The only thing Anthony was concerned about now was finding the right words to tell her folks the truth about their relationship—or rather the lack of one. Anthony didn't want to leave this place tomorrow morning on a bad note, but he figured that would probably end up being the case. The main thing, though, was to make sure that Rosa's family knew the ruse had been his idea, not hers.

When Rosa entered the house, she hung up her outer garments and went from room to room, looking for her mother. She knew Mom had to be here somewhere, because her horse was in the barn. Since she wanted to speak to her mother as soon as possible, and since Anthony was still in the barn putting Rosa's horse away, she figured this was a good time to catch her mother alone. There was no point in involving him in this particular conversation. They would both have their chance to talk to her parents after supper tonight.

When Rosa entered the kitchen where the nutty aroma of peanut butter wafted, she was glad to see that her mother was alone and in the midst of baking cookies. It was too early for Alvin to be home from school, and since Tena wasn't helping Mom, Rosa figured her sister had either gone out somewhere or was busy doing something in another room in the house.

"Oh, you're home," Mom said, turning to face Rosa. "How'd it go at the greenhouse? Did you have a chance to see Ada?"

"Yes, I did, and I found out that she's expecting a baby."

"Oh, how nice for her and Ephraim. I'm sure they're both happy and looking forward to the arrival of their first child." Mom smiled. "Just like you and Anthony are excited about the upcoming birth of your baby."

Anthony is not the father of my child, so he has no reason to share in my joy over becoming a parent. Rosa wanted to blurt the truth out here and now, but Anthony had made it clear that he wanted to be there when Rosa told her parents. In fact, before their conversation had ended, he'd even said that he planned to do most of the talking.

No, this conversation Rosa wanted to have with her mother had nothing to do with the lie they'd told Mom and Dad and what all would be said this evening.

"I need to talk to you about something." Rosa pulled out a chair at the table. "Can you please set your baking aside for a few minutes and listen to what I have to say?"

"Of course." Her mother placed the empty cookie sheet on the counter and sat down.

Rosa seated herself in a chair on the other side of the table. She leaned slightly forward with both elbows on the table. "Would you mind telling me why you thought it was necessary to ask Melvin Peachey to come over here this morning and talk to Anthony about our marriage?"

Mom blinked rapidly, then quickly looked away. "Didn't the minister speak to you as well?"

"No. This happened while I was at the greenhouse. He spoke to Anthony without me being present." Rosa lifted her elbows and crossed her arms. "Why would you send Melvin here, Mom?"

"Because after our talk yesterday, I figured you and Anthony were having some issues and could use a little counseling from someone who's been happily married for a good many years." Mom's chin quivered a bit, like it always did whenever she was upset or felt remorseful for something she'd said or done. "I'm very sorry, Rosa, if I overstepped my bounds. I was concerned for you and Anthony, and I thought it would help if you could speak to someone outside of our family about whatever problems you may be facing."

"Oh, we've got problems, all right. More than you can imagine."

"Would you like to talk with me about it? I promise not to be judgmental, and I won't offer my advice unless you want me to."

Rosa shook her head. "Not right now, Mom, but after supper tonight, Anthony and I would like to speak with both you and Dad."

"Oh, okay, if that's what you'd prefer." Mom got up from the table and went back to her baking project.

Rosa left the room, wondering if she should have told her mother the truth and been done with it, but it wouldn't be right to tell Mom before Dad. Besides, she and Anthony had agreed to tell them together after supper. It would be their last evening meal together, because Anthony planned to leave early tomorrow morning, most likely without even eating breakfast. Rosa had been able to tell from the few things he'd said to her in the barn that he was eager to be on his way home. She couldn't blame him for that. He should have left weeks ago, but the car dying, his sprained ankle, and a nasty case of the chicken pox had kept him here much longer than either of them had planned. It would be sad to see him go, but Anthony didn't belong here, whereas Rosa did. Before her great escape, she'd thought she wanted to be as far from Mifflin County and her Amish family as she could get. But the two-plus years she'd been away and on her own had proved otherwise. Coming home and seeing her family again had given Rosa the confirmation that she was exactly where she needed to be and that this Plain community was a good place to raise her baby. Rosa could only hope and pray that after tonight's conversation, she would be allowed to stay.

She closed her eyes briefly. *Oh Lord, please let it be so.*

That evening after supper, Rosa told her parents that she and Anthony would like to speak with them about something important and suggested that the four of them go to the living room.

"Do you want the rest of us there too?" Susan asked.

Before Rosa could respond, Mom quickly said, "You and Tena need to do the dishes." She looked across the table at Alvin. "And I want you, young man, to go upstairs and take a bath. You smell like a goat, and I have a hunch you were out there playing with them before you came inside for supper."

Alvin gave a sheepish grin and bobbed his head. "I wasn't playin', though. I was tryin' to teach one of the younger goats to come to me when I whistle."

Tena rolled her eyes. "That's *dumm*, little brother. No goat is gonna come to the sound of a whistle."

Alvin's nose wrinkled as he looked at his sister. "It's not dumb, Tena, and a lot you know. I read in one of the books I checked out at the library that you can train your goats to come when they hear you whistle. But you gotta do it regularly and offer them a treat so they'll race toward the sound."

"So who cares about that?" Susan got up and grabbed a few of the dishes, which she promptly carried to the sink. When she turned on the water to fill the dish tub, she looked over her shoulder and said tersely, "Are you going to help, Tena, or just sit there like a slug?"

Rosa looked at Mom to see if she would say anything, but it was Dad who spoke first. "Just mind your own business and start filling the dishpan. You should not talk to your sister like that."

"Sorry," Susan mumbled as she came back to the table to pick up some more dishes.

Dad looked at Tena. "Your mamm asked you and your sister to do the dishes, so that means she wants them done now."

Wordlessly, Tena left her seat and carried four plastic tumblers by the rims over to the sink.

Dad looked at Mom. "Come on, Elsie, let's go find out what Rosa and her *mann* want to talk with us about."

Rosa cringed. She could only imagine what either of her folks would have to say when they found out that Anthony was not her husband.

"What are you up to?" Tena asked when Susan stopped drying the dishes, headed across the room, and pressed her ear against the kitchen door.

Susan put a finger to her lips. "Shh. . ."

"Are you trying to hear what Rosa and Anthony are saying to Mom and Dad?"

"Jah, and with good reason."

"There's no good reason to be eavesdropping on someone."

Susan's brows furrowed. "Will you please keep your voice down? They might hear you."

Tena dried her hands and stomped across the room. "So what? You're listening to them, right?"

"I'm trying to, but you are making it difficult." Susan spoke quietly between clenched teeth. Sometimes Tena got on her nerves. Of course, not nearly as much as Rosa did. What frustrated her the most was that all she could hear were muffled voices and nothing of what was actually being said in the living room. If she were standing in the hall, she'd have a better chance.

Susan pointed to the sink. "Please finish washing the dishes. When I get back, I'll dry all of them."

"Get back from where?"

"I'm going to the bathroom down the hall."

"Can't it wait till after you're done helping me with the dishes?"

"No, it can't—nature calls, and I need to go now." Susan didn't wait for her sister's response. She pushed open the kitchen door and stepped into the hallway. Not wishing to be seen or heard by her parents or the supposed young husband and wife, Susan stood close to one side of the living room door and listened, pleased that she could now hear clearly every word being said.

⁂

"What is it that you're trying to tell us, Rosa?" Elsie questioned. "We can't understand you when you're crying."

Anthony, who had remained quiet during supper and even when the four of them had first come into the living room, spoke up. "Rosa and I have a confession to make, and since she's having trouble getting the words out, I'll be the one to tell you."

"Tell us what?" This question came from Mahlon.

"I believe it's about the fact that these two young people are having some marital problems," Elsie interjected. "Rosa admitted it to me yesterday, and this morning, I went to ask Melvin Peachey if he would offer them some counsel."

Mahlon's eyes narrowed and he scowled at her. "You went behind my back and asked one of the ministers? Have you forgotten, Wife, that I am the bishop in our church district?"

Elsie's chin dipped, and she tucked her elbows against her sides. "No, Mahlon. . .I just thought. . ."

Anthony figured it was best to set the record straight right away before Mahlon and Elsie ended up with marital problems of their own. He held up one hand and blurted out, "Rosa and I are not having marital issues, because we're not married."

Rosa dabbed at the tears on her cheeks and looked at Anthony with wide eyes. She'd obviously not expected him to blurt out the truth so bluntly to her parents. No doubt she felt an obligation to do it herself, but she'd been through enough emotional angst, and Anthony wanted to take the brunt of as much of this as possible. After all, it was his idea to accompany Rosa to her home in the Big Valley and pretend to be her husband. And now that her parents knew he and Rosa were not husband and wife, he admitted to them that the whole idea was his and why he and Rosa had felt it was the best thing for her and the baby.

Now it was time for Rosa to make another admission. "Anthony is not the father of my baby," she said.

Mahlon pointed a finger at her and said, "Is that a fact?"

She nodded.

"I see. Guess we can talk about that later."

Elsie sat with her lips pressed together and hands clasped tightly in her lap. Anthony figured she might be in shock from hearing this news, or perhaps very disappointed in both of them. He couldn't quite read her expression.

Mahlon, however, was clearly angry. His hazel eyes appeared as though they could bulge right out of the sockets, and he pounded his right fist against his left thigh. "How could you come in here and bold-faced lie to us like this? You accepted our hospitality, slept in our daughter's room, and pretended to be our son-in-law, when the whole time you were nothing but a conniving liar." He smacked his fist a little harder this time. "I'm beginning to think no one in this house is capable of telling the truth." He turned to glare at Elsie. "Even my own wife has gone behind my back and secretly asked my friend and fellow minister to speak to you and Rosa about your troubled marriage." He rose to his feet, tromped across the room to where Anthony sat, and stared down at him, like an angry tiger ready to attack. "You are no longer welcome in this house, Mr. Reeves. I want you to pack up your things and clear out now!"

Rosa leaped out of her seat, dashed over to her father, and clasped his arm. "Please, Dad, don't ask Anthony to leave now. It's late, and it wouldn't be good to travel at this time of night."

Rosa was right, but Anthony figured in order to keep things here a bit calmer, he would go upstairs, grab his clothes and personal items, and head in the direction of home. He wouldn't make it there tonight, of course, but surely he could find a hotel to stay at and then head for New York in the morning.

"What Rosa and Anthony did was wrong, for sure, but we can't ask him to leave right now, Mahlon," Elsie spoke up. "It would be safer for Anthony to head out in the morning."

"I agree with Mom," Rosa said. "Please, Dad, say he can stay till tomorrow."

Mahlon released a strange, guttural sound and then gave a nod. "All right, but you'll sleep down here on the sofa, not upstairs with my daughter."

"Dad," Rosa was quick to say. "The entire time Anthony has been here, we have not slept together. I slept in the bed and he had a piece of foam so he could sleep a little more comfortably on the floor. During the time when Anthony was sick with the pox, I slept on the foam and gave him my bed."

Mahlon shook his head vigorously. "I don't care who slept on the floor or in the bed. He's sleeping down here tonight, and nowhere else. Is that clear?"

"That's fine, sir," Anthony was quick to say. "And please, even if you can't forgive me, I hope you will find it in your heart to forgive Rosa for her part in the untruth we told."

Mahlon tapped his foot a couple of times and grunted. "I don't need you telling me what to do, young man. My wife and I will work things out with Rosa after you're gone."

"I understand. I'll head upstairs and get my things to bring down here right now." Anthony glanced at Rosa and cringed when he saw her trembling lips. If ever he wished he could take back something he'd done that was wrong, it was now. All he could really hope for at this point was that after he was gone, Rosa's parents would forgive her and allow her to continue living here. And when the time came for her to have the baby, her entire family would be there to love and support her.

She deserves that much, doesn't she? Anthony asked himself. *Just the fact that Rosa swallowed her pride and came home to the family she loved to seek help from them in her time of need should have proved something to them.*

Anthony's shoulders rose as he heaved a sigh. *I can only hope that my dad will be forgiving when I get home and explain to him and Mom the real reason for my absence. With the way my luck's been going, Pop might cut me out of his life and never let me work in his restaurant again.*

CHAPTER 25

SUSAN GASPED AND QUICKLY STEPPED aside to avoid being knocked over when Anthony rushed out of the living room and raced up the stairs. Rosa was right behind him and didn't appear to notice her either. Since Susan had been listening to their conversation, she knew her parents were finally aware of the truth. Well, it was about time.

Susan also figured that after Dad told Anthony he would have to leave, the big pretender had been in a hurry to get out of the room. Was it wrong to hope that Rosa would leave too and never come back?

Now is my chance to set things right with my folks. With no thought of any consequences, Susan burst into the room. "See, I told you so, Mom and Dad. You should have believed me when I said Anthony and Rosa weren't really married." She moved close to her father. "I'm glad you told Anthony that he needs to go, but in my opinion, you should throw Rosa out too."

"We don't need your opinion, Susan, and what your mother and I say or do concerning your sister is none of your business." The wrinkles in Dad's forehead deepened. "You're not without fault, you know."

Susan lifted her chin. "I'm a better daughter than Rosa will ever be. I did lots of things to help Mom after Rosa disappeared, and—"

Dad clapped his hands together, causing Susan to jump. "That'll be enough! It's up to your mamm and I to decide how we are going to deal with this, so go on back to the kitchen and help Tena finish the dishes."

"She's probably done with them now," Susan muttered.

"Do as your father said." It was the first Susan's mother had spoken since Susan had burst into the room.

"Okay, whatever." Holding both arms firmly at her sides, Susan hurried off to the kitchen. *I hope Rosa doesn't think Mom and Dad are gonna let her keep living here or that they'll help her raise that baby after it's born.*

Susan swung the kitchen door open and stepped inside as another thought popped into her head. *If Anthony's not the father of Rosa's baby, then who is?*

With the early morning light filtering into the living room through the two large windows, Anthony squinted and sat up from the couch where he'd spent a miserable night. It wasn't just the backache he felt. Anthony had been awake half the night thinking about the conversation that had transpired in this room between him, Rosa, and her parents. He could still picture the shocked expression on her mother's face and hear her father's commanding voice as he'd ordered Anthony to sleep on the couch and leave his house in the morning. There had been no apologies accepted, even though both he and Rosa had said they were sorry for their actions.

"I thought churchgoing people who called themselves Christians were supposed to be forgiving," Anthony muttered as he rose to his feet. He didn't care if anyone was up and heard what he'd said. He just wanted to see Rosa, tell her goodbye, and head on out to his car. The sooner Anthony left this place, the sooner he could put all thoughts of Rosa and her family out of his mind.

When Rosa came down the stairs and saw Anthony by the front door with his duffel bag, she hurried toward him, reached out, and tapped his back. "Hey! You're not leaving without saying goodbye, I hope."

He whirled around. "Of course not. I was just going to put my stuff in the car and turn on the ignition to warm it up. Then I was planning to see if you were awake so I could say a proper goodbye."

"What if I was still asleep in my bed?" She tipped her head back and looked into his eyes. *Oh, those beautiful blue eyes.* Rosa felt like she could drown in the depths of them.

"If you'd been sleeping when I knocked on your bedroom door, I would have written you a note and slipped it under the door."

"If you had knocked, I'm sure it would have awakened me. I'm a light sleeper, you know."

Anthony nodded. "That's for sure. If I made the slightest noise from my foam mattress on the floor, your sleep was disturbed."

"I always went right back to sleep, though."

"True." Anthony shifted his weight from one leg to the other and then cleared his throat. "Well, guess I ought to get going before any of your family wakes up. I'm sure they'll be glad when they do get up and see that I'm gone."

Rosa blinked in succession, trying to keep the tears that were stinging her eyes from spilling out. "Thank you for everything, and I hope you'll keep in touch."

"You have nothing to thank me for, Rosa. If anything, I made things worse for you by coming here and pretending to be your husband." He leaned a bit closer and whispered, "And I don't think your father would like it if I called or wrote you a letter."

"I—I guess you're right." She paused and drew in a shaky breath. "Dad can be harsh with his words at times, but I think it's because he wants us all to live a godly life and not stray from the church rules." Rosa placed a hand against her chest and grimaced. "Out of all his children, I'm pretty certain that I'm the one who has disappointed him the most."

"I wouldn't be too sure about that," Anthony countered. "From what I've seen and heard, I don't think he's too happy with Susan either."

"Probably not, but at least she didn't run away from home and cause our family so much grief."

"Well, you're back now, and you must do whatever you can to keep the peace and make your folks see that you're sorry for hurting them."

"You are right—I am very sorry, and I plan to do everything I can to regain their trust."

Anthony leaned forward and pulled Rosa gently into his arms. "You'll be fine." He held her for a few more seconds and then pulled away. "I've gotta go. If you think you can go back to sleep, I'd recommend returning to bed." He brushed a wayward strand of hair off her face. "Have a nice life, Rosa. I hope everything works out well for you and your baby." Before Rosa could respond, Anthony turned and rushed out the front door.

Rosa grabbed a woolen shawl hanging on a wall peg in the hall and wrapped it around her shoulders. Then she stepped out onto the porch and watched as Anthony got into his vehicle. When he pulled out of the yard and started down the driveway, she lifted her hand in a wave. Her friendship with Anthony was over now, and she needed to keep her focus on the future and the life she would have here in the Big Valley with her baby.

As Anthony drove onto the main road, his stomach tightened. In some ways he knew he'd miss this place, but in another way he was glad to be heading for home. At least there he wouldn't have to pretend anymore. He'd simply be accepted for who he was.

Of course, Pop might not accept me at all, he thought. *My relationship with him could easily be toast. But there's nothing I can do about that right now, not until I see him face-to-face and try to talk things out. I just hope he's willing to listen to what I have to say.*

Anthony turned his radio on and cranked up the volume, hoping it would drown out his thoughts. He'd fulfilled his duty almost to the last and wondered now if it would have been better to stage their breakup instead of telling Rosa's parents the truth.

It was too late for second guesses or reversing his decision. Anthony would keep driving until he made it to New York and then see how things panned out between him and his folks.

I'm sure Mom will be on my side, he thought. *She'll no doubt welcome me home with open arms. Maybe she'll even go to bat for me and speak up to Pop on my behalf. One thing is for sure. Once I return to New York City and everything that's familiar to me, I'll forget all about Rosa Petersheim and her Amish family.*

⁓⁓

Rather than going back to bed, Rosa went to the living room and took a seat on the couch where Anthony had slept last night. Her eyelids felt hot and gummy, from struggling to hold back the tears. She reached for a tissue from the small square box on the side table and blew her nose. It was impossible to see where her future or that of her unborn baby might go. Rosa felt a strong desire to escape the sadness that had welled up in her soul.

I brought this all on myself, she thought. *If only I'd stayed home instead of running off, I'd never have met Anthony, and I wouldn't even be pregnant right now.*

As much as Rosa hated to admit it, she'd foolishly allowed herself to fall in love with Anthony. "And where did that get me?" she murmured, burying her face in her hands.

"Is Anthony gone?"

Rosa lifted her head and nodded as she looked up at her mother standing a few feet away. She'd been so caught up in her sorrow that she hadn't even heard Mom come into the room. "Jah, he left a while ago."

Mom took a seat beside Rosa on the couch and reached over to take hold of her hand. "You're in love with him, aren't you?"

Rosa couldn't deny it as she moved her head slowly up and down. "But it doesn't matter how I feel, because Anthony doesn't love me, and besides, he's gone and won't be coming back."

"How can you be so sure?"

"Because his parents, as well as the job he used to have, are waiting for him in New York."

"But how can you be certain that Anthony doesn't love you?"

"If he did, I'm sure he would have said so." Rosa nearly choked as she tried to swallow the lump in her throat.

"Does he know you love him?"

"No, Mom, I never said the words to him, so it doesn't matter how I feel." Her shoulders lifted. "Anthony and I are from two different worlds, so it's really quite simple. We were never meant to be together, and I need to accept that fact and move on with my life."

Mom slipped her arms around Rosa and gave her a tender squeeze. "I'm so glad to have you back home with us, and I'm sure that whatever God has planned for your life will eventually be revealed to you."

Rosa felt a flutter in her belly and placed both hands across her middle. She hoped what Mom had said was correct and that she would make the right decisions for herself, as well as for her little one, when the time was right. Rosa was determined to do something good in her life—if not for herself, then for the precious child that would be born in about four months.

When Susan and her father entered the Meat and Cheese Store, she was surprised to discover that Norman wasn't there yet. Usually he arrived at least fifteen minutes before them to open the store. Fortunately, there weren't any customers waiting outside in the parking lot. Of course, that wasn't much of a surprise, considering how cold it was this morning. To Susan's way of thinking, nobody in their right mind would want to go shopping for meat or cheese when the weather was so frigid. She had hoped her dad would have closed the store today so they could stay home and gather around the fireplace, where it was warm and toasty.

When Susan had come downstairs this morning, she'd seen her mother and Rosa in the living room with their heads together. Susan was pretty sure she knew what they were talking about, especially when she'd looked outside and seen that Anthony's car was gone.

I hope Mom sees Rosa for what she is, Susan thought as she put the OPEN sign in the front window. *I'm getting tired of Mom and Dad's accusations against me. The truth is, Rosa's a bigger liar than I'll ever be.*

THE PRETENDER

It was pretty nervy of her to bring that English fellow into our house, posing as her husband. I'm almost sure the whole idea was Rosa's. Anthony probably went along with it to prove that he was a nice guy.

Susan turned away from the window in time to see Dad head toward the back of the store and disappear into his office. *Or maybe Rosa gave Anthony some money to play the part of her doting husband. Sure wish I had some proof of that to tell Mom and Dad about.*

Susan slipped behind the checkout counter and took a seat on the wooden stool. As far as she could tell, there wasn't much to do today, so she may as well sit here and wait until Norman arrived. Susan figured that unless Mom or Dad had called late last night or early this morning and left Norman a message, he had no clue what had transpired at their house last night. So maybe. . .just maybe. . .she would get the opportunity to tell him about it.

After several minutes had passed, Susan turned and looked at the clock on the wall behind her. Still no Norman, and he was now almost thirty minutes late. *I wonder what could be keeping him. Maybe I should go mention Norman's absence to Dad.*

Susan slid off the stool and had just stepped out from behind the counter when the front door opened and Norman rushed in.

"Whew! It's sure bitter cold out there," he said, following a low whistle.

"Yeah, and we'll be lucky if we have any customers at all today. Maybe you can talk Dad into closing the store for the rest of the day." Susan gestured to the back of the building. "He's in his office if you care to suggest that idea to him."

"Nope." Norman shook his head. "If Dad thinks the weather will keep customers away, he'll make the decision to go home without either of us suggesting it to him."

"You're probably right." She moved closer to Norman and spoke quietly, hoping her father wouldn't hear. "You'll never guess what transpired at our house last night."

"No, I can't, but I'm sure you plan to tell me."

"Well. . .Anthony blurted out something I already knew, but of course, when I had tried to tell Mom and Dad, they wouldn't believe me."

"What did he say?" Norman took off his stocking cap and placed it on the counter.

"He admitted that he and Rosa aren't even married. They were just pretending all along."

Norman's eyes widened. "Seriously?"

"Yep. Can you believe that he and Rosa, the perfect daughter, would do such a thing?"

"You and I both know that Rosa's not perfect, Susan, and neither is anyone else in our family. Only Jesus is perfect."

Susan anchored one hand against her hip. "I don't need a sermon."

"Wasn't giving you one. Just stating facts as they are."

"Yeah, okay. . .whatever."

"Did Anthony or Rosa explain why they had pretended to be married?"

"Anthony said it was all his idea—that he thought Rosa would be accepted back into the family if Mom and Dad believed he was her husband." Susan scrunched up her face. "The truth is, Anthony is not even the father of that baby Rosa's carrying."

"Wow! That's quite a story you're telling. Are you sure you have all your facts straight?"

"Of course I do!" Susan's face heated. "Why would I lie about something like this? If you don't believe me, you can go ask Dad." She gestured to the back part of the store.

"That won't be necessary!" Dad shouted as he strode down the aisle toward them. He pointed at Susan. "I'm here now to set the record straight." He eyeballed Susan. "With all the stinking lies you've told me and your mother, you have no right to criticize your sister, and it's not your place to be telling Norman or anyone else about our family business. It was my responsibility to let your brother know the facts since he is part of our family, and if I want anyone else to know, I'll do the telling. Is that clear, Susan?"

She lowered her gaze to the floor. "Jah, Dad."

He pointed to the storage closet. "Now go find a broom and dustpan and get busy cleaning the floor."

Susan hurried off without saying another word. She figured Dad would probably tell Norman everything that had been said last night, and he'd no doubt say a few more negative things about her too.

CHAPTER 26

New York City

AFTER NEARLY FIVE HOURS ON the road due to heavy traffic, as well as some icy patches on the rural roads in Pennsylvania, Anthony drove down the alley behind his father's restaurant. He parked his vehicle in one of the spots reserved for employees. Anthony wasn't sure he was still an employee or that his dad would hire him back if he'd truly been replaced. But he'd never have an answer to that question without going inside.

Anthony had to admit he was a bit nervous about seeing his folks again—especially Pop. In some ways, Anthony's father reminded him of Mahlon Petersheim. They were both stubborn and opinionated and could be rather harsh when speaking to someone while offering their biased opinion.

"And both men seem to have it in for me," Anthony muttered as he got out of his car and headed for the restaurant's back entrance.

Anthony wasn't perfect, but he wasn't a bad guy either. He cared about people and liked to help solve their problems whenever he could. *I'm also a pretty good cook*, Anthony reminded himself. *Too bad my dad's never appreciated that fact.*

When Anthony opened the door and stepped inside, he was greeted by the tantalizing aroma of savory pasta sauce and aromatic herbs. Someone was in the kitchen, no doubt about it. Anthony was eager to find out who and quickly headed in that direction. Before he could get there, however, he was stopped short by his mother, who greeted him with a wide smile and open arms.

"Anthony, my dear boy, welcome back. We have missed you so much."

We? As in you and Pop, or are you the only parent who has missed me? Anthony chose not to ask the question at the forefront of his mind. Instead, he accepted his mother's embrace and patted her back a few times. "I've missed you too, Mom."

"Why didn't you let us know you were coming?" She looked up at him. "Was it supposed to be a surprise?"

"Not exactly, Mom, although I'm sure it is. Things got kind of crazy last night, and I was almost kicked out of the Petersheim home by Rosa's father. Thankfully, I was granted the right to spend the night, but I left early this morning before anyone but Rosa was up."

With a puzzled expression, Mom slanted her head to one side. "Who is Rosa? When we've talked on the phone, you never mentioned anyone by that name. Is Rosa one of Eileen's relatives?"

Anthony shook his head. "Eileen and Rosa are one and the same. The waitress we knew went by Eileen, which is actually Rosa's middle name. Oh, and her last name is not Peterson. It's Petersheim."

Mom's fingers touched her parted lips. "Oh my. I had no idea."

"Neither did I. It wasn't until we were at her parents' house in Belleville, Pennsylvania, that she sprung it on me. But I don't want to talk about that right now. I'll give you all the details this evening after the restaurant closes. Right now, I need to talk to Pop and see if I still have a job."

Anthony turned toward the kitchen, but she caught hold of his arm. "Things have been really busy here, Anthony, and since we had no idea if or when you might return, your father had to hire another cook. His name is Billy Adams."

Anthony frowned. "I figured he would need to hire someone part-time, but I didn't think it would be to actually replace me." His shoulders lifted as he released a groan. "I told you I'd be coming back, but things kept getting in the way, so I couldn't give you or Pop an exact day or time that I would return to New York."

She reached up and patted both of his cheeks, the way she'd often done when Anthony was a child and she was trying to be supportive. "It's okay, Son. You're here now, and that's what counts."

"Thanks, Mom. I'll let you get back to work now, and we can talk more when I return later on." Anthony gave his mother another hug and went quickly to the kitchen area, where he found Pop and a red-haired fellow with a face full of freckles. Both men were cooking at their respective stoves. The young man glanced at Anthony for a few seconds, but then he returned his focus to whatever he'd been stirring in a pot. Anthony was tempted to introduce himself, but he wanted to speak to his dad first.

" 'Bout time you showed up," Pop said, barely looking at Anthony. He gestured to the fellow with red hair. "That's my new chef. Since you didn't come back when you were supposed to, I hired Billy Adams to take your place."

"There were good reasons why it took me so long to return to New York." Anthony felt his defenses rise. "It's not like I stayed away on purpose, you know." He moved closer to his father and lowered his voice to a near whisper. "Now that I'm here, I'd like my job back."

"Is that so?"

"Yeah."

"Well, as you can see, the position has already been filled."

"How about I take over for you as head cook, and then you and Mom can take an extended vacation? You've talked about doing some traveling, right?"

Pop stared at Anthony with an emotionless expression. Then he muttered something Anthony couldn't understand and turned back to his job at the stove.

Anthony figured this wasn't a good time to take their conversation any further, so he forced a smile and said, "It's good be back, Pop, but I'll let you focus on your job right now, and we can talk more after the restaurant closes this evening."

Pop shrugged and said in a monotone voice, "Suit yourself, but there really isn't much to talk about."

Oh yes there is, and I plan to do plenty of talking. Anthony whirled around and marched out of the kitchen. *I just hope my stubborn father will listen to me.*

When Anthony caught sight of his mother waiting on one of the tables, he waved at her and mouthed, *"I'll return in a few hours."*

She gave a nod and blew him a kiss.

Anthony went out the back door and climbed into his car. As soon as he got to his apartment he planned to call the Petersheims' number and leave a message for Rosa, so she would at least know that he'd made it home safely.

Belleville

When Susan arrived home from work that afternoon, she went out to the phone shed to check for messages. She found one from Caroline, one of the young women who attended their church, inviting her to an ice-skating party. Disinterested, Susan simply deleted the message.

There weren't any other messages, which meant Anthony hadn't called Rosa. *Good. If she's worried about him and disappointed that he hasn't called, that's just too bad.*

Shivering against the cold that had invaded the phone shed, Susan got up and left the small building. Whether she liked it or not, it was time to help Mom start supper.

Trudging up the path toward the house, Susan's boots crunched in the snow. Halfway there, her foot slipped on a patch of ice and she nearly lost her balance but caught herself in time. "Stupid snow," she muttered. "I hate winter and all the nasty cold weather it brings. I wish we lived someplace where it stayed warm all year."

"Who ya talkin' to, Sister?"

At the sound of her younger brother's voice, Susan turned to the left and saw Alvin rolling a snowball, which would no doubt become a snowman once he had finished. "I was talking to myself. Is that okay with you?"

He stopped what he was doing and looked up at her with raised brows. "I don't have a problem with it, but I think it's kinda weird."

"Don't you ever talk to yourself?" Susan countered.

Alvin shrugged. "Sometimes, I guess, but not when other people are around, and I mostly do it in my *kopp*." He pointed to his head.

"I don't normally talk to myself when others are around either," she said, "but I didn't know you were out here in the yard until you spoke to me." Susan pointed to the lightweight jacket her brother wore. "Aren't you feeling *kelt*?"

Alvin gave a vigorous shake of his head. "Nope. I ain't one bit cold."

Susan shrugged, and when she started moving toward the house again, she called over her shoulder, "Better hurry and get your snowman made before Mom calls you in for *nachtesse*, because I doubt she'll let you go out after it gets dark and the temperature drops even farther."

"No need for you to worry about that. I'll have this finished long before it's time to eat supper."

"Okay, little bruder, whatever you say."

"I ain't little," Alvin hollered in response.

She chuckled and stepped onto the front porch. When Susan entered the house, she was surprised that there were none of the usual aromas coming from the kitchen. Instead, she found Mom, Rosa, and Tena in the living room, sitting near the fireplace, all holding teacups in their hands.

"What's going on?" Susan asked. "I figured the three of you would have supper started by now."

"Not tonight," Mom responded. "We've been invited to eat at Norman and Salina's home this evening."

"Oh, I see."

"You don't sound too excited about the idea," Tena commented. "Would you rather stay here by yourself and fix a cold sandwich to eat?"

Susan drew close to the fireplace, turning her back toward the flames. "No, I'll join you. I'm just not looking forward to going outside in the cold again and riding in Dad's drafty buggy. It's chillier than the inside of the phone shed I just came from."

"Were there any messages for me?" Rosa questioned. "Anthony said he would call when he got to New York to let me know that he'd arrived safely." She glanced at the clock on the mantel. "Surely he must be back there by now."

Susan shook her head. "Nope. There were no messages from anyone today." She took pleasure in seeing the disappointed look on her sister's face. *Rosa deserves to be as miserable as I've been since she came home to spin her web of lies.*

⁓⌇

"It's really strange that Anthony hasn't called. He should have been home by now, and I can't help but be worried about him." Rosa grimaced as she clutched the neckline of her dress.

"Don't you have Anthony's cell number?" Mom asked.

"Yes, I do."

"Then why don't you give him a call? Wouldn't that put your mind at ease?"

"I think it would. Guess I can put my boots and outer garments on, then go out to the phone shed to make the call. I'll dress warmly so that when Dad comes inside to let us know that he has the horse and buggy ready to go, I'll be all set."

"While you're out there, would you tell Alvin to quit playing in the snow and come inside so he can get washed up and into some clean, dry clothes?"

"Sure, Mom. I'll deliver your message."

"And do be careful," Mom hollered when Rosa got up from her chair and left the room. "The packed snow and patches of ice could be dangerous, and you sure don't want to slip and fall."

"I'll watch out for any slick patches," Rosa responded before disappearing into the hall.

When Rosa stepped out the front door, she spotted Alvin in the yard next to a pretty good-sized snowman. She smiled, remembering the days when she and Norman had built snowmen together, before Susan or Tena had been old enough to join them. Those were fun times, when life was carefree and less complicated. It wasn't until she'd become a teenager that Rosa had begun to question their church rules and Dad's expectations of her joining the church. Rebellion had set in by the time she'd turned sixteen and desired to sow her wild oats.

I was a fool, Rosa thought as she approached Alvin. *All those rebellious things I wanted to do so badly only led to trouble and heartache for my parents.* She glanced down at her growing baby bump. *I hope I can instill good behavior in my child, and that when he or she becomes a teenager, good decisions will be made.*

"Wanna help me put a face on my snowman?" Alvin asked.

"That sounds like fun, but I don't have time for that right now, and neither do you."

His round face contorted. "How come?"

"We'll be going to Norman and Salina's for supper soon."

Alvin reached under his knitted stocking cap. "Oh yeah. I forgot about that. Figured we'd be eating here like usual."

"I have a message for you from Mom," Rosa said. "She wants you to quit what you're doing and go inside to wash up and change clothes. We all need to be ready to leave as soon as Dad gets the horse and buggy ready."

Alvin's shoulders slumped. "Guess I'll have to finish it in the morning before I leave for school, 'cause it'll probably be time for bed when we get back from Norman's place this evening."

"That's true." Rosa began walking down the driveway.

"Where ya going?"

"To the phone shed to make a call."

When Rosa entered the chilly building, she was disappointed that the light on the answering machine was not blinking, which meant that no messages had come in since Susan had checked.

Rosa picked up the receiver and dialed Anthony's cell number. When he didn't answer, she left a message. "Hi, it's Rosa. I'm hoping you made it home by now, and if you have, I would appreciate it if you'd give me a call. My family and I will be gone for the rest of the evening, but I'll check for messages again in the morning."

Rosa wanted to say that she missed Anthony already, but what would be the point? He really had no choice but to leave, and he was probably looking forward to being home with his parents and going back to work at a job he really enjoyed. Although he'd never come right out and said so, Rosa figured Anthony had been bored while staying with them. He might have even wished that he'd never come to her parents' home in the Big Valley, pretending to be someone he wasn't.

New York City

That evening, after spending the afternoon getting settled into his apartment along with searching for his cell phone, which he'd somehow misplaced and had yet to find, Anthony returned to the restaurant. He had every intention of speaking to his parents about the reason he'd gone to Belleville. He also planned to admit that while he was there, he had pretended to be Rosa's husband.

Anthony wasn't sure they would understand the reason behind his decision to do such a thing, but he felt he needed to explain anyway. Anthony hoped that his dad would understand about the things that had kept him in Belleville longer than he'd planned.

I hope if I ever become a parent, I'll be understanding when my children come to me to discuss something and seek my approval, Anthony thought as he approached his mother and father at the table where they sat eating a late meal. He'd seen them do this many times over the years—always after the restaurant had closed for the day.

"I see you two are enjoying a plate of Pop's tasty lasagna," Anthony said when he approached their table.

"Actually, it was Billy who made this batch." Anthony's father looked at him with a smug expression. Was he trying to rub it in? If so, Anthony refused to let it ruffle his feathers.

"There's still some lasagna left in the kitchen," Mom said. "Would you like me to fix you a plate?"

"No thanks. I'm fine. Just came here to do some explaining to you and Pop about my trip to Pennsylvania with Rosa."

"Who's Rosa?" Pop asked. "I thought you left here with that flighty waitress, Eileen."

"Her real name is Rosa, and she's not flighty." Anthony pulled out one of the empty chairs and took a seat. "I mentioned that to Mom when I was here earlier. Figured she would tell you about it."

Pop grabbed his glass of red wine and took a drink. "Nope, your mother never said a word."

"I didn't have the chance," Mom explained. "We were super busy all day."

Anthony shrugged. "That's okay. No problem." Not sure where to begin, he drew in a quick breath and spilled the whole story about how he'd pretended to be Rosa's husband and why.

His mother's eyes widened, and Pop stared at Anthony with a stony face. Good or bad, Anthony wished one of them would say something, but maybe the shock of all this was too much information to digest in one sitting.

Maybe they think I made the whole thing up, Anthony reasoned. *It is pretty unbelievable.*

Rather than wait to see if either of them would comment on the role he'd played as a pretender, Anthony shared the details about his car that had taken so long to be repaired. He also mentioned his sprained ankle that had occurred when he'd fallen off a trampoline. The last thing Anthony brought up was a description of how miserable he'd felt having to deal with chicken pox.

Deep wrinkles appeared in Pop's forehead. "I know that much already, Anthony. You told your mother about the things keeping you from coming back to work here when you spoke to her on the phone."

He leaned closer to Anthony with both elbows on the table. "Didn't you think she would share that information with me?"

"Well, yes, but—"

"If you want my opinion, those were just made-up excuses so you could hang out with that pretty waitress."

Anthony gave a vigorous shake of his head. "No way, Pop! Each of those events actually happened. Everything I've told you tonight is the truth."

Pop raised both hands above his head. "Doesn't matter. You were foolish for running off with Eileen—Rosa—or whatever she calls herself now, and pretending to be married to her was even more stupid. On top of that, if you'd really wanted to come home and keep your job here at the restaurant, you'd have found some way to get here. When the car died, you could have had it towed to a garage here in the city, and I'm sure they would have been able to get the part and fix it quickly." He paused to take another drink of wine. "And if you'd done that, the sprained ankle and chicken pox breakout would not have happened to you."

"That's not fair, Herb," Mom said. "Anthony could have been exposed to the chicken pox anywhere, anytime, and been laid up for a few weeks." She shrugged her shoulders. "For that matter, he could have sprained an ankle doing anything right here in his hometown."

Anthony appreciated his mother sticking up for him, but he was fairly sure he would not garner his dad's sympathy or understanding. "I guess, then, you're not planning to give me my old job back," he said, directing his statement to his father.

Pop shook his head. "Nope. Not unless Billy quits for some reason."

Yeah, like that's gonna happen. Anthony pushed away from the table and stood. "Guess I'd better start looking for another job in the morning."

"You don't have to do that," Pop said. "We need another busboy. You can take that position if you want to."

Anthony felt his facial features tighten, right along with his fingers pressing into the palms of his hands. "No thanks—not interested!" He looked at his mother and saw the look of compassion on her face, but to his disappointment, she said nothing. Was she afraid to take a stand and go against his father's wishes? Wasn't this restaurant just as much hers as it was his father's?

"Give me a call if you change your mind, Pop. Of course, I'll need to find my cell phone first." Anthony started to walk away, but Mom stopped him.

"You left your phone here earlier, and I put it in the office for safekeeping. I can go get it for you, Son."

"No thanks, Mom. I'll get the phone myself." Anthony turned away and stalked off toward the office. What a great ending to a not-so-perfect day! He wished now that he'd never come here and tried to explain things to his parents. In truth, Anthony wished he hadn't bothered to come back to New York at all.

CHAPTER 27

Belleville

THE FOLLOWING DAY, WHEN THERE still had been no word from Anthony, Rosa went to the phone shed to call him again. She felt relieved when he responded.

"Oh hey, Rosa," Anthony said. "Sorry for not calling to let you know I made it home, but I misplaced my cell, and by the time I found out where it was, the battery had died; plus it was late. I did plan to call you this morning, but you beat me to it."

"It's okay. I'm just glad to know that you made it back to New York. I'm sure it feels good to be home."

"In some ways not so much, but I'm sure that I'll feel better about things once I find a job."

"What about your job at your parents' restaurant?" Rosa pulled her jacket collar a little tighter to keep the cold draft off her neck. It was so chilly in the phone shed this morning that she could see her fog-like breath every time she opened her mouth to speak.

"The job's been filled. My dad hired a young fellow to take my place, and the restaurant doesn't get enough activity to keep three cooks working." There was a pause, followed by a groan. "Oh, I forgot to mention—Pop did offer me a job—as a busboy, no less. Can you believe that?"

"Did you accept the offer?"

"Of course not! There's no way I could work for lower wages, doing something I'm overqualified for. Nope. I turned the job down flat, so I'll be heading out soon to see if I can find a chef's position at one of the other restaurants here in the city."

Rosa heard the frustration in Anthony's voice. She couldn't blame him for being upset. A chef who cooked as well as he did deserved to be doing something better than bussing tables, and she told him so.

"I agree," he countered, "but that doesn't change the facts."

"I bet you'll find something soon." Rosa's fingers felt so numb she could barely hold on to the phone's receiver. "I'd better let you go, Anthony, so you can begin your day and find the perfect job. I'm sure that whichever restaurant you end up cooking for, the owners will be glad they hired you."

"I hope so. And you're right. I do need to get going pretty soon. But before we hang up, I'd like to know how things are going there for you. Are your folks still pretty upset about me pretending to be your husband?"

"I'm sure they are—especially my father, but Mom is a little more understanding and has been trying to offer me some support."

"So you don't have to worry about being asked to leave?"

"I don't think so, but I know it'll be an embarrassment for them when the word gets out that you and I were just pretending to be married." Her voice faltered, and she paused for a breath. "They know you're not my baby's father, but I haven't given them all the details yet about the affair I had with Jeff."

"Sorry I can't be there to help shield you from that."

"It's okay. You're not at fault, and this is something I'll have to deal with. What I did was wrong, and I've confessed my sin to God. Next, I'll be asking Mom and Dad's forgiveness for that as well."

"I'm sure once the baby comes and they get to enjoy the experience of being grandparents, things will be better and they'll find it in their hearts to forgive you for anything they disapprove of."

"I hope you're right. I can't imagine going through this without their support."

"I believe my mom's on my side, but I wish I had my dad's support." Anthony spoke quietly, almost mumbling his words. "Pop's never been the understanding type, and it seems like his impatience and intolerance of me has gotten worse over the years."

"You never know. Some things do improve with the passing of time." Rosa shifted her body on the unyielding chair she sat upon. It was getting more difficult to remain in the phone shed, but it was nice talking to him, so she had endured the discomfort. "I'll be praying for you, Anthony—that you find the right job and that things get better between you and your dad."

"Thanks. Take care, Rosa. I'll let you know if anything changes, and I hope you'll do the same on your end."

"I will. Bye for now." Rosa hung up the phone and swiped at the tears that had escaped her eyes and felt as though they were frozen to her face. Anthony had only been gone a day, but she missed him already. Part of Rosa wanted to suggest he come back to the Big Valley and try to find a job at one of the restaurants in the area. But she reminded herself, yet again, that they were from different worlds and were not meant to be together.

"I need to forget about Anthony and the strong feelings I have for him. It's best for both of us if we move on with our lives and focus on the paths we were meant to take." Rosa's words were spoken out loud. Her throat felt clogged, and she swallowed hard as she uttered her final words before leaving the shed. "I am sure that after Anthony finds a job and moves forward, he will be glad that I'm no longer a burden for him." Truthfully, Rosa figured she would probably never hear from Anthony again.

New York City

Anthony entered his apartment and flopped onto the couch with a moan that reverberated off the walls. He'd spent the entire morning and most of the afternoon looking for a job and finding nothing. It was hard to believe that none of the restaurants he'd visited needed a cook. In a city the size of New York, with its many eateries, surely there must be at least one chef's position open. *I can't stop trying. I'll need to keep looking*, Anthony told himself.

As he lay staring at the ceiling, Anthony's thoughts went to Rosa and the conversation he'd had with her early this morning. It had felt good to talk to her, and he appreciated her encouragement about finding the right job, as well as the hope of the relationship he had with his father improving. Anthony wanted to believe her, but knowing how stubborn his father could be, he doubted that anything would ever change between them. When Pop made up his mind about something, it wasn't likely that he could be persuaded to change it—not even with Mom's encouragement.

Why does life have to be so difficult? Anthony wondered. *I always try to be a nice guy, and I took pity on Rosa when I heard she was expecting a baby and wanted to go home. And look where that got me—Rosa's dad and mine are mad at me, and I'm out of a job.*

Anthony sat up and plodded out to the kitchen in his bare feet to see if there was anything in the refrigerator he could eat. It was the first time he'd bothered to check out the contents since his arrival. This morning, in a hurry to start job hunting, Anthony had showered, gotten dressed, and rushed out the door. His first stop was the neighborhood coffee shop, where he'd purchased a latte and one raspberry-filled donut. He'd figured that would hold him over till he'd grown tired of job hunting for the day. Anthony had also hoped there would at least be something in his refrigerator to get him by for a day or so.

When Anthony grabbed the handle and jerked open the door, he slammed it shut just as quickly. "Phew! What a stench! I bet nearly everything in there went bad while I was gone." He was in no mood to go grocery shopping right now or clean out the spoiled contents in the fridge. However, the rumbling in Anthony's belly spoke loud enough that he knew he had to make a choice. He would pitch all the food that had gone bad and clean and sanitize every shelf, tray, and drawer in the refrigerator. Once that chore was done, he would go to one of the fast food places nearby for a bite to eat. After that, he'd stop by the grocery store and buy enough food to last him for at least a week.

"It's a good thing I have some money saved up, or I might have had to let my apartment go and sleep in my car," Anthony muttered as he opened the cupboard and grabbed a plastic garbage bag to put the smelly contents in before hauling it outside to the dumpster, located behind the apartment building. Fortunately, while Anthony had been gone, he'd been able to use his cell phone to pay his rent and utilities via his bank account. One thing was for sure: It would be a cold day in the hottest part of Arizona before Anthony would ask his folks if he could move in with them. Nope, that would never work out.

Seeing his duffle bag in a corner of the living room, Anthony picked it up and hauled it to his bedroom. After dumping the contents out onto the bed, he was taken by surprise when he noticed a black book that tumbled out among his clothes.

"What in the world?" He picked the book up, turned it over, and stared at the title: Holy Bible.

His lips compressed. "For goodness' sake," Anthony muttered. "I wonder how that got in there. Could Rosa have put the Bible in the bottom of my bag, thinking I might miss the time of morning devotions, when her father read a portion of scripture from the Bible before everyone began their day?"

Anthony put the book on his nightstand. He might open it one of these days, but not right now.

***

When there was a lull between the lunch and supper crowd, Lavera headed to the kitchen to speak with Herb. Upon arrival, she was glad to see that Billy was not in sight. She figured he had probably gone to the restroom or was on a late lunch or early dinner break.

Lavera spotted her husband across the room, standing near the stove, so she went over to him. "Herb, I need to talk to you about something."

"Can it wait?" he asked without turning to look at her. "I'm heating up the new sauce I created and need to keep an eye on it."

"It could wait, I suppose, but it's important, and I would really like to talk about it now."

"Well, spit it out, then, because I'm not gonna leave this sauce unattended."

Lavera knew that when her husband said he wasn't going to do something, he meant it. This was her biggest worry about the topic she wished to discuss with Herb, but she planned to carry through anyway.

She moved close to the stove and stood with her arms hanging loosely at her sides. "I really think you should hire Anthony back, Herb. It's not his fault that several unexpected things got in the way of him returning to New York by the date he'd originally planned."

Herb shrugged his shoulders. "It's not my fault either." He glanced her way. "As I told Anthony last night, I hired Billy in his absence and I'm not about to fire him now just so Anthony can have his old job back."

"But Herb. . ."

"And as I'm sure you recall, I did offer him a job bussing tables."

Lavera lifted her gaze to the ceiling. "That's ridiculous, Herb! Our son's culinary skills lie here in the kitchen, not clearing dirty dishes off the tables."

"It's the best I can offer, so as far as I'm concerned, this topic is over. Now please find something to keep yourself busy till the dinner crowd arrives, and let me take care of my special pizza sauce."

It was all Lavera could do to hold her tongue, but she felt sure that, no matter how hard she pleaded their son's case, Herb was not going to budge. She sincerely hoped Anthony would be able to find another chef's position soon. Otherwise, he might end up leaving New York for good, and that would break her heart.

Belleville

Since Tena was in the basement checking on the clothes she'd hung up after washing several loads and Rosa had gone to her room to take a nap, Elsie decided this was a good chance to catch up on her letter writing. Several of her friends and relatives who didn't live in the area had written notes and letters with the Christmas cards they'd sent in December, and she'd been too busy since the holidays to respond to all of them.

She opened the desk drawer and took out a writing tablet, along with her favorite pen, and placed them on the kitchen table. The teakettle whistled, so she fixed herself a cup of tea and set it on the table, along with a few gingerbread cookies. Taking a bite of a cookie, she washed it down with a few sips of tea. Although the quiet time was pleasant, it would have been nice to have either one of her daughters join her. Most likely, Tena would do that once she'd finished checking on the laundry. But it wasn't likely that Rosa would come out of her room until it was time to help fix supper.

The poor girl had opened her heart last night before bedtime and confessed to Elsie and Mahlon that she'd had an affair with a married man, who had fathered her baby. Lots of tears had fallen from Rosa's eyes as she'd begged for their forgiveness. Elsie had shed a few tears of her own and assured Rosa that she was loved and they would do whatever they could to help her raise the baby. Mahlon hadn't disagreed, which she took as a sign that he too would offer his support to Rosa in her time of need. But he did quote some scriptures and instruct their daughter that she needed to get right with God and change her ways. After her father's lecture, Rosa assured him that she had confessed to God and wanted to move forward, putting her trust in the Lord.

Elsie released a heavy sigh. All that was good, but even so, she couldn't help being concerned about her eldest daughter. Not only was Rosa expecting a baby in May without the support of a husband, but it was also obvious that she pined for a love she couldn't have.

What a shame that Anthony is English. If he were Amish or even willing to become part of the Plain community, perhaps things could have worked out between them.

While Anthony had been staying with them, posing as Rosa's husband, Elsie had seen the looks of endearment that passed frequently between him and Rosa. *I'm sure what I observed was real,* she mused. *Although I know now that they were just pretending to be married, I don't think either of them realized that they'd fallen in love with each other. But as Rosa's mother, I knew from their actions and the expressions I observed on their faces that they both cared deeply for one another.*

Elsie remembered how during her own courting days and the early part of her marriage, she and her husband had looked at one another in a way that communicated to each other, as well as to others, that their love went deep. And even though Elsie's husband might not always say the words or look at her with the same tenderness in his eyes, she knew he still loved her. Mahlon's concern for Elsie during her battle with Graves' disease had been proof of that. He'd made sure that she got her proper rest, took her medicine regularly, and did everything the doctor had instructed her to do to help reduce some of her stress. Mahlon had also made sure that Elsie kept every one of her doctor's appointments, and he almost always went along to ask questions of the doctor.

Elsie picked up her pen and tapped it along the edge of the tablet. *I wish there was something I could do to ease Rosa's sorrow. It is my mother's prayer that she will be able to move on with her life and perk up soon.*

The sound of knocking on the front door pushed Elsie's thoughts aside. Since Tena was still in the basement and wasn't likely to hear the knock and Rosa was no doubt asleep, Elsie got up and rushed out of the kitchen to see who was on the front porch.

After opening the door, she was surprised to find Margaret, the young woman who taught the older grades at the schoolhouse where Alvin attended. Margaret's face looked flushed. She stood there, taking in deep, calming breaths.

"What is it, Margaret?" Elsie asked, a sense of concern welling in her soul. "Did something happen at the schoolhouse today that I should know about?"

The teacher slowly nodded. "It's your boy Alvin. Some of the scholars were sledding down the hill on the left side of the schoolhouse during their afternoon recess, and Alvin had an accident. Right now, he is on his way to the hospital via ambulance."

Elsie put one hand against her mouth and gasped. "Is it serious? Is my son going to be all right?"

"I hope so. One of the paramedics who arrived soon after we called for help said it looked like Alvin might have a concussion, as well as a broken arm." Margaret paused for a few seconds and clasped her hands together. "The driver who brought me here is waiting outside to give you a ride to the hospital. Are you free to come with me right now?"

"Of course. I just need to tell Tena, and then we can be off." All thoughts of letter writing or her concern for Rosa were set aside, as Elsie opened the basement door and hollered down to Tena. As soon as she arrived at the hospital, she would call Mahlon at the Meat and Cheese Store so he could get a driver to take him there too. Elsie's brain felt so rattled, she could barely think. *Maybe it would be best to ask Margaret's driver to stop by the store. That way Mahlon could accompany me to the hospital. Jah,* she told herself. *That makes more sense.*

CHAPTER 28

Lewistown, Pennsylvania

ELSIE SAT BESIDE MAHLON in one of the waiting rooms at the hospital, eager to learn how badly their son had been hurt. It was never easy to wait for answers—especially when one of her children was involved.

Unable to sit any longer, Elsie stood and began pacing the room, thankful that there were no people here at the moment to occupy any of the other chairs. It was bad enough that Mahlon kept eyeballing her; she didn't need strangers watching her every move too.

"Walking the floor won't give us the answers we seek one bit sooner," Mahlon called from the other side of the room. "Why don't you sit back down and try to relax? If you keep moving around like that, you'll wear out your shoes or maybe the floor."

Elsie stopped pacing and squinted at him. Wasn't he, too, apprehensive about the outcome of Alvin's injuries? Maybe Mahlon simply had more patience than she did when it came to waiting. Either way, it didn't matter. Elsie was a basket of nerves, and she couldn't help it.

She glanced at her husband, and seeing that his hands were folded and his eyes had closed, she felt certain that he was praying for Alvin. With all the strength she could muster, Elsie took a seat in the chair beside him and bowed her head in prayer. She should have been doing that in the first place, but for some reason, Elsie always spent time worrying and anticipating the outcome of things before finally resorting to prayer. How many times had she heard Mahlon or one of the other ministers in their church speak on this very topic?

Dear Lord, Elsie prayed silently, *please be with my youngest child, as he endures the tests that must be run in order to learn the extent of his injuries. And guide the doctors and nurses who are caring for him.*

Her eyes sprang open as negative thoughts pushed her prayer aside. She remembered last year reading one of the scribe's posts in *The Budget* newspaper, where he wrote about his young daughter who had been severely injured during a sledding accident that had occurred on their neighbors' property. Several children, including the scribe's daughter, had been taking turns sliding down a hill that was on the north side of their home. When it was his daughter Abby's turn, the poor child lost control, swerved, and slammed full speed into the bulky trunk of an unyielding tree. The girl was rushed to the hospital emergency room, just like Alvin had been a few hours ago. The poor child narrowly escaped with her life and ended up with some serious injuries including a skull fracture, crushed nose, broken collarbone, and dislocated shoulder. It took a skilled surgical team to repair the damage done to her face and head. But for the grace of God, the scribe said they could have lost his daughter.

I hope Alvin's injuries aren't that serious. Elsie struggled to hold back her tears. *I wish we could have been here to see our boy when he was first brought to the hospital. Maybe they don't want us to see him because his injuries are so severe.*

Elsie shifted her body to the right, trying to find a more comfortable position on the chair, as more doubts and fears set in. Tears continued to sting the back of her eyes, and she squeezed them shut. *These negative thoughts don't come from You, do they, Lord? Isn't that just like the enemy to sidetrack a person when they are praying, while trying to trust and seek God's will?*

Elsie heard their names called, and her eyes snapped open. A tall man with light brown hair and a mustache approached them. "Mr. and Mrs. Petersheim, I'm Dr. Yealey. Your son's CT scan and X-ray results are in, and I'm here to inform you that Alvin's right arm is broken, and he has a mild concussion." He paused briefly, then continued. "We will be setting his arm and putting it in a cast, and I feel that it's best to keep Alvin overnight for observation."

"If it's not a serious concussion, why can't we take him home this evening?" Mahlon asked.

"It's a precautionary measure," the doctor replied. "Just in case a problem should arise. We will be keeping a close watch on him, so try not to worry." He spoke with an air of assurance that gave Elsie some measure of comfort. It would be hard to go home without their son, but she understood the doctor's reasoning. Better to be safe than sorry. If they brought Alvin home too soon and he lost consciousness, she would never forgive herself for not listening to the doctor's advice.

"We understand," Mahlon said before Elsie could get the words out. "We'll be back tomorrow morning, and please give us a call right away if there are any problems we should know about."

Another thought popped into Elsie's head. "Dr. Yealey, would it be all right if I stayed here at the hospital all night and slept in a chair next to my son's bed? As his mother, I would feel better if I could see for myself that he's doing okay."

"I suppose that would be all right, but you probably won't rest well in a chair. I'll see if one of the nurse's aides can find a cot for you to sleep on." The doctor looked at Mahlon then. "Did you wish to stay the night too? If so, you might have to sleep out here in the waiting room, because Alvin's hospital room is too small for more than one cot."

Mahlon looked at Elsie. "What do you think? Will you be okay here by yourself, or would you prefer that I stay?"

She shook her head. "There's no need for that, Mahlon. You have chores to do at home, and someone needs to go home and give the girls a report on how Alvin's doing." Elsie gave his arm a few taps for added assurance. "I'll be fine."

"Okay then," he said. "I promise I'll be back early in the morning.

And don't worry about the store either," he added. "I'm sure that Norman and Susan can cope just fine without my help tomorrow."

Elsie nodded and managed to muster a brief smile. Although she probably wouldn't get much sleep tonight, at least she'd be in Alvin's room and could keep an eye on her precious boy. One thing was for sure, Alvin wouldn't be doing any more sledding for the rest of this winter. And if Elsie had her way, his sled would be put up in the hayloft where it would be out of sight and hopefully out of mind.

Belleville

"I could not believe it when Mom rushed in here to get Dad because Alvin's been hurt." Susan folded her arms and glared at Norman. "We weren't that busy, and you should have insisted that Dad put the CLOSED sign in the window so we could both go to the hospital with them. How are we supposed to get anything done when all we're thinking about is our little bruder?"

"You need to settle down and stop being so worked up about this." Norman spoke in a calm but firm tone. "We ought to pray, because there's nothing else we can do for Alvin right now. Even if we had gone along with our folks, all we could have done was sit with them in the waiting room and pray."

Susan's lips compressed into a thin line. "That may be, but I can't help wondering how badly Alvin was hurt, and if we'd gone to the hospital I'm sure we would have heard something by now."

Norman nodded. "I'm concerned about the state of his condition too. Sledding's a lot of fun, but it can also be dangerous."

Susan looked out the front window at the snow that had begun to fall. "I hate winter! There are too many dangerous things that can occur during the nasty, cold weather." She thumped the windowpane and turned to face Norman again. "Ice-skating and sledding are just two examples."

"You're right," he agreed. "Which is why anyone who chooses to engage in winter sports needs to be careful and take extra precautions."

Susan marched back over to the checkout counter where Norman stood. "You know who I blame for Alvin's accident?"

He shook his head.

"His teacher—that's who! She should not have allowed the kids to do any sledding in the schoolyard." Susan gave a huff. "Salina was a much better teacher than Margaret is, and I don't think the accident would have happened if Salina was still Alvin's teacher."

"What are you saying—that Salina should not have married me?"

Susan shrugged. "She was a good teacher, you know, and now she's trapped in the house, cooking, cleaning, mending your clothes, and doing all kinds of unpleasant chores." She leaned slightly forward, looking directly at her brother. "I'll tell you what, Norman—I never plan to get married. And I don't believe in true love anymore either. I'm not even looking for anyone to go on dates with. Even if some fellow were to ask me out, I'd say no, because after what Ben put me through, I'll never be able to trust another man."

"You can't compare all men to the way Ben acted, Susan. Lots of fellows are honest, kind, and good. You just need to be willing to give one of them a chance, if they should be interested in you."

She shook her head vigorously. "No way! Never! It's not gonna happen!"

"Okay then, but I know something that does need to happen."

Susan tipped her head. "What's that?"

"We both need to find something to do for the rest of the day, even if we have no customers." Norman pointed to the back section of the Meat and Cheese Store. "Why don't you check the expiration dates on all the dairy products, and I'll go to Dad's office and get some paperwork done."

Susan groaned. "Oh wow, those jobs sound like so much fun."

"We're not here to have fun," Norman reminded her. "We are employees in this store, and it's our job to see that it's running smoothly."

"Okay, big brother—whatever you say." Susan ambled off toward the back of the store. This day couldn't end soon enough. She hoped that by the time they were ready to put the Closed sign in the window, they'd have heard from Mom or Dad with some news about Alvin. Although Susan had teased her younger sibling many times over the years, Alvin was still her little brother, and she cared about him.

"Too bad no one cares about me," Susan mumbled as she approached the dairy case. "I'm not the number one daughter—that's for sure."

Rosa yawned, stretched her arms over her head, and pulled herself to a sitting position. She'd had a good long nap, and looking at the alarm clock on the nightstand near her bed, she realized that it was getting close to suppertime.

I need to get up and help Mom and Tena prepare our meal, she told herself. Angling her legs toward the side of the bed, she wiggled her toes a few times and stood. Her room was chilly, so she put on a sweater and stepped into a cozy pair of fleece-lined slippers. Since she had no plans to go outside, Rosa figured slippers were a better choice than putting on a pair of socks and shoes.

Rosa left the bedroom and went to the bathroom to freshen up. She'd taken her head covering off before lying down, and after a quick look in the mirror, she realized that her hair was a mess. She brushed her silky tresses and pulled them back into a bun, then set the white, heart-shaped head covering in place. She'd gone without any kind of head covering during the two-plus years she'd been away and had only worn modern, English clothes. After returning home and deciding it was best to wear Amish clothing some of the time, Rosa almost felt Amish again, even without having joined the church.

Becoming a member in the Amish church is something I still need to consider, Rosa told herself. *I'm sure it's the only way Dad will ever fully accept me.*

Rosa still missed some things about the English world, like electricity and the opportunity to drive a car and wear more stylish-looking clothes. But clothes weren't everything, and there were also some nice things about living the Amish way, such as the community spirit of the church people and a quiet, more simplified way of daily living. When any church member needed help, they could count on others to pitch in as needed. That was not always the case among those outside the Plain communities. Rosa had seen it in her travels. Yet until she'd gotten pregnant, she hadn't seriously considered returning home and joining her father's church.

If I do become a church member and raise my baby in the Amish lifestyle, will the child be better for it? Rosa moved away from the mirror. *Guess I should stop thinking so much and take one day at a time. It's not good to think too far ahead anyway. So many unexpected things can occur that a person has no control over.*

Rosa turned off the battery-operated light that had been placed on the bathroom vanity and left the room.

Downstairs in the kitchen, Rosa found Tena at the sink, rinsing several red-skinned potatoes she'd probably retrieved from the root cellar. No doubt they were some that Mom had grown in her garden this summer, because it wasn't likely that they had come from the grocery store.

"Where's Mom?" Rosa asked her sister. "Is she in her sewing room?"

Wearing a somber expression, Tena turned from her job at the sink to face Rosa. "Alvin got hurt while sledding in the schoolhouse yard this afternoon, and Mom and Dad are at the hospital with him."

Rosa's mouth went dry. "Oh my! How serious are his injuries?"

"I checked the phone shed a short time ago, and there was a message from Dad. He said Alvin has a concussion and a broken arm."

"Oh no! I'm so sorry to hear that. Do you know how long he will be at the hospital?"

"Dad said they are keeping him overnight, and Mom's gonna stay there with him. Dad should be coming home soon, and I'm sure his driver will stop and pick up Susan too. Since Norman has his own driver, he'll probably go home and give Salina the news."

Rosa drew in a deep breath and released it. "Thank the Lord our brother's injuries aren't any worse. Even though Alvin has been hurt, with some time and proper care, I'm sure he will heal and be right back to his playful self."

Tena nodded. "Jah, you can't keep our little bruder down very long."

Rosa thought about Anthony and wondered if she ought to make a trip to the phone shed to let him know about Alvin. It had been obvious during Anthony's stay here that he'd taken an interest in her young brother. She'd known that the feeling was mutual, because Alvin had hung on Anthony's every word.

But even if I did let Anthony know, Rosa thought, *there's nothing he can do about Alvin's injuries, and since he is not coming back here and will never be a part of this family, there's really no point in calling him. I'll just let the idea go and get busy helping Tena fix supper.*

CHAPTER 29

ALVIN HAD BEEN HOME FROM the hospital for three days, and Elsie was having a hard time keeping him down. The head injury had been a little worse than previously thought, so the doctor had sent explicit discharge orders that Alvin should stay home from school until he returned to the hospital for further testing in two weeks. Elsie had sent Tena to the schoolhouse to fetch whatever assignments Alvin would be expected to do, as she didn't want him to get behind. It was hard to keep the boy from becoming bored, however, because other than his arm hurting, Alvin said he felt fine. But he wasn't fine yet, and the fact that the doctor wanted them to bring Alvin back in two weeks for more tests was proof of that.

"I won't worry, Lord. I'll trust," Elsie murmured as she moved about the living room, washing the windows that faced their front yard. Today was another snowy day, and even though the snowflakes looked like delicate crystals dropping from the sky, she felt no joy in watching them. Elsie was eager for sunshine, blue skies, and warm spring days, when the trees and flowers would awaken from their winter sleep. She yearned to be on her knees in the garden again, turning over the dirt and planting seeds. What happiness it always brought when new shoots started popping through the soil, with the hope of becoming a strong, healthy plant. The sense of satisfaction that toiling in the garden brought to Elsie was beyond description. While others might have seen it as backbreaking, dirty labor, gardening brought her great pleasure.

Elsie leaned closer to the window she'd finished cleaning and craned her neck to gain a partial view of her spacious vegetable garden plot. Caring for it involved a lot of work, but she looked forward to the abundance of produce it would eventually bring. Hours of canning and freezing done in her kitchen during the summer months would be worth every hour spent when winter came again and the family could enjoy the fruits of Elsie's and her daughters' labor.

Elsie thought about Rosa and how she planned to have her baby here at home, with the help of the midwife Ida who lived a ways down the road. The middle-aged woman had come by a few times to see Rosa, and Elsie was glad that her daughter felt comfortable with the idea of having the baby here, rather than in a hospital.

Elsie's musings came to a halt when Alvin approached, touching her elbow with his good arm. "I'm *hungerich*, Mom. Will you have lunch ready for me to eat soon?"

"Tena and Rosa are in the kitchen, Son. They offered to fix the noon meal without my help today, so I could get the windows done."

He pointed at one glass pane and then the other. "They both look pretty clean to me."

"That's true, because I just finished washing them, but I have more windows to do yet in some of the other downstairs rooms."

Alvin looked up at her and said, "I'd help ya, but I can't do much with my broken *aarem*."

She patted his shoulder. "I know, and I don't expect you to do any work. There will be plenty of chores for you to do once your arm and head injury have healed."

"I hate bein' laid up right now. I'm bored, and I'd rather be in school or out playin' in the *schnee*." His youthful facial features sagged.

"As you may recall, Alvin, it was playing in the snow that sent you to the hospital."

He bobbed his head. "I know, but I wasn't playing, Mom. I was ridin' on a sled."

"Same difference." Elsie gestured to the kitchen door. "Now why don't you go see if your sisters have lunch ready?"

"Okay, Mom. I'll make sure they save you something to eat, 'cause I'm sure you'll be plenty hungerich by the time you're done with the windows."

"Jah, I'm sure that's true." Elsie smiled as she watched Alvin exit the room. He was a thoughtful boy, and someday she hoped he would grow up to be an equally considerate man.

New York City

Anthony unlocked the door to his apartment and was about to step inside when a familiar voice called out to him. He turned and saw the tall, shapely blond who lived a few doors down from him heading his way. He shifted the grocery sack he held into the other hand and waited for her.

"It's nice to see you again, Anthony." She batted the long lashes above her sky-blue eyes and smiled. "I haven't seen you around for some time. A few days ago, I stopped by the Italian restaurant where you work as a cook, and the woman who waited on me said you had taken an extended vacation. Is that true?"

"Yeah, Cindy, it was something like that. Oh, and to set the record straight, I don't work at that restaurant anymore. The owner of the place—who happens to be my father—fired me and hired someone to take my position."

"Seriously?"

"Yep."

"What made him do that? I mean, if you were on vacation, he had to know you'd be coming back."

Anthony didn't feel like going into detail about the length of his so-called vacation. So he replied with a shrug, "Guess things were busy, and my dad couldn't wait for me to get back." Anthony entered his apartment and was surprised when Cindy followed.

"Even so, I would think your dad would give your job back to you and let the other guy he hired go." Cindy joined Anthony in the kitchen, where he placed the sack on the counter near the sink.

"Yeah, that's what I figured too, but I've been known to be wrong, especially where my dad is concerned."

"What are you going to do now, Anthony? Will you look for another chef's position?"

"Yeah, and I found one this morning." He pulled a few canned items from the bag. "Well, it's not actually a chef's position, but I will be cooking."

"What's the name of the restaurant where you've been hired?"

"It's that fast food place on the corner of Thirteenth and Main."

Cindy's pale eyebrows shot up. "That's a big step down from the kind of cooking you're used to doing, wouldn't you say?"

"True, but it's better than no job at all." Anthony deliberately avoided looking at her as he unloaded his groceries. He hoped Cindy would take the hint and head on back to her own apartment or wherever she'd been going to when she spotted him.

"Are you low on money? Is that why you took a job beneath your abilities? If so, maybe I could give you a loan."

"No, I'm fine. I accepted the job offer so I'd have something to do." *Something other than think about Rosa and how much I miss her.* Anthony kept that thought to himself. Cindy didn't know anything about Rosa, and he planned to keep it that way. He'd been on a few dates with the attractive blond, but he didn't know her well enough to share the story about how he'd gone to the Big Valley with a waitress who had worked at his folks' restaurant and posed as her husband.

Now wouldn't that make a juicy piece of gossip to get going around the apartment complex, and who knows where else it could spread?

Anthony glanced at his watch then back at Cindy. "I'd like to chat more," he said, "but I have a ton of things to get done before the day is over." He gestured to the grocery items sitting on the counter. "Including figuring out what I'm going to have for supper."

"I can solve that problem for you," she said, moving closer to him. "Why don't you come over to my place for the evening? I'll fix you a

233

nice big juicy steak with some baked potatoes and a tossed green salad. I'll even serve some spumoni ice cream, if you're hungry enough to eat dessert after the meal."

Anthony's mouth watered at the mention of steak, and spumoni was one of his favorite ice cream flavors. But he wasn't in the mood for idle chitchat this evening, much less with a young woman whose interest in him seemed to go further than simply being apartment neighbors. The last thing Anthony needed was a romantic involvement with any woman right now.

"I appreciate the offer, Cindy," he stated, choosing his words carefully. "But as I said, I have a lot I need to do here this evening, so can I take a rain check?"

Her mouth opened slightly as she lowered her head a bit. "Sure. We'll get together another time. Just let me know when you're not so busy." Cindy turned and rushed out the door before Anthony could say anything more.

"Whew!" he exclaimed as a feeling of relief rushed over him. "I'm just not up to spending a few hours this evening with Cindy Duncan . . .or anyone else, for that matter."

Anthony pulled out a package of noodles and was about to put a kettle of water on the stove when his cell phone rang. He clasped his hands under his chin in a prayerlike gesture, although he didn't know why, because he wasn't a praying man. *Maybe it's Rosa, calling to give me an update on how she's doing.*

He eagerly pulled the phone out of his pocket, but when he saw his mother was calling, he let it go to voicemail. Anthony was in no mood for another pep talk from Mom, and he wasn't ready to tell her that he'd found a job cooking at a fast food restaurant either. The only person he wanted to speak with was Rosa, but unless she was, by some chance, sitting in the phone shed right now, it wasn't going to happen.

Guess I could call anyhow and leave a message for Rosa, asking her to give me a call. It would sure be nice to hear her voice.

Anthony punched in the Petersheims' number, and when their

voicemail came on, he left a message asking Rosa to give him a call. He figured she probably wouldn't get the message until sometime later today or maybe not even until tomorrow morning. Either way, at least she would know that he was thinking of her and hopefully would call him back. Anthony felt sure that even a few minutes of talking to Rosa would make him feel better, and maybe she might enjoy visiting with him too.

Belleville

When their driver dropped Susan and her father off from work that afternoon, while Dad went to the barn to check on the horses, Susan headed straight for the phone shed to see if there were any important messages.

Upon entering the frigid shack and seeing the light blinking on the answering machine, she discovered a message for Rosa from Anthony, which she promptly deleted.

"That guy left here after pretending to be someone he wasn't, for goodness' sake! Why is he bothering to keep in touch with my sister now?"

Then another idea hit Susan like a bolt of lightning. *Maybe Anthony's developed feelings for Rosa. He might even believe that he's in love with her. Well, if he is, that's just too bad. Rosa left home once, and it could have cost our mother her life. My sister doesn't deserve to be happy.*

Susan remained stiffly in place on the cold wooden chair, pondering things a few minutes, until tears gathered in the corners of her eyes. *Why does everyone love Rosa, and no one care about me? If Ben had truly loved me the way he'd said he did, he wouldn't have done something so horrible that it sent him to prison. Now we can never be together, and even if it were possible, I wouldn't want to be with someone like him, who I could never trust.*

After what Ben had pulled, by burning down numerous barns in Mifflin County, Susan didn't think she could ever trust another man not to betray her.

Of course, no one has shown an interest in me since Ben left, Susan reminded herself. *So I guess I have nothing to worry about. I just wish I could come up with some way to make my life more fulfilling, because I'm bored out of my mind and can't imagine any kind of a happy future. I will certainly never get married or have children. At least Rosa has the birth of her baby to look forward to. I, on the other hand, have no hope of becoming a mother.*

Tears coursed down Susan's cheeks and dripped onto her woolen jacket. *Maybe I should start reading the Bible on my own and stop tuning out the verses Dad reads to us after breakfast every morning. Who knows? Maybe I'll find some answers from God's Word.*

༺ ༻

Rosa woke up the following morning, and when she pulled her covers aside, she was shocked to discover several blood spots in her bed. She rushed out of the room, hollering, "Mom, I need you right now. Please hurry, and come *schnell*!"

"What is it, Rosa?" Mom questioned after hurrying up the stairs.

On the brink of tears, Rosa heard her voice tremble as she exclaimed, "Mom, I'm bleeding, and I'm afraid I may lose the baby."

Mom gasped, and she covered her mouth with one hand. "Let's get you back to bed and off your feet, and I'll send your daed out to call for a driver. We need to get you to the hospital right away!"

Rosa quivered as she made her way back to her room and crawled into bed. *Heavenly Father*, she prayed fervently, *please don't let me lose this baby.*

CHAPTER 30

"I'M REALLY SCARED, MOM." Rosa's chin trembled as she reclined on the downstairs guest bed, where she'd been placed when they got home from the hospital. "I don't want anything to happen to my unborn baby."

Mom took a seat beside Rosa and rubbed her legs gently. "The doctor will keep a close eye on things, and he did say that there's a good chance that the baby will be fine if you do everything he suggested."

Rosa heaved a sigh. "How long do you think I'll have to be on full bed rest?"

"I don't know, dear one. Guess it all depends on whether the bleeding subsides and how well you obey the doctor's orders not to be up and around for anything except use of the bathroom or to take a shower. Once the bleeding stops, I'm sure you'll be allowed to be on partial bed rest, which means it will likely be okay to sit, stand, or even walk around for short periods of time. Of course," Mom added, "you won't be able to resume regular household duties—at least not until the doctor says it's safe to do so."

"Thanks for allowing me to move down here to the guest room and for bringing down all the things I need as well."

"It wouldn't be good for you to go up and down the stairs," Mom responded with furrowed brows. "Also, having you here will make it easier for me to tend to your needs, and you won't have to share a *baadschtubb* with your siblings upstairs—just me and your daed in the bathroom down here."

"True. And since Dad's not home when he's working at the store, I'll only have to share the downstairs necessary room with you and Tena."

Mom grinned. "Good point."

"It's gonna be hard to lie around in bed all day." Rosa leaned into the bed pillows Mom had plumped up for her. "It'll be boring, and I'll end up feeling sorry for myself."

"You can read or write letters to your friends—maybe even send one to Anthony," her mother suggested. "Do you have his address?"

Rosa shook her head. "No, and I've never been to his place. All I know is that he lives in an apartment a few blocks from his parents' restaurant." She discovered she was crying, and she rubbed at the tears on her cheeks. *Great—now I'm crying. Mom probably thinks I'm nothing but a big baby.*

"It's okay, Daughter," Mom said, stroking Rosa's face. "You have every right to shed a few tears today. "But fear not, Rosa, once the word gets out about you being bedridden, many people will pray for you."

"I hope God will listen."

"Of course He will. Our Father in heaven hears every believer's prayer, and He always answers too, although sometimes His ways are not our ways, and His answer might not be what we want."

Rosa bit the inside of her lower lip. "What are you saying, Mom? Do you think God wants my baby to die? Would He cause me to lose the child in order to punish me for becoming pregnant out of wedlock?"

"I'm not saying that at all." Mom clasped Rosa's trembling hand. "The fact is the Lord knows what is best for each of us, and if by some chance you do end up losing the baby, God will give you the strength to deal with it."

"I don't want to deal with it." Rosa's voice caught on a sob as she placed her free hand against her protruding belly. "I want this child growing inside of my womb, and with every ounce of my being, I shall pray and ask God to stop the bleeding and allow me to carry my little one to full term."

"I will pray for that as well." Mom rose from the bed. "I'm going to the kitchen to fix you a cup of herbal tea. Hopefully it will help you relax so you can take a much-needed nap." She started across the room but paused at the door and turned around. "Is Anthony's phone number posted somewhere out in the shed?"

"Jah, I wrote it on one of the empty index cards and put it in the small wooden box where all our important phone numbers are kept."

"Well, good. Sometime today, either when Tena gets back from the errands I sent her on a while ago or Susan returns home from work, I'll ask one of them to put in a call to Anthony so he'll be aware of what's happened with you."

"That's really not necessary, Mom. Anthony is just a good friend who cared enough to try to solve my concerns about returning home. I had told him that as an unwed mother, I would probably not be accepted here." Tears clogged the back of Rosa's throat, and she was unable to say anything more.

"Rosa, my dear daughter—we would have accepted you back without you and Anthony pretending to be married." Now it was Mom's turn to tear up, and she sniffed a couple of times. But it was no use—a few slipped out and splashed onto the bodice of her solid-gray dress. "I am sorry, Rosa," she said. "It looks like we're both letting our emotions get the best of us today. But on the other hand, it's not good to keep things bottled up inside."

Rosa had to admit that her mother's statement was correct. Even so, there was no way she would reveal to Mom or anyone else in the family the way she truly felt about Anthony.

⁓♥⁓

When Susan arrived home after another boring workday and entered the house with her father, she was surprised to find out from Tena that Rosa had been put on bed rest due to unexpected bleeding. While she took no pleasure in knowing that her sister could lose the baby, Susan couldn't help wondering if, should she lose her child, Rosa might abandon her family and strike out on her own again. Susan felt certain that the only reason Rosa had returned home in the first place was because she needed her family's help to raise the child that had been conceived out of wedlock.

"Where's your mamm?" Dad asked Tena. "Is she with Rosa?"

"I don't believe she's with her at the moment," Tena replied. "When I got home from running errands this afternoon, Mom was in one of the downstairs guest rooms with Rosa, but then she went to the other guest room to check on Alvin, so she's probably still with him."

"Oh boy! This is not what your mother needs right now." Dad sank into a chair at the kitchen table with a groan. "She's been running herself ragged waiting on Alvin and making sure that he does his homework, and now she has Rosa to take care of."

Tena stepped up beside their father's chair with one hand anchored against her hip. "Aren't you even concerned about Rosa, Dad? Don't you realize that if the bleeding doesn't stop, she could lose her baby?"

"Of course I'm concerned. It's just that—"

"Since I don't have a job outside of the home, I'll be here to help Mom take care of Alvin and Rosa," Tena was quick to say. Then she glanced over at Susan. "I'm sure that Susan will also help out whenever she's not working at the store. "Right?"

Susan bobbed her head. What else could she do, with both Tena and Dad looking at her with expectant expressions?

"Good to know." Dad reached behind his head and began massaging his neck.

Susan figured he was probably feeling as stressed as she was right now, only for different reasons. She didn't need more work piled on her right now. Between her hours at the Meat and Cheese Store and her chores at home, Susan had enough work to do.

It's not fair, she thought. *I never get any time for myself.* Susan couldn't remember the last time she'd done something fun. *It was probably back when Ben and I were a couple—before I knew what he was really like. Guess I should have listened to Norman's and Salina's warnings about Ben Ebersol. But I was so taken with him—and thought I was in love. Was it any wonder that I didn't believe anything negative that was said about him?* Susan's shoulders slumped as her gaze fell to the floor.

"Susan, did you hear what I said?"

Her head came up. "Huh? What was that, Dad?"

"I asked you to go see if your mamm needs any help with Alvin, while I go check on Rosa."

"Oh...umm...okay. I'll go see her right now." Susan darted out of the kitchen and went straight for the smaller of the two guest rooms. She found Alvin sitting at a small study table Dad had brought into the room the day Alvin came home from the hospital. Mom stood beside him with a book in her hand.

"Sorry. Did I interrupt something?" Susan asked, quickly moving to her mother's side.

"Not really," Mom replied. "I was reading one of the assignments to your brother that his teacher sent home with Tena when she went by the schoolhouse earlier today." She turned her head toward Susan. "I presume Tena told you and your daed about the situation with Rosa?"

"Jah. It's too bad. What brought it on, do you know?"

"No, but the doctor said it could have been one of several possibilities that started the bleeding. He's put Rosa on full bed rest for now, and I moved several of her things to the other downstairs guest room, because in her present condition, she shouldn't be going up or down the stairs."

"That makes sense. Will she be staying there until the baby's born, or do you think she night miscarry?" Susan questioned.

"She'll be staying in the room down here for as long as necessary. I hope and pray, as we all should, that Rosa will carry her baby to full term."

"Jah, of course. We all wish that." Susan considered the best way to form her next question. "Umm...since Rosa will be staying down here, probably for the next few months, and her room upstairs will be sitting empty, would it be okay if I moved my things in there and took over her room?"

Mom opened her mouth as if to respond, but Susan cut her off. "Even after the baby comes, it would make more sense for Rosa to remain in the downstairs bedroom, where she wouldn't have to go up and down stairs. Don't you think?"

Bright pink circles erupted on Mom's cheeks, and she shook her finger at Susan. "I cannot believe you would ask me such a question, but since you did, then I will make sure to say this clearly enough so you won't bring the topic up again. You may not move your things into Rosa's room unless at some point after the baby comes she decides to remain downstairs permanently and agrees to give up her room."

Mom spoke with such conviction and in a louder voice than usual, which let Susan know she'd lost the battle. Once again, Rosa the favored one had won out without even knowing it.

"Guess I'll go help Tena get supper started," Susan mumbled.

"That would be appreciated," Mom said. "Oh, and would one of you please go out to the phone shed and call Anthony? His number is posted in the shed near the phone. I'm sure he would want to know about Rosa's condition."

"Sure, Mom. I'll take care of that myself."

"Danki, I appreciate it."

Why does Anthony need to know anything about Rosa? He's not her husband, for goodness' sake, Susan thought as she left the room and returned to the hallway where she'd hung her outer garments when first arriving home. *Tena can start supper while I'm outside in the frigid weather. That's just fine with me.*

New York City

Anthony was about to start cooking supper when his cell phone rang. He picked it up from the counter near the sink to see who was calling. He'd hoped it might be Rosa, responding to his last message, but no, it was Mom.

"I suppose I may as well answer it," Anthony muttered. "If I don't, she'll just keep calling, wanting to know how I'm doing." Anthony couldn't fault her for that, because if he were a parent, he'd be interested in how his children were doing, even if they were fully grown and living on their own.

"Hi, Mom," Anthony said after he'd answered the call. "How's it going?"

"Fine on this end, I suppose, but the reason I called is to ask how you're doing. Any prospects of a job yet?"

"Uh. . .yeah. . .in fact, I landed one yesterday."

"Oh, good. Which restaurant owner is the lucky person to have hired my son, the brilliant and talented chef?"

Anthony lifted his gaze toward the ceiling. "Come on, Mom. Don't you think you're just a wee bit prejudiced?"

"It's a mother's prerogative to be proud of her son, so it's okay for me to do a little bragging when I want to."

He chuckled. "Okay."

"So where will you be cooking from now on?"

Anthony grimaced. *Guess I may as well tell her and get it over with, 'cause it's not likely that she'll drop the subject till I do.*

"I'll be cooking at one of the fast food places not far from here."

"What? Would you please repeat that?"

"I said, I'll be cooking at one of the fast food places not far from here."

There was silence on the other end, and Anthony figured his mother was trying to process this and would no doubt have something to say about it once the shock wore off. He wasn't wrong.

"You've got to be kidding, Son. That position is beneath your abilities as a mighty fine chef. What were you thinking, accepting a job at a fast food restaurant? If you can even call it a restaurant," she added.

"I was thinking that I needed to earn a living, and this was the only place willing to hire me, so I took it."

"Oh, Anthony—I'm so sorry your dad won't consider giving you your job back. I'm sure we could make it work if he'd be willing to take some time off and let you act as head chef, with Billy working under you."

"Yeah, right, Mom. Like that's ever gonna happen. You know how stubborn Pop can be once he makes up his mind about something. Besides, I can't imagine him taking any time off and turning things over to me." Anthony paused to formulate his next sentence. "Let's face the facts, Mom—Pop's mad at me for leaving New York and going with Rosa to see her folks. And the fact that I got stuck there due to circumstances that were not of my making and were out of my control doesn't mean a thing as far as Pop is concerned. I have to wonder if he thinks that I planned it that way, just to make his life difficult at the restaurant." Anthony's face heated, and he knew it wasn't from the warmth in the room.

"Listen, Mom, there's no point in going over all this. I lost my job at the restaurant, Pop's not going to hire me back, and I am moving on with my life. Even if the new job isn't to my liking, I'm gonna do my best to make it work. Do you understand and support me in that decision?"

"Well, since you put it that way, as your mother, who loves you very much and cares about our relationship, I don't have any choice but to accept whatever decision you have made."

"Thanks, Mom, I appreciate that." Anthony glanced across the room at the circular pan he'd set out in preparation for creating one of his favorite pizza pies. "It's been nice talking to you, Mom, but I'm getting ready to fix my supper, and I'm hungry."

"I understand, so I won't keep you any longer, but please keep in touch. Okay?"

"Of course. Bye for now, Mom." Anthony clicked off and silenced his phone, although he figured his mother probably wouldn't call again tonight. All he wanted right now was some peace and quiet and to be left alone to create and eat the kind of mouthwatering meal he'd become so good at making.

"Mom's right," Anthony said aloud. "I shouldn't be working somewhere like a fast food place. But it'll have to do until something better comes along, so I'll make the best of it until that time."

Belleville

When Susan entered the phone shed, she found Anthony's number, but instead of making the call to him, she sat there on the frosty chair, shivering while mulling things over. *If I make the call, Anthony might be worried and head right on back here to see how Rosa is doing. If I'm not mistaken, he had a thing for her, although I don't know if he ever confessed his feelings to her.*

Susan tapped her cold fingers on the wooden shelf where the phone sat. *On the other hand, if I don't let Anthony know about Rosa's condition, I will have to lie to Mom when she asks if I made the call.*

Susan shrugged her shoulders. *Well, I've lied to her before, so what's one more untruth gonna hurt? I'll just say I made the call and left him a message, and Mom will be none the wiser.*

She stared out the small window at the dense fog that had found its way into the valley and flexed her fingers a few times. It made no sense that her sister could have bold-faced lied to their parents about Anthony and been forgiven—at least by Mom. Susan wasn't sure how Dad felt about Rosa these days. But he hadn't thrown her out of his home—only Anthony had been given the boot. And it certainly wasn't fair that Mom had always seemed to care more about Rosa than she did Susan.

There's absolutely no reason I can't have Rosa's room now that she isn't sleeping there. It's not fair. Nothing in my life has ever been fair, so why should I be fair to others?

When the frigid temperature inside the phone shed got to be more than Susan could handle, she opened the door and stepped outside. Walking as fast as her cold legs would allow and being careful of her footing, she soon entered the house.

After removing her outer garments, Susan went to the kitchen.

She was surprised to see her mother there, helping Tena peel and cut potatoes.

"Did you reach Anthony?" Mom asked, glancing at Susan.

"Jah, it's done." Susan approached her mother. "You look really tired, Mom. If you want to go rest awhile or check on Rosa, I'll help Tena make our supper."

Mom offered Susan a weary smile. "Danki, Daughter. That's thoughtful of you. Think I will go to the living room and sit by the fire for a while. But please call me if you need my help, okay?"

"I'm sure we won't need your help, Mom," Susan was quick to say. "Go enjoy the warmth of the fire. We'll call you and Dad when supper is ready."

"And we'll let Alvin know too," Tena interjected. "At least he's able to come to the table." She heaved a sigh. "I feel so sorry for Rosa. It can't be easy to be confined to her bed. I'll take her a tray as soon as the meal is ready to serve."

"I'm sure she'll appreciate that." Mom smiled at both Susan and Tena before leaving the kitchen.

Susan grabbed a peeler and, holding it over the sink, started working on one of the larger potatoes. She was glad Mom hadn't asked her what Anthony's response had been when she'd told him about Rosa.

Susan began peeling hard and fast. *If she had asked, I was prepared to say I didn't talk directly to Anthony but left him a message. At least I wouldn't have had to make up anything about Anthony's response, and for that, I'm thankful.*

CHAPTER 31

Allensville

"Before you leave for work this morning, would you mind hitching my horse to the buggy?" Ada asked Ephraim as they ate breakfast together.

He yawned and stretched his jaw. "I thought you were planning to stay home all day and rest."

"There's too much going on around here for me to spend the day sitting or doing nothing. Besides, I want to head over to the Petersheims' to see how Rosa is doing. She's been confined to her bed for a week now, and I haven't gone to see her yet."

"I'm sure she would appreciate a visit from you," Ephraim said as he reached for his cup of coffee. "But if you keep doing so much around here, plus running errands and taking the time to visit people, you might end up on bed rest too."

Ada waved away his concerns. "You worry too much, Husband. I know my limits, and I'm feeling just fine."

"I'm sure Rosa's husband must be worried about her." Ephraim took a drink of coffee and shrugged his shoulders. "Well, at least I was able to talk you into quitting your job at the greenhouse and staying home where you can rest when you feel mied." His brows furrowed. "Of course, you always seem to find something to keep yourself busy, so you're probably tired most of the time and just won't admit it."

"I'm not always tired, and it's not in my nature to sit around and

247

do nothing. As you know, I enjoy keeping busy, and I'd be bored silly if I wasn't doing something beneficial."

Ephraim reached over and laid his hand on her arm. "I am well aware." He finished his coffee and put on his hat and jacket. "I'll get your horse ready for you now, and then I'd better be on my way to the harness shop."

When Ada stood, Ephraim came around and gave her a kiss. "Be careful today, okay? Not only while driving the horse and buggy, but in everything else you do."

"I will, and I hope you'll do the same." She stroked his chin where his beard had begun to grow nicely. "And I hope things go well for you at work."

He kissed her again. "They'll be even better when I get home this evening and can spend time with my sweet *fraa*."

When Ephraim went out the back door, Ada headed to the sink with her empty plate and silverware. There weren't too many breakfast dishes, so she'd have plenty of time to get them washed, dried, and put away before leaving for Belleville. She looked forward to seeing Rosa and offering some words of encouragement.

Belleville

"Rosa, are you awake? You have a visitor," Mom called from the hallway outside the bedroom door where Rosa lay, propped against two supporting pillows.

"*Jah*, I'm awake." Although Rosa had no idea who'd come to see her, she welcomed the company, knowing it would help stamp out her boredom, if only for a little while.

The door opened and Mom entered the room with Ada. The sight of her dear friend's pretty face brought tears of appreciation to Rosa's eyes.

"It's so good to see you," she said, reaching her hand toward Ada.

"It's wonderful to see you as well. I was sorry to hear about your condition and wanted to come by and offer my support."

Mom pulled the desk chair close to the bed for Ada and suggested that she sit down. "I have some things to do in the kitchen, so I'll leave you two alone to chat."

After Rosa's mother left the room, Ada took a seat and clasped Rosa's hand. "How are you feeling? Has the bleeding stopped?"

"I'm still spotting, but it's not as heavy as it was." Rosa heaved a sigh. "I hate having to spend all my time in bed, but I will do anything to make sure I don't lose my baby."

"I would too, if faced with the same situation." Ada's gentle brown eyes matched the sincere tone of her voice.

They both sat quietly for a few seconds, and Ada spoke again. "I've been praying for you, Rosa, but if there's anything else I can do, please let me know."

"I don't know what it would be. You're expecting a baby too, and you shouldn't be worried about taking care of anyone but yourself." Rosa leaned back against her pillows again. "Besides, between Mom and Tena, I have plenty of help with my care."

"What about your husband? I'm sure he's deeply concerned and has probably been waiting on you hand and foot."

Rosa shook her head. "Anthony returned to his home in New York, and..." She paused to compose herself.

"And what?"

"The truth is, Ada, Anthony and I are not married, and we never were. He's not even my baby's father."

"What?" Ada's mouth formed an O, and her eyebrows shot straight up. "Are you serious, Rosa?"

"Yes, I am finally telling you the truth." More words rushed out of Rosa's mouth as she filled Ada in on the details of how she had come to know Anthony when she'd been hired as a waitress at his parents' restaurant.

"Our original plan," Rosa went on to say, "was for Anthony to stay for only a few days. Then we would stage a big argument and tell my parents that we'd made a mistake getting married and that Anthony would be going back to New York to get a divorce. Of course, he couldn't really get one, since we had never gotten married."

Ada's eyes widened, and she blinked rapidly. "Why would you make up such a story?"

"We came up with the idea, figuring that if my folks thought we were married and believed Anthony was the father of my child, they would allow me to come home." Rosa swallowed against the constriction in her throat. "I figured that if my parents believed our story, they would allow me to stay on after Anthony returned to New York. I also needed their help raising my baby."

Rosa lowered her hand to her belly and gave in to the tears forthcoming. "Only now there may not be a baby, and even though Mom has forgiven me for lying to them, I'm not sure about Dad."

Ada leaned forward and then back, as though she were in a rocking chair. "Oh, Rosa, I had no idea all of this was going on." She pulled her fingers through the ends of her head-covering ties. "Surely your parents didn't accept the idea of you and Anthony getting a divorce."

"They didn't have to accept it, Ada, because Anthony and I owned up to everything. Instead of faking a breakup, we told them the truth—that we had never gotten married and what we had made plans to do."

"I'll bet that didn't go over well."

"No, it did not, and Dad ordered Anthony to leave, which he did the following morning." Rosa reached for a tissue from the table beside her bed and blew her nose. "Beginning with the rebellious years of my Rumspringa all the way up to now, I've made such a mess out of my life." She paused to wipe her eyes. "What's wrong with me, anyhow? Why can't I make the right decisions?"

"We all make wrong decisions," Ada said. "I have found that the best way to stay on track and do right is to keep my focus on God and not my own selfish ambitions. Reading the Bible, and spending time in prayer, helps me stay on the straight and narrow."

"You've certainly done that well, Ada, and now you are married to Ephraim and expecting your first child. I'm happy for you, and I believe you will both make good parents."

"With God's help, I hope so, but I'm sure we will make some mistakes along the way. That's just how it is, because none of us humans are perfect."

Rosa lowered her head. "I'm certainly not, but I'm trying to do better, and with God's help, I want to raise my baby in the best way possible."

Ada leaned closer. "Can I ask you a personal question?"

"Of course."

"You've admitted that you and Anthony are not married, and that he isn't the father of your baby."

"That's correct. My relationship with the baby's biological father, who I never should have been with, was wrong." Rosa sniffed, hoping to avoid further tears. "I've confessed my sin to God and asked Him to forgive me."

"That's good. That's what God's Word says we should do when we sin."

They sat quietly for a while, and then Ada posed a question. "How do you feel about Anthony?"

"He's a kindhearted friend."

"Okay, but how do you *feel* about him?"

"I'm grateful he cared enough to bring me here."

Ada's mouth opened as if she was prepared to say something more, but then she closed it.

"Is there something else you wanted to say?" Rosa questioned.

"Yes, and I would like you to be completely honest with your answer."

"Okay."

"Are you in love with Anthony?"

"Well...umm..."

"The expression I saw on your face when the two of you came to the greenhouse together was very convincing."

"How so?" Rosa turned her head to the left to glance out the window before looking back at Ada.

"What I saw was a look of love. Can you deny that you have strong feelings for Anthony?"

"It wouldn't matter if I did." Rosa lowered her gaze to the Lone Star quilt covering the lower half of her body. "Anthony doesn't love me, and except for the one brief conversation we had on the phone when he returned to New York, he's made no effort to contact me."

"He must feel something for you, Rosa, or he wouldn't have brought you home. And although it was wrong, he did try to protect you from any disapproval of your parents by pretending that the two of you were married."

"He only did that because he's a nice guy, who cares about people. I witnessed that plenty of times at the restaurant in New York where he cooked. Sometimes a homeless person would come in, just to get out of the weather for a bit, and Anthony would cover the cost of their meal. And he always spoke kindly to everyone."

Ada began rocking in the chair again. Rosa wondered if she might be practicing for the time when her own baby would be born. Or maybe her dear friend rocked in an effort to keep the air between them peaceful. It wasn't that they'd never had any big disagreements, but things had become strained when Rosa became so rebellious during their teen years. Ada had tried to reason with Rosa several times back then, especially regarding some wrong choices she'd made. Perhaps she had come here to do that again, only this time it had to do with Anthony. Maybe Ada thought Rosa should admit her true feelings for him, but that was not going to happen, because admitting it to her friend would be admitting it to herself. Rosa was not willing to do that—especially when it served no purpose, since Anthony was never coming back to the Big Valley.

It's better that way, Rosa thought. *If I saw him again, I might drown in a puddle of tears.*

⁓⁓

"I'm bored, Mom. When can I go back to school?"

Elsie slipped a tray of peanut butter cookies into the oven and moved over to the table to stand beside the chair where Alvin sat working on an assignment for school. "The doctor said you could return to school on Monday, and that's just a few days from now, so you won't be bored much longer."

He let out a noisy snort. "I wanna go to school, but it'll be just as bad as stayin' home all day 'cause I'll be stuck inside." He lifted his broken arm and with his good arm pointed to the cast. "The teacher's not gonna let me go outside and play in the schnee with the other kids."

"That's true, Son. When I saw your teacher after church last Sunday, I reminded her to keep you in during recess, so there is no chance of you getting hurt again."

Alvin's lips pressed into a tight grimace as he sagged against the back of his chair. "It ain't fair, Mom. I'm sure not looking forward to standin' at the window and watchin' all the other *kinner* outside having fun in the schnee. Pretty soon, it'll be spring, and then there'll be no snow to play in."

"There's always next year." Elsie gave his shoulder a tender squeeze and went back to the counter to start placing more cookie dough on a second tray. Having two people in the house suffering from boredom at the same time was a bit too much for her to cope with. Thankfully, Ada had come by earlier, so Elsie figured Rosa's boredom had been put aside, at least until her friend went home.

New York City

Anthony didn't have to be at work until noon, so he took a seat in his favorite reclining chair and pulled the handle on the side to put up his feet. He was about to reach for the remote to turn on the TV when he caught sight of the Bible Rosa must have put in his duffel bag. He'd placed it there the other day but hadn't looked at it since. He felt a strange pull to pick it up and read a few verses. Anthony had never been that interested in what the Bible had to say before now. Even while staying in the Petersheims' home, Anthony hadn't been inclined to really listen when Mahlon read some passages of scripture each morning. And as far as getting anything out of the messages the Amish ministers had preached during church services, Anthony hadn't the foggiest notion of what was being said. With the preaching and reading from the Bible being done in German, he couldn't understand any of the words.

Why am I curious now, though? he wondered. *Am I really so bored that I would turn to the Bible for entertainment, or is it possible that there's an unknown voice in my head directing me to read from this book because I'm lacking something in my life?*

Anthony thumbed through a few pages in the Old Testament, where some verses had been underlined with a red pen. "Strange. Really strange," he said aloud. *Why would anyone underline these particular verses?*

Feeling a need to do so, Anthony read the first verse out loud. "'For I know the thoughts that I think toward you, says the Lord, thoughts of peace and not of evil, to give you a future and a hope.' Jeremiah 29:11."

"Hmm. . .I wonder if that verse applies to me, or was it meant for someone in the Bible? Maybe God was talking to a man named Jeremiah, and it has nothing to do with me or anyone else who might read the Bible."

With the way things had been going in Anthony's life, he certainly needed some peace and a hope for his future. But was this scripture something he could cling to? Were any of the verses in the Bible meant for him, or were they only for religious folks, like the Amish people who attended the Petersheims' church?

Anthony set the Bible aside, clicked the lever, and rose from his chair. Like it or not, the only future he had today was going to work at a job he didn't like.

CHAPTER 32

Belleville

After the weeks of winter had faded away, bringing warmer days in the early part of May, Rosa's condition had improved. She was now able to sit, walk, and do a few easy tasks when she wasn't resting. The doctor said she should remain downstairs for the rest of her pregnancy and that if things kept going well, it shouldn't be a problem for Rosa to have a home birth in the care of her midwife.

Alvin seemed to enjoy being back in school, and he said he was thankful that he no longer had to wear his cast. For a while, his arm had been stiff, but certain exercises had helped to get his range of motion back.

Overall, things were back to normal in the Petersheim household, except for the ache Rosa had felt in her heart ever since Anthony returned to New York. Rosa had known when he left that she'd probably never see him again, but she'd hoped he might keep in touch by calling once in a while to see how she was doing.

It's probably just as well, Rosa told herself as she sat on the front porch the first Saturday of May, watching numerous birds flitter from tree to tree as they took their turn at the various feeders Tena had set out.

"Mind if I join you?" Mom asked, taking a seat next to Rosa.

"Of course not." Rosa mustered a smile.

"The weather is quite nice today, jah?"

"For sure, and it's good to spend a few minutes outside where we can watch the birds and breathe in some fresh air."

"Speaking of birds," Mom said, pointing to the grassy area of their front yard, "do you see those two frisky robins that have both pulled up fresh worms?"

Rosa eyed the birds in question and nodded. "Those busy birds showed up soon after all the winter snow melted."

"That's usually how it goes." Mom glanced at the empty wrought-iron shepherd's hooks closest to the porch. "Soon it'll be time to get the hummingbird feeders out and fill them with nectar. I always look forward to that."

"Me too. Or at least I did before I took off on my own." Rosa pulled in some air and released it with a groan. "I've said it before, but I can't begin to tell you how guilty I feel for running off like that and causing you and the rest of the family to worry about me." *Well, maybe not Susan*, Rosa thought. *I doubt that she missed me at all.*

Mom reached for Rosa's hand and gave her fingers a gentle squeeze. "What's done is done, Rosa. You can't change the past, and you've apologized. It's time to move forward with your life and look to the future."

"I know, and I'm trying. It's just hard to forgive myself for hurting you."

"I've forgiven you, Daughter, but have you asked God's forgiveness?"

"Yes, but. . ."

"There are no buts. If you have confessed your wrongs to the Lord, and asked Him to forgive you, then your wrongdoing has been forgiven and you must stop dwelling on it." Mom spoke with conviction. "What you must do now is be a good mother to your child when it's born in a few months and commit your life to the heavenly Father."

Rosa's head moved slowly up and down. "Must I join the Amish church in order to do that?"

Mom tapped her fingers on the arms of her chair. "Your *daed* would probably say that in addition to confessing your sins, you should take classes in preparation of joining the church and becoming a baptized member."

"Is that what you believe I should do, Mom?"

"Only if you truly want to, but if you don't feel led to join the Amish church, there are other options."

"Such as?"

"You could attend, and eventually join, one of the Mennonite churches in the area, or perhaps one of the evangelical churches that preach holiness." Rosa's mother looked at her with a steady gaze. "I have to admit, it would be nice if you became a member in our Amish church district, but it's entirely up to you. I don't think you should be pressured either way. The decision must be yours."

Rosa appreciated her mother's understanding, and she said so. "I hope during the years when I am raising my child that I'll be as thoughtful and supportive as you are, Mom."

"If you give God first place in your life, He will guide and direct you all the days of your life."

Rosa nodded. "Yes, Mom, that's exactly what I plan to do. I just don't know yet if it will include joining the Amish church."

"Well, whatever decision you make, I'll be praying that it will be the right one for both you and the baby."

◈

"How come you hardly ever smile?" Noah Esh asked as he stood in front of the checkout counter inside the Meat and Cheese Store, waiting for Susan to bag up the items he'd purchased.

Susan wrinkled her nose as she squinted at him. "There's not much to smile about."

He reached under his straw hat and tweaked his left earlobe. "Are you serious? If you look around, there's always something to smile or laugh about."

"Like what?"

"For one thing, this beautiful weather we're having. Blue skies and sunshine—those two things alone are enough to make me feel joyous."

"Good for you. The weather's still a little too chilly for my liking." She slipped the meat and cheese packages into a paper sack and handed it to him.

"So you prefer the warmer months of summer?"

Susan shrugged. "Mostly. But not when it gets too hot or so muggy that your clothes stick to your skin like flypaper."

He leaned forward a bit, arms resting on the counter. "If I'm hearing you right, it's only perfect weather—not too hot—not too cold—that would put a smile on your face?"

Susan took a step back. She didn't appreciate having someone in her space—especially a good-looking fellow like Noah, with hair the color of straw and eyes so blue a person could get lost in the depths of them. It wasn't that Susan had any interest in the young harness maker's apprentice. Or maybe he'd surpassed that title by now and had become a full-fledged, able-bodied harness maker. For all Susan knew, Noah might be as good at the trade as Ephraim Peight and his dad. Either way, it didn't matter, because she had no interest in him at all, other than to take his money whenever he came into the store for meat and cheese. Susan was pretty sure that Noah probably had a girlfriend, anyway. Most young Amish women her age were looking for nice-looking fellows with a steady job, hoping for a marriage proposal if they found an acceptable man. Not Susan, though. After what Ben had put her through, she was done with men.

"How come you're looking at me so strangely?"

Noah's question put an end to Susan's musings. "Oh, I was just thinking about something. It didn't pertain to you, though."

"That's good. I thought maybe part of my lunch had been left on my face." Noah chuckled.

Susan made no comment, nor did she crack a smile.

"Do you like to fish?" he asked, making no move to leave the store.

Susan shook her head. "Not particularly. Why do you ask?"

"Because fishing can be a lot of fun, and it sure makes me smile."

Smile...smile...smile... Is that all Noah can think to talk about? And why is he still standing here, looking at me with such a smug expression?

"I can't imagine what would be so fun about sitting for hours, waiting for a stupid fish to bite." Susan wrinkled her nose once again.

"And having to clean and cook the smelly thing would definitely not be my idea of fun."

"What is your idea of fun?" he asked.

"I don't know. Maybe volleyball, but I'm not that good at it. I could never compete with my sister Rosa, that's for sure. She's always been a champion at the game."

"I don't think you'll have to worry about competing with her for a while, since from what I've heard, she's in a family way."

"That's true."

"What? That she's expecting a baby, or that you won't have to compete with her?"

"Both. I'm sick of walking in my sister's shadow and trying to make people notice me."

"You have a pretty face, so I'm sure there are plenty of guys who have noticed you."

A feeling of warmth started at the base of Susan's neck and quickly traveled up to her face. Was Noah flirting with her or simply teasing and trying to get a rise out of her, like Alvin often did? Norman used to do it sometimes too, but since he'd married Salina and settled into being a husband, he rarely teased Susan anymore. If anything, the only thing Susan got from her older brother was "do this" or "do that" at the store, or comments about Susan's negative attitude. She was tired of being put down or ignored. Since Rosa had come home, things had gotten even worse for Susan, because all Mom talked about these days was the excitement of becoming a grandmother once Rosa's baby was born. Her mother also went on and on about how nice it was to have Rosa living at home again. Susan wondered what was so special about Rosa. And how come their mother accepted Rosa's apology so easily when she returned home after being absent for such a long time?

I'll bet if that had been me who'd run away, I wouldn't have been welcomed home so easily.

Noah snapped his fingers, bringing Susan's thoughts to a halt once again. "Hey! You looked like you were spacing off again, and you didn't answer my last question."

"Umm. . .what did you want to know?"

"I was wondering if you'd like to go to the next young people's singing with me."

Susan's eyes opened wide, and she clamped her teeth together to keep her mouth from dropping open. "You're kidding, right?"

"Nope. I meant every word."

"Why would you want to go anywhere with me? I don't smile, remember?"

"Exactly." He tipped his hat in her direction. "And I'd like a chance to prove that you do have the ability to crack a smile once in a while."

"How is attending a young people's singing going to make me feel happy enough to smile?"

"You'll see. There's a gathering next Sunday night. I'll come by your place around five to pick you up, so you'd better be ready on time." Noah whirled around and sashayed out the door before Susan could form a single word.

"Who does that guy think he is, anyway?" Susan muttered when the door shut behind him.

"What guy?" Norman asked as he approached from the back of the store.

"Noah Esh." Susan pressed both arms tightly against her thighs. "Can you believe he asked me to go to a singing with him next Sunday evening?"

Norman opened his mouth and released a round of laughter.

"What's so funny?"

He pointed at her. "If you could see your red cheeks and the flustered expression on your face, you'd understand the reason I laughed."

"Well, there's nothing humorous about it."

"Did you agree to go with him?"

She shook her head. "Not hardly, but he didn't take no for an answer. In fact, Noah said he'd be by our place to pick me up around five next Sunday evening."

"I guess you'd better be ready, then. Sure don't want to keep the nice fellow waiting." Norman put his hand over his mouth, as though to hide the snicker that Susan heard anyway.

What should I do? Susan questioned herself. *If I hide out in the house and refuse to go with Noah when he comes to pick me up, the news will spread like wildfire that Susan Petersheim is unsociable, and then Dad will hear about it and get on my case.* Susan pinched the bridge of her nose while squeezing her eyes shut. *And if I go to the singing with Noah, people might think I'm his girlfriend.* It was a no-win situation, and Susan only had until a week from tomorrow to make up her mind about what she should do.

New York City

Anthony had only been home from work a few hours when a knock sounded on his apartment door. He was tired and didn't feel up to company, so he was tempted not to answer. But his curiosity got the best of him. When he opened the door, Cindy Duncan stood in the hall, wearing faded blue jeans and a T-shirt of the same color. Cindy held a cardboard box in her hands.

"I hope you haven't eaten supper yet," she said with a dimpled smile. "I made too much chicken-and-rice casserole, and thought it would be nice to share it with someone. Oh, and I also have a tossed green salad and some brownies for dessert."

Anthony was tempted to say no thanks, but his empty, rumbling stomach won out. He could have grabbed a bite at the fast food place where he worked, but nothing on the menu there appealed. Never mind that he'd had his hand in cooking everything from hot dogs with sauerkraut to burgers cooked on the grill. Something different for supper would be nice for a change—especially when he hadn't been involved in making it.

"No, I haven't eaten yet," Anthony answered. "I just got home from work." He held the door open for her. "Come on in, and thanks for thinking of me."

The shapely blond strode across the room and entered his small but well-equipped kitchen. She placed the box on the counter and quickly removed the contents.

"Guess I should get busy and set the table." Anthony hurriedly got out two plates, silverware, glasses, and napkins, which he promptly placed on the table. Steam escaped from the casserole, indicating that it was still warm, and his stomach growled as he inhaled the tantalizing aroma. "If it tastes as good as it smells, guess I'm in for a treat."

Cindy offered Anthony another friendly smile as she placed the casserole dish on a hot pad Anthony had placed in the middle of the table. After she set out the salad and he poured purified water into their glasses, they took seats opposite each other.

As though he'd been doing it his whole life, Anthony automatically closed his eyes and bowed his head. After a short silent prayer, he lifted his head and looked up, surprised to see her staring at him with raised brows.

"Were you praying?" she asked with her head angled slightly to one side.

"Yep. It's something I started doing while staying for a while with an Amish family in Mifflin County, Pennsylvania, a few months ago." He reached for his glass of water and took a drink. "They pray silently before every meal."

"Seriously?"

"Yeah."

"How come?"

"You mean why do they pray, or why do they do it silently?"

"Both. Seems kind of strange to me."

Anthony blotted his lips with the napkin next to his plate. "Well, they pray to thank God for the food on the table, and I suppose they pray about some other things too." He paused to drink some more water. "I guess the reason it's done silently is so that others at the table don't know what each of them is praying about."

She rolled her pretty blue eyes. "That does seems odd."

Anthony made no comment as he dished himself some of the casserole and passed the serving dish to Cindy.

She smiled and leaned closer to him. "So my next question is, why were you staying with an Amish family?"

Anthony wasn't comfortable telling Cindy the reason he'd stayed with the Petersheims, and he wasn't about to go into the story of pretending to be Rosa's husband. So to satisfy her curiosity and end the topic quickly, he said in a casual voice, "Oh, I just thought it would be interesting to observe an Amish family's way of life. I learned a lot about their cooking methods too."

"Oh, I see." Cindy looked away for a few seconds while dishing up some salad, and then she passed the bowl to Anthony. As he put some on his plate, he noticed that the leafy greens were covered with some kind of salad dressing he didn't recognize. Anthony was about to ask what kind it was when Cindy spoke again.

"So what exactly did you learn while observing the Amish people's way of life? Did they eat by candlelight, and was there an outhouse out back?"

He shook his head. "I guess there are some Amish communities that are very Plain and might live that way, but this group that drives black-topped buggies is a little more progressive than that."

"I watched a documentary on TV once about some Amish people who live in the backwoods of Kentucky." Cindy wrinkled her nose like some foul odor had permeated the room. "I could never live without modern conveniences. Could you?"

"Well, I did, and it wasn't too bad, and maybe if I'd been raised in an Amish home, I would never have missed what the world has to offer in the way of modern technology."

She snickered while shaking her head. "Not me. I'd never make it without all the modern conveniences."

"I bet you could if you had to."

"Nope. Think I'd have to run away from home if I was forced to live like a pioneer woman."

Cindy had touched on a nerve when she'd mentioned running away from home, and a vision of Rosa came to mind. Had she left her home in Belleville because she wanted modern conveniences, or did it have more to do with a rebellious streak? During the time Anthony had lived in her parents' home, Rosa had seemed content. She'd even put on her Amish garb when attending church and a few other events. Anthony had a hunch that she planned to join the Amish church.

As much as he hated to admit it, Anthony missed Rosa and thought about her frequently. He wondered if she ever thought about him, but if she did, why hadn't she returned any of his calls?

When Cindy clinked her glass with the handle of her fork, Anthony's thoughts about Rosa ended.

"You looked like you were someplace else for a few minutes," she said. "Am I a boring supper companion?"

"Certainly not." Anthony picked up his fork and dived into the food on his plate. Maybe a little more eating and a little less talking would be the best thing all the way around. Too much thinking about Rosa might give Anthony the stupid notion that he should jump on his motorcycle sometime when he had two days off in a row and head back to Mifflin County just to see how Rosa was doing. But most likely that wasn't going to happen, because really, what would be the point?

CHAPTER 33

Rosa had been tossing and turning for nearly an hour, but she couldn't find a comfortable position and had been unable to fall asleep. The baby had been kicking a lot too, and Rosa's back ached. She'd resigned herself to the fact that she probably wouldn't get much sleep tonight.

Guess I may as well get used to this, Rosa told herself. *Once my little one is born, I'll no doubt be up several times during the night, feeding the baby and doing diaper changes. I hope the baby's crying won't keep my parents awake. With Dad getting up early every morning to do chores and go to the store to work five days a week, not to mention rising early for Sunday church services, he needs to get good-quality sleep.*

Rosa sat up and swung her legs over the side of the bed. A cramp in her right leg meant the other leg would likely cramp up soon too. Knowing the best way to deal with it was to get up and walk around the room until it subsided, that's exactly what she did.

It was hard to believe it was the second week of May already, and with Rosa's due date only a few weeks away, even if the baby came a little early Rosa was sure it would be fine. Her large belly that had dropped considerably was an indication that the infant was getting ready to meet the world. Rosa figured the baby might make his or her appearance on or even before her due date.

After walking around the room long enough to release the leg cramp, Rosa ambled over to the window, lifted the shade, and looked out. The night sky was as black as ink, and a bright, full moon set among twinkly stars gave the appearance of a picture postcard Rosa had bought once on her travels and sent home to her parents. She'd included a note telling them where she was and assuring Mom and Dad that she was okay and would write or call again soon. Rosa was still perplexed that no one in the family had acknowledged receiving any written messages or phone calls from her during the two-plus years she'd been gone. It didn't add up, and she felt sure that someone had received those messages and had not owned up to it.

Rosa tapped one of her bare feet against the cold hardwood floor. *Surely if Mom or Dad had received my messages, they would have admitted to that. And if Mom had known I was doing okay, she wouldn't have been so worried about me and gotten sick from not knowing what had happened to me.*

She touched the cold window glass with the palms of her hands and shivered. *Someone must have discovered my messages and destroyed them. But who, and more importantly, why? Could it have been Dad? Would he have been so angry at me for leaving home that he would have kept my whereabouts from Mom and the rest of the family?*

Rosa shook her head. *I don't think so. Dad would never be that cruel—especially to Mom. I'm sure Alvin wouldn't have done it either. He's just a kid, and when I returned home, he said that he'd missed me. Same thing with Tena. The two of us have always gotten along.*

Despite the chilly room, Rosa felt a sheen of sweat erupt on her face. *I bet it was Susan. She and I never saw eye to eye on much of anything, and out of everyone in the family, she's been the coldest toward me since I returned home. Sometimes she seems almost hostile.*

Rosa moved away from the window and took a seat on the edge of her bed. *I wonder how it would go if I came right out and confronted Susan about it—asked if she hid my letters and postcards and deleted my messages from phone calls. Would she deny it or admit that she was responsible?*

Rosa clutched the part of the quilt on her bed that almost hung down to the floor. *I've put it off long enough. When I feel that the time is right, I'm going to have a serious talk with Susan.*

After Rosa climbed back into bed and pulled the covers up to her chin, her thoughts changed direction. Once more, she focused on the future. If she continued to live here with her folks, it would be necessary to join the Amish church. That would probably be the best thing for her and the baby.

What should I name my little one if I end up having a girl? she wondered. *Or what's a good name if it's a boy?* Although Mom had brought the topic up a few times, Rosa had no idea what to call the child. If the baby turned out to be a boy, Rosa would certainly not name him after his biological father. Even thinking about the relationship she'd had with a married man made Rosa feel sick to her stomach. She had asked God to forgive her for the sin she had committed, but it had been hard for Rosa to forgive herself. She knew it did no good to keep beating herself up over her transgression. It was in the past, and she had turned over a new leaf, committing her life to the Lord.

Rosa thought about Anthony, as she often did. She hoped things were going well for him. It was a good thing they hadn't established a relationship that went deeper than friendship, because it never could have worked out between them. Rosa would be joining the Amish church, and she felt sure that Anthony could never be one with the Plain people. He'd been raised differently, with all the modern conveniences, which would be difficult to give up.

"Enough thinking now," Rosa murmured. "It's time for me to leave my concerns in God's hands."

She closed her eyes and prayed for Anthony, as well as each member of her family, until she finally drifted off to sleep.

New York City

Anthony had gone to bed around eleven o'clock, but unable to fall asleep, he'd gotten up and made his way out to his favorite reclining chair in the living room. The Bible he'd found in his duffel bag still lay on the small table next to the chair, and he picked it up, certain that there was a lot more to learn inside the pages of this interesting book.

After leafing through several pages in the Old Testament again, Anthony discovered a strip of paper tucked inside the book of Proverbs. In chapter 3, verses 5 and 6 had been underlined. He read them out loud. "Trust in the Lord with all your heart, and lean not on your own understanding; in all your ways acknowledge Him, and He shall direct your paths."

Last night Anthony had read John 3:16–17, and he'd taken those verses to heart. In verse 16, Anthony had substituted his own name to replace the word *whoever*, making it read: "For God so loved the world that He gave His only begotten Son, that if Anthony believes in Him, he should not perish but have everlasting life."

Still holding the Bible in his hands, Anthony bowed his head and closed his eyes. "Dear Lord, I do believe in You. Please help me to trust You in all things. I ask, Lord, that You will guide and direct my path in the days ahead and give me the wisdom to make good decisions."

Anthony was beginning to realize why Rosa must have felt it necessary to put a Bible in his duffel bag, and he appreciated it more than she would ever know. Or if it wasn't Rosa who had done it, then he owed a debt of thanks to whoever had put the one true book there.

Anthony closed the Bible, set it back on the table, and stretched his arms over his head. He felt both rejuvenated and peaceful.

"Think I'm ready now to head on back to bed." Anthony was fairly certain that he could sleep peacefully, but he also knew that when he woke up in the morning, he'd have some important decisions to make.

Belleville

Sunday morning, as Susan sat beside Tena, it was hard to keep her focus on the song the congregation was singing from the *Ausbund*. She tried not to look across at the men's section of the building, where Noah Esh sat with some other young men his age. She still couldn't believe he had come into her father's store last week and boldly invited her to go to the young people's singing with him this evening.

What in the world was Noah thinking? Susan wondered, clasping the hymnal tightly in her hands. *Surely it couldn't be because he is interested in me. No, that would be ridiculous, especially after I've made it abundantly clear to anyone who will listen that I have no interest in getting married or even dating. I'm sure by now the news has spread from one end of Mifflin County to the other that Susan Petersheim plans to remain single for the rest of her life.*

The words blurred on the page before her as Susan toyed with the idea of hiding upstairs in the room she shared with Tena when five o'clock came around. Susan figured it would be easy enough to fake a headache and ask Tena or Mom to let Noah know that she wasn't up to going to the singing. *Jah, that would be the best way, all right. I just hope Mom doesn't insist that I take an aspirin and go to the event anyway. Both she and Dad are always after me to take part in some of the young people's activities.*

Tena bumped Susan's arm and whispered, "We're done singing now and the first sermon's about to begin, so you'd better pay attention and quit staring off into space."

Susan flinched as a warm flush crept across her cheeks. She handed her hymnal to Tena, who passed it to the next person in line, a process that continued until every *Ausbund* had been picked up and put away.

Henry Graber, a visiting minister, stood up and began to preach. He stated that his sermon was on the subject of lying and that he would share what God's Word had to say about the issue.

Susan squirmed on the backless wooden bench she sat upon. This was not a topic she wished to hear about. But what choice did she have, unless she got up and went out to use the restroom? If she did that, she would draw attention to herself, and she didn't relish that idea either.

Susan tried to focus on something else, like the back of the young girl's head in front of her, but it was no use. The minister, with his booming voice, quoted scripture after scripture, and each one pierced

Susan's soul like a two-edged sword. One passage in particular, Proverbs 6:16–19, really spoke to her heart.

"These six things the Lord hates," Minister Graber quoted. "Yes, seven are an abomination to Him: a proud look, a lying tongue, hands that shed innocent blood, a heart that devises wicked plans, feet that are swift in running to evil, a false witness who speaks lies, and one who sows discord among brethren."

Henry paused a few seconds, as if to let his words sink in, before continuing. "Proverbs 25:18 says, 'A man who bears false witness against his neighbor is like a club, a sword, and a sharp arrow.' From this we should safely conclude that God hates lying in any form. He hates it because our heavenly Father is the source of all truth."

Another pause preceded the minister's next words. "So what do we do when we are guilty of lying? Do we shrug it off and say, 'It doesn't matter. The person I lied about had it coming'? I ask you now, is that kind of attitude pleasing to God?"

He looked Susan's way, as though speaking directly to her, and Susan's body broke out in a cold sweat. The word *guilty. . .guilty. . .guilty. . .*swam in her head. Replaying some of her lies—especially those involving Rosa, made the minister's teaching reach deep into Susan's soul. For the first time since she'd destroyed her sister's note and chosen not to tell her parents about it, Susan's thoughts were filled with self-loathing. God had known all about her lies. There was no way she could hide them from Him. It hadn't taken Mom and Dad long to catch Susan in the lies she'd told regarding Ben either, and because of it, she'd lost their trust. Even when she'd told them things that were true, they didn't believe her.

Susan felt a burning at the back of her throat, and she tried to squelch it by swallowing several times. But it was no use. *If my parents knew that I'd discovered a few notes from Rosa in our mailbox during her absence and destroyed them, plus deleted all of Rosa's phone messages, they'd probably never speak to me again.*

To make matters worse, after Anthony left Belleville, Susan had also gotten rid of his voicemail messages. She'd even pretended to call Anthony to let him know how Rosa was doing, but she hadn't, and afterward, she'd confirmed to her mother that she'd made the call, even though she hadn't.

I'm a terrible person, Susan admitted to herself. *I can tell God I'm sorry and really mean it, but if I confess my sins to Mom, Dad, and Rosa, they'll probably never forgive me.*

Tears clouded Susan's vision, and she looked down at her lap while clenching her fingers. Her shoulders trembled as she tried to gain control, but it was no use. Susan's guilt felt like a heavy weight pressing down on her body and piercing her broken heart.

Dear Lord, Susan prayed silently, *forgive me for the horrible lies I have told, and please show me what I should do to make restitution.* Maybe, just maybe, there was something Susan could do to help make up for her past failures. If not, she might have no other recourse than to move out of her parents' home and strike out on her own, someplace where no one knew her and she could begin anew. Of course, that would mean losing touch with her family, and the thought of that gave Susan a headache that was not made up. What she needed to do now was figure out when to make her confession and how to bring up the topic without falling apart.

Susan was certain about one thing: She wouldn't have the desire or strength to go anywhere with Noah Esh this evening. When he arrived, she would need to come up with the right words to convey that fact, without telling another lie.

CHAPTER 34

Soon after Susan's family arrived home from church that afternoon, Susan decided she must tell her parents and Rosa about the lies she'd told and beg for their forgiveness. Her stomach felt like it had been tied up in knots, and her mouth was so dry she could barely swallow. But she couldn't wait any longer to unburden her soul. Fortunately, Tena and Alvin had changed out of their church clothes and gone for a walk to one of the neighbors' homes to see the new pony that had recently been purchased for one of their children. The last thing Susan wanted was for her younger sister and brother to hear her confession. They might need to know eventually, but not today.

"Mom, Dad, I need to talk with you both, and also Rosa," Susan said when she entered the living room, where her parents sat.

"Rosa is resting in the guest room right now," Mom responded. "She had a restless night, which is why she didn't go to church with us this morning."

"What I have to say is really important, and it involves her."

"Is it a matter of life and death?" Dad asked, looking at Susan over the magazine he'd been reading.

"Well, no, but..."

"Then it can wait till Rosa comes out of her room."

"Maybe you can tell us whatever you have on your mind during supper this evening," Mom suggested.

Susan shook her head. "No, it can't wait that long. Besides, Noah

Esh will be coming here at five to take me to a young people's singing tonight." Her heart began to race, and she drew in a few quick breaths, wishing she could take back what she'd just blurted out. *Why did I tell them that? I don't even want to go, and I was hoping I could find some way to get out of it.*

Mom's eyes opened wide, and she got up from her seat and came over to give Susan a hug. "That's wunderbaar! I'm happy to hear that you'll be attending a young people's function." She smiled widely. "And with a nice young man like Noah, no less. I hope you'll have an enjoyable evening."

Dad set his magazine aside and looked at Susan with raised brows. "Have you and Noah been seeing each other on the sly?"

She gave a quick shake of her head. "No way! He came into the store a week ago Saturday, and while I was packaging up the items he'd bought, right out of the blue, he asked if I'd go to the singing and said he'd be by to get me at five o'clock this evening."

"I see. Well, your mother's right—it will be good for you to attend the event."

Oh, great! Now I'm stuck going to the singing, and unless Rosa comes out of the bedroom soon, I won't get this confession off my mind before Noah shows up.

⁌⁍

Rosa didn't know how long she'd been sleeping, but her room had darkened, so she rolled over and clicked the battery-operated light on the table by her bed. It was nearly four o'clock, and even though it might not be dark outside yet, her blinds were closed, which she figured might have accounted for the darkened room.

Rosa heard voices, which she assumed came from the living room down the hall, but she couldn't make out what was being said.

I wonder if anyone has started fixing a light supper yet. She sat up, smoothed the wrinkles in her dress, put her head covering in place, and went out the door.

Upon entering the living room, Rosa saw Mom and Dad sitting

together on the sofa, while Susan stood off to one side with her arms folded. It was hard to read her sister's expression, but if Rosa had to guess, she would say that it was one of apprehension. Rosa wondered if Mom or Dad may have scolded Susan regarding something she'd said or done. Unfortunately, that had happened frequently since Susan was a child.

But then who am I to judge my sister or anyone else? Rosa thought. *Our parents, especially Dad, have been displeased with many things I've done over the years, and with good reason.* She placed both hands against her stomach. *The truth is, I didn't always make good choices.*

"I'm glad you're awake," Susan said, approaching Rosa. "I have something to tell you, Mom, and Dad, and I need to do it right now, before I lose my nerve."

Rosa looked directly at her sister. "Are you in some kind of trouble?"

"No, but I probably will be after I tell you the truth."

"The truth about what?" Dad questioned.

"It's regarding all the lies I told you concerning Rosa when she had disappeared." Susan lowered her gaze.

"What lies did you tell about me?" Rosa's voice cracked as she posed the question.

"Well, I...umm..."

"Girls, I think it would be good if you both took a seat." Mom gestured to the two vacant chairs in the room.

Feeling a bit wobbly on her feet, Rosa didn't hesitate, and she seated herself in the rocking chair. Susan shuffled over and sank into their father's recliner.

"Go ahead, Susan," Dad spoke up. "Tell us what lies you told about Rosa."

No doubt feeling quite apprehensive, Susan gripped her hands together and glanced at the clock on the far wall. "To start with, Rosa was right when she said that she did leave a note in her room that explained that she was leaving home and listed her reasons."

"How do you know this?" The question came from their mother, as she leaned slightly forward and cupped her right elbow with her left hand.

"Because I found the note and destroyed it."

"Why would you do that?" The muscles along the midsection of Rosa's back tightened.

"I—I didn't want Mom and Dad to know you had left of your own accord or that you had planned to keep in touch."

Dad's right fist came down hard in his left palm. "That's *lecherich*, Susan!"

"Your *daed* is correct," Mom interjected. "That is just plain ridiculous. Why would you not want us to know the reason your sister left home? Didn't you realize how worried we were?"

"And not just worried, but the stress of not knowing where Rosa was caused your mamm to get sick because she was concerned that something horrible may have happened to her." Dad's voice became louder with each word he spoke.

"I know, and I'm sorry." Susan slumped in her chair. "The sermon we heard today on the subject of lying caused me to realize what a horrible thing I had done."

"But why?" Mom asked once more. "What reason did you have for destroying Rosa's note?"

"I already said it—I didn't want you to know that she'd left of her own accord." Susan put a hand against her mouth as a muffled sob came forth. "I figured if I kept the truth to myself, you might come to care more for me than her."

Mom blinked rapidly. "Are you serious, Susan? Did you actually think I favored Rosa over you?"

"Jah, I did, and I still do." Tears coursed down Susan's red face.

"It's not true," Mom said. "I love all my children equally. Each one of you has a special place in my heart, and I've never intentionally played favorites."

Susan reached for a tissue from the box on the little table beside the recliner and blew her nose. "Well, it hasn't always seemed that way.

After Rosa left, you paid me more attention than you had before, and I did everything I could think of to be supportive and help out around here in order to make it easier for you."

"And your actions were appreciated," Mom said.

"Wait a minute." Rosa held up her hand. "There's something else we need to talk about."

"What's that?" Dad asked.

"How about the letters and postcards I mailed home to give an update on where I was, so you wouldn't worry about me?"

"We told you before, Rosa—we never got any of them," Mom replied. "Nor did we receive phone calls or voicemail messages from you."

"Would you know anything about that?" Dad pointed at Susan.

She slunk a little farther down in her chair. "Jah, Dad, I do."

"Well then, tell us."

"I deleted all of Rosa's phone messages, and when I found letters or cards from her in the mailbox, I destroyed those too. After a while, the letters and calls quit coming, so I figured Rosa had given up trying to reach anyone and wasn't coming home." Susan reached for another tissue and blotted the tears on her cheeks. "I'm an unworthy daughter and a terrible sister, and I don't know if any of you can find it in your hearts to forgive me. Even so, I am truly sorry for all the lies I told, and for not letting you know when Rosa's messages came in." She looked at their father. "If I was a child, I would willingly go out to the woodshed so you could punish me, Dad. But I guess I'm too old for you to *bletsche* me."

"You are right, Susan," Dad agreed. "A spanking would not be appropriate at your age, nor would it change what you have done to hurt your sister, not to mention your mamm, me, and your other siblings. You need to apologize to them as well, because everyone was worried sick about Rosa."

"And don't forget that your brother Norman spent many hours searching for Rosa," Mom said. "His determination to find Rosa almost cost him the relationship he had established with Salina."

Susan bobbed her head. "I am well aware, and I will apologize to each of my siblings. I doubt that anyone will forgive me, though." She looked at Rosa. "Least of all, you."

The clock's chime struck five, and Susan's eyes widened. "Oh no! Noah will be here soon, and I'm in no condition to go with him to the singing. When he gets here, could someone please tell him that I'm unable to go?"

"Unable or unwilling?" Dad questioned.

"Umm...well...look at me." She gestured to her tearstained face. "If Noah were to see me like this, he'd know I've been crying and expect me to explain."

"Maybe discussing this with him would do you some good," Mom stated.

Susan's eyes widened even farther, and Rosa figured her sister might dash out of the room. She didn't, though. Instead, Susan remained in her chair. "I need to say one more thing. I don't expect any of you to forgive me, and I'll pack up my things and move out of the house if you say so. But I do want you all to know that I am truly sorry for my wrongdoings, and I confessed my sins to the Lord during church in a silent prayer."

A horse whinnied from outside, and Susan finally rose from her chair. "Noah must be here. I need to go wash my face, and then I'll go with him, because it's the right thing to do." She looked at their parents. "Besides, I'm sure you both need some time to decide if you'd like me to move out of the house. You can leave a note for me on the kitchen table, and when I get home from the singing tonight, I'll see if Noah will give me a ride to the bus station." Without waiting for anyone's response, Susan dashed out of the room. Soon, her footsteps could be heard running down the hall and then tromping up the stairs.

A knock sounded on the front door, and Mom rose from her chair. "I'd better answer that and let Noah know that Susan is upstairs and will be ready to go in a few minutes." She looked over at Rosa. "After your sister leaves with Noah, the three of us will need to talk about all of this."

"You're right," Rosa replied. *Although I'm really too exhausted to think clearly, let alone talk.*

⁓⁓

When Elsie opened the door, she found Noah holding the brim of his hat in one hand. The battery-operated lantern on the porch provided enough additional light for her to see the eager expression on the young man's face. With his feet pointing forward and his shoulders straight and back, Noah announced, "I'm here to pick up Susan. Is she ready to go?"

"Almost. She's upstairs at the moment, but I believe she will be down soon. Would you like to come in and wait for her in the living room?"

"Naw, that's okay. I'll just stay right here till she comes out."

"All right. I'm sure it won't be too long." Elsie stepped back inside and closed the door. She hoped her daughter hadn't changed her mind and decided to stay upstairs in her room. If she did, Elsie would feel obligated to offer the young man some kind of an explanation, but it wouldn't be an outright lie. They'd had enough of that in this family.

Elsie returned to the living room and took her seat next to Mahlon.

"Was that Susan's escort to the singing?" her husband asked.

"Jah. I invited him in, but he said he'd rather wait for her on the porch." Elsie glanced toward the door leading into the hallway. "I hope our daughter doesn't disappoint Noah. He wore an eager expression, and if Susan doesn't come down, I'll have to offer him an explanation."

"No need to worry about that," Mahlon was quick to say. "I will take care of the problem if it becomes necessary."

"What will you say, Dad?" Rosa asked from her chair. "Surely you won't tell Noah about Susan's confession."

"No, but I won't make up a lie either. I'll just say that Susan's not up to going anywhere this evening."

"That would definitely be true," Elsie said with a nod. She sat quietly, fiddling with her head-covering ties and wondering how long Mahlon would wait before he gave up on Susan and went out to speak with Noah. This was a very awkward situation, and Elsie was still in shock from hearing Susan's confession. She glanced over at Rosa and noticed the lines of fatigue etched on her face. Her sister's revelation had no doubt shaken her to the core.

If only Susan had been honest and shown us the note she'd found that Rosa had left. If we'd received Rosa's letters and phone messages, none of us would have been so worried about her. Disappointed that she'd gone off on her own, yes, but not in a panic because we thought she might be dead.

Elsie felt her pulse begin to race, and she knew she needed to calm herself before anxiety took over and she'd have to go lie down. *Just breathe and try to relax. And most of all, don't forget to pray*, the voice in her head reminded her.

Several minutes passed, and then Elsie heard steady footsteps coming down the stairs. A few seconds later, Susan entered the room. The tears had been washed away, but the area beneath Susan's eyes still looked a bit puffy. Hopefully Noah wouldn't notice or ask about it, so Susan wouldn't have to offer an explanation.

"Where's Noah?" Susan asked, looking in Elsie's direction. "Did you tell him I wasn't going?"

"No, I said you were upstairs getting ready."

"Okay. I'll just get my shawl now and go with Noah. I guess a few hours with other young people singing songs that bring glory to God will be good for me."

Elsie nodded. "Jah. I hope the evening goes well."

Susan glanced at her father and then Rosa, but when neither of them said anything, she hurried out of the room.

Elsie heard the front door open and close, and a short time later the whinny of Noah's horse, followed by a steady *clip-clop, clip-clop* as the horse trotted down the driveway.

Mahlon cleared his throat and drew his fingers through the ends of his full beard. "Well, ladies, should we get on with our discussion about how we're going to handle this situation with Susan?"

Elsie nodded, as did Rosa. There was no doubt—this was a subject they needed to talk about, and it should be done before Tena and Alvin got home.

CHAPTER 35

"Y<small>OU LOOK KIND OF MIED</small> tonight," Noah commented as they walked out to the hitching rail where his horse and buggy waited.

"Jah, I am a bit tired," Susan responded.

"I guess maybe you didn't have time to take a nap after church today."

"No nap for me." *Just a confession, and now I don't know what my future holds.*

"I didn't take one either." He chuckled. "But then I rarely do. Didn't even like to sleep during the daytime when I was a boy."

Susan made no comment as she climbed into the passenger side of Noah's buggy. She didn't feel like talking and hoped he wouldn't ask her a bunch of questions as they traveled to the home where the singing would be held.

Noah climbed in and gathered up the reins, then backed up his horse so they were positioned to head down the driveway. "Are you looking forward to more spring weather, Susan? I sure am."

She shrugged.

"When the weather gets even warmer, maybe we could check out some of the ponds in our area and do a bit of fishing."

Susan spread her fingers out like a fan against her breastbone. Was he asking her out? Did Noah want to spend more time with her? If so, she couldn't understand his reasons. Although he and his family often attended church services in her family's district on their off Sundays, Noah had never shown any interest in her.

Maybe he feels sorry for me because I'm alone most of the time and don't go to many of the young people's functions, Susan thought. *Noah could be the nurturing type, who likes to make people like me feel better about themselves. If he knew the real me, who was capable of telling so many lies that I almost believed them myself, I bet he wouldn't want anything to do with me.*

"Susan, did you hear what I said?"

"Oh, uh—what was that?"

"I mentioned going fishing sometime this spring. Thought maybe you'd like to go with me sometime."

She turned her head to look at him directly. "How come?"

"How come fishing, or are you wondering why I asked you to join me?"

"The second part." Susan sucked in some air and blew it out quickly. "I'm not a nice person, Noah. You don't want to go anywhere with me."

"Jah, I do. That's how we can get to know each other better."

She shook her head so hard that the ties on her head covering flipped back and forth, just missing her mouth. "Knowing me better would not be a good thing."

"Why not?"

"It just wouldn't. That's all."

"You should allow me to be the judge of that."

Susan flexed her fingers a few times and then drew them into the palms of her hands. She was tempted to tell Noah, right then and there, that she was a liar and had told some things that weren't true during the time her sister had gone missing.

But if I tell him, she reasoned, *he'll probably never speak to me again, much less want to take me fishing or anyplace else.*

Susan sat quietly for a few minutes until Noah nudged her arm. "So how about it, Susan? Should I start planning a fishing date?"

"No, you shouldn't, so please drop the subject. In fact," Susan added, "I'd prefer not to talk at all." Her tone was sharp, and she felt bad about that, but how else was she supposed to get through to him? Somehow, Susan needed to make Noah understand that she was not a fit date, for him or anyone else.

She bit her lower lip until she recognized the metallic taste of blood. *The truth is, I'm no better than Ben. Maybe I ought to be in jail too. At least there, I'd know my sins were being punished.*

Susan's thoughts turned to something else. *I wonder if Mom, Dad, and Rosa are sitting there at home, talking about me. I bet they're trying to decide whether they should accept my apology or not. Maybe when I get home from the singing tonight, my bags will be packed and waiting for me at the door.*

"Well, guess we'd better get busy and have this discussion now, before Tena and Alvin show up," Rosa's father announced. "We each need to decide if we're willing to forgive Susan for her deceit and all of the lies she told while Rosa was gone." He got up and reached for his Bible, which had been lying on the table near his recliner; then he took a seat in the chair.

Rosa shifted uneasily on the sofa, where she'd moved to sit beside her mother. Although Dad was a bishop in their church, he could be harsh sometimes. She figured he would not go easy on Susan and would come up with some way to make her pay for her transgressions. Even so, Dad studied the Bible a lot and was well versed in what God's Word had to say about a good many topics. And since he had picked the Bible up and was now thumbing through the pages, she felt sure that he was about to read them one or more verses of scripture, most likely on the topic of lying.

Once Dad found the page he apparently sought, he turned and faced Rosa and her mother. "Before we resume our discussion about Susan, I'm going to read a few verses that apply to all of us and must be taken to heart."

"Jah, please do," Mom said.

Rosa bobbed her head in agreement.

Dad stood, like he would if he were preaching during one of their church services, and said, "Rosa, since you didn't feel up to going to church with us this morning, as Susan had stated, our guest minister preached on the topic of lying. He quoted several verses of scripture to remind us that lying is wrong—a sin, in fact—an abomination to God. Susan said she took the verses to heart, felt guilty for her lies, and came to the realization that she must come forth and tell us the truth. As you know, she also apologized for her misdeeds. Do you believe her apology was heartfelt, or did she merely tell us what she thought we wanted to hear?"

Rosa looked at her mother, wondering if she would respond first, and she did.

"Jah, Mahlon, I believe that Susan was truly repentant."

"And you, Rosa? What do you think about your sister's apology?"

"It seemed genuine."

"All right then, since we are all in agreement, let's listen to what the Bible says about forgiveness." He opened the black book to the page he'd been holding with his index finger and read, "'For if you forgive men their trespasses, your heavenly Father will also forgive you. But if you do not forgive men their trespasses, neither will your Father forgive your trespasses.' Matthew 6:14 and 15."

Dad paused and remained quiet. Rosa figured he wanted to allow them some time to digest and ponder God's Word. "Those two verses pretty much said it all," he said. "Forgive others or God won't forgive you."

"There is no might or maybe. It is spelled out clearly, and the choice is up to each individual. In this case, we could either forgive Susan or not forgive her, in which case our own sins would not be forgiven by God.

"I would like to read another passage of scripture," Dad continued. "This one is found in Luke 23, verse 34, and the words are written in red, indicating that Jesus was speaking. Listen to what He said when he was on the cross, close to death." He paused before reading: "Then Jesus said, 'Father forgive them, for they do not know what they do.'" Dad paused again, and Rosa saw tears glistening in his eyes. "If our Lord could forgive those who had put Him to death, why do we find it so difficult to forgive others? Since God forgives our sins, we must offer forgiveness to those who have wronged us." He pointed to himself. "I, for one, am going to forgive Susan, but each of you will have to make that decision for yourself, just as Norman, Tena, and even Alvin will need to when Susan apologizes to them, which I feel sure she will do."

Rosa was on the verge of commenting, but Dad spoke again. "Susan is not the only person in this family who needs to apologize. I owe the two of you, as well as the rest of the family, a heartfelt apology for being so harsh and often saying things that I am sure must have hurt you deeply. If there is anything specific that I may have said or done, please feel free to discuss it with me, and I will apologize once more."

Tears welled up in Rosa's eyes, and she noticed that Mom was crying softly too. The fact remained that no one was perfect, and when a sinner repented, God would forgive them. So did Rosa have any right to withhold forgiveness when Susan said she was sorry? The answer was a resounding no, and Rosa immediately bowed her head in prayer. *Dear Lord, I believe my sister was sincere in her apology, and even though I was deeply hurt when she admitted what she had done and said while I was away from home, I need to find it in my heart to forgive her. Please help me do that, and also to remember that I am not perfect either. I ask You to forgive me for my shortcomings and all the pain I put my family through by selfishly running away from home. I hurt not only my family but also my friends Ada and Ephraim. Although I have apologized to everyone involved, the one person I still need to forgive is myself. I am asking Your help with that.*

When Rosa's prayer ended and she opened her eyes, she realized that her mother's head was bowed too. She sat quietly until Mom looked up and reached for Rosa's hand. "I had a little talk with Jesus," she said, "and I have found it within my heart to forgive Susan."

Rosa nodded. "Me too."

"All right then," Dad exclaimed. "Having forgiven Susan, we must express that to her, and then we all need to put the past behind us, move on from here, and try to be more supportive of each other."

"I couldn't agree more," Mom said. She gave Rosa's fingers a tender squeeze. "Right, Daughter?"

Rosa smiled and nodded. "Absolutely."

THE PRETENDER

Susan felt about as out of place as a mouse on a lily pad as she sat at a table with several other young Amish women, eating the light meal that had been served to those who had come to the gathering. The main dish was haystack, and it consisted of several bowls filled with everything from cut-up lettuce, diced tomatoes, cucumbers, and celery to onions, green peppers, and anything else one might put on a tossed salad. In addition to the vegetables, there was cooked ground beef, steamed rice, and homemade cheese sauce. A few jars of salsa and two big bottles of ranch dressing rounded out the selection.

After everyone had helped themselves, the women had taken seats at two long tables, and the young men all sat together in another area. Since most of the young people were from Noah's church district, Susan didn't know any of them well. So she sat quietly eating her food and wishing she was anywhere else. The other girls at the table were all busy talking to one another, and nobody seemed to pay any attention to Susan. She glanced over at the men's tables and caught Noah looking at her. He gave a nod, and she forced a smile.

Why did I allow Noah to bring me to this gathering? Susan asked herself. *I should have made up some excuse not to go, but that would have been telling another lie, and I'm done with that. I need to be honest now and try to treat people better. I have to stop feeling jealous of Rosa too.* Truthfully, Susan wouldn't want to be in her sister's shoes—expecting a child in a few weeks without a husband. Susan actually felt sorry for Rosa. *I'll need to be a better sister. Maybe when the baby comes I can babysit when I'm not working at Dad's store.*

When the singing was over and everyone was preparing to leave, Noah approached Susan. "Ready to go?" he asked.

She nodded. *I was ready to go the minute I got here.*

"Sorry we didn't get to spend much time together," he said as they headed out to his horse and buggy. "But now that we're going back to your house, we have plenty of time to talk."

Susan made no comment as she climbed into his carriage. As far as she was concerned, there wasn't much to talk about.

Noah gathered up the reins, and soon they were heading down the road in the direction of her home.

He tried to make conversation a few times and even asked her a few questions, but Susan kept her answers short.

As they approached her home, Noah slowed his horse and guided the gelding slowly up the driveway. Stopping at the hitching rail, he bumped shoulders with Susan. "Is it all right if I drop by your home sometime soon to see you? We could just sit and talk or maybe play a board game."

"I may not be here much longer," she replied in a voice barely above a whisper.

He leaned closer to her. "What was that?"

"I might not be living in the Big Valley much longer."

"I'm confused. Are your folks planning to move?"

"No, but they might ask me to leave."

"How come?"

Susan threw caution to the wind and blurted everything out about all the lies she'd told. A lump formed in her throat, and she swallowed hard, hoping to push it down. "I told Rosa, as well as Mom and Dad, that I'm very sorry, but I can't seem to forgive myself."

"We've all done things we regret, Susan."

She felt his hand on her trembling shoulder, which brought tears to her eyes. "Jah, I regret everything I did, but unfortunately, I can't take it back or make up for any of it."

"If you've asked God and your family to forgive you, then you need to forgive yourself. There are some verses in the Bible that say so."

"Really? Which ones?"

"Acts 3:19 says, 'Repent therefore and be converted, that your sins may be blotted out, so that times of refreshing may come from the presence of the Lord.'"

"I haven't heard that verse before."

"Well, it's there in the Bible, and you must remember that after you've confessed your sin, it's blotted out, to be remembered no more."

"That's easier said than done."

"Susan, you need to forgive yourself, just as God forgave you as soon as you repented. It's time for you to move forward, asking the Lord to help you be a better person in the days ahead."

Susan sat for several minutes, pondering all the things Noah had said. "I will do my best," she murmured, "but it might not be good enough. My family may not forgive me, and they could very well ask me to leave."

Noah reached for her hand and gave it a squeeze. "Well, if they do, you can come to my folks' house and sleep on the sofa tonight. Want me to go inside with you?"

She shook her head. "No, that's okay. I appreciate the offer, but I need to face this by myself."

"All right then. I'll sit out here for a while, and if you don't come out with your suitcase in the next half hour or so, I'll head on home."

Susan held in a chuckle. "How are you gonna tell how long half an hour is?"

"I have a flashlight in the buggy and my pocket watch."

"Oh, okay." Susan was about to get out, but he put his hand on her shoulder again. "Can I see you again, Susan?"

"I—I guess so."

"Okay, good. Unless you come outside, I'll call and leave you a message tomorrow or the day after."

"Danki." Susan stepped down from the buggy and quickly made her way to the house. When she opened the front door, she was surprised to find Rosa, Mom, and Dad sitting in the living room.

"We waited up for you," Dad said.

Susan's spine stiffened. *Here it comes.*

Rosa got up from her chair and gave Susan a hug. "I forgive you, Susan." Then Mom and Dad did the same, both proclaiming that they loved Susan and forgave her for the lies she had told.

"With God's help, I'm going to do better now," she said tearfully. "I want to start over, and to show you how truly sorry I am, I'll do whatever any of you ask."

"All right," Dad said. "Why don't you start by going up to bed so we can all get some sleep?"

"I don't have a problem with that." Susan hugged them again and practically skipped out of the room and all the way up the stairs. She was ever so thankful that she hadn't been asked to leave, and for once, she didn't mind sharing a room with Tena. In fact, she welcomed the idea of sleeping across from her sister's bed and hearing Tena's gentle breathing.

CHAPTER 36

New York City

ANTHONY ROLLED OVER IN BED, squinted at his alarm clock, and groaned. Seeing that it was nearly 10:00 a.m., he jerked the covers back and jumped out of bed. He had been exhausted last night and forgot to set the clock so he could get up early this morning. Today was his birthday, and following the tradition he'd started five years ago, Anthony liked to begin the day by taking a motorcycle ride.

Last night at the invitation of his mother, Anthony had eaten a late supper at his parents' restaurant after closing hours. Mom called it an "early birthday celebration," and she'd gone all out, with a bouquet of pink carnations in the center of the table and a candle on either side of the vase. She had also used a white linen tablecloth with matching cloth napkins, as well as their best dishes and silverware.

Anthony's father's contribution to the celebration was the meal he had fixed in the restaurant's well-equipped kitchen. The first course was a caprese salad. Pop had created a spectacular twist on the Italian classic salad that consisted of tomato, mozzarella, and basil with the addition of crispy prosciutto shards. The main dish was one of Anthony's favorites—pork sausage and tomato rigatoni. In addition to the sausage, Pop had included grape tomatoes. He'd also prepared cheesy garlic bread with slabs of semisoft herbed butter. For dessert, Anthony's mother had brought out cannoli with vanilla custard, which Mom had declared she'd made with no help from her husband. The tantalizing delicacy definitely reflected her Italian heritage.

Anthony could still picture the gleam in his father's eyes when he brought the food to the table. Even now, it put a smile on Anthony's lips. If there was ever a time when he could count on Pop giving him some extra attention, it was on his birthday. In fact, Anthony's father had always made sure that every year when they celebrated Anthony's birthday, something special transpired. Pop did the same thing for both of Anthony's sisters when their birthdays rolled around.

Too bad my sisters couldn't have taken part in my birthday supper, Anthony thought with regret. *Seems like Connie and Eva always have something going on in their lives.* He gave a huff. *My life seems boring in comparison to those young women and their busy schedules.*

"Well. . .I'd better quit thinking and get myself fully awake with a cup of coffee and a piece of raisin-bread toast topped with peanut butter. Then I'll need to get in my riding clothes and head on out the door," Anthony said aloud, as a feeling of excitement welled up in his chest. "Time's a-wasting, and I need to fire up my bike and head out on the road for another thrilling birthday ride. Guess my sisters don't have anything on me—at least not today."

Belleville

"Mom, I need you," Rosa called from the guest room. "I need you right now!"

In the living room, Elsie dropped what she'd been doing when she heard Rosa's cries. "Oh dear, something must be wrong with your sister," she said to Tena. She handed her the dustrag. "Please take over my job. I need to go check on her right away."

Elsie quickly rushed down the hall. When she entered the guest room and saw Rosa sitting on the edge of the bed in a bent over position, she knew something was wrong. "Has your labor started?"

Rosa nodded and pointed to a puddle on the floor. "My water broke, Mom, and the contractions are coming fast. Is it supposed to be this way?"

"Not always. Labor can be different for everyone," Elsie replied. "Are your contractions coming regularly?"

"Yes, and I believe it's time to call my midwife."

"I agree with you. I'll send Tena out to the phone shed to call Ida, and then I'll come right back to the room with something to clean up the floor."

"What should I do while you're gone?" Rosa's eyes were wide with obvious concern. "Should I get into bed, walk around the room, or sit on the end of the bed, holding my belly and trying to be brave?"

"Do whatever makes you the most comfortable." Elsie gave her daughter's back a few gentle pats and quickly left the room. She fully understood the fear Rosa must feel, because she felt the same way when she was in labor with her firstborn.

Rosa's hands and legs shook in tandem. She was a ball of nerves. Never having been pregnant before, she hadn't really known what to expect, and so many questions ran through her head. *What if the midwife doesn't get here before the baby decides to make his or her appearance? What if she does come but I have a serious problem and can't get to the hospital in time? What if Alvin gets home from school before the baby is born and he hears me screaming in pain? That would probably scare the wits out of my little brother.* Rosa squeezed her eyes shut and tried to block out all the what-ifs.

For a while, Rosa wasn't sure that she could even use the services of the midwife she had chosen soon after Anthony returned to New York. When the bleeding had started and she'd been on bed rest several weeks, Rosa figured she might need to have her baby in the hospital with a doctor present. But once the bleeding had stopped and she'd been allowed to be out of bed, Rosa was thankful the doctor had given her permission to have the birth at home with the help of her capable midwife. But he'd cautioned Rosa not to overdo it and said she should seek emergency help immediately if any problems arose.

Rosa began to pace, striding barefoot from the end of the bed over to the window and back. She hoped walking wouldn't cause the baby to come too soon, but she couldn't sit still and do nothing, so there was no point taking a seat on the bed. And for sure, she wouldn't be able to sleep.

Another pain shot through her abdomen, and she winced. *I hope Tena gets in touch with Ida right away and she comes here real soon. I can't imagine doing any of this without her help.*

⁓⁓

"What did the midwife say?" Elsie asked when Tena entered the house. "Is Ida available to come right away?"

"Apparently not, because she didn't answer her phone," Tena replied.

"Did you leave a message?"

"I tried to, but her voicemail was full."

Elsie heaved a weighted sigh. "Oh dear, that's not good. Not good at all."

"Maybe Ida is doing something outside and didn't take her cell phone into the yard with her. Or maybe she went to town to do some shopping today."

With a shake of her head, Elsie said, "That's doubtful. When Ida was here a few days ago to check on Rosa, she clearly stated that since the baby had dropped, she'd be staying close to home and would come right away when we called." She pursed her lips tightly. "If Rosa's midwife lived closer, we could run right over there, but Ida's home is nearly five miles from here."

"I could hitch one of our horses to the buggy and go see if she's home."

"Jah, I suppose you'd better do that, but you should try to call her again first."

"Okay, Mom. I'll do that right now." Tena started for the door but turned back around. "If she still doesn't answer her phone, should I come back here and notify you, or would you rather that I just get the horse and buggy ready to head over to Ida's place?"

"Please come back in and let me know that you're going. In the meantime, I need to get back into Rosa's room to clean up the floor and see how she's doing."

Tena hesitated a few seconds, like she might have more to say, but then she gave Elsie a quick hug and dashed out the front door.

Elsie paused briefly to say a quick prayer before grabbing the cleaning supplies and hurrying back to the guest room. She sure didn't relish the idea of having to tell Rosa that they hadn't been able to get ahold of her midwife. No doubt that would not sit well, and it would probably cause Rosa to feel even more stressed than she already was.

⁓⁓

Anthony had been on the road for four hours, and he was more than ready to get off his bike. When his destination came into view, he heaved a sigh of relief. *Thank You, Lord, for giving me a safe trip. Now please give me the right words when I go inside. If I'm allowed to go in*, he added before ending the prayer.

Anthony slowed the motorcycle as he turned onto the driveway and came to a stop when he saw Rosa's sister Tena come out of the phone shed. He leaned forward and hollered, "Is Rosa here? I need to talk to her."

The young woman's hand came up as she shielded her eyes against the glare of the sun and squinted. "Anthony?"

"Yeah, it's me." He removed his helmet and grinned at her.

"I didn't know you had a motorcycle." Before Anthony could respond, Tena added, "What are you doing here?"

"I just told you, Tena. I came to see Rosa."

Her brows pulled downward as she stared at him. "After the made-up story you told my folks about being married to Rosa, I'm surprised you had the nerve to come back here. And furthermore, how do you know that Rosa will even want to talk to you?"

"I don't, but I'll take my chances. And I'm not leaving till I have the opportunity to tell Rosa what's on my mind." Anthony drew a quick breath and released it before speaking again. "Pretending to be Rosa's husband was wrong, but I'm here now to try and make things right. Is she at home or not?"

"Yes, my sister is here, but you can't talk to her right now."

"How come?"

"She's in labor, and we can't reach her midwife on the phone, so I need to get a horse and buggy ready so I can go to the woman's house and see if she's there."

"There's no need for that. I can take you there."

With widened eyes, Tena pointed to Anthony's bike. "On that?"

"Well, sure, but you're not really dressed for it."

She looked down at her Plain dress and grimaced. "You're right, and I don't have a helmet either."

"Can you give me the woman's name and address?"

"I suppose, but—"

"I can get there a lot faster on my motorcycle than you can by horse and buggy."

"You're right, but I'm not sure—"

"Rosa needs the midwife, correct?"

"Yes, she does, and from my mother's wide-eyed expression when she asked me to call the midwife, I'd have to say that Rosa's contractions are moving along quickly."

"Okay then. You'd better give me the midwife's name and address."

"All right, I'll get a piece of paper and pen from the phone shed and write it down for you." Tena stepped inside the small building and returned moments later. "Here you go." She handed him the slip of paper. "I hope for Rosa's sake that you'll find Ida at home when you get there."

He nodded. "I hope so too."

As Anthony headed out of the yard and onto the main road, he prayed for Rosa and that he would find the midwife at home.

⁓⁓

Rosa stopped pacing and turned to look at her mother when she entered the room.

THE PRETENDER

"How are things going?" Mom asked as she bent down to clean up the floor.

"The contractions are coming quicker." Rosa spoke forcefully, through clenched teeth. "Is Ida coming?"

"Not yet. Your sister couldn't reach her on the phone, but she's trying again. She said that if she still doesn't make contact with her, she'll come back to the house and let me know."

"Then what?" Rosa's chin trembled.

"Tena will hitch one of our horses to the buggy and be on her way to Ida's house."

"But that will take a while. And what if Ida's not home?" Rosa grimaced as another contraction overtook her. Each one was getting more painful, and they were coming closer together, which she knew was not a good thing.

"Try not to worry," Mom said, gently rubbing Rosa's back. "If by some chance Tena doesn't find Ida at home, I'll do my best to deliver your baby."

"Seriously?"

"Jah. I'll have no other choice, and neither will you, so you need to calm down and try to relax."

"Calm down? How can I do that, Mom?" Rosa pinched the skin at her throat, hoping the pain from that might take her mind off the situation at hand. "Have you ever delivered a baby before?" she questioned.

"Well, no, not a human baby, but I've had plenty of experience helping mama katze and a few of our hund when they had trouble giving birth to their little ones."

Rosa clutched the bedpost with both hands. "Bringing a human baby into the world is a little more complicated than helping a kitten or a puppy get born, don't ya think?"

"Well, yes, but. . ."

Mom stopped talking, and Rosa angled her head toward the bedroom door. Someone was knocking on it, really hard.

"Who's there?" Mom called.

"It's me, Tena."

"Did you reach Ida on the phone?"

"No, I didn't, but I'm going back outside to hitch a horse to the buggy, like we talked about, but..."

Rosa screeched as another pain overtook her. The sound of her scream reverberated on the bedroom walls, drowning out whatever else her sister may have said. Part of Rosa wanted Mom to deliver this baby right now, but the fearful part of her dreaded the thought of her own mother delivering this baby who seemed so determined to make his or her entrance into the world.

"Never mind, Tena, It's too late for trying to get the midwife," Rosa heard her mother say. With a steady, lower-pitched voice, Mom took Rosa by the shoulders and said, "We need to get you in position, Rosa, because there's not enough time for Tena to go after Ida now. Like it or not, it appears I'll be the one who helps you bring this baby into the world."

CHAPTER 37

Anthony didn't have a bit of trouble finding the home Tena had written out for him, as it was on the same road where the Petersheims lived. As he drove up the driveway, he spotted a dark-haired woman on her hands and knees, digging in the front flower bed.

When Anthony stopped his bike in front of the house, she rose to her feet and approached him. "Hello. May I help you with something?" she asked.

"Are you Ida, the midwife?"

"Yes, I am."

"I'm Rosa Petersheim's friend, and her sister tried to call to let you know that Rosa is in labor and needs you to come right away."

"Oh, I'm so sorry," she apologized. "I left my cell phone in the house, thinking I'd only be out here a short time, but once I started digging in the soil, I got carried away. I'll go inside to get my things, and then I'll hop in my car and head right over to the Petersheims' place."

"Thank you." Anthony got his motorcycle going again and headed out onto the road. He hoped he would have the opportunity to see Rosa before the baby was born.

Anthony made it back to the Petersheims' house before the midwife, and after he parked his bike, he ran up the porch steps and jerked the front door open without bothering to knock.

Tena greeted him in the entryway. "Did you find Ida's house? Was she at home?"

"Yes to both, and she's on her way over here."

"Oh good, that's a relief."

"Has Rosa had her baby yet?"

"No, but I think she's getting really close. Hopefully the midwife will be here soon and can deliver the infant so Mom doesn't have to." Tena rubbed her hands along the sides of her blue dress. "I sure hope my sister and her baby will be all right."

"We need to pray for a safe delivery."

Tena looked up at Anthony with creases across her forehead. "Have you been praying for Rosa?"

"Of course, and I'm sure you've been doing the same."

"Definitely, but I didn't know if you believed in God, let alone offered prayers to Him."

There was a time when Anthony could have been offended by her statement, but that was before he'd spent time reading the Bible and accepted Jesus as his Savior. So Anthony just smiled and said, "I didn't always, but I'm a Christian now."

"Oh, that's good to hear."

A knock sounded on the front door, and when Tena answered it, the midwife rushed in. "Where's Rosa?" she asked. "Has the baby come?"

Tena shook her head. "No, not yet. Rosa's in the guest room down the hall, and my mother is with her. Come with me. I'll take you there."

"I'd like to go too." Anthony stepped forward. "There's something important I'd like Rosa to know."

Ida paused and looked at Anthony. "You said you were a friend, so I assume that means you're not Rosa's husband?"

"That's correct."

"Sorry, sir, but you'll have to wait out here."

Anthony began to sweat profusely. Although he wasn't the father of Rosa's child, he was desperate to speak to her, if only for a few minutes. Anthony waited until Tena and the midwife headed down the hall and then followed quietly. When Ida opened the door and entered the bedroom, Anthony grabbed hold of the doorknob and held the door partway open, but not enough so he could see what was going on inside. "Rosa, it's me!" he shouted.

"Anthony?" Her voice sounded strained, like she might be having a difficult time breathing.

"Yeah, it's me. I came here to say that I love you, and if you'll have me, I want us to get married. In fact, I'd do it right now, if we had a preacher."

"There's no time for talk. Can't you see that this woman is about to give birth?" Ida whirled around, gave Anthony an icy stare, and slammed the door in his face.

Feeling like a scolded pet with its tail between its legs, Anthony followed Tena into the living room.

"I don't know what you're up to," Tena said, taking a seat on the couch, "but this was not a good time to be asking my sister to marry you. What's the matter with you, anyway?"

"What's the matter? I'll tell you what the matter is. I'm in love with Rosa, and I should have come here sooner to tell her that." Anthony plopped down in the recliner. He wasn't sure if Rosa had heard his declaration of love or his proposal. More importantly, he didn't know if she loved him. He'd taken a chance coming here, but it had been worth the risk. Once the baby had been safely delivered and he was allowed to talk to Rosa, he would ask her to marry him again, with much more feeling this time. He just hoped she loved him too and wouldn't turn him down flat.

∽∾

"I'm ever so glad you're here," Elsie said when Ida took over. "Do you need my help? Would you like me to stay?" Her thoughts were in a whirl with concern about Rosa. And then there was that intrusion by Anthony Reeves. *Or did I imagine that he was here?* Elsie pondered. *Why would he show up out of the blue and propose marriage to Rosa?*

Elsie looked at her daughter's corded neck and clenched jaw as she struggled with the pain of her next contraction. A sheen of perspiration covered Rosa's forehead, and the hair on her forehead, peeking out from the black scarf on her head, was a matted mess. Elsie would give anything if she could take away her daughter's discomfort. But it was all part of childbearing that each mother must endure. Elsie had been through it five times, but at that moment, it felt like yesterday, as she observed her daughter and relived her own pain.

"I can always use an extra pair of hands," Ida said, pushing Elsie's thoughts aside. "And yes, of course I think it would be good if you remain here with your daughter. She needs your support right now."

Elsie took hold of Rosa's hand. "Don't try to talk, dear one, and don't think about anything except doing whatever Ida tells you."

⁓

"Don't push yet," Ida instructed. "I'll tell you when it's time."

Rosa pulled in several deep breaths as Mom placed a cool cloth on her forehead and told her to try to relax. "It won't be much longer, Rosa." She spoke with assurance, but Rosa wasn't convinced. Although she probably hadn't been in labor very long, her pains had gone on much longer than she expected. In some ways Rosa felt like she was in the middle of a bad dream, but then she remembered hearing Anthony's voice.

Or did I imagine it? Surely Anthony couldn't be here right now. In my state of mind, I must have been hearing things.

"All right, Rosa, it's time to push," Ida announced. "Bear down now and keep pushing until I tell you to stop."

Rosa did as her midwife instructed, and she gave it her all. Moments later, she heard the cry of a baby, and Ida proclaimed, "It's a boy, Rosa. Your son has arrived, and he's breathing on his own."

Tears welled in Rosa's eyes and trickled onto her hot cheeks. *Thank You, Lord. Thank You for my baby's safe entry into this world.*

⁓

Anthony drummed his knuckles along the arm of the chair, where he sat waiting impatiently for some word. Tena had tried to carry on a conversation with him, asking questions about New York, his parents, and the motorcycle parked out front. But it was all Anthony could do to answer each query when his thoughts were on Rosa.

If we were actually married, I could be in there with her right now, offering my love and support. I'd be holding Rosa's hand and soothing her brow. I'd say over and over how much I love her. I would be doing everything I could to make my wife more comfortable, and I'd be cheering her on with each contraction.

Anthony's head jerked and he sat up straight when he heard the cry of a baby.

Tena must have heard it too, because she gave a small yelp, jumped off the couch, and clapped her hands. "Did you hear that, Anthony? Rosa's baby has been born."

"Yes, I heard the baby's cry." He got up and walked across the room to stand in front of the fireplace. "Sure wish I could see Rosa right now. I bet she looks beautiful, holding the baby in her arms."

"This is so thrilling. I wonder what she had." Tena's broad smile mirrored her excitement.

A short time later, Rosa's mother entered the room. Her lips were parted in a pleasant smile. "It's a boy," Elsie announced, looking only at Tena. Her head swiveled when she caught sight of Anthony. "So it really was you I heard when Ida came into the room. I thought I must have been hearing things." She pointed at Anthony. "What are you doing here?"

"I came to see Rosa and confess my love for her." Anthony swiped a palm over his sweaty forehead. "Does she know I'm in the house? Did she hear when I asked her to marry me?"

Elsie's brows furrowed. "Is that what you said?"

"Yes, I did, and I meant it. She means the world to me, and I plan to stay here in Belleville to prove it."

"No more pretending? Is that what you're saying?"

"That's exactly what I'm saying." Anthony took a few steps forward. "Is there any chance I can see her now?"

"We need to give the midwife a chance to finish all that needs to be done, and it's important for Rosa to get some rest."

"I understand, and I won't stay in there long. I just need to see her for a few minutes."

"I want to see Rosa and the baby too," Tena was quick to say.

"And you shall, but first I'm going back to see what else Ida wants me to do. When she says it's all right, I'll come back to get Anthony, and then Tena, you can go in for a few minutes to see your nephew."

A sense of hope mixed with trepidation flooded Anthony's soul. It had taken him too long to reach the decision to come here, and he didn't know what he would do if Rosa rejected his proposal or said she didn't love him.

But I need to be patient, he told himself. *Patient for the go-ahead to see her, and patient as I spend time in prayer while waiting for my answer.* Anthony closed his eyes. *Please Lord, let it be Your will for Rosa and me to be together as husband and wife.*

Rosa stared lovingly at the precious baby in her arms. "A son. I have a son," she murmured.

"You sure do," Mom said, "and he's perfect."

"Thank you for being here with me the whole time. I couldn't have it done it without you."

Her mother smiled. "Ida was more help than I was."

"I'm glad Tena went and got her, or you might have had to deliver the baby alone."

"It wasn't your sister who went to Ida's house."

"Who was it, then?"

"Anthony."

Rosa's fingers touched her parted lips. "Anthony was here?"

"Jah. He arrived on his motorcycle while you were in labor, and then he went to get Ida because it was much quicker than Tena going by horse and buggy."

Rosa pondered her mother's words. "When I was getting close to having the baby, I thought I heard Anthony's voice, but I figured I'd imagined it because of the pain I felt."

Mom shook her head. "No, he's here now in the living room, and he wants to see you if you're willing."

"I—I must look a mess, Mom. I'm sure Anthony wouldn't want to see me this way."

Mom put her hand on Rosa's shoulder. "And I'm equally sure that he would. Can I send him in?"

"Yes, please do. I'm eager to find out how he's been doing and ask why he came here."

"He came to see you."

"But I don't understand why. All the time since he's been gone, we only spoke on the phone once, and he never said anything about coming to see me."

"It doesn't matter," Mom said. "He's here now, and if it's okay with you, I'm going to send him in."

"All right."

After her mother left the room, Rosa drew in some deep breaths in an effort to calm herself. Of all the times to hear from Anthony, why now, on the day she'd given birth to her son?

Only a few minutes passed before Rosa heard a knock on her door. "Come in," she called, looking up expectantly. Her breath caught in her throat at the sight of the man she'd foolishly allowed herself to fall in love with.

"Rosa."

"Anthony."

"It's so good to see you," he said, approaching her bed.

"It's good to see you too, but why are you here?"

"I've missed you, Rosa, and I had to see you and say what's been on my mind for weeks." Anthony looked at her baby boy and grinned. "But before I do, let me give my congratulations on the birth of your son. He looks like a strong, healthy baby."

She nodded.

"How are you doing?" he asked.

"Thanks to Ida and Mom, I'm doing well. Giving birth wasn't easy, and I'm glad it's over, but I'd do it again if I could have another child as precious as this little guy." She stroked the baby's dark hair.

"You're right. He is pretty special, and so is his mama." Anthony reached for Rosa's free hand. "I didn't come here for a casual visit, Rosa. I came to say something I should have told you sooner."

"What's that?"

"I'm in love with you, and if you'll have me, I want to be your husband, for real this time—no pretending at all."

"Oh, Anthony, I love you too. I knew it before you left Belleville, but I didn't feel I had the right to tell you."

"You had every right, sweet Rosa." He let go of Rosa's hand and stroked the side of her face with a gentle touch. "Not only do I want to marry you, Rosa, but I want to be your little boy's father."

"Really?"

"Absolutely. Of course you first have to accept my proposal of marriage. So what do you say?"

"I say yes, Anthony Reeves, I would be honored to be your wife."

He bent down and kissed her gently. "Now all we have to do is tell your folks. My only concern is how well this news will go over with your dad."

"I'm sure it'll be fine. Dad has softened considerably since you left the Big Valley. He forgave Susan for the lies she told about my disappearance, but I'll tell you all about that another time."

"I look forward to hearing it." Anthony stroked the baby's forehead with his thumb. "So what are you going to name this little boy of yours?"

"I hadn't really put much thought into it yet, but now that you're here and soon to be my husband, I was thinking maybe we could call the baby Richard Louis. Richard was my grandfather's name, and I remember you had mentioned once that your grandpa was Louis."

"Yeah, that's right. I'm sure both of our grandpas would be honored to have your little guy named after them." Anthony kissed Rosa again.

"There's something else I need to tell you."

"What's that?"

"I wanted to say thank you for the Bible you put in my duffel bag. After reading it, I learned a lot about God, and I now have a personal relationship with Jesus."

Rosa's eyes filled with tears. "That's wonderful, Anthony. But just so you know, it wasn't me who put the Bible in your bag."

He tipped his head to one side. "Oh? Who was it, then?"

"It was my dad. He said a fellow like you needed the Lord in your life, and he hoped when you found the Bible you might read it and figure out what kind of plan God might have for you."

"Seriously? He told you that?"

"No, but I overheard him telling Mom one evening when they thought I was asleep in bed."

"That's amazing. I never would have guessed that Mahlon placed that Bible in the bottom of my duffel bag. I guess God works in mysterious ways His wonders to perform."

"Amen," Rosa said as she closed her eyes and clung to Anthony's hand.

"There's one more thing I need to tell you, Rosa."

She opened her eyes. "What's that?"

"Using some money my grandfather left me that I didn't know about until recently, I've been able to purchase a restaurant in Allensville that recently went out of business. As soon as I do some repairs and fix things up, I plan to cook and serve Italian cuisine there. What do you think of that?"

"It sounds like a great idea, and I'm sure it'll be a success," she responded.

"Before we can start planning our wedding, there's one more thing I need to talk to you about."

"Which is?"

"It's about what church we should get married in and attend regularly as a family." Anthony shifted his body on one side of the bed where he sat. "I'm pretty sure you know that I wouldn't be comfortable joining the Amish church, because the truth is, having grown up English, I'd never really fit in."

"I understand, and it won't be a problem, Anthony. Whatever church you feel comfortable attending, as long as they preach the truth from God's Word, I'll be right there beside you."

"I was hoping you would say that, future wife of mine." He kissed Rosa a third time and stood. "And now, if you don't mind, I'm going outside to call my folks. I need to let them know you accepted my proposal and that I'm planning to stay in the Big Valley permanently."

"I hope they'll be okay with it."

"They will, because last night during my prebirthday supper, I told them what I planned to do today."

"Prebirthday?"

"Yeah. Today's my birthday, and I did what I've been doing for the last five years."

"What's that?"

"I got on my motorcycle and took a birthday ride. Only this was the best one ever!"

Rosa smiled as she pointed to little Richard Louis. "From now on, you and our boy will be able to celebrate your birthdays together, as father and son."

EPILOGUE

Allensville, one year later

Pushing her one-year-old son's stroller ahead of her, Rosa entered her husband's restaurant, which he had named Anthony's Italian Bistro. Today was Anthony's birthday, and rather than going for his yearly motorcycle ride, he'd chosen to be in the kitchen, cooking. In fact, he'd sold the bike a month after he and Rosa got married.

This evening at her parents' home, they would have a family dinner to celebrate both Anthony's and Richard's birthdays. Rosa looked forward to the occasion, and she was sure her husband did too. Rosa's whole family would there—including Norman, Salina, and their two-month-old baby boy, Samuel.

Rosa smiled when she saw her dear friend Ada waiting for her at one of the tables near the front window. Ada's eight-month-old daughter, Jenna, also in a stroller, was with her. What a blessing it was to be able to meet like this, especially since they both lived in Allensville and didn't have far to go whenever they wanted to see each other. And what better place to visit than right here, where the food was delicious and tantalizing smells wafted out of the kitchen.

"It's good to see you. How are things going?" Ada asked after Rosa took a seat across from her.

"Fine as feathers." Rosa grinned. "How about you?"

"We're doing well, and my husband's busier than ever at the harness shop. It's a good thing he has Noah Esh working for him, because now that Ephraim's dad has officially retired, Ephraim would never be able to keep up with all the work without Noah's help."

"Same here for my dear husband. Thomas, the young man Anthony hired to help in the kitchen, spent a year in Italy, and while he was there, Thomas learned a thing or two about Italian cooking. So Anthony is glad he hired him."

"That's good."

Rosa pointed to Ada's daughter. "Your little girl is sure growing, not to mention getting cuter all the time."

Ada nodded. "I hope it doesn't sound like I'm bragging, but Ephraim and I think Jenna is pretty smart for her age. He's taught her how to wave bye-bye, and is working with Jenna to say 'Da-Da.'"

Rosa laughed. "That was Richard's first word, but now he's saying other words, and I made sure that Ma-Ma was one of them."

Ada leaned over and tickled Rosa's son under his chin. "Who knows, Rosa, maybe someday when our two are old enough, they'll end up getting married. Now wouldn't that be something?"

"It sure would." Rosa looked up when their waitress came to the table to take their order. "Please tell my husband that I'll have the usual," she said with a wink.

"What's your usual?" Ada questioned.

"It's sort of a toss-up between the farfalle pasta salad with sun-dried tomato pesto and Anthony's original German pizza. But the pizza usually wins out." Rosa looked back at their waitress. "So yeah, that's what I'd like to order. There will be enough for both of us if you'd like to have that too," she said to Ada.

Her friend nodded. "Sounds good to me."

After the waitress left, Rosa and Ada got out a few toys they'd brought for their little ones to play with and resumed their conversation.

"When I was in the harness shop the other day, I heard Noah mention to Ephraim that he had another date with Susan," Ada commented.

"It's probably true," Rosa said. "Those two have been seeing a lot of each other this year, and I wouldn't be surprised if a wedding is in the works sometime soon."

"That would be nice." Jenna started fussing, and Ada put a pacifier in her daughter's mouth, which she happily accepted.

"Does Anthony hear much from his parents or sisters?" Ada asked.

"His mother mostly, because his sisters are busy with their own lives, and Anthony's father's life is pretty much centered around his restaurant." Joyful tears sprang into Rosa's eyes. "I'm ever so thankful that Anthony takes time off from the restaurant to be with me and our son. He has said many times that there is no reason for his business to be open seven days a week. Five is plenty, and the restaurant is always busy, so we are making a decent living."

"That's good, and I'm glad my husband feels that way too. Ephraim loves spending time with me and our daughter, and we enjoy being with him as well." Ada leaned a little closer to Rosa and spoke in a serious tone. "I love Ephraim so much, and I'm thankful that you don't feel any resentment toward me for marrying your ex-boyfriend."

"None at all," Rosa responded. "I'm happy for both of you, and grateful that I met Anthony and the two of us fell in love. When I left home and was out on my own, I never expected that the Lord would bless me so. I'm thankful that I had the good sense to return to my parents' home, and even more grateful that God showed me the error of my ways and brought me into a close relationship with Him."

Rosa placed her hands together in a prayerlike gesture and quoted John 8:32, a Bible verse that had become important to her: "And you shall know the truth, and the truth shall make you free."

"That is a good one," Ada agreed.

Rosa nodded. "God's truth will always win out, and with His help and guidance, I will strive to let my light shine so that others will see Jesus living in me."

Anthony's German Pizza

Ingredients:

1 pound ground beef
½ medium onion, chopped
½ green pepper, diced
1½ teaspoons salt, divided
½ teaspoon pepper
2 tablespoons butter
6 raw potatoes, shredded
3 eggs, beaten
⅓ cup milk
2 cups shredded cheddar or mozzarella cheese, divided

Directions:

In 12-inch skillet, brown ground beef with onion, green pepper, ½ teaspoon salt, and pepper. Remove beef mixture from skillet. Drain skillet and melt butter. Spread potatoes over butter and sprinkle with remaining teaspoon of salt. Top with beef mixture. Combine eggs and milk and pour over all. Top with half of cheese. Cook, covered, on medium heat until potatoes are tender, about 30 minutes. Top with remaining cheese. Cover and heat until cheese is melted, about 5 minutes. Cut into wedges or squares to serve. Makes 4–6 servings.

Discussion Questions:

1. Rosa Petersheim had been gone more than two years, and her family didn't know if she was dead or alive. The tragedy of her disappearance had affected each of Rosa's family members differently. How would you react if a loved one went missing and the case hadn't been solved?

2. When Rosa showed up at her parents' house unexpectedly, she was welcomed by most of the family, but her father and sister Susan weren't quite as sociable. Do you think the reason behind their distance was justified? If so, in what way? If not, why not?

3. When Anthony first said he would go with Rosa to see her family and pose as her husband, she was hesitant to accept his offer. Why do you think Rosa changed her mind? Was it a wise decision?

4. What makes a person like Anthony willing to set aside his own needs to help someone he didn't know all that well?

5. It was a surprise and a cultural shock for Anthony to discover that Rosa's family was Amish. The fact that they didn't have electricity and he was expected to attend Amish church with the family were also factors he hadn't expected when agreeing to pose as Rosa's husband. If you had not grown up in an Amish home, how hard would it be for you to adopt their lifestyle, even for a short time? How would you try to adapt to such drastic changes?

6. How did you feel about the unwelcoming way Rosa's father, Mahlon, a bishop in the Amish church, acted toward Rosa and Anthony?

7. Have you ever experienced a similar reaction with a member of your family who claimed to be a Christian? Do you think Mahlon's actions were justified? How could he have done better and still let his daughter know that she was loved?

8. When Anthony returned to his home in New York, he discovered that his father had hired someone else to cook at his restaurant. How would you feel if you'd been in Anthony's place, losing a job you loved? Was his father justified in hiring someone to take Anthony's place when he didn't return home on time? Should Herb have let the new employee go so Anthony could cook in the restaurant again, or would there be some other way to deal with the situation?

9. Anthony's father offered him a job as a busboy, but Anthony turned it down because it didn't involve cooking. Have you ever lost a job to someone else and been unable to find another? If so, were you willing to take a position outside of your scope of talents?

10. Rosa's sister Susan had been harboring a secret the entire time Rosa was missing. She knew where Rosa was and had been keeping her whereabouts from their parents by deleting Rosa's phone messages and destroying Rosa's letters and notes. The guilt Susan felt for the lies she had told finally caught up with her and she confessed, begging for her family's forgiveness. Even though her parents, Rosa, and Susan's other siblings forgave Susan for having kept the truth about Rosa from them, Susan had trouble forgiving herself. Have you ever felt like that about another person or done something you knew had hurt someone? If so, were you able to forgive yourself and move forward, resolved to do better?

11. Rosa felt betrayed when she learned about her sister's lies, but she chose to forgive Susan. What does the Bible say about forgiving others when they have wronged us? How important is forgiveness in mending a relationship?

12. When Anthony returned to the Big Valley, he set his original plans for the future aside and agreed to help Rosa raise her child, even though the baby wasn't his. What does that say about Anthony? How do you think it made Rosa feel to know that Anthony was willing to raise another man's child?

13. Did you have a favorite character in this book? If so, what made them special to you?

14. Did you learn anything new about the Amish way of life while reading this book?

15. Do you think Rosa did the right thing by choosing not to become a member of the Amish church? How do you think it affects Amish parents when one of their children chooses not to join or even leaves the church after they have already become a member?

16. Were there any Bible verses in this story that spoke to you personally? If so, in what way did those scripture passages minister to your heart or help you deal with a particular situation?

New York Times bestselling and award-winning author Wanda E. Brunstetter is one of the founders of the Amish fiction genre. She has written more than one hundred books, with several translated in four languages. With over twelve million copies sold, Wanda's stories consistently earn spots on the nation's most prestigious bestseller lists and have received numerous awards.

Wanda's ancestors were part of the Anabaptist faith, and her novels are based on personal research intended to accurately portray the Amish way of life. Her books are read and trusted by many Amish people, who credit her for giving readers a deeper understanding of the people and their customs.

When Wanda visits her Amish friends, she finds herself drawn to their peaceful lifestyle, sincerity, and close family ties. Wanda enjoys photography, ventriloquism, gardening, bird-watching, beachcombing, and spending time with her family. She and her husband, Richard, have been blessed with two grown children, six grandchildren, and three great-grandchildren.

To learn more about Wanda, visit her website
at www.wandabrunstetter.com.

A MIFFLIN COUNTY MYSTERY

A Mysterious Disappearance Shakes a Family's Faith in Pennsylvania's Amish Country

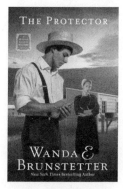

The Protector
Book 1

Rosa Petersheim disappeared without a trace. Norman always considered himself his sister's protector and can't believe she would have left home of her own accord—so he must have failed her. He throws all he has into helping the authorities search for Rosa, while trying to support his parents and siblings who are struggling both mentally and physically. Salina Swarey loves Norman and hopes they are headed toward marriage, but his obsession with Rosa's whereabouts is driving them apart. Can Norman find a place of peace and contentment if he never learns where Rosa is?

Paperback / 978-1-63609-760-2

The Peacemaker
Book 2

Ada's best friend, Rosa, disappeared a year ago and still has not been found. In their grief and confusion, Ada and Rosa's boyfriend, Ephraim, have grown very close. But some in the community feel Ephraim is responsible for Rosa's disappearance. Now Rosa's younger sister is making accusations against Ephraim that can't be true, and he pulls away from Ada, feeling betrayed. A fire set by an arsonist might finally be the thing to reveal secrets that have long been dividing this community of friends and family. But will it be too late for love between the peacemaker and the suspect?

Paperback / 978-1-63609-920-0

Find This and More from Barbour Publishing at Your Favorite Bookstore or at www.barbourbooks.com